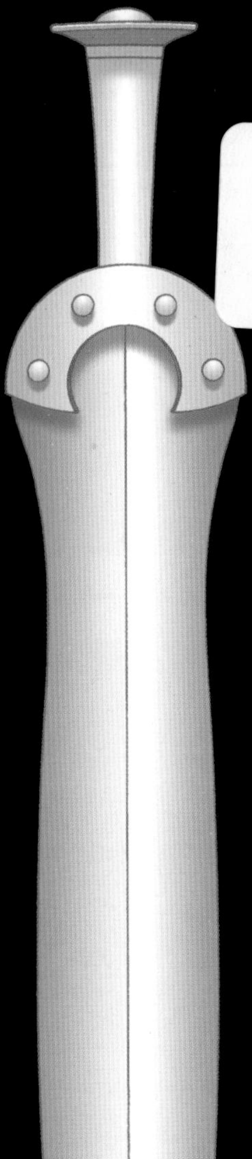

THE SWORD

WATER

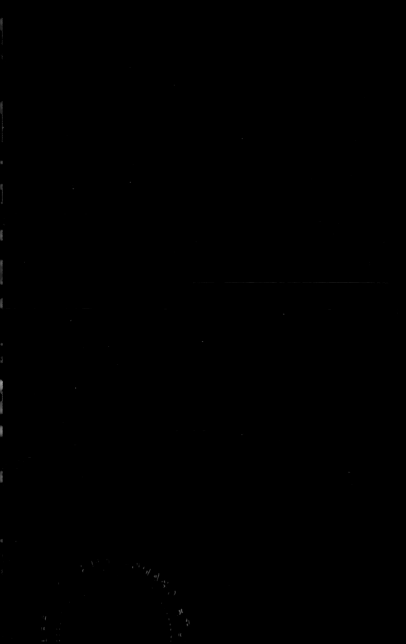

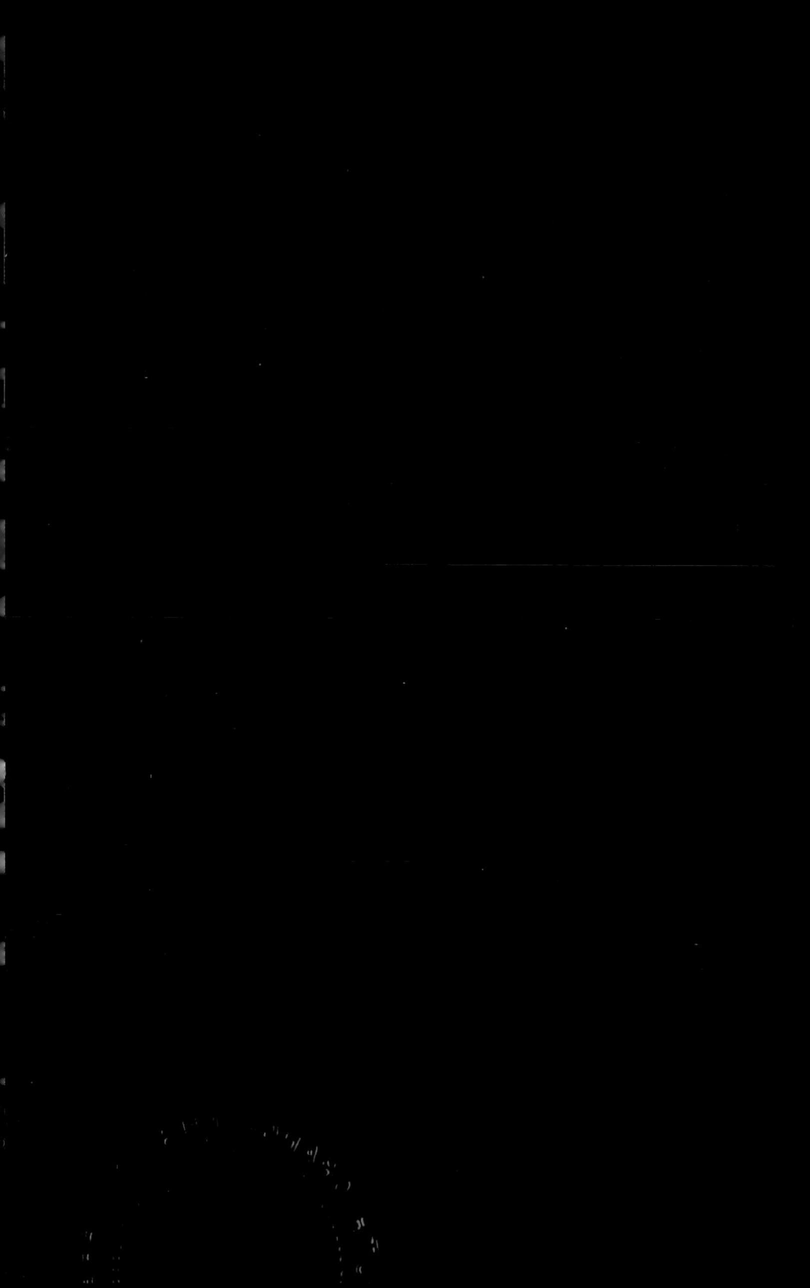

JOSHUA LUNA
Story, Script, Layouts, Letters

JONATHAN LUNA
Story, Illustrations, Book Design

SPECIAL THANKS TO:

Rommel Calderon
Randy Castillo
Dan Dos Santos
Timothy Ingle
Jenn Kao
Marc Lombardi
Victoria Stein
Giancarlo Yerkes

IMAGE COMICS, INC.

Robert Kirkman Chief Operating Officer
Erik Larsen Chief Financial Officer
Todd McFarlane President
Marc Silvestri Chief Executive Officer
Jim Valentino Vice-President
ericstephenson Publisher
Joe Keatinge PR & Marketing Coordinator
Branwyn Bigglestone Accounts Manager
Tyler Shainline Administrative Assistant
Traci Hui Traffic Manager
Allen Hui Production Manager
Drew Gill Production Artist
Jonathan Chan Production Artist
Monica Howard Production Artist

www.imagecomics.com
www.lunabrothers.com

THE SWORD, VOL. 2: WATER
ISBN: 978-1-58240-976-4
First Printing

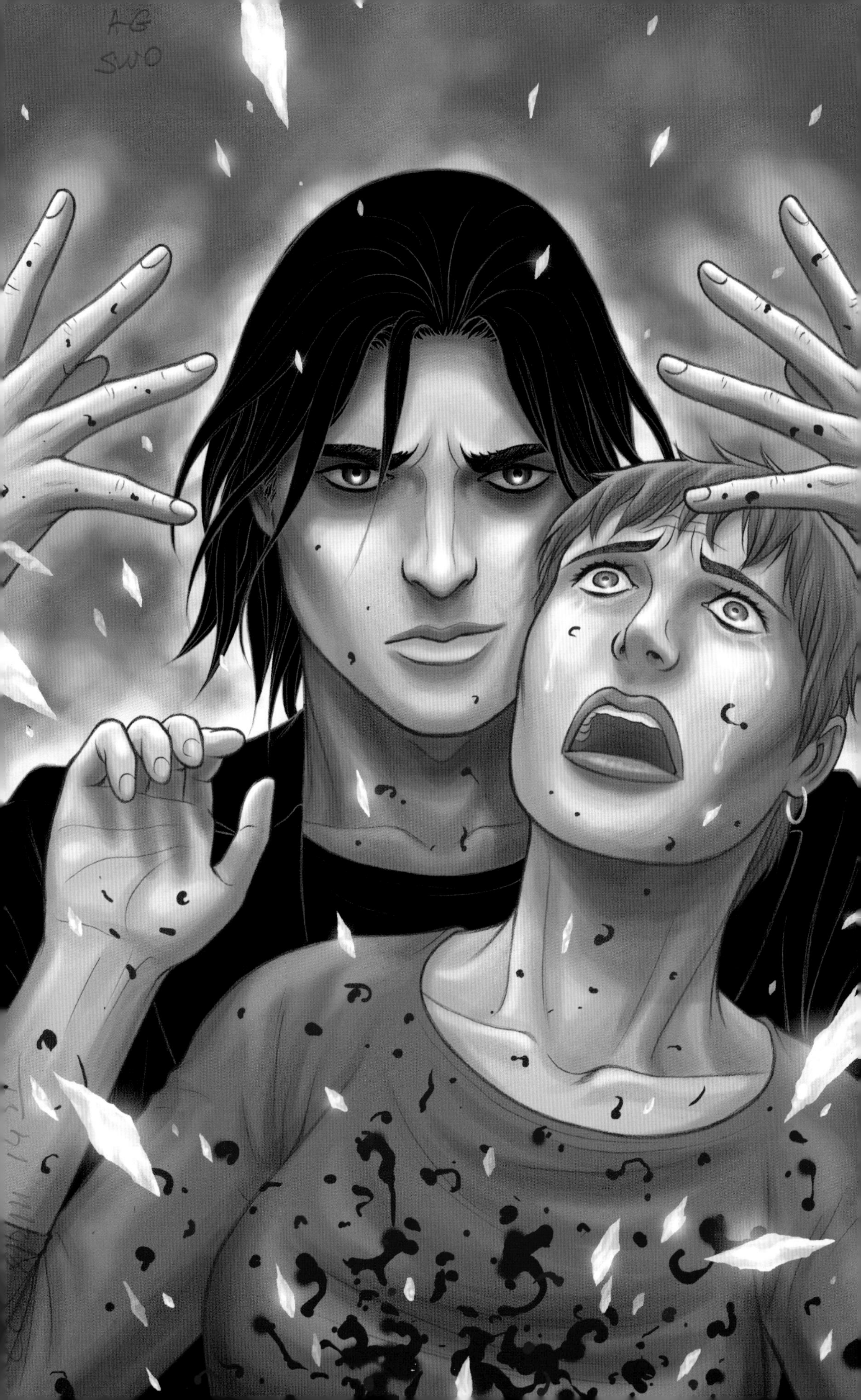
AG
SWO

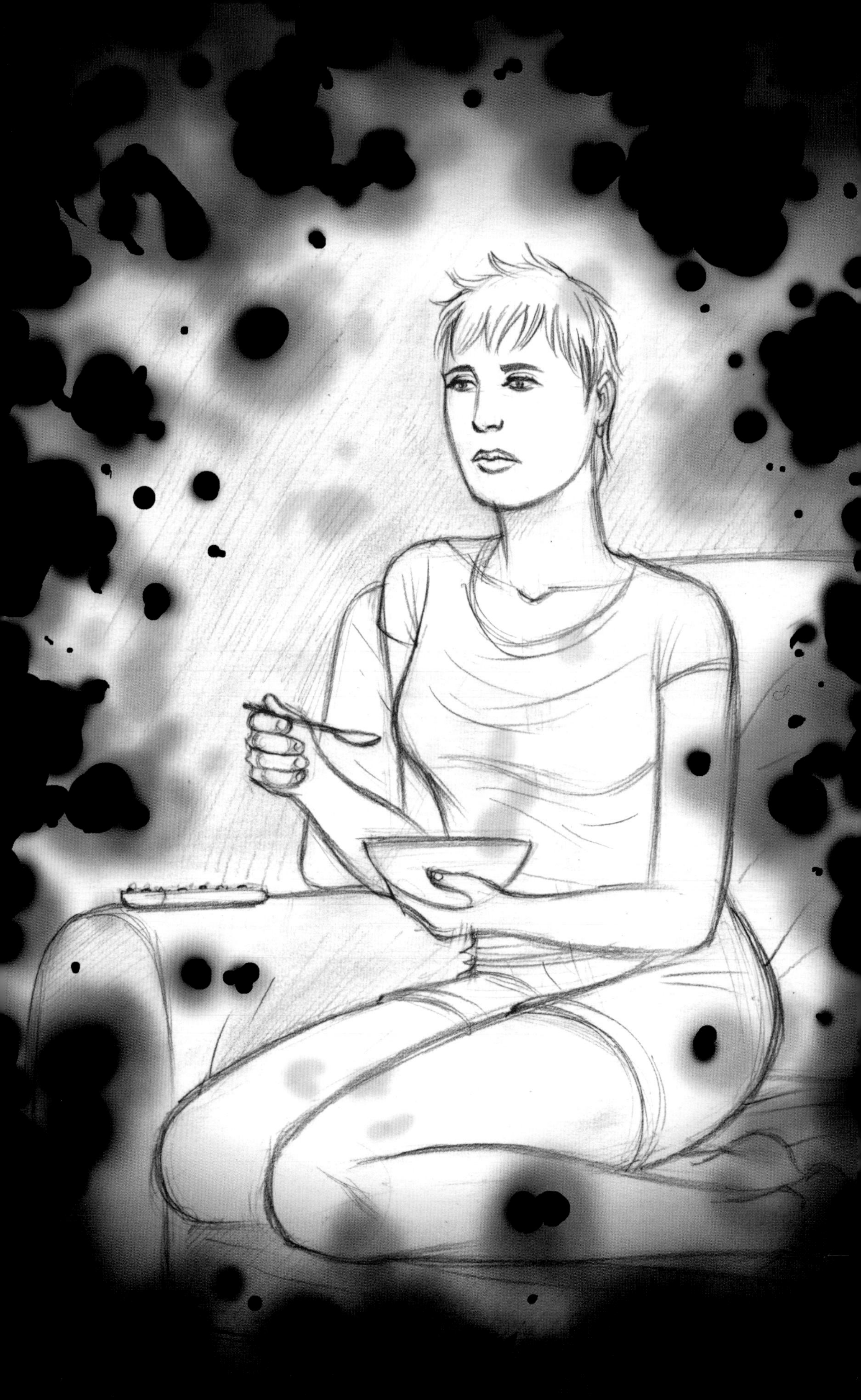

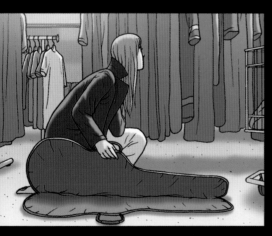

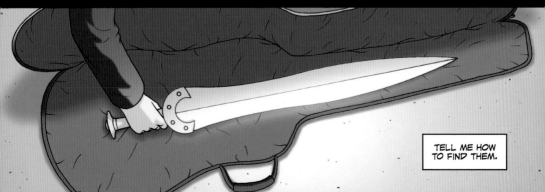

TELL ME HOW
TO FIND THEM.

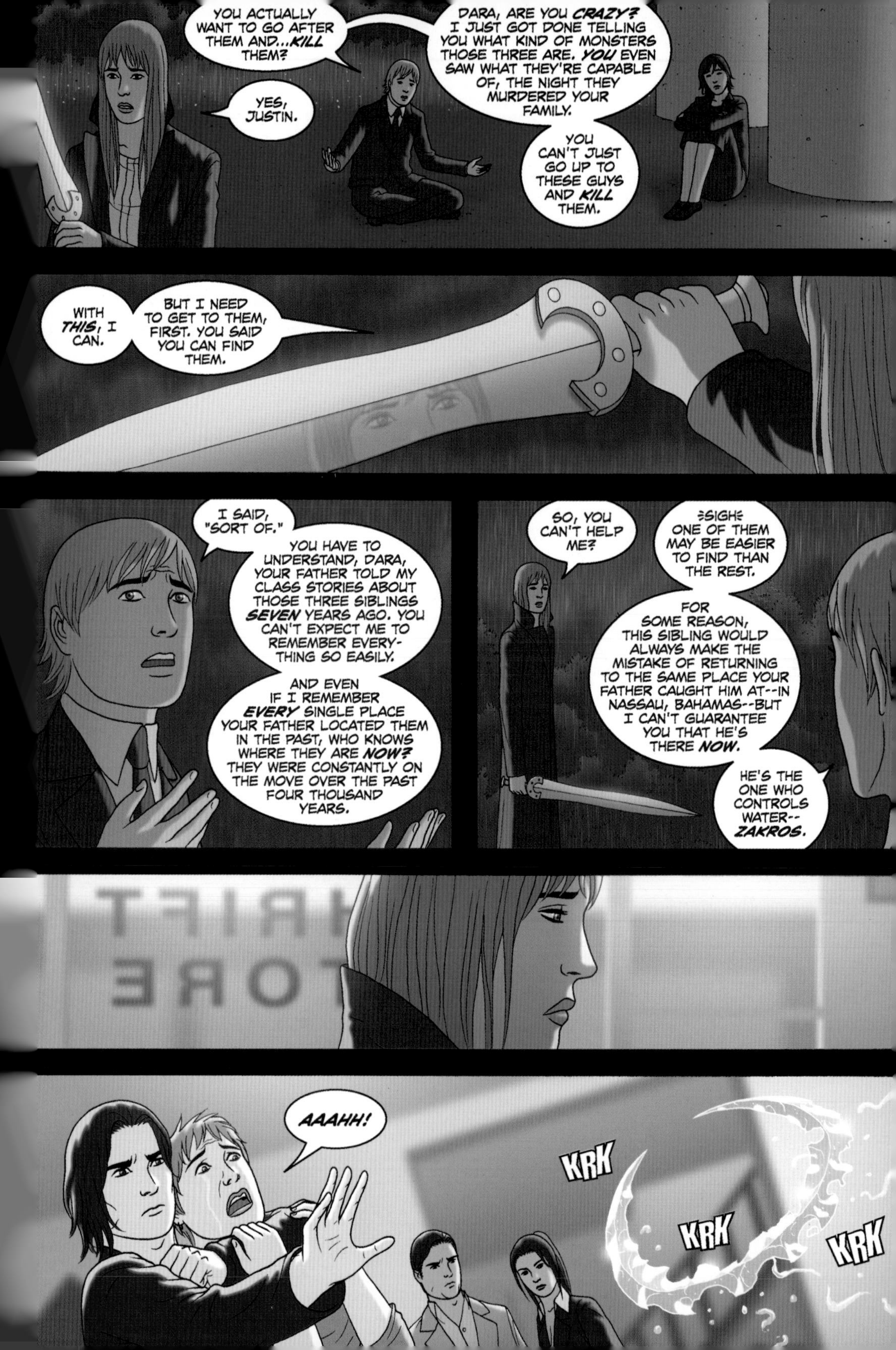

YOU ACTUALLY WANT TO GO AFTER THEM AND...KILL THEM?
YES, JUSTIN.
DARA, ARE YOU CRAZY? I JUST GOT DONE TELLING YOU WHAT KIND OF MONSTERS THOSE THREE ARE. YOU EVEN SAW WHAT THEY'RE CAPABLE OF, THE NIGHT THEY MURDERED YOUR FAMILY.
YOU CAN'T JUST GO UP TO THESE GUYS AND KILL THEM.
WITH THIS, I CAN.
BUT I NEED TO GET TO THEM, FIRST. YOU SAID YOU CAN FIND THEM.
I SAID, "SORT OF."
YOU HAVE TO UNDERSTAND, DARA, YOUR FATHER TOLD MY CLASS STORIES ABOUT THOSE THREE SIBLINGS SEVEN YEARS AGO. YOU CAN'T EXPECT ME TO REMEMBER EVERY-THING SO EASILY.
AND EVEN IF I REMEMBER EVERY SINGLE PLACE YOUR FATHER LOCATED THEM IN THE PAST, WHO KNOWS WHERE THEY ARE NOW? THEY WERE CONSTANTLY ON THE MOVE OVER THE PAST FOUR THOUSAND YEARS.
SO, YOU CAN'T HELP ME?
SIGH
ONE OF THEM MAY BE EASIER TO FIND THAN THE REST.
FOR SOME REASON, THIS SIBLING WOULD ALWAYS MAKE THE MISTAKE OF RETURNING TO THE SAME PLACE YOUR FATHER CAUGHT HIM AT--IN NASSAU, BAHAMAS--BUT I CAN'T GUARANTEE YOU THAT HE'S THERE NOW.
HE'S THE ONE WHO CONTROLS WATER--ZAKROS.
AAAHH!
KRK
KRK
KRK

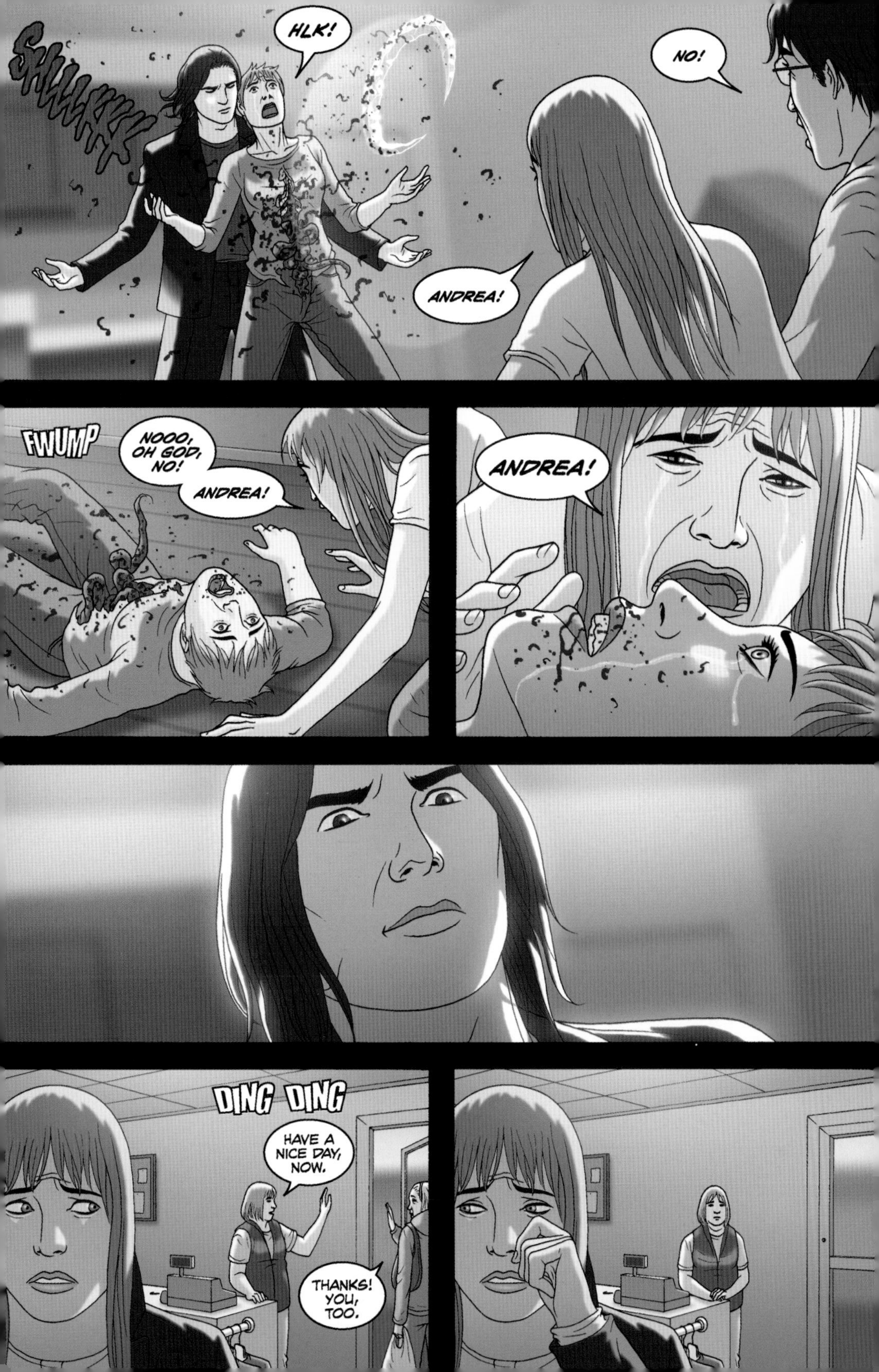
SHLLKKK
HLK!
NO!
ANDREA!
FWUMP
NOOO, OH GOD, NO!
ANDREA!
ANDREA!
DING DING
HAVE A NICE DAY, NOW.
THANKS! YOU, TOO.

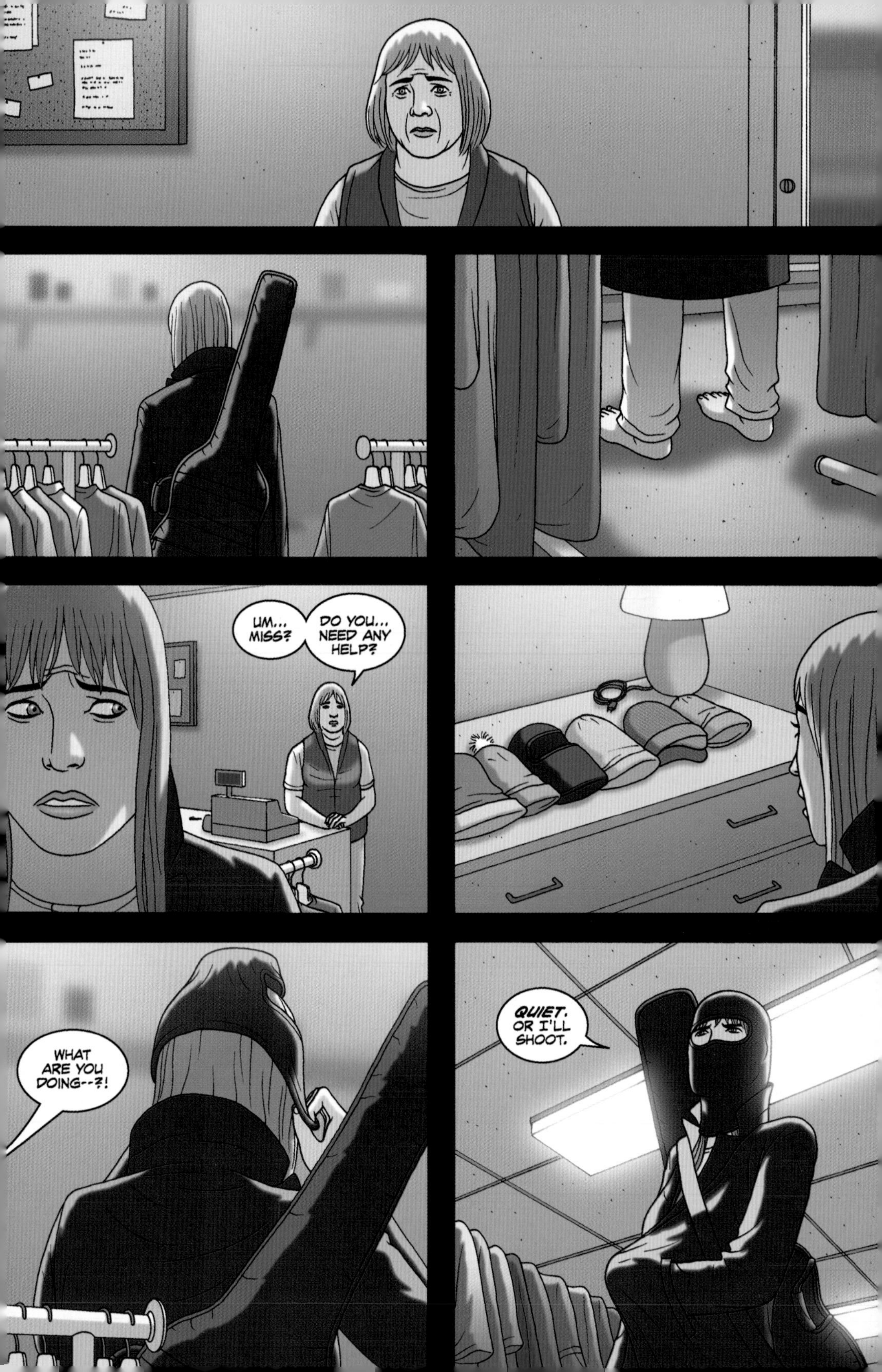
UM... MISS?
DO YOU... NEED ANY HELP?
WHAT ARE YOU DOING--?!
QUIET. OR I'LL SHOOT.

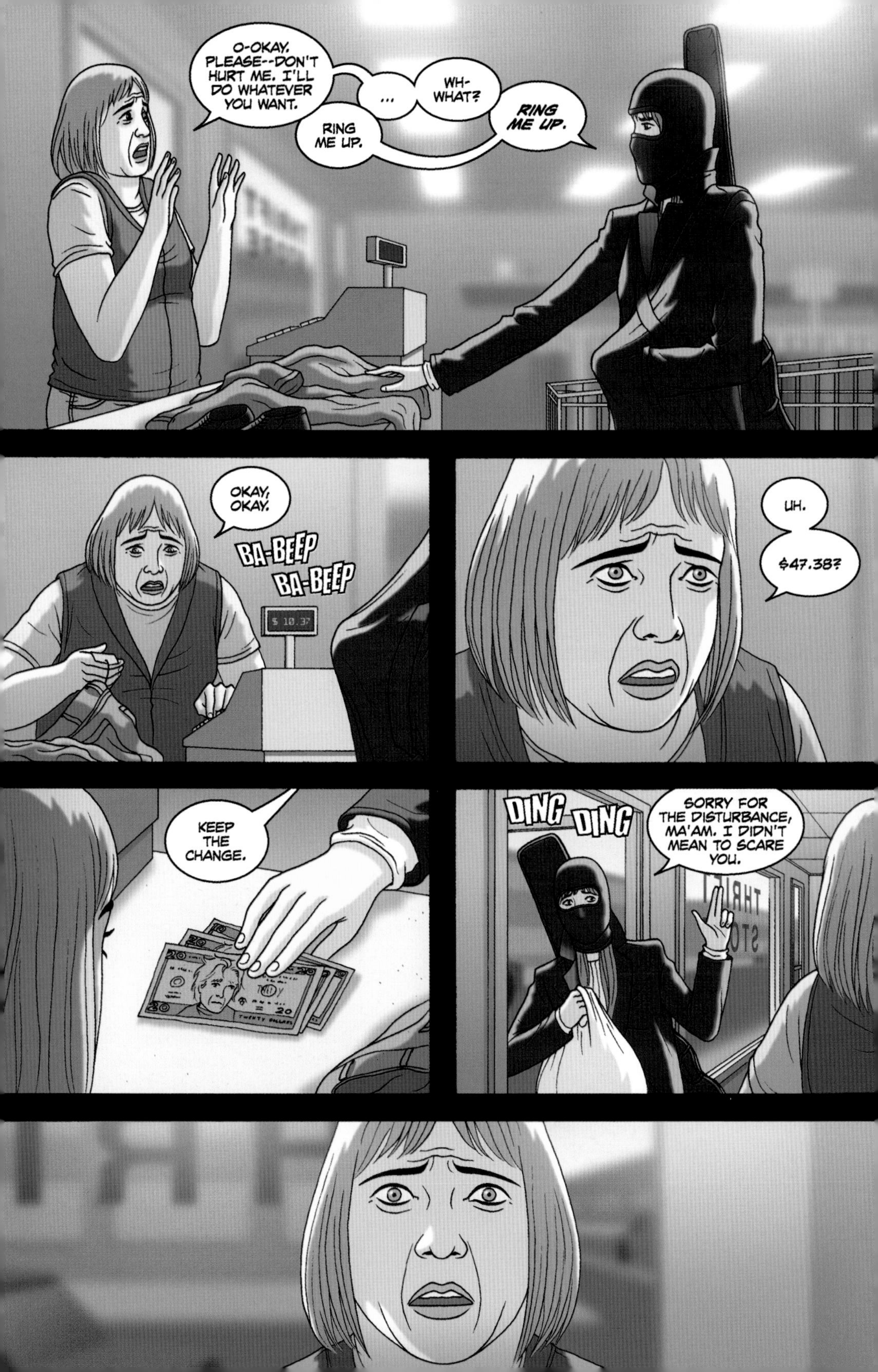
O-OKAY. PLEASE--DON'T HURT ME. I'LL DO WHATEVER YOU WANT.
...
WH-WHAT?
RING ME UP.
RING ME UP.
OKAY, OKAY.
BA-BEEP
BA-BEEP
$ 10.37
UH.
$47.38?
KEEP THE CHANGE.
DING
DING
SORRY FOR THE DISTURBANCE, MA'AM. I DIDN'T MEAN TO SCARE YOU.

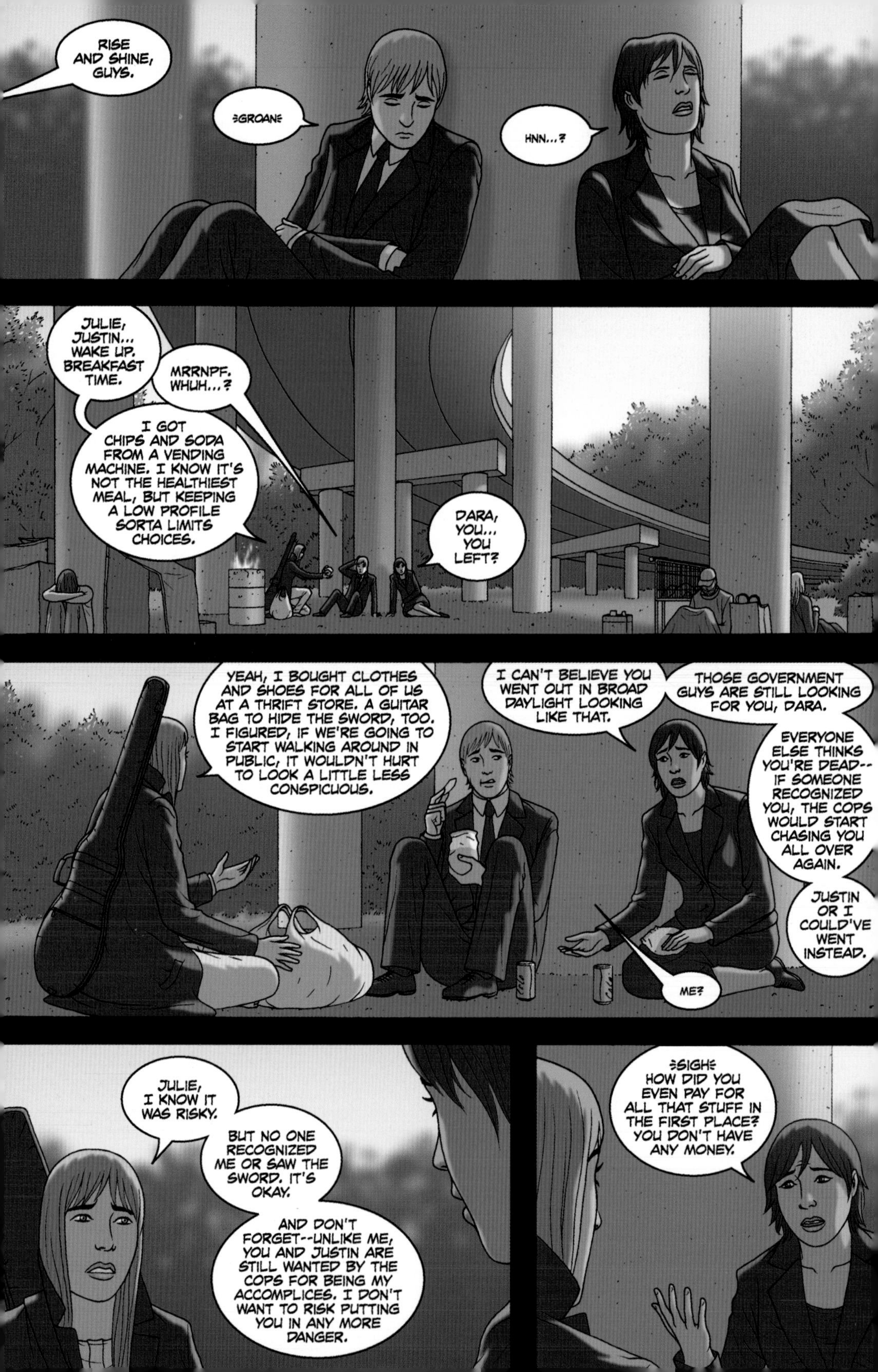
RISE AND SHINE, GUYS.
≷GROAN≶
HNN...?
JULIE, JUSTIN... WAKE UP. BREAKFAST TIME.
MRRNPF. WHUH...?
I GOT CHIPS AND SODA FROM A VENDING MACHINE. I KNOW IT'S NOT THE HEALTHIEST MEAL, BUT KEEPING A LOW PROFILE SORTA LIMITS CHOICES.
DARA, YOU... YOU LEFT?
YEAH, I BOUGHT CLOTHES AND SHOES FOR ALL OF US AT A THRIFT STORE. A GUITAR BAG TO HIDE THE SWORD, TOO. I FIGURED, IF WE'RE GOING TO START WALKING AROUND IN PUBLIC, IT WOULDN'T HURT TO LOOK A LITTLE LESS CONSPICUOUS.
I CAN'T BELIEVE YOU WENT OUT IN BROAD DAYLIGHT LOOKING LIKE THAT.
THOSE GOVERNMENT GUYS ARE STILL LOOKING FOR YOU, DARA.
EVERYONE ELSE THINKS YOU'RE DEAD--IF SOMEONE RECOGNIZED YOU, THE COPS WOULD START CHASING YOU ALL OVER AGAIN.
JUSTIN OR I COULD'VE WENT INSTEAD.
ME?
JULIE, I KNOW IT WAS RISKY.
BUT NO ONE RECOGNIZED ME OR SAW THE SWORD. IT'S OKAY.
AND DON'T FORGET--UNLIKE ME, YOU AND JUSTIN ARE STILL WANTED BY THE COPS FOR BEING MY ACCOMPLICES. I DON'T WANT TO RISK PUTTING YOU IN ANY MORE DANGER.
≷SIGH≶ HOW DID YOU EVEN PAY FOR ALL THAT STUFF IN THE FIRST PLACE? YOU DON'T HAVE ANY MONEY.

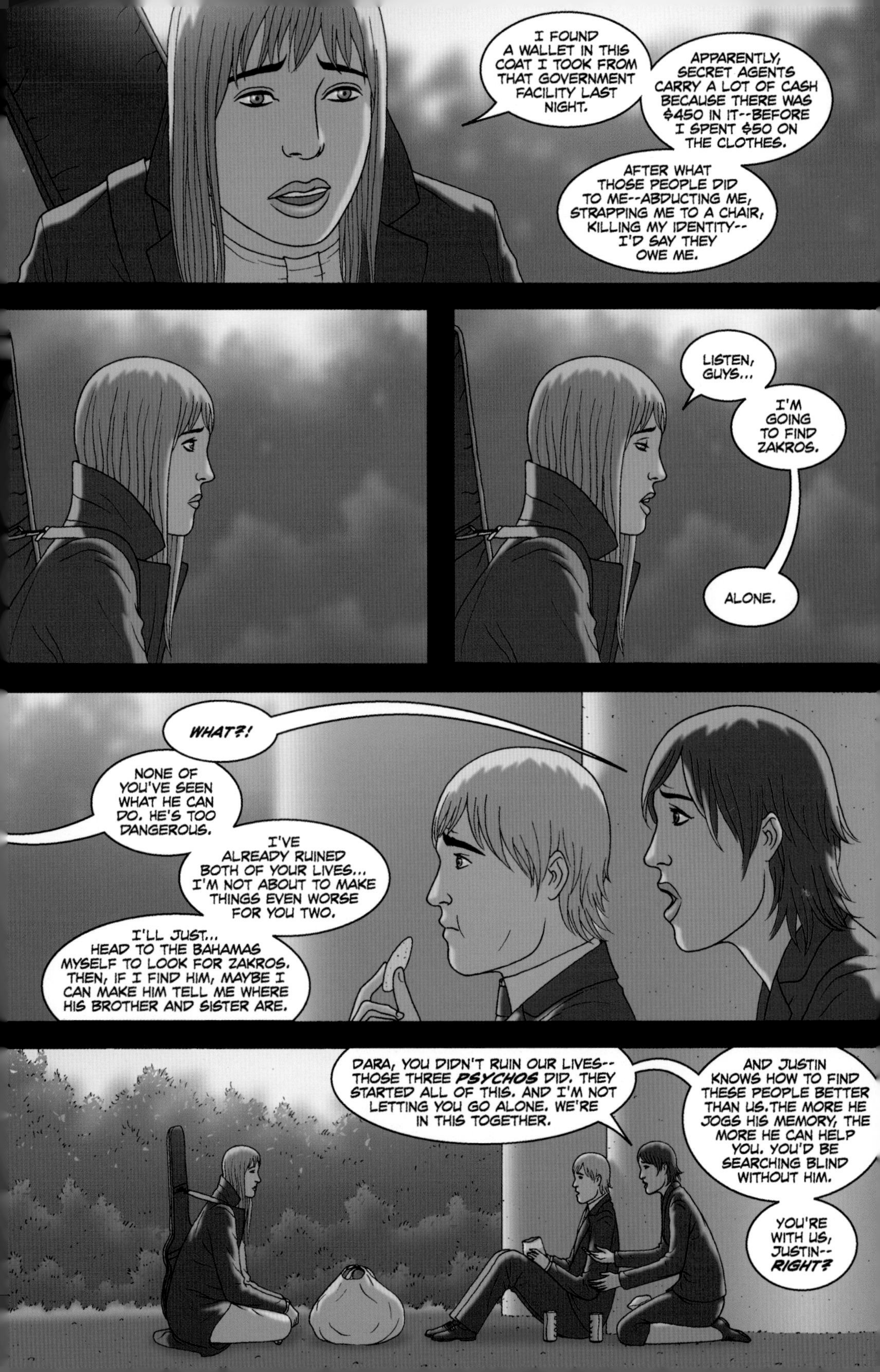
I FOUND A WALLET IN THIS COAT I TOOK FROM THAT GOVERNMENT FACILITY LAST NIGHT.
APPARENTLY, SECRET AGENTS CARRY A LOT OF CASH BECAUSE THERE WAS $450 IN IT--BEFORE I SPENT $50 ON THE CLOTHES.
AFTER WHAT THOSE PEOPLE DID TO ME--ABDUCTING ME, STRAPPING ME TO A CHAIR, KILLING MY IDENTITY--I'D SAY THEY OWE ME.
LISTEN, GUYS...
I'M GOING TO FIND ZAKROS.
ALONE.
WHAT?!
NONE OF YOU'VE SEEN WHAT HE CAN DO. HE'S TOO DANGEROUS.
I'VE ALREADY RUINED BOTH OF YOUR LIVES... I'M NOT ABOUT TO MAKE THINGS EVEN WORSE FOR YOU TWO.
I'LL JUST... HEAD TO THE BAHAMAS MYSELF TO LOOK FOR ZAKROS. THEN, IF I FIND HIM, MAYBE I CAN MAKE HIM TELL ME WHERE HIS BROTHER AND SISTER ARE.
DARA, YOU DIDN'T RUIN OUR LIVES--THOSE THREE PSYCHOS DID. THEY STARTED ALL OF THIS. AND I'M NOT LETTING YOU GO ALONE. WE'RE IN THIS TOGETHER.
AND JUSTIN KNOWS HOW TO FIND THESE PEOPLE BETTER THAN US. THE MORE HE JOGS HIS MEMORY, THE MORE HE CAN HELP YOU. YOU'D BE SEARCHING BLIND WITHOUT HIM.
YOU'RE WITH US, JUSTIN--RIGHT?

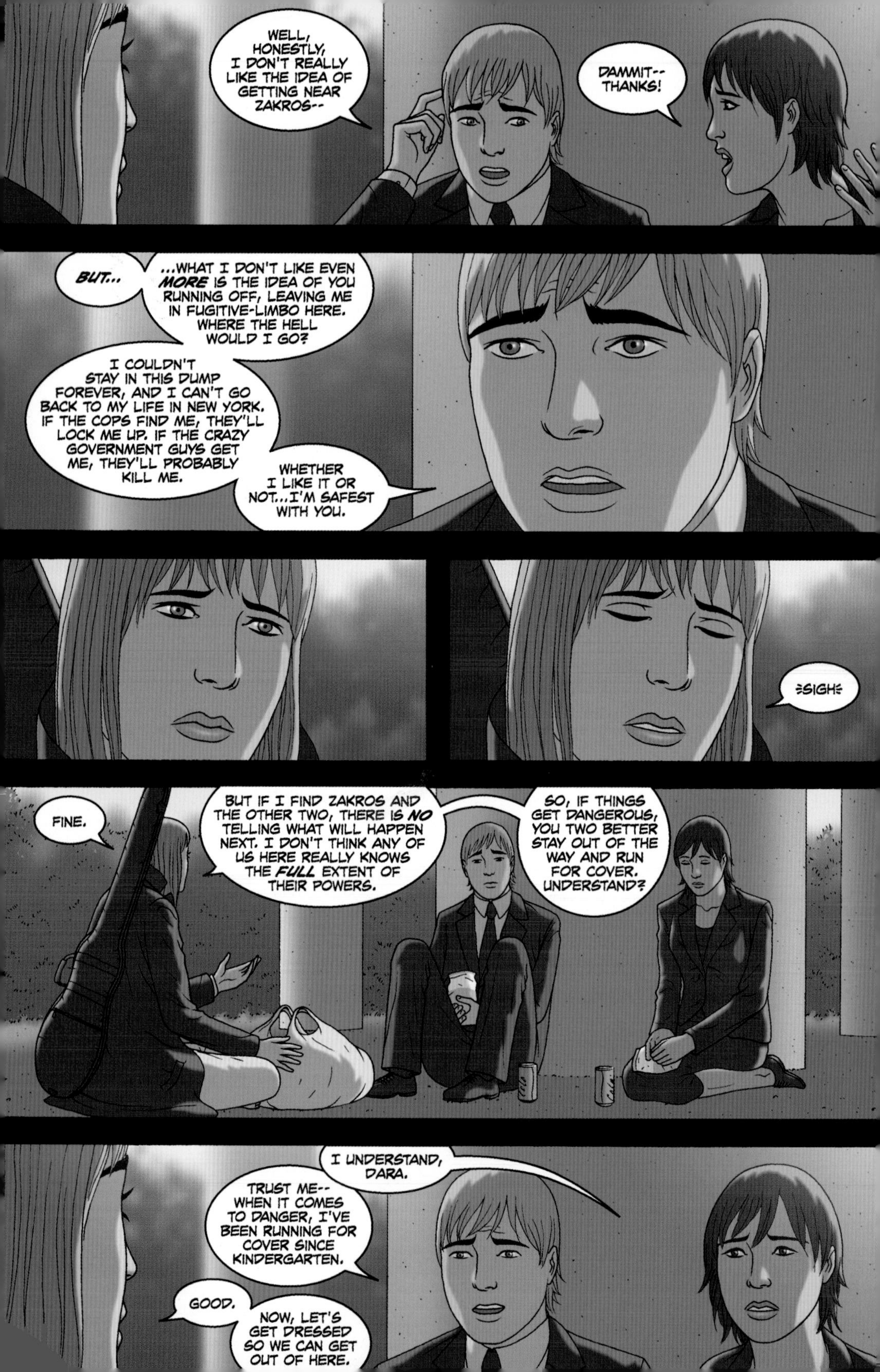
WELL, HONESTLY, I DON'T REALLY LIKE THE IDEA OF GETTING NEAR ZAKROS--
DAMMIT-- THANKS!
BUT...
...WHAT I DON'T LIKE EVEN MORE IS THE IDEA OF YOU RUNNING OFF, LEAVING ME IN FUGITIVE-LIMBO HERE. WHERE THE HELL WOULD I GO?
I COULDN'T STAY IN THIS DUMP FOREVER, AND I CAN'T GO BACK TO MY LIFE IN NEW YORK. IF THE COPS FIND ME, THEY'LL LOCK ME UP. IF THE CRAZY GOVERNMENT GUYS GET ME, THEY'LL PROBABLY KILL ME.
WHETHER I LIKE IT OR NOT...I'M SAFEST WITH YOU.
SIGH
FINE.
BUT IF I FIND ZAKROS AND THE OTHER TWO, THERE IS NO TELLING WHAT WILL HAPPEN NEXT. I DON'T THINK ANY OF US HERE REALLY KNOWS THE FULL EXTENT OF THEIR POWERS.
SO, IF THINGS GET DANGEROUS, YOU TWO BETTER STAY OUT OF THE WAY AND RUN FOR COVER. UNDERSTAND?
I UNDERSTAND, DARA.
TRUST ME-- WHEN IT COMES TO DANGER, I'VE BEEN RUNNING FOR COVER SINCE KINDERGARTEN.
GOOD.
NOW, LET'S GET DRESSED SO WE CAN GET OUT OF HERE.

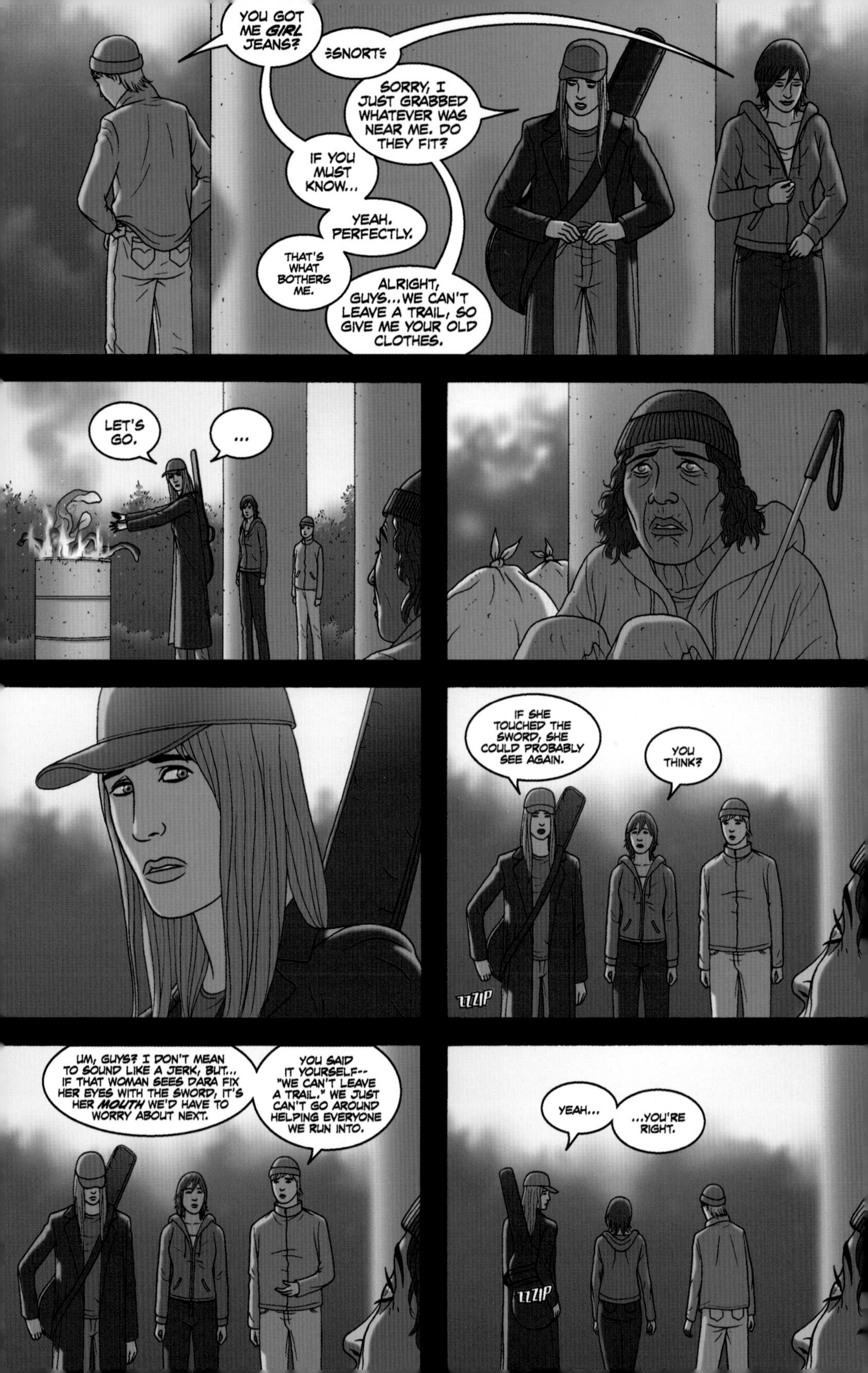
YOU GOT ME GIRL JEANS?
SNORT
SORRY, I JUST GRABBED WHATEVER WAS NEAR ME. DO THEY FIT?
IF YOU MUST KNOW...
YEAH. PERFECTLY.
THAT'S WHAT BOTHERS ME.
ALRIGHT, GUYS...WE CAN'T LEAVE A TRAIL, SO GIVE ME YOUR OLD CLOTHES.
LET'S GO.
...
IF SHE TOUCHED THE SWORD, SHE COULD PROBABLY SEE AGAIN.
YOU THINK?
ZZZIP
UM, GUYS? I DON'T MEAN TO SOUND LIKE A JERK, BUT... IF THAT WOMAN SEES DARA FIX HER EYES WITH THE SWORD, IT'S HER MOUTH WE'D HAVE TO WORRY ABOUT NEXT.
YOU SAID IT YOURSELF-- "WE CAN'T LEAVE A TRAIL." WE JUST CAN'T GO AROUND HELPING EVERYONE WE RUN INTO.
YEAH...
...YOU'RE RIGHT.
ZZZIP

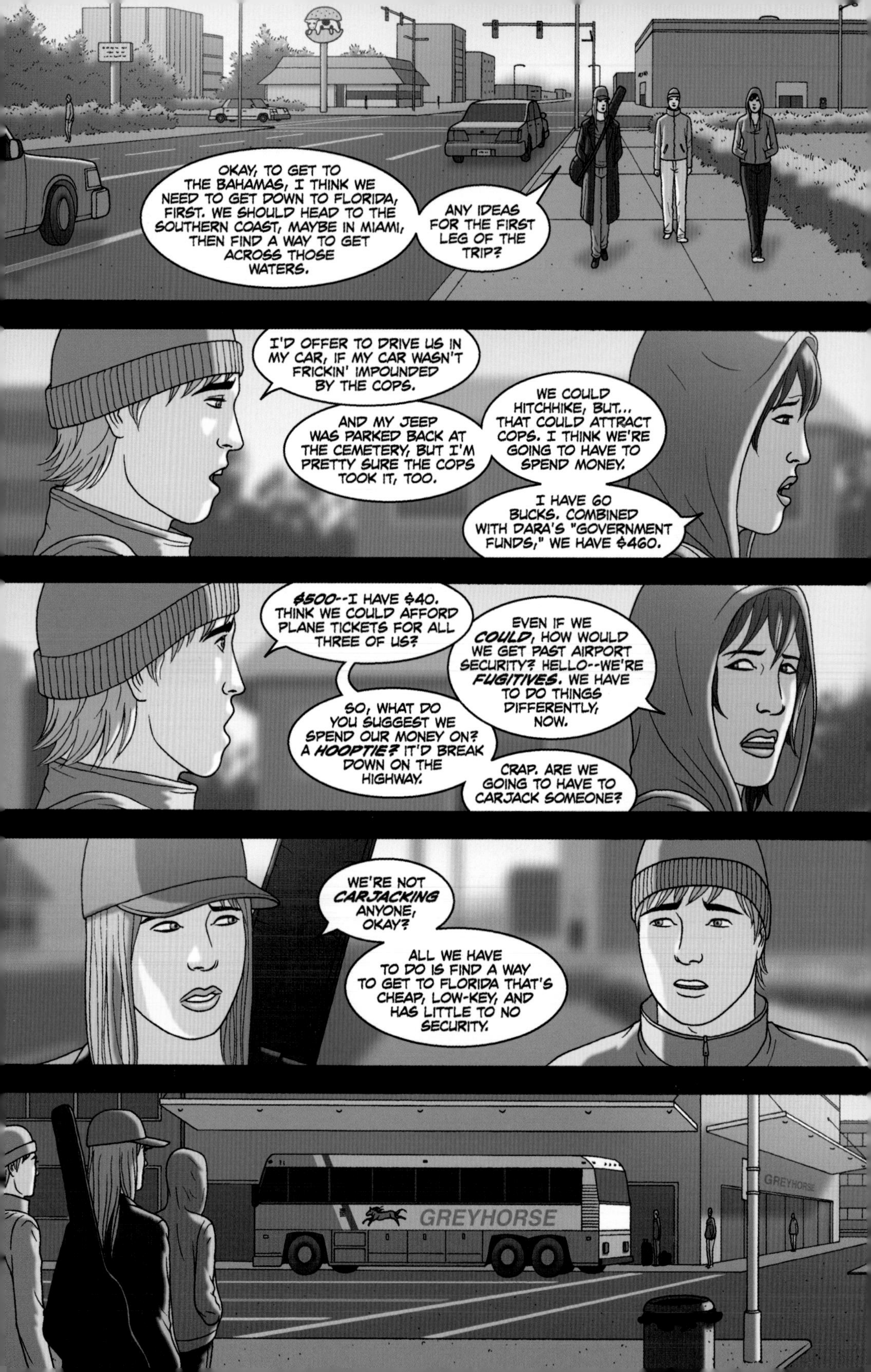
OKAY, TO GET TO THE BAHAMAS, I THINK WE NEED TO GET DOWN TO FLORIDA, FIRST. WE SHOULD HEAD TO THE SOUTHERN COAST, MAYBE IN MIAMI, THEN FIND A WAY TO GET ACROSS THOSE WATERS.
ANY IDEAS FOR THE FIRST LEG OF THE TRIP?
I'D OFFER TO DRIVE US IN MY CAR, IF MY CAR WASN'T FRICKIN' IMPOUNDED BY THE COPS.
AND MY JEEP WAS PARKED BACK AT THE CEMETERY, BUT I'M PRETTY SURE THE COPS TOOK IT, TOO.
WE COULD HITCHHIKE, BUT... THAT COULD ATTRACT COPS. I THINK WE'RE GOING TO HAVE TO SPEND MONEY.
I HAVE 60 BUCKS. COMBINED WITH DARA'S "GOVERNMENT FUNDS," WE HAVE $460.
$500--I HAVE $40. THINK WE COULD AFFORD PLANE TICKETS FOR ALL THREE OF US?
EVEN IF WE COULD, HOW WOULD WE GET PAST AIRPORT SECURITY? HELLO--WE'RE FUGITIVES. WE HAVE TO DO THINGS DIFFERENTLY, NOW.
SO, WHAT DO YOU SUGGEST WE SPEND OUR MONEY ON? A HOOPTIE? IT'D BREAK DOWN ON THE HIGHWAY.
CRAP. ARE WE GOING TO HAVE TO CARJACK SOMEONE?
WE'RE NOT CARJACKING ANYONE, OKAY?
ALL WE HAVE TO DO IS FIND A WAY TO GET TO FLORIDA THAT'S CHEAP, LOW-KEY, AND HAS LITTLE TO NO SECURITY.
GREYHORSE
GREYHORSE

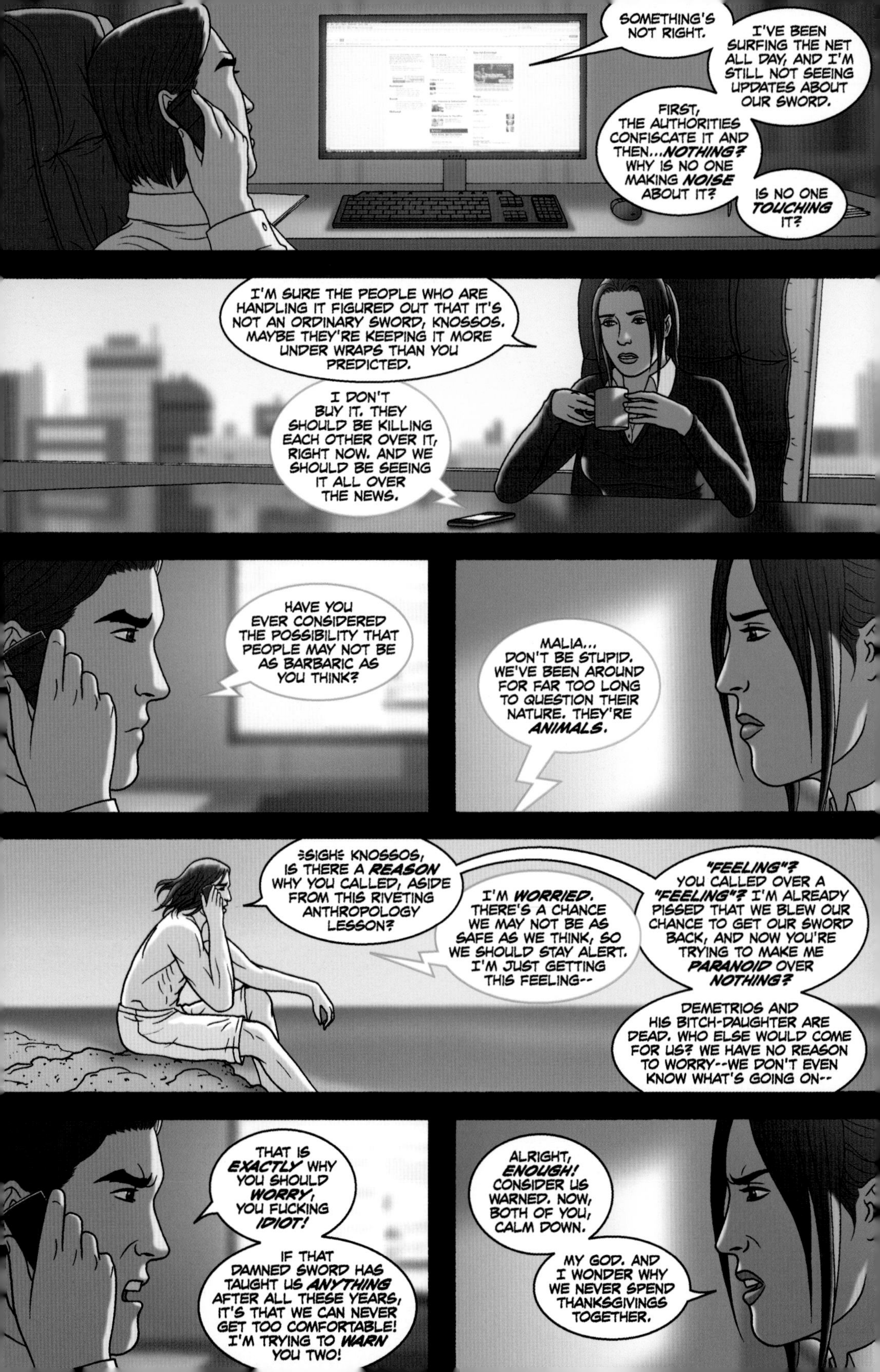
SOMETHING'S NOT RIGHT.
I'VE BEEN SURFING THE NET ALL DAY, AND I'M STILL NOT SEEING UPDATES ABOUT OUR SWORD.
FIRST, THE AUTHORITIES CONFISCATE IT AND THEN...NOTHING? WHY IS NO ONE MAKING NOISE ABOUT IT?
IS NO ONE TOUCHING IT?
I'M SURE THE PEOPLE WHO ARE HANDLING IT FIGURED OUT THAT IT'S NOT AN ORDINARY SWORD, KNOSSOS. MAYBE THEY'RE KEEPING IT MORE UNDER WRAPS THAN YOU PREDICTED.
I DON'T BUY IT. THEY SHOULD BE KILLING EACH OTHER OVER IT, RIGHT NOW. AND WE SHOULD BE SEEING IT ALL OVER THE NEWS.
HAVE YOU EVER CONSIDERED THE POSSIBILITY THAT PEOPLE MAY NOT BE AS BARBARIC AS YOU THINK?
MALIA... DON'T BE STUPID. WE'VE BEEN AROUND FOR FAR TOO LONG TO QUESTION THEIR NATURE. THEY'RE ANIMALS.
SIGH KNOSSOS, IS THERE A REASON WHY YOU CALLED, ASIDE FROM THIS RIVETING ANTHROPOLOGY LESSON?
I'M WORRIED. THERE'S A CHANCE WE MAY NOT BE AS SAFE AS WE THINK, SO WE SHOULD STAY ALERT. I'M JUST GETTING THIS FEELING--
"FEELING"? YOU CALLED OVER A "FEELING"? I'M ALREADY PISSED THAT WE BLEW OUR CHANCE TO GET OUR SWORD BACK, AND NOW YOU'RE TRYING TO MAKE ME PARANOID OVER NOTHING?
DEMETRIOS AND HIS BITCH-DAUGHTER ARE DEAD. WHO ELSE WOULD COME FOR US? WE HAVE NO REASON TO WORRY--WE DON'T EVEN KNOW WHAT'S GOING ON--
THAT IS EXACTLY WHY YOU SHOULD WORRY, YOU FUCKING IDIOT!
IF THAT DAMNED SWORD HAS TAUGHT US ANYTHING AFTER ALL THESE YEARS, IT'S THAT WE CAN NEVER GET TOO COMFORTABLE! I'M TRYING TO WARN YOU TWO!
ALRIGHT, ENOUGH! CONSIDER US WARNED. NOW, BOTH OF YOU, CALM DOWN.
MY GOD. AND I WONDER WHY WE NEVER SPEND THANKSGIVINGS TOGETHER.

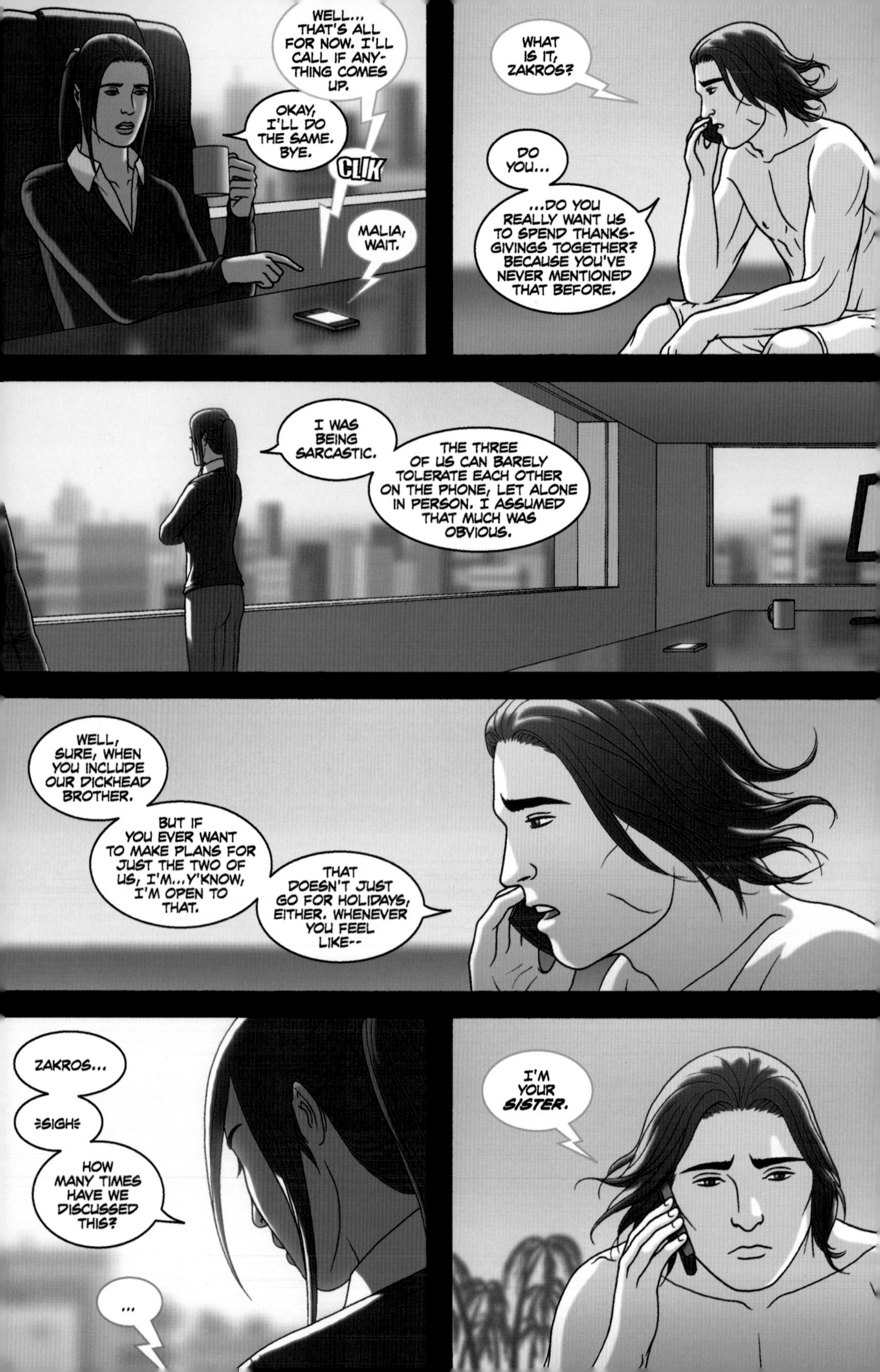
WELL... THAT'S ALL FOR NOW. I'LL CALL IF ANY-THING COMES UP.
OKAY, I'LL DO THE SAME. BYE.
CLIK
MALIA, WAIT.
WHAT IS IT, ZAKROS?
DO YOU...
...DO YOU REALLY WANT US TO SPEND THANKS-GIVINGS TOGETHER? BECAUSE YOU'VE NEVER MENTIONED THAT BEFORE.
I WAS BEING SARCASTIC.
THE THREE OF US CAN BARELY TOLERATE EACH OTHER ON THE PHONE, LET ALONE IN PERSON. I ASSUMED THAT MUCH WAS OBVIOUS.
WELL, SURE, WHEN YOU INCLUDE OUR DICKHEAD BROTHER.
BUT IF YOU EVER WANT TO MAKE PLANS FOR JUST THE TWO OF US, I'M...Y'KNOW, I'M OPEN TO THAT.
THAT DOESN'T JUST GO FOR HOLIDAYS, EITHER. WHENEVER YOU FEEL LIKE--
ZAKROS...
SIGH
HOW MANY TIMES HAVE WE DISCUSSED THIS?
...
I'M YOUR SISTER.

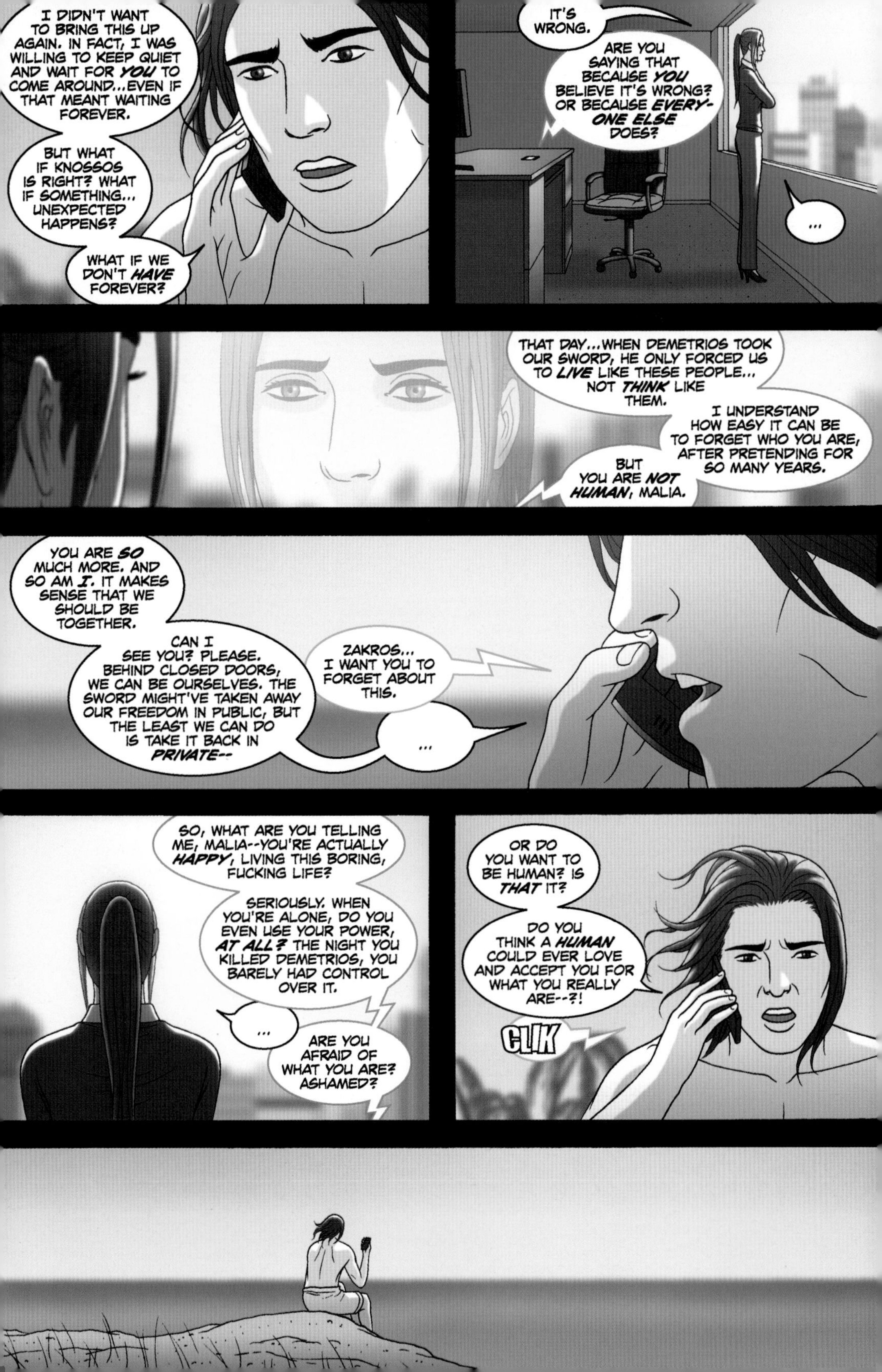
I DIDN'T WANT TO BRING THIS UP AGAIN. IN FACT, I WAS WILLING TO KEEP QUIET AND WAIT FOR YOU TO COME AROUND...EVEN IF THAT MEANT WAITING FOREVER.
BUT WHAT IF KNOSSOS IS RIGHT? WHAT IF SOMETHING... UNEXPECTED HAPPENS?
WHAT IF WE DON'T HAVE FOREVER?
IT'S WRONG.
ARE YOU SAYING THAT BECAUSE YOU BELIEVE IT'S WRONG? OR BECAUSE EVERY-ONE ELSE DOES?
...
THAT DAY...WHEN DEMETRIOS TOOK OUR SWORD, HE ONLY FORCED US TO LIVE LIKE THESE PEOPLE... NOT THINK LIKE THEM.
I UNDERSTAND HOW EASY IT CAN BE TO FORGET WHO YOU ARE, AFTER PRETENDING FOR SO MANY YEARS.
BUT YOU ARE NOT HUMAN, MALIA.
YOU ARE SO MUCH MORE. AND SO AM I. IT MAKES SENSE THAT WE SHOULD BE TOGETHER.
CAN I SEE YOU? PLEASE. BEHIND CLOSED DOORS, WE CAN BE OURSELVES. THE SWORD MIGHT'VE TAKEN AWAY OUR FREEDOM IN PUBLIC, BUT THE LEAST WE CAN DO IS TAKE IT BACK IN PRIVATE--
ZAKROS... I WANT YOU TO FORGET ABOUT THIS.
...
SO, WHAT ARE YOU TELLING ME, MALIA--YOU'RE ACTUALLY HAPPY, LIVING THIS BORING, FUCKING LIFE?
SERIOUSLY. WHEN YOU'RE ALONE, DO YOU EVEN USE YOUR POWER, AT ALL? THE NIGHT YOU KILLED DEMETRIOS, YOU BARELY HAD CONTROL OVER IT.
...
ARE YOU AFRAID OF WHAT YOU ARE? ASHAMED?
OR DO YOU WANT TO BE HUMAN? IS THAT IT?
DO YOU THINK A HUMAN COULD EVER LOVE AND ACCEPT YOU FOR WHAT YOU REALLY ARE--?!
CLIK

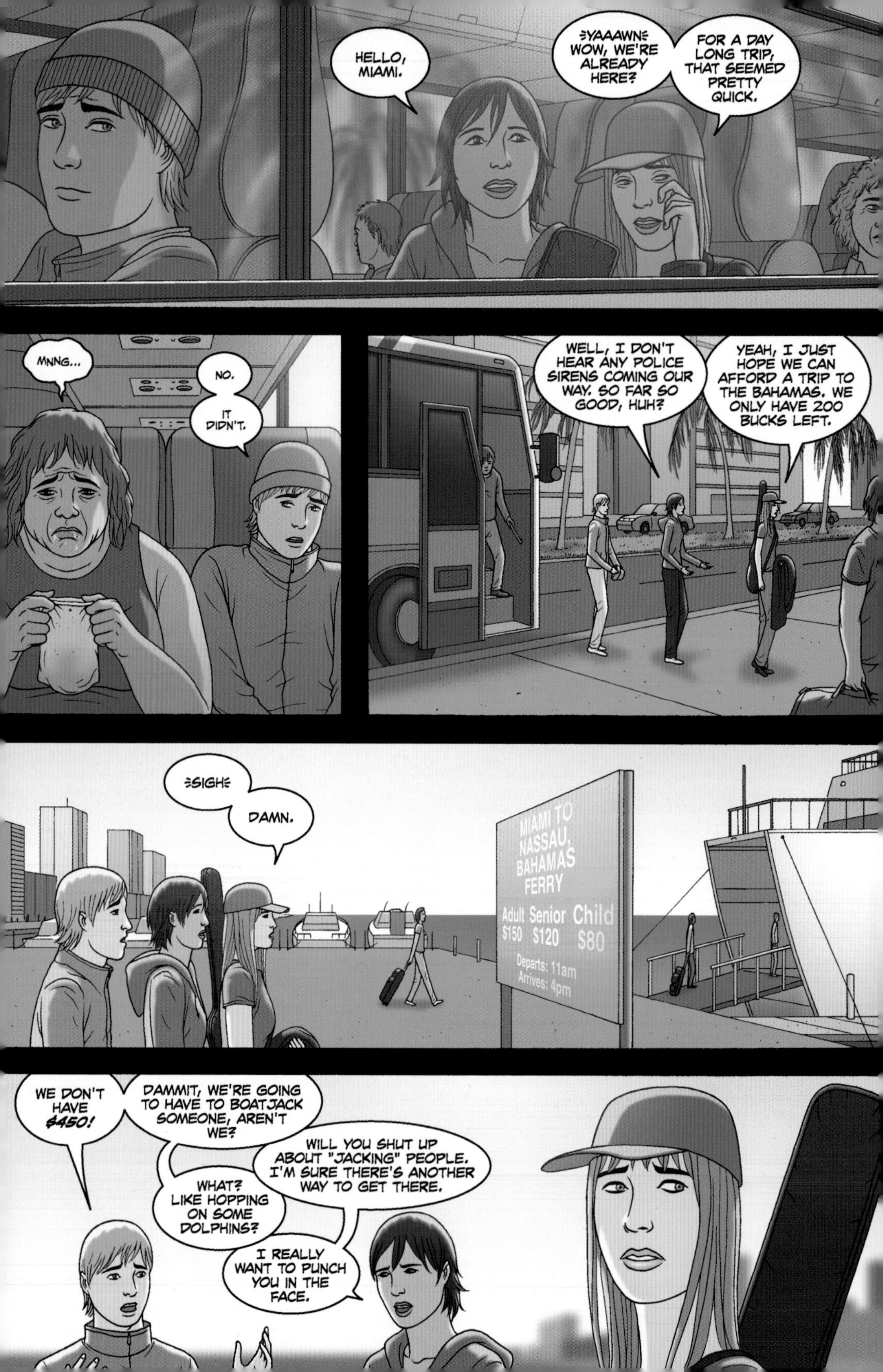

HELLO, MIAMI.
=YAAAWN= WOW, WE'RE ALREADY HERE?
FOR A DAY LONG TRIP, THAT SEEMED PRETTY QUICK.
MNNG...
NO.
IT DIDN'T.
WELL, I DON'T HEAR ANY POLICE SIRENS COMING OUR WAY. SO FAR SO GOOD, HUH?
YEAH, I JUST HOPE WE CAN AFFORD A TRIP TO THE BAHAMAS. WE ONLY HAVE 200 BUCKS LEFT.
=SIGH=
DAMN.
MIAMI TO NASSAU, BAHAMAS FERRY
Adult $150 Senior $120 Child $80
Departs: 11am
Arrives: 4pm
WE DON'T HAVE $450!
DAMMIT, WE'RE GOING TO HAVE TO BOATJACK SOMEONE, AREN'T WE?
WILL YOU SHUT UP ABOUT "JACKING" PEOPLE. I'M SURE THERE'S ANOTHER WAY TO GET THERE.
WHAT? LIKE HOPPING ON SOME DOLPHINS?
I REALLY WANT TO PUNCH YOU IN THE FACE.

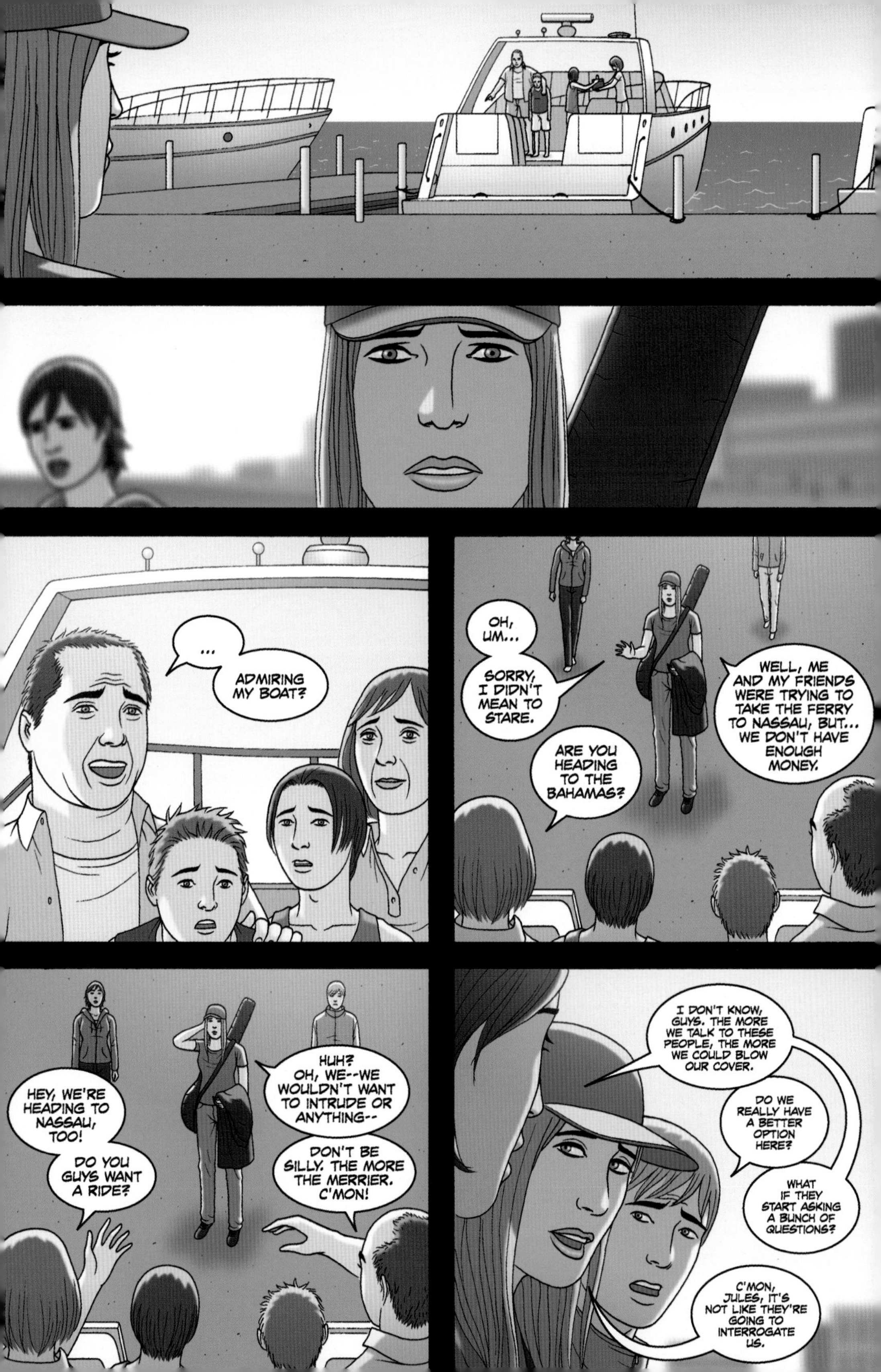
...
ADMIRING MY BOAT?
OH, UM...
SORRY, I DIDN'T MEAN TO STARE.
ARE YOU HEADING TO THE BAHAMAS?
WELL, ME AND MY FRIENDS WERE TRYING TO TAKE THE FERRY TO NASSAU, BUT... WE DON'T HAVE ENOUGH MONEY.
HEY, WE'RE HEADING TO NASSAU, TOO!
DO YOU GUYS WANT A RIDE?
HUH? OH, WE--WE WOULDN'T WANT TO INTRUDE OR ANYTHING--
DON'T BE SILLY. THE MORE THE MERRIER. C'MON!
I DON'T KNOW, GUYS. THE MORE WE TALK TO THESE PEOPLE, THE MORE WE COULD BLOW OUR COVER.
DO WE REALLY HAVE A BETTER OPTION HERE?
WHAT IF THEY START ASKING A BUNCH OF QUESTIONS?
C'MON, JULES, IT'S NOT LIKE THEY'RE GOING TO INTERROGATE US.

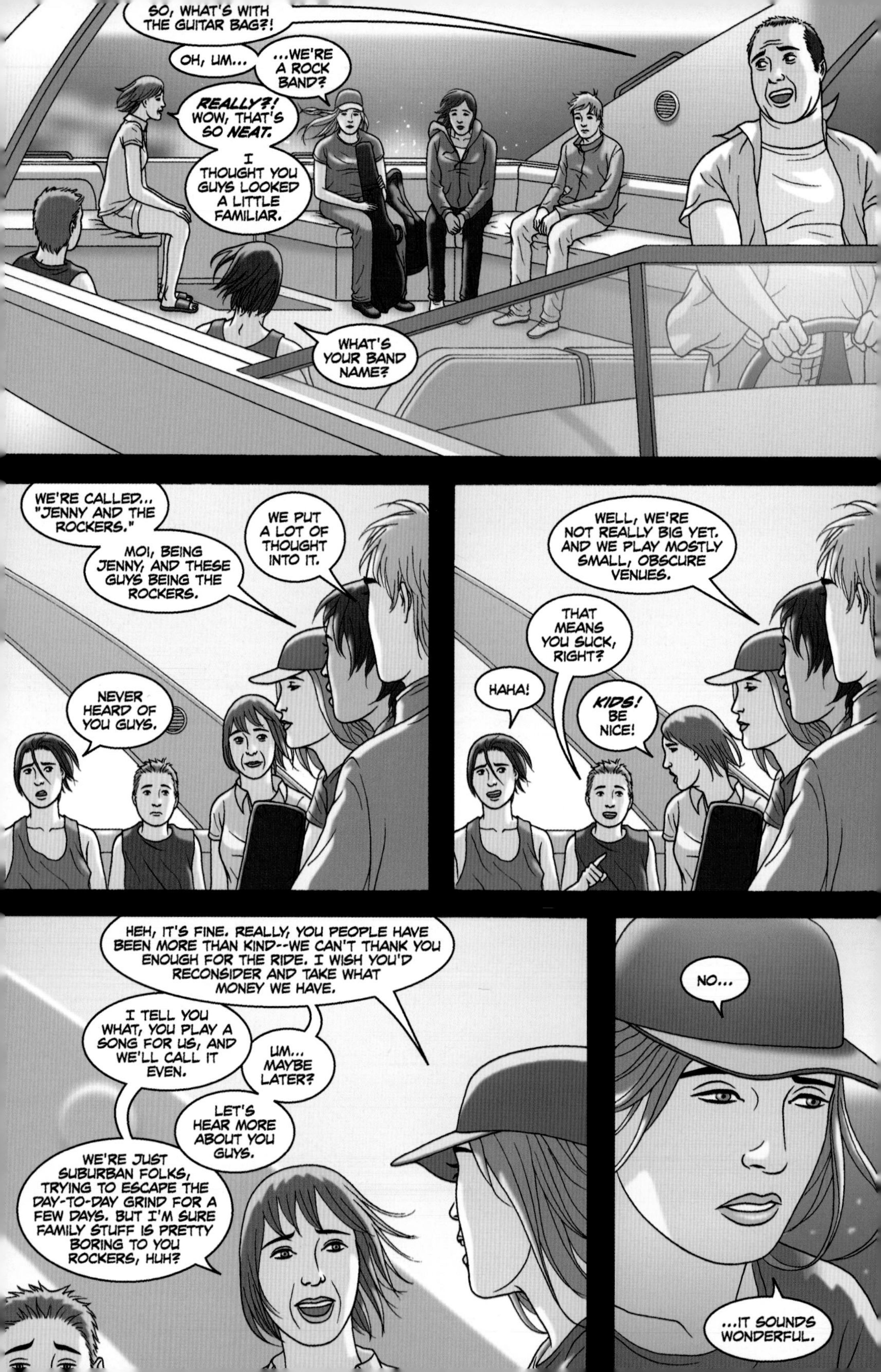

SO, WHAT'S WITH THE GUITAR BAG?!
OH, UM...
...WE'RE A ROCK BAND?
REALLY?! WOW, THAT'S SO NEAT.
I THOUGHT YOU GUYS LOOKED A LITTLE FAMILIAR.
WHAT'S YOUR BAND NAME?
WE'RE CALLED... "JENNY AND THE ROCKERS."
MOI, BEING JENNY, AND THESE GUYS BEING THE ROCKERS.
WE PUT A LOT OF THOUGHT INTO IT.
NEVER HEARD OF YOU GUYS.
WELL, WE'RE NOT REALLY BIG YET. AND WE PLAY MOSTLY SMALL, OBSCURE VENUES.
THAT MEANS YOU SUCK, RIGHT?
HAHA!
KIDS! BE NICE!
HEH, IT'S FINE. REALLY, YOU PEOPLE HAVE BEEN MORE THAN KIND--WE CAN'T THANK YOU ENOUGH FOR THE RIDE. I WISH YOU'D RECONSIDER AND TAKE WHAT MONEY WE HAVE.
I TELL YOU WHAT, YOU PLAY A SONG FOR US, AND WE'LL CALL IT EVEN.
UM... MAYBE LATER?
LET'S HEAR MORE ABOUT YOU GUYS.
WE'RE JUST SUBURBAN FOLKS, TRYING TO ESCAPE THE DAY-TO-DAY GRIND FOR A FEW DAYS. BUT I'M SURE FAMILY STUFF IS PRETTY BORING TO YOU ROCKERS, HUH?
NO...
...IT SOUNDS WONDERFUL.

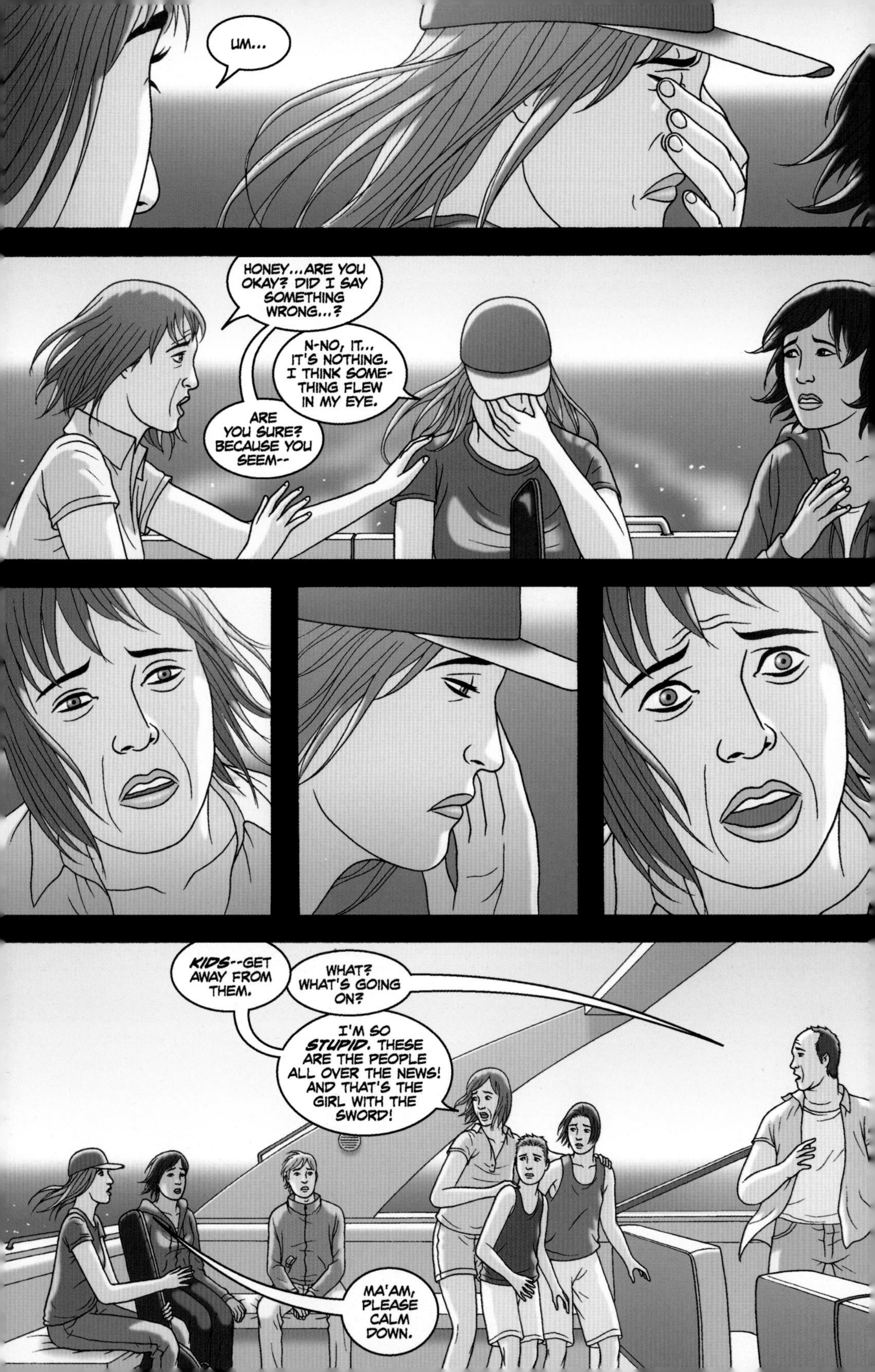
UM...
HONEY...ARE YOU OKAY? DID I SAY SOMETHING WRONG...?
N-NO, IT... IT'S NOTHING. I THINK SOME-THING FLEW IN MY EYE.
ARE YOU SURE? BECAUSE YOU SEEM--
KIDS--GET AWAY FROM THEM.
WHAT? WHAT'S GOING ON?
I'M SO STUPID. THESE ARE THE PEOPLE ALL OVER THE NEWS! AND THAT'S THE GIRL WITH THE SWORD!
MA'AM, PLEASE CALM DOWN.

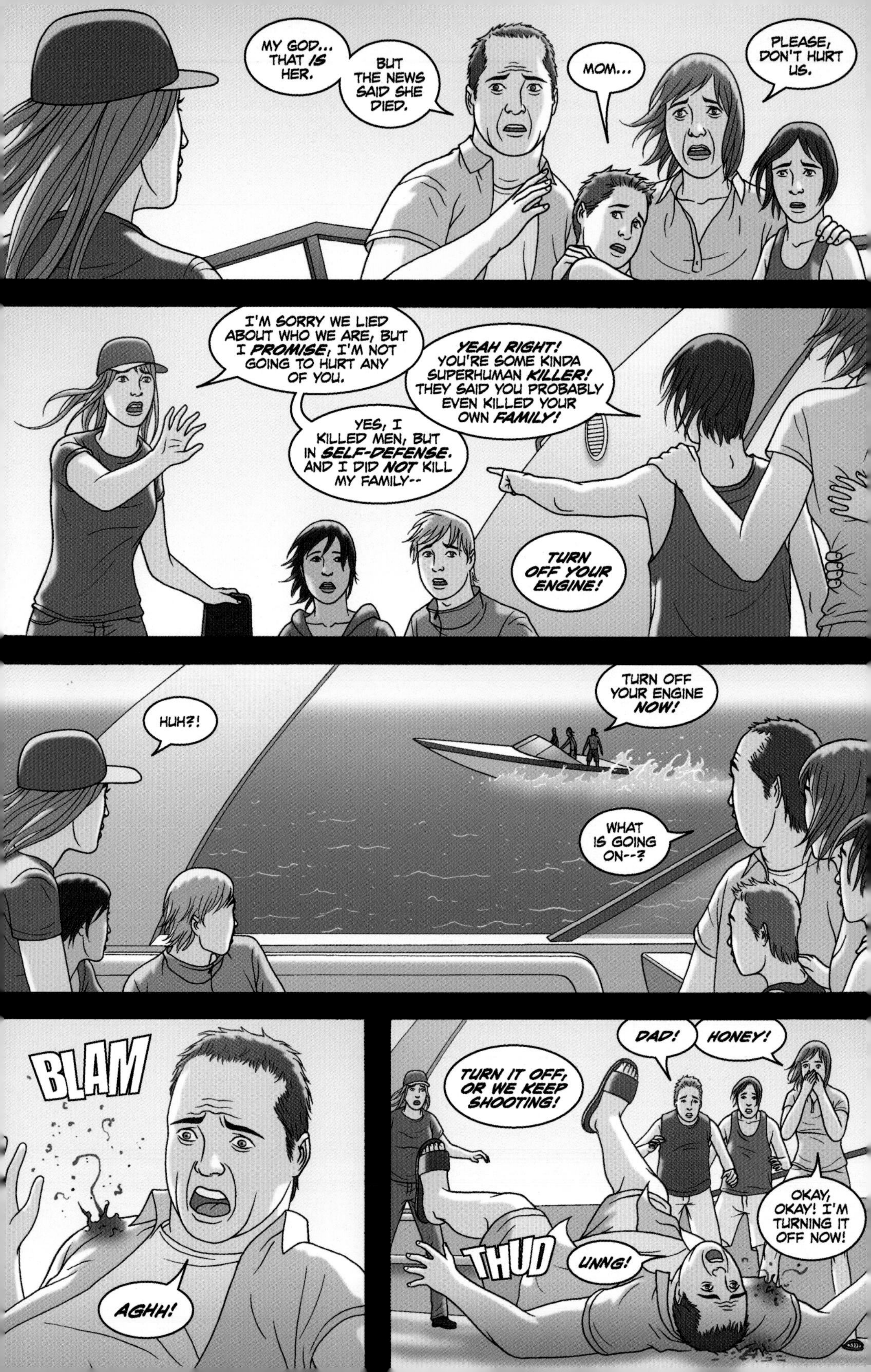
MY GOD... THAT IS HER.
BUT THE NEWS SAID SHE DIED.
MOM...
PLEASE, DON'T HURT US.
I'M SORRY WE LIED ABOUT WHO WE ARE, BUT I PROMISE, I'M NOT GOING TO HURT ANY OF YOU.
YEAH RIGHT! YOU'RE SOME KINDA SUPERHUMAN KILLER! THEY SAID YOU PROBABLY EVEN KILLED YOUR OWN FAMILY!
YES, I KILLED MEN, BUT IN SELF-DEFENSE. AND I DID NOT KILL MY FAMILY--
TURN OFF YOUR ENGINE!
HUH?!
TURN OFF YOUR ENGINE NOW!
WHAT IS GOING ON--?
BLAM
AGHH!
TURN IT OFF, OR WE KEEP SHOOTING!
DAD!
HONEY!
OKAY, OKAY! I'M TURNING IT OFF NOW!
THUD
UNNG!

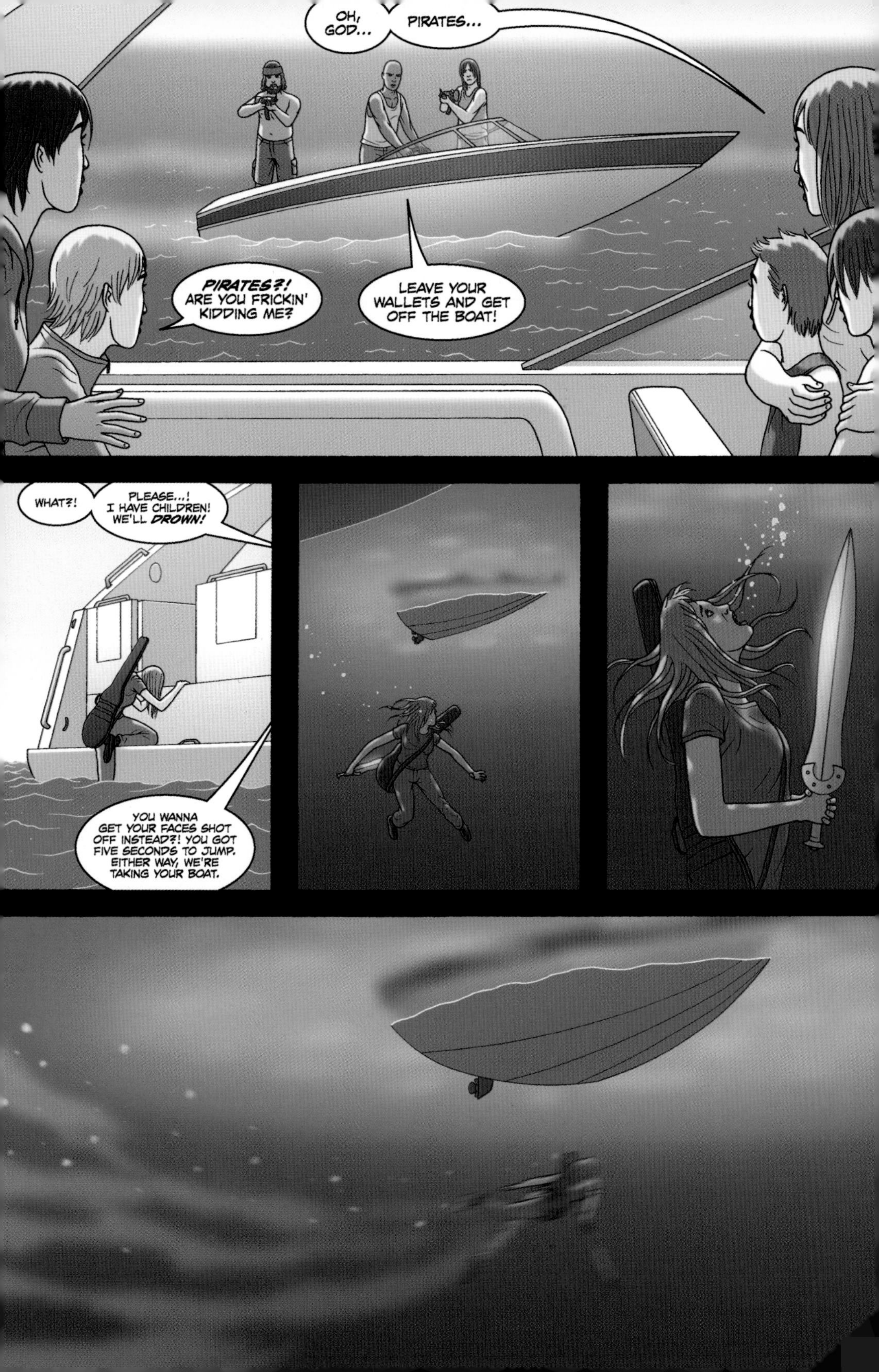
OH, GOD...
PIRATES...
PIRATES?! ARE YOU FRICKIN' KIDDING ME?
LEAVE YOUR WALLETS AND GET OFF THE BOAT!
WHAT?!
PLEASE...! I HAVE CHILDREN! WE'LL DROWN!
YOU WANNA GET YOUR FACES SHOT OFF INSTEAD?! YOU GOT FIVE SECONDS TO JUMP. EITHER WAY, WE'RE TAKING YOUR BOAT.

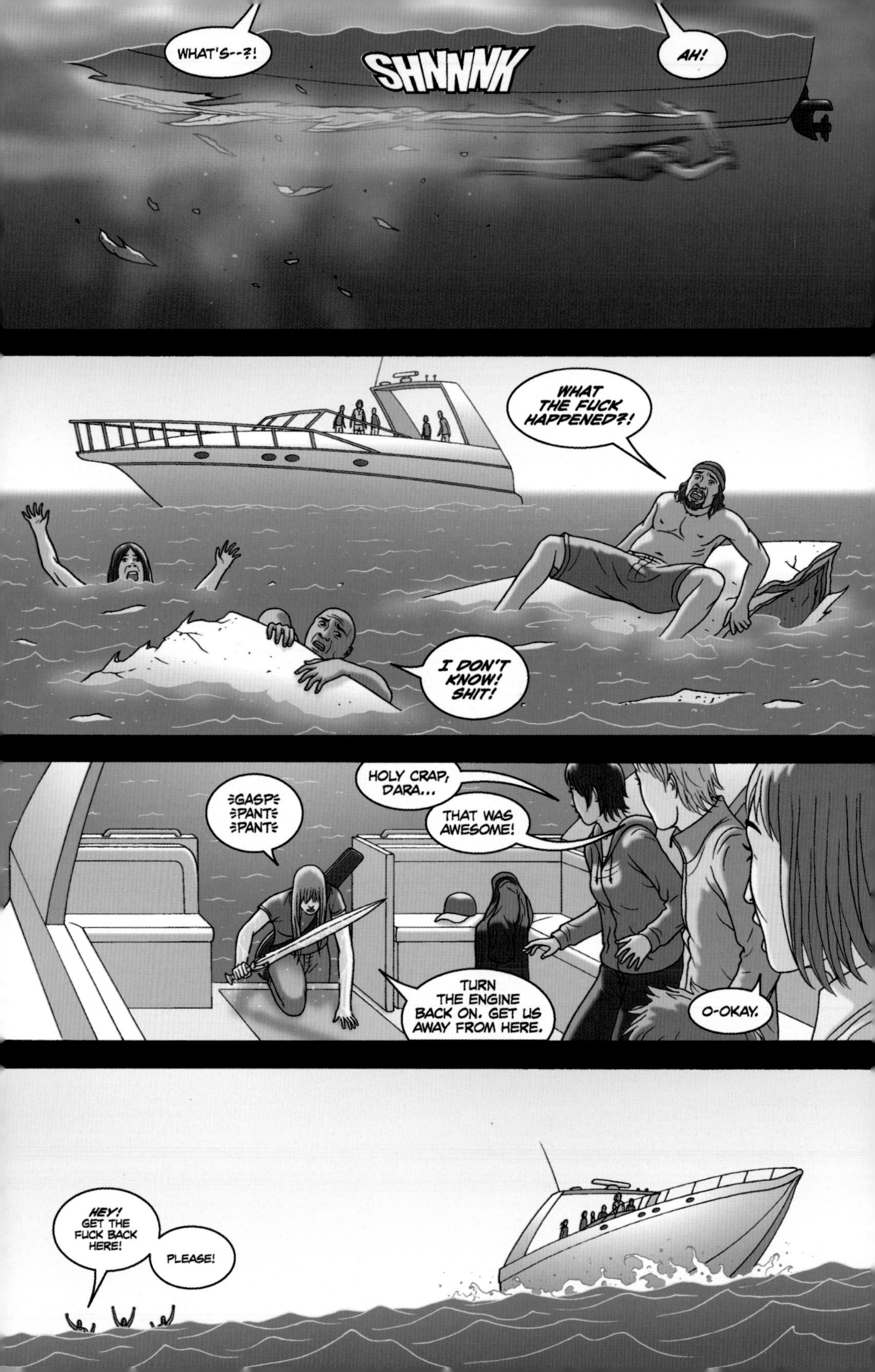
WHAT'S--?!
SHNNNK
AH!
WHAT THE FUCK HAPPENED?!
I DON'T KNOW! SHIT!
HOLY CRAP, DARA...
THAT WAS AWESOME!
GASP PANT PANT
TURN THE ENGINE BACK ON. GET US AWAY FROM HERE.
O-OKAY.
HEY! GET THE FUCK BACK HERE!
PLEASE!

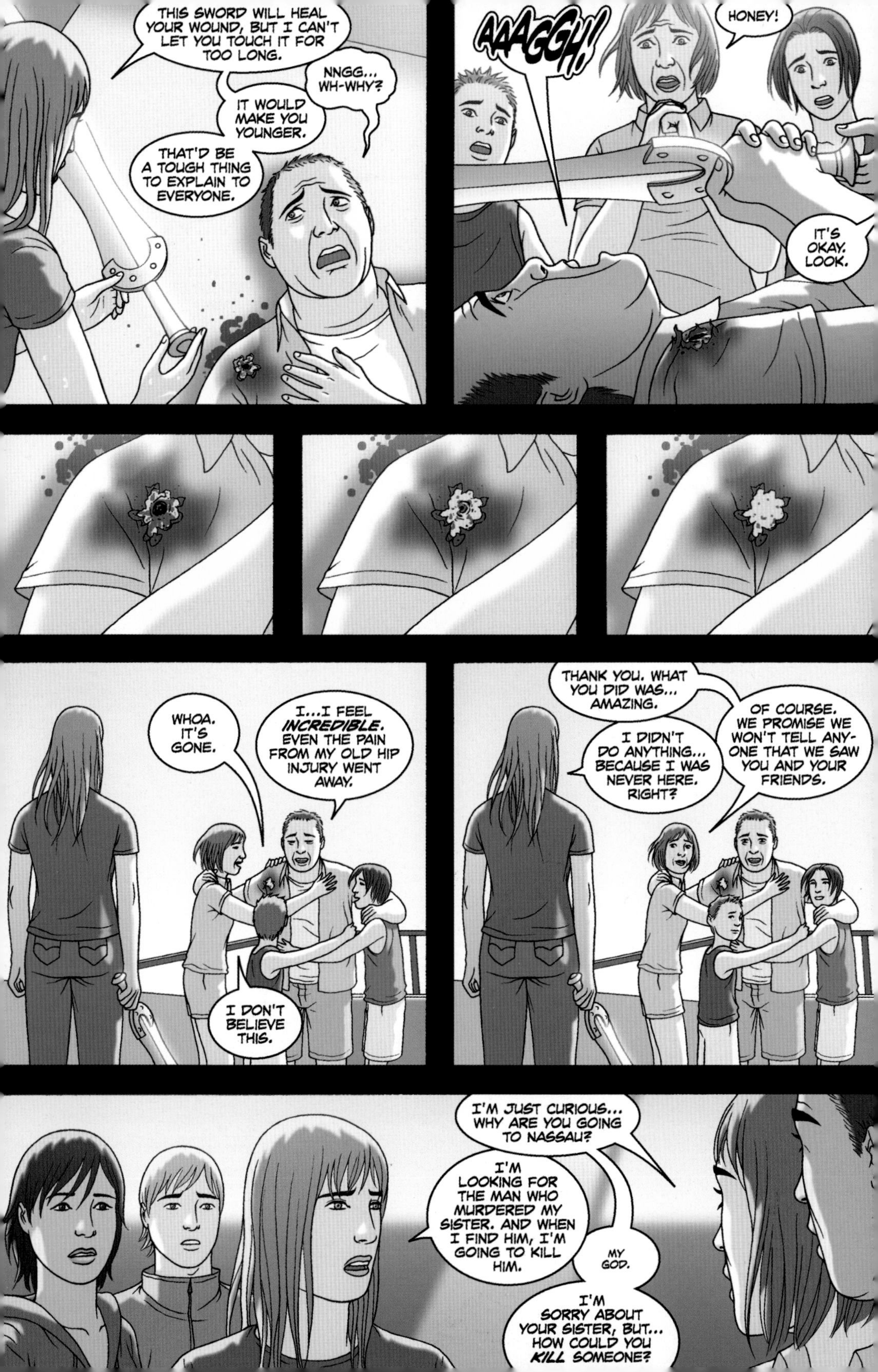
THIS SWORD WILL HEAL YOUR WOUND, BUT I CAN'T LET YOU TOUCH IT FOR TOO LONG.
NNGG... WH-WHY?
IT WOULD MAKE YOU YOUNGER.
THAT'D BE A TOUGH THING TO EXPLAIN TO EVERYONE.
AAAGGH!!
HONEY!
IT'S OKAY. LOOK.
WHOA. IT'S GONE.
I...I FEEL *INCREDIBLE.* EVEN THE PAIN FROM MY OLD HIP INJURY WENT AWAY.
I DON'T BELIEVE THIS.
THANK YOU. WHAT YOU DID WAS... AMAZING.
I DIDN'T DO ANYTHING... BECAUSE I WAS NEVER HERE. RIGHT?
OF COURSE. WE PROMISE WE WON'T TELL ANY-ONE THAT WE SAW YOU AND YOUR FRIENDS.
I'M JUST CURIOUS... WHY ARE YOU GOING TO NASSAU?
I'M LOOKING FOR THE MAN WHO MURDERED MY SISTER. AND WHEN I FIND HIM, I'M GOING TO KILL HIM.
MY GOD.
I'M SORRY ABOUT YOUR SISTER, BUT... HOW COULD YOU *KILL* SOMEONE?

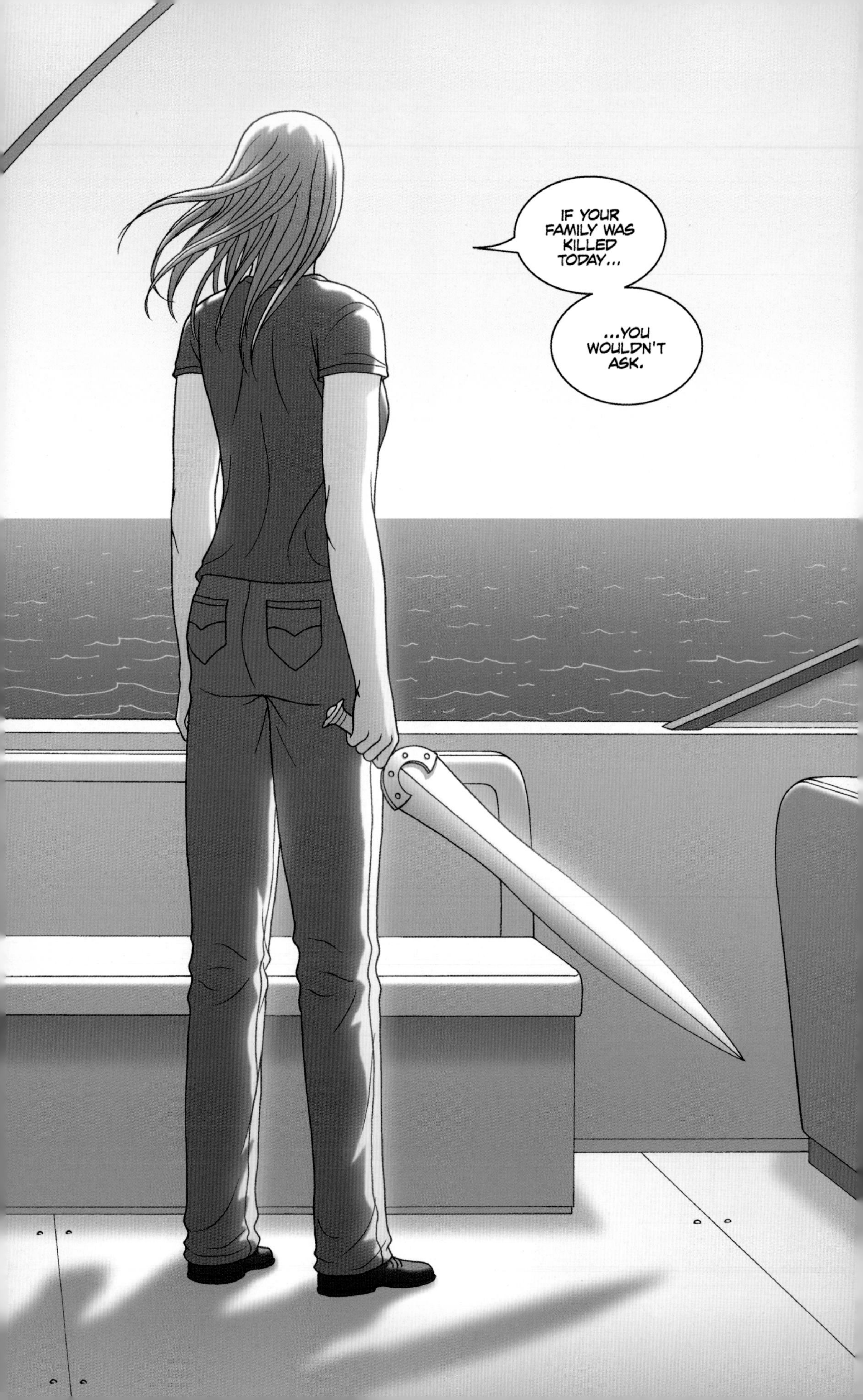
IF YOUR FAMILY WAS KILLED TODAY...
...YOU WOULDN'T ASK.

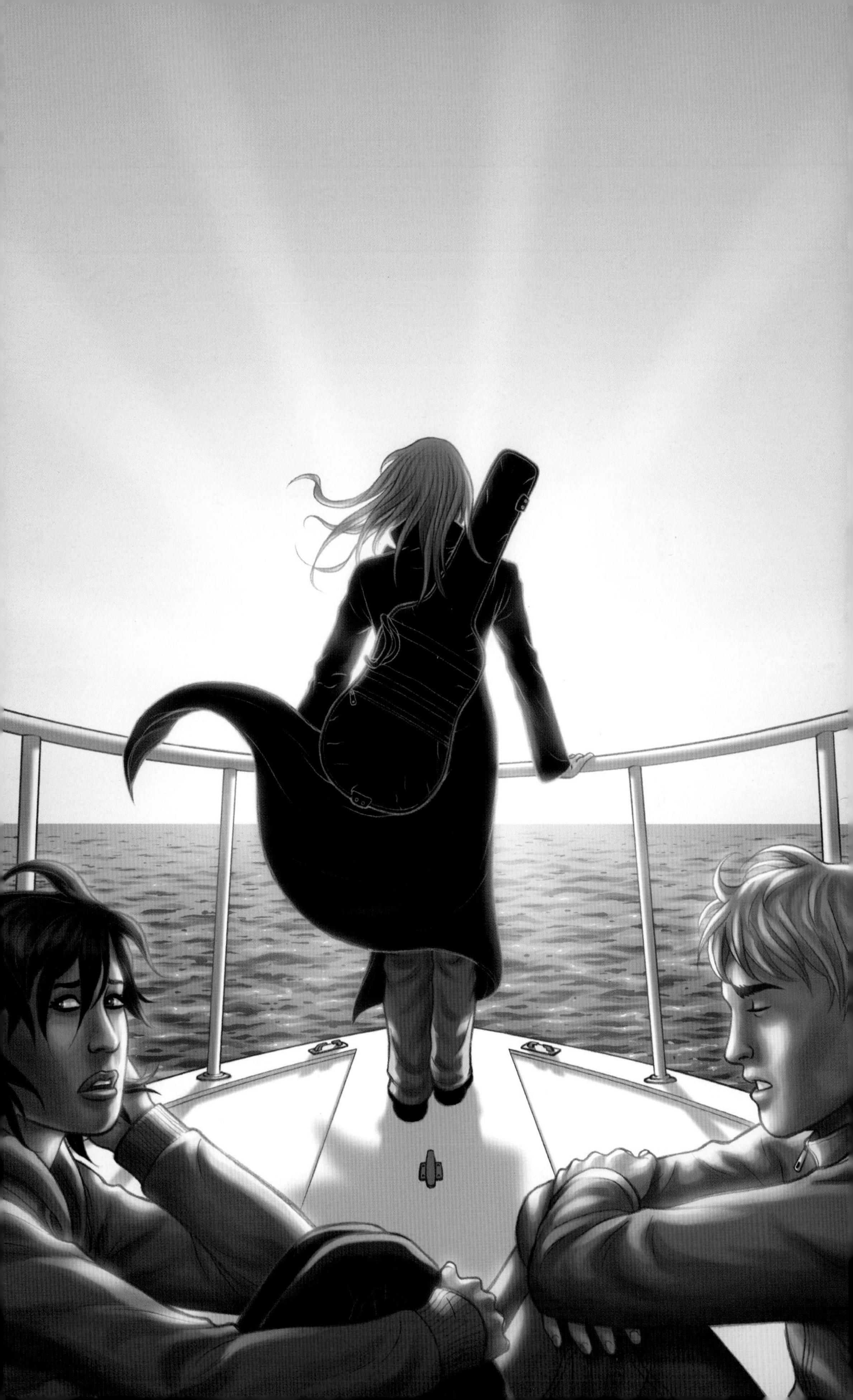

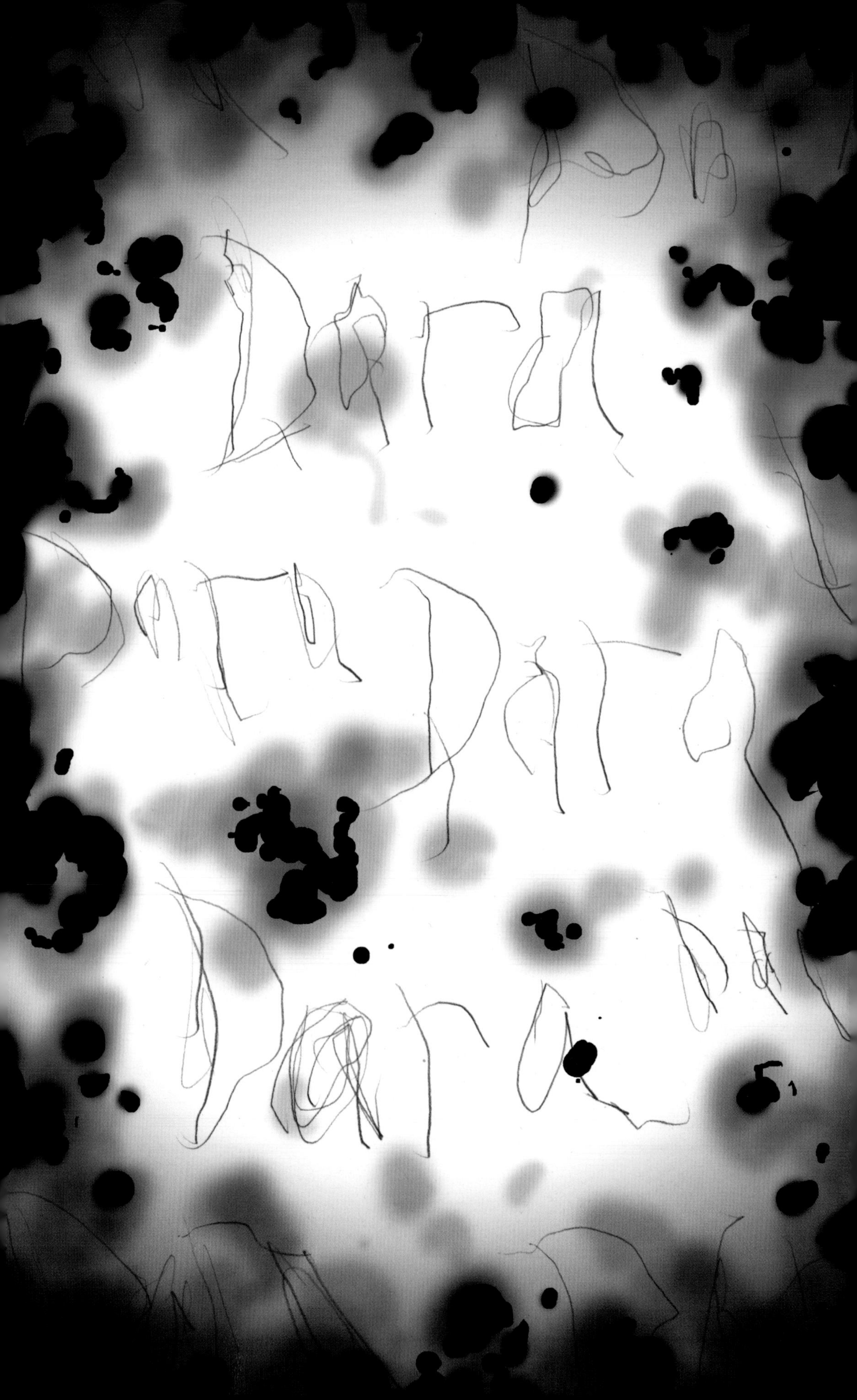
Dora
Dora Dora
Dora

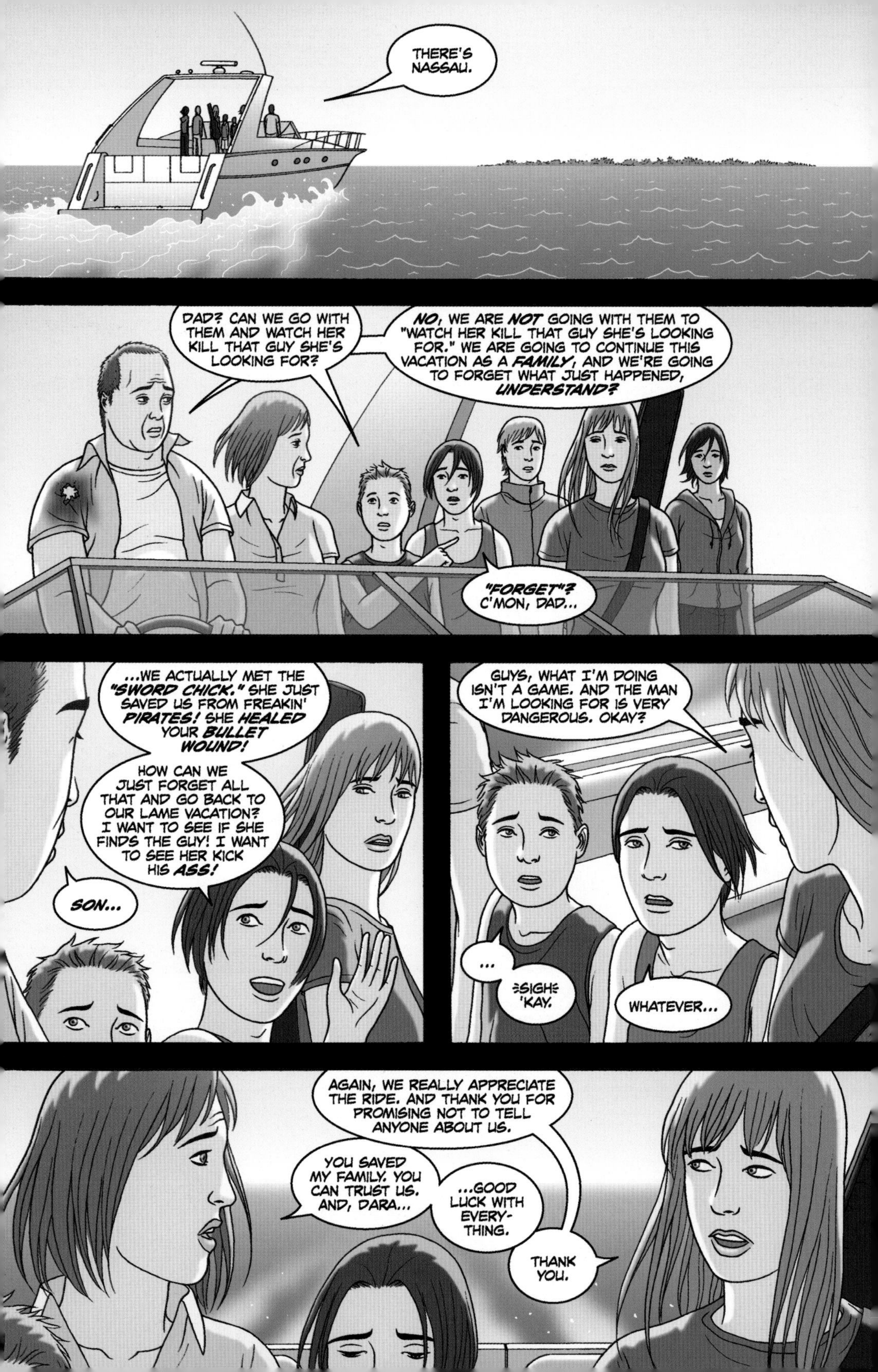
THERE'S NASSAU.
DAD? CAN WE GO WITH THEM AND WATCH HER KILL THAT GUY SHE'S LOOKING FOR?
NO, WE ARE NOT GOING WITH THEM TO "WATCH HER KILL THAT GUY SHE'S LOOKING FOR." WE ARE GOING TO CONTINUE THIS VACATION AS A FAMILY, AND WE'RE GOING TO FORGET WHAT JUST HAPPENED, UNDERSTAND?
"FORGET"? C'MON, DAD...
...WE ACTUALLY MET THE "SWORD CHICK." SHE JUST SAVED US FROM FREAKIN' PIRATES! SHE HEALED YOUR BULLET WOUND!
HOW CAN WE JUST FORGET ALL THAT AND GO BACK TO OUR LAME VACATION? I WANT TO SEE IF SHE FINDS THE GUY! I WANT TO SEE HER KICK HIS ASS!
SON...
GUYS, WHAT I'M DOING ISN'T A GAME. AND THE MAN I'M LOOKING FOR IS VERY DANGEROUS. OKAY?
...
SIGH 'KAY.
WHATEVER...
AGAIN, WE REALLY APPRECIATE THE RIDE. AND THANK YOU FOR PROMISING NOT TO TELL ANYONE ABOUT US.
YOU SAVED MY FAMILY. YOU CAN TRUST US. AND, DARA...
...GOOD LUCK WITH EVERY-THING.
THANK YOU.

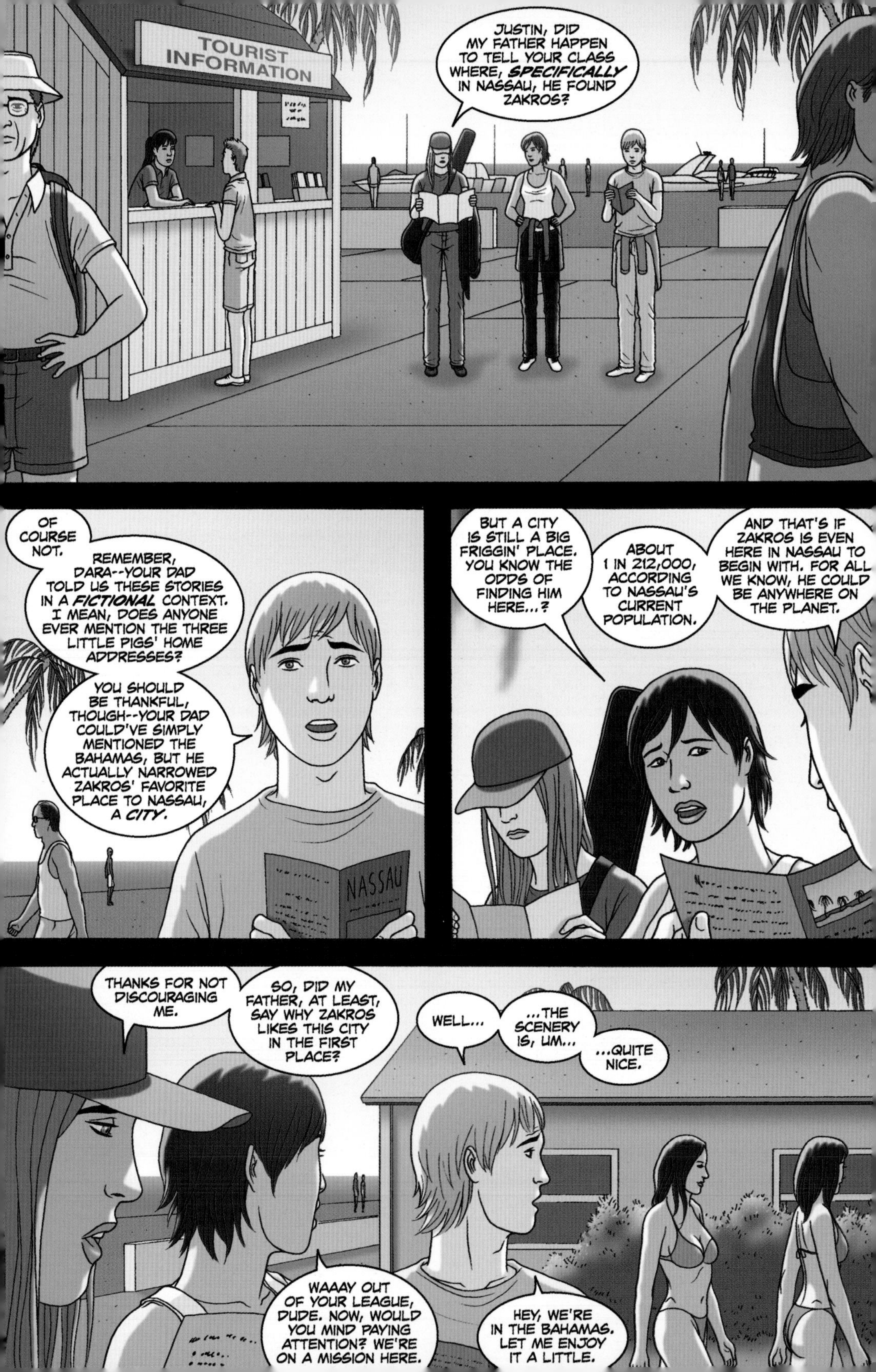
TOURIST INFORMATION
JUSTIN, DID MY FATHER HAPPEN TO TELL YOUR CLASS WHERE, *SPECIFICALLY* IN NASSAU, HE FOUND ZAKROS?
OF COURSE NOT.
REMEMBER, DARA--YOUR DAD TOLD US THESE STORIES IN A *FICTIONAL* CONTEXT. I MEAN, DOES ANYONE EVER MENTION THE THREE LITTLE PIGS' HOME ADDRESSES?
YOU SHOULD BE THANKFUL, THOUGH--YOUR DAD COULD'VE SIMPLY MENTIONED THE BAHAMAS, BUT HE ACTUALLY NARROWED ZAKROS' FAVORITE PLACE TO NASSAU, A *CITY*.
NASSAU
BUT A CITY IS STILL A BIG FRIGGIN' PLACE. YOU KNOW THE ODDS OF FINDING HIM HERE...?
ABOUT 1 IN 212,000, ACCORDING TO NASSAU'S CURRENT POPULATION.
AND THAT'S IF ZAKROS IS EVEN HERE IN NASSAU TO BEGIN WITH. FOR ALL WE KNOW, HE COULD BE ANYWHERE ON THE PLANET.
THANKS FOR NOT DISCOURAGING ME.
SO, DID MY FATHER, AT LEAST, SAY WHY ZAKROS LIKES THIS CITY IN THE FIRST PLACE?
WELL...
...THE SCENERY IS, UM...
...QUITE NICE.
WAAAY OUT OF YOUR LEAGUE, DUDE. NOW, WOULD YOU MIND PAYING ATTENTION? WE'RE ON A MISSION HERE.
HEY, WE'RE IN THE BAHAMAS. LET ME ENJOY IT A LITTLE.

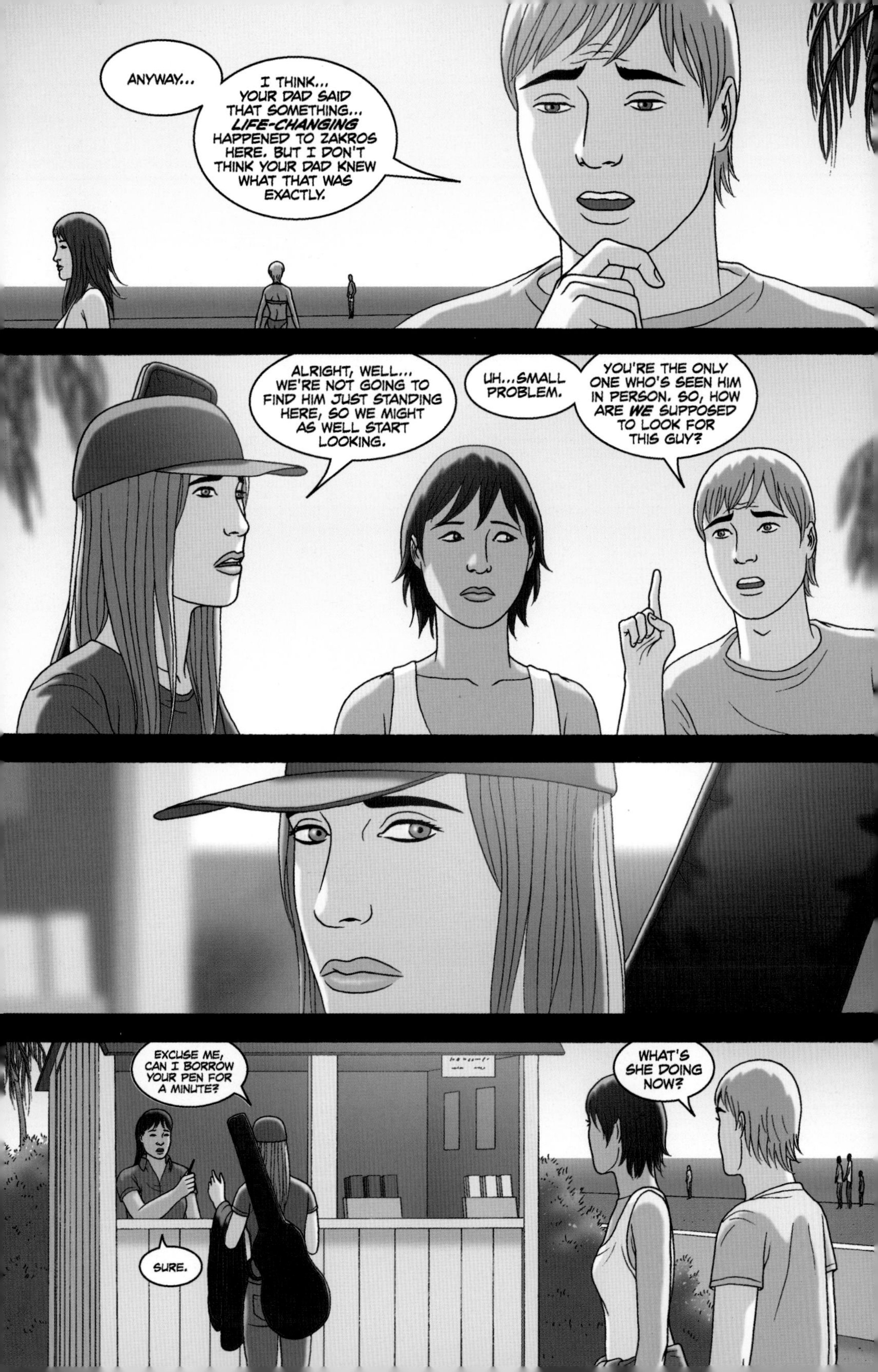
ANYWAY...
I THINK... YOUR DAD SAID THAT SOMETHING... LIFE-CHANGING HAPPENED TO ZAKROS HERE. BUT I DON'T THINK YOUR DAD KNEW WHAT THAT WAS EXACTLY.
ALRIGHT, WELL... WE'RE NOT GOING TO FIND HIM JUST STANDING HERE, SO WE MIGHT AS WELL START LOOKING.
UH...SMALL PROBLEM.
YOU'RE THE ONLY ONE WHO'S SEEN HIM IN PERSON. SO, HOW ARE WE SUPPOSED TO LOOK FOR THIS GUY?
EXCUSE ME, CAN I BORROW YOUR PEN FOR A MINUTE?
SURE.
WHAT'S SHE DOING NOW?

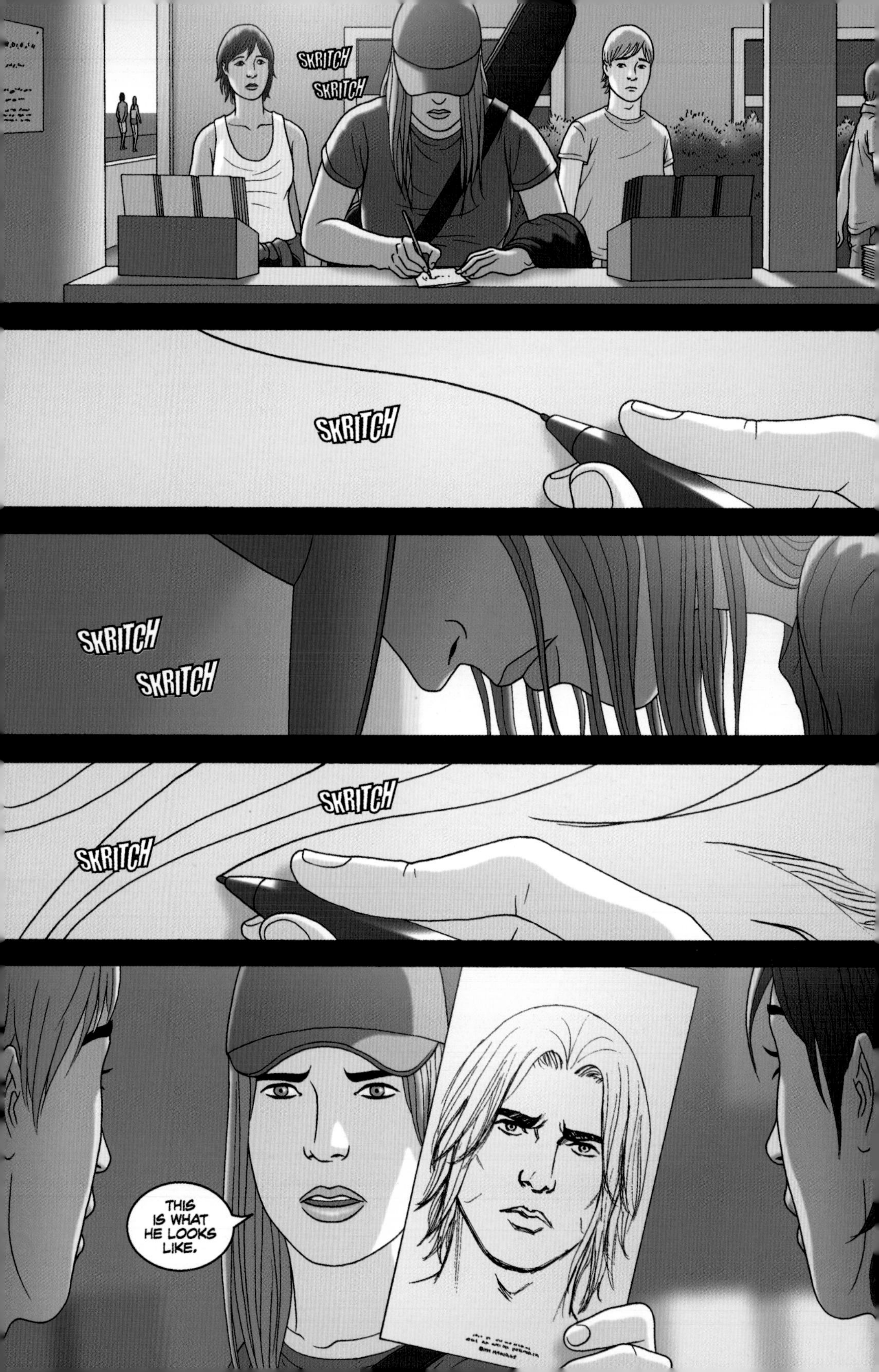
SKRITCH
SKRITCH
SKRITCH
SKRITCH
SKRITCH
SKRITCH
SKRITCH
THIS IS WHAT HE LOOKS LIKE.

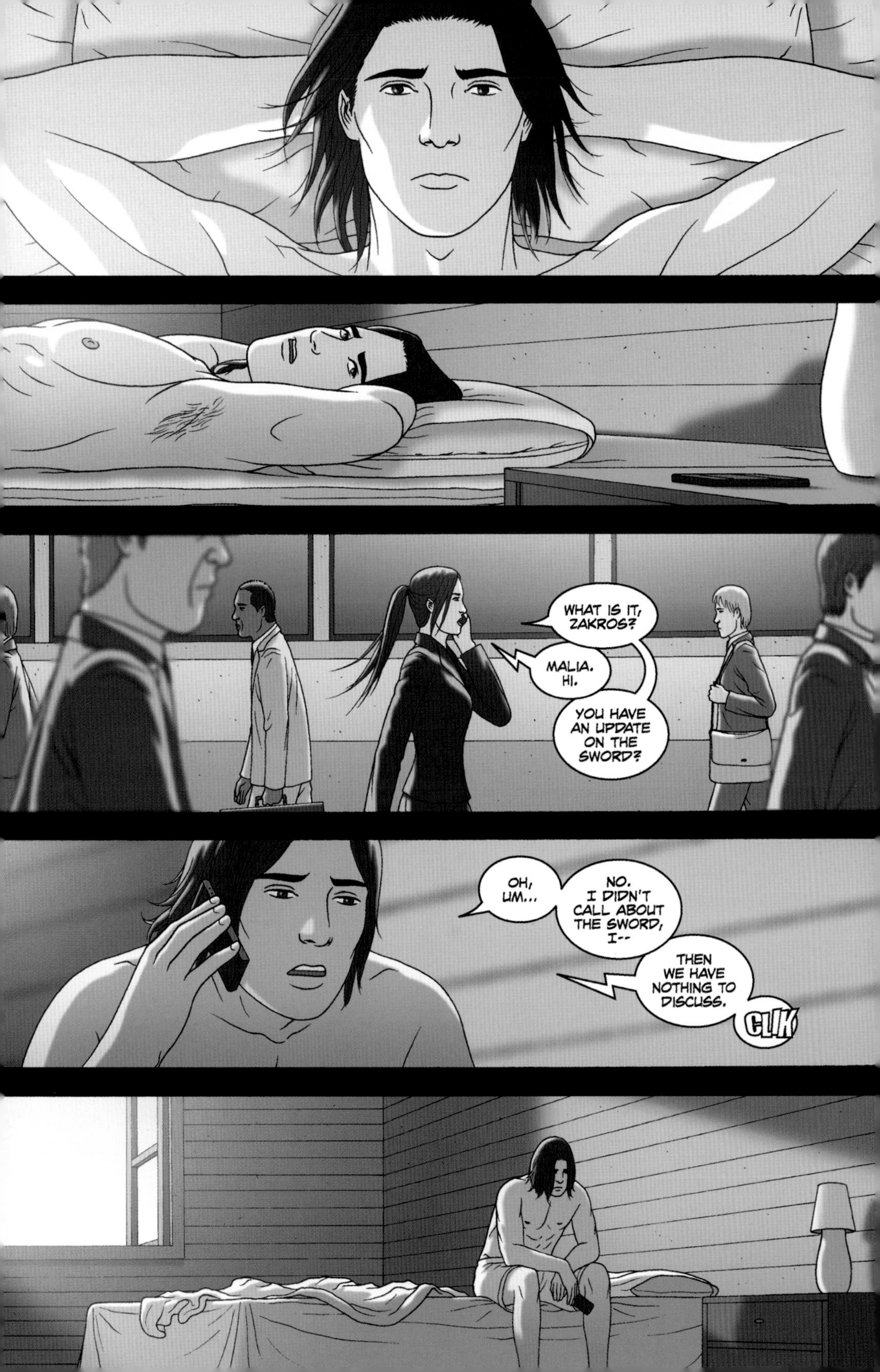
WHAT IS IT, ZAKROS?
MALIA. HI.
YOU HAVE AN UPDATE ON THE SWORD?
OH, UM...
NO. I DIDN'T CALL ABOUT THE SWORD, I--
THEN WE HAVE NOTHING TO DISCUSS.
CLIK

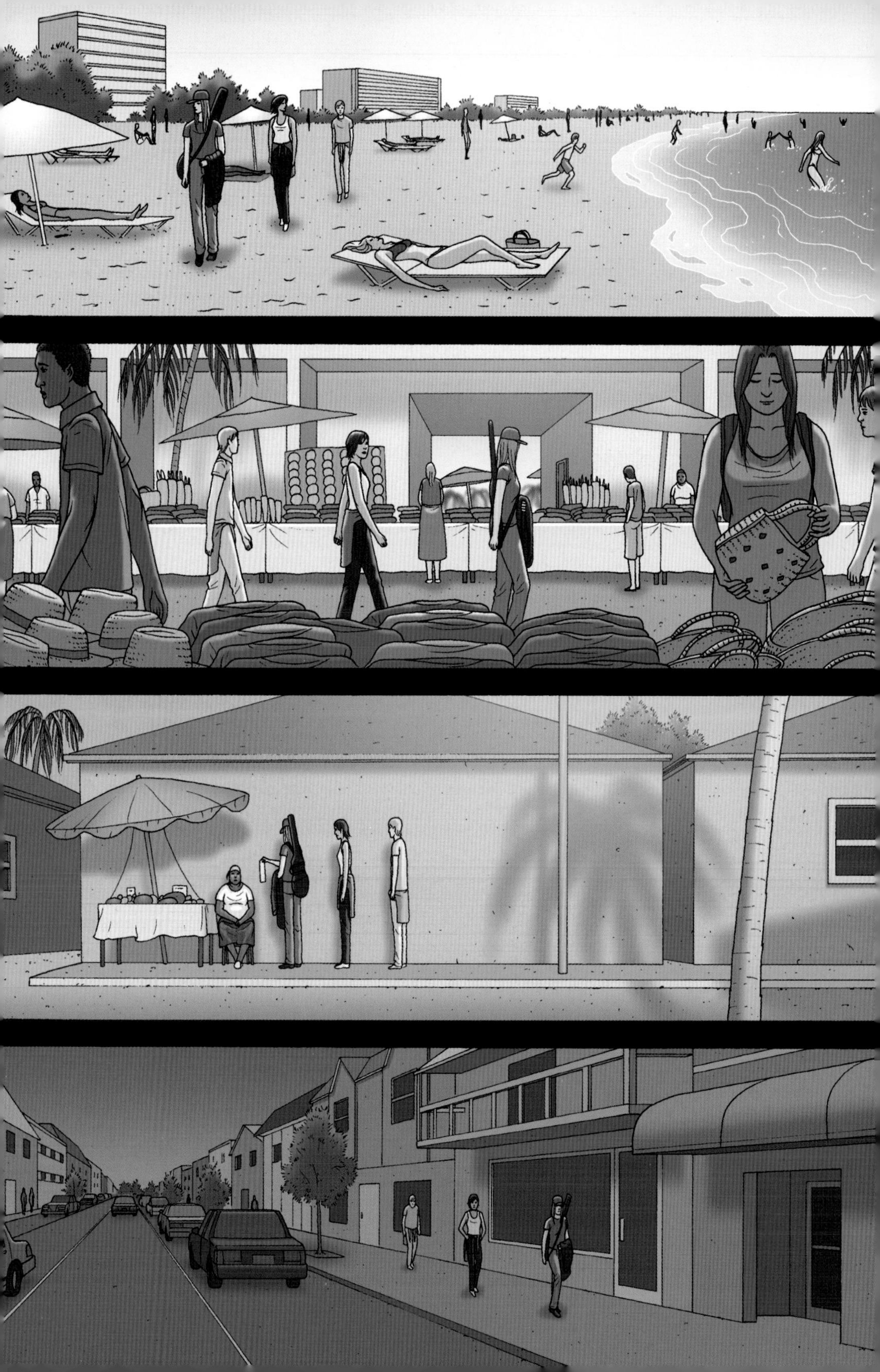

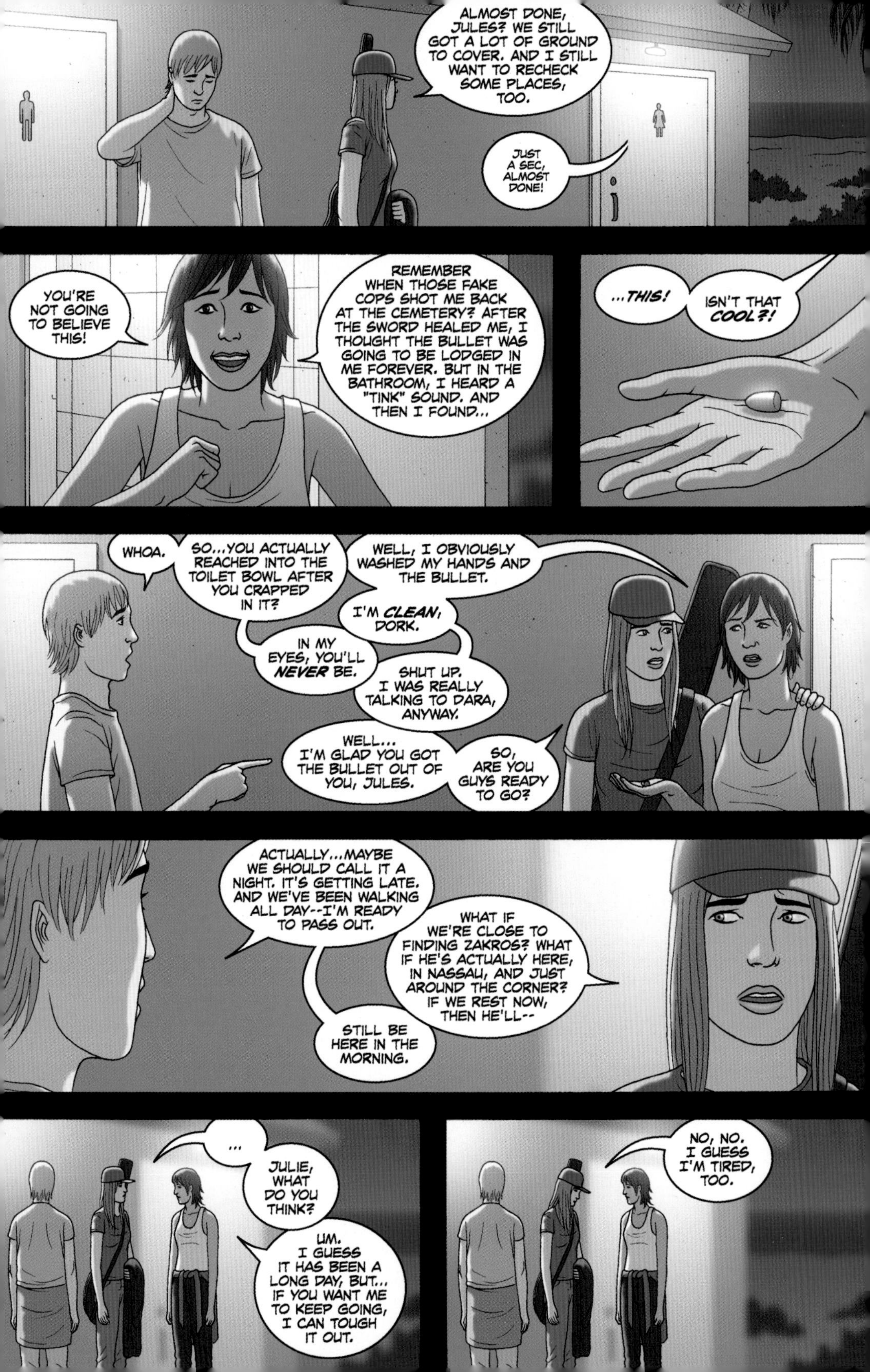
ALMOST DONE, JULES? WE STILL GOT A LOT OF GROUND TO COVER. AND I STILL WANT TO RECHECK SOME PLACES, TOO.
JUST A SEC, ALMOST DONE!
YOU'RE NOT GOING TO BELIEVE THIS!
REMEMBER WHEN THOSE FAKE COPS SHOT ME BACK AT THE CEMETERY? AFTER THE SWORD HEALED ME, I THOUGHT THE BULLET WAS GOING TO BE LODGED IN ME FOREVER. BUT IN THE BATHROOM, I HEARD A "TINK" SOUND. AND THEN I FOUND...
...*THIS!*
ISN'T THAT *COOL?!*
WHOA.
SO...YOU ACTUALLY REACHED INTO THE TOILET BOWL AFTER YOU CRAPPED IN IT?
WELL, I OBVIOUSLY WASHED MY HANDS AND THE BULLET.
I'M *CLEAN*, DORK.
IN MY EYES, YOU'LL *NEVER* BE.
SHUT UP. I WAS REALLY TALKING TO DARA, ANYWAY.
WELL... I'M GLAD YOU GOT THE BULLET OUT OF YOU, JULES.
SO, ARE YOU GUYS READY TO GO?
ACTUALLY...MAYBE WE SHOULD CALL IT A NIGHT. IT'S GETTING LATE. AND WE'VE BEEN WALKING ALL DAY--I'M READY TO PASS OUT.
WHAT IF WE'RE CLOSE TO FINDING ZAKROS? WHAT IF HE'S ACTUALLY HERE, IN NASSAU, AND JUST AROUND THE CORNER? IF WE REST NOW, THEN HE'LL--
STILL BE HERE IN THE MORNING.
...
JULIE, WHAT DO YOU THINK?
UM. I GUESS IT HAS BEEN A LONG DAY, BUT... IF YOU WANT ME TO KEEP GOING, I CAN TOUGH IT OUT.
NO, NO. I GUESS I'M TIRED, TOO.

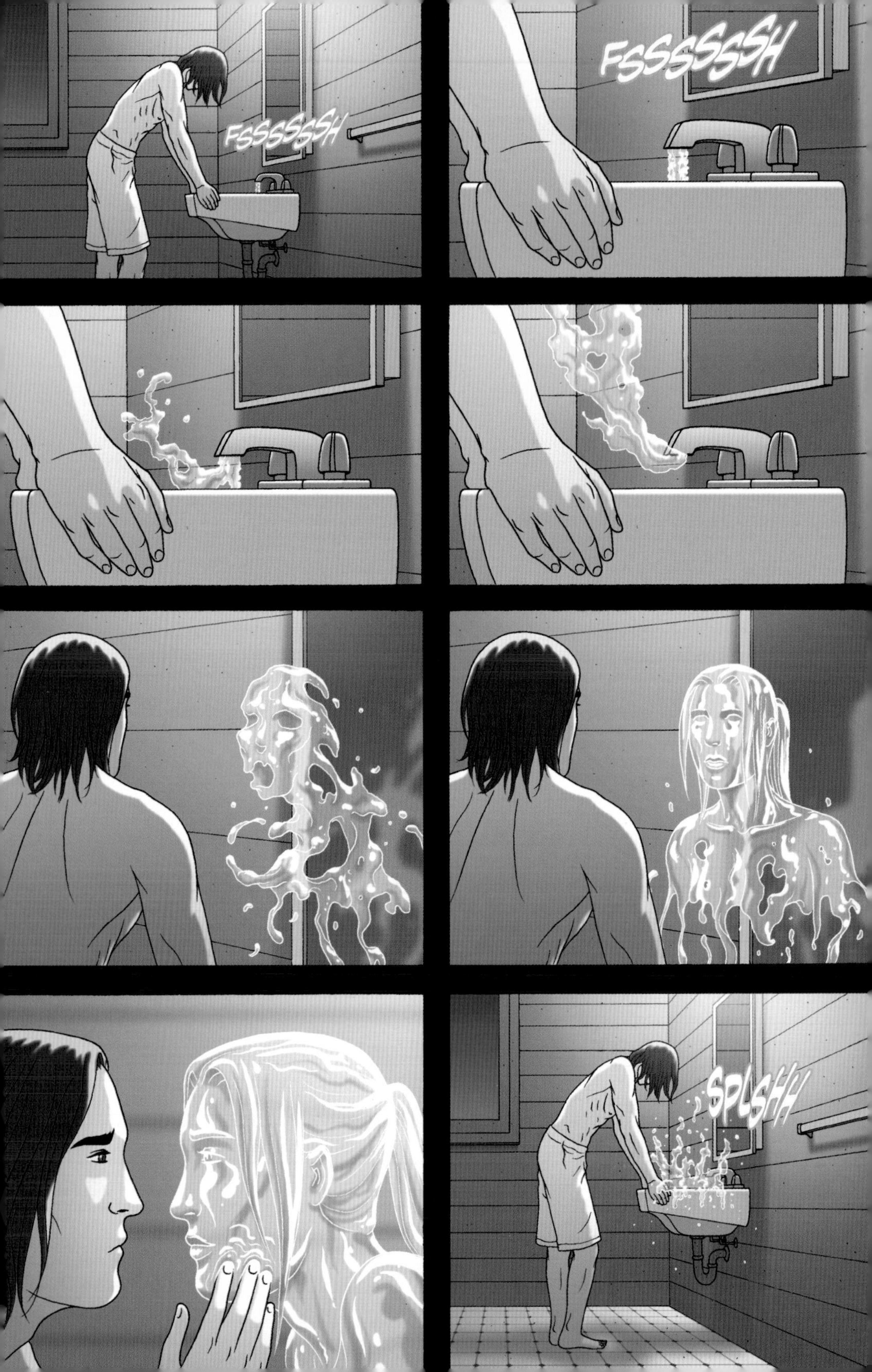
FSSSSSSH
FSSSSSSSH
SPLSHH

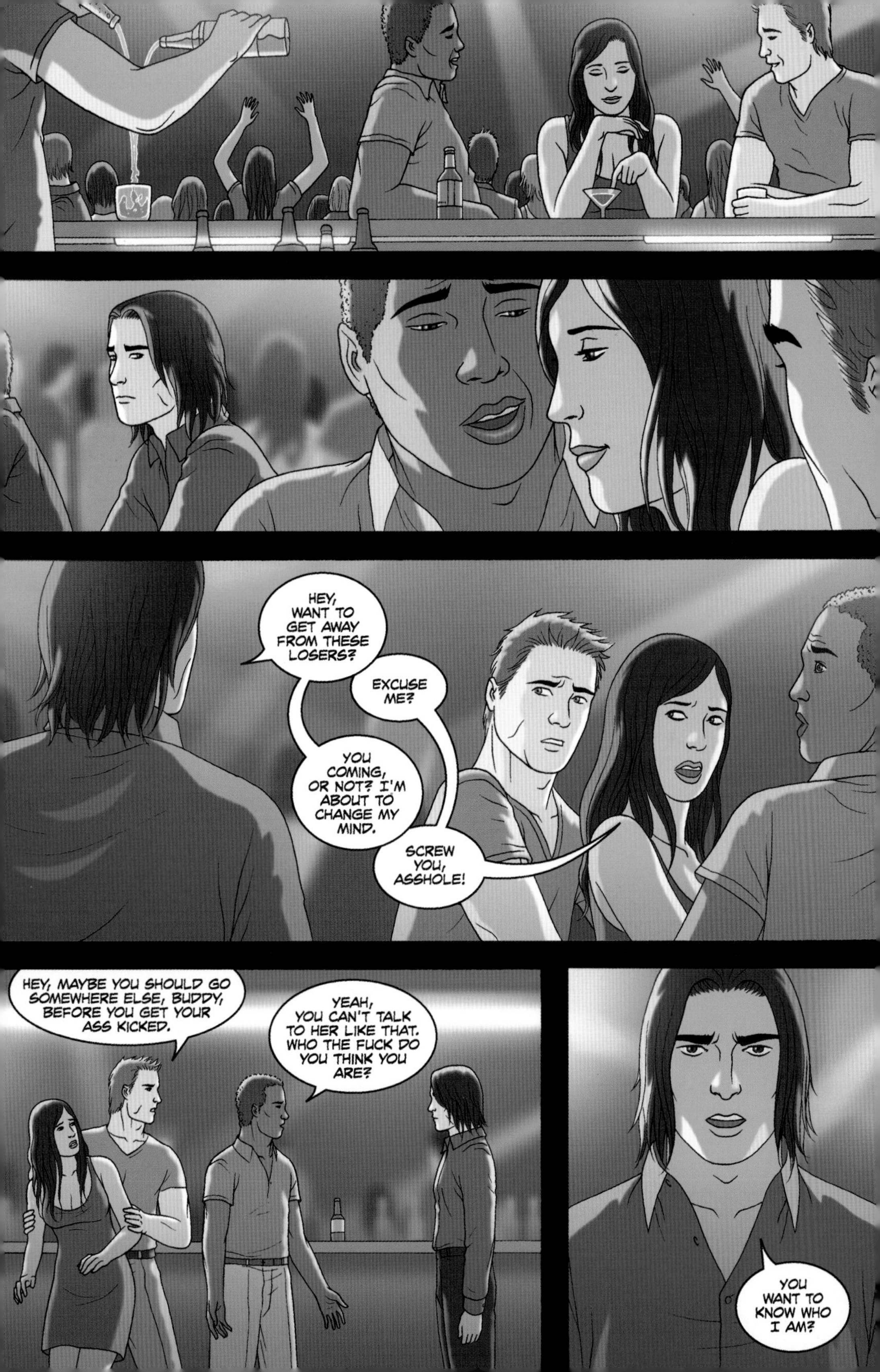
HEY, WANT TO GET AWAY FROM THESE LOSERS?
EXCUSE ME?
YOU COMING, OR NOT? I'M ABOUT TO CHANGE MY MIND.
SCREW YOU, ASSHOLE!
HEY, MAYBE YOU SHOULD GO SOMEWHERE ELSE, BUDDY, BEFORE YOU GET YOUR ASS KICKED.
YEAH, YOU CAN'T TALK TO HER LIKE THAT. WHO THE FUCK DO YOU THINK YOU ARE?
YOU WANT TO KNOW WHO I AM?

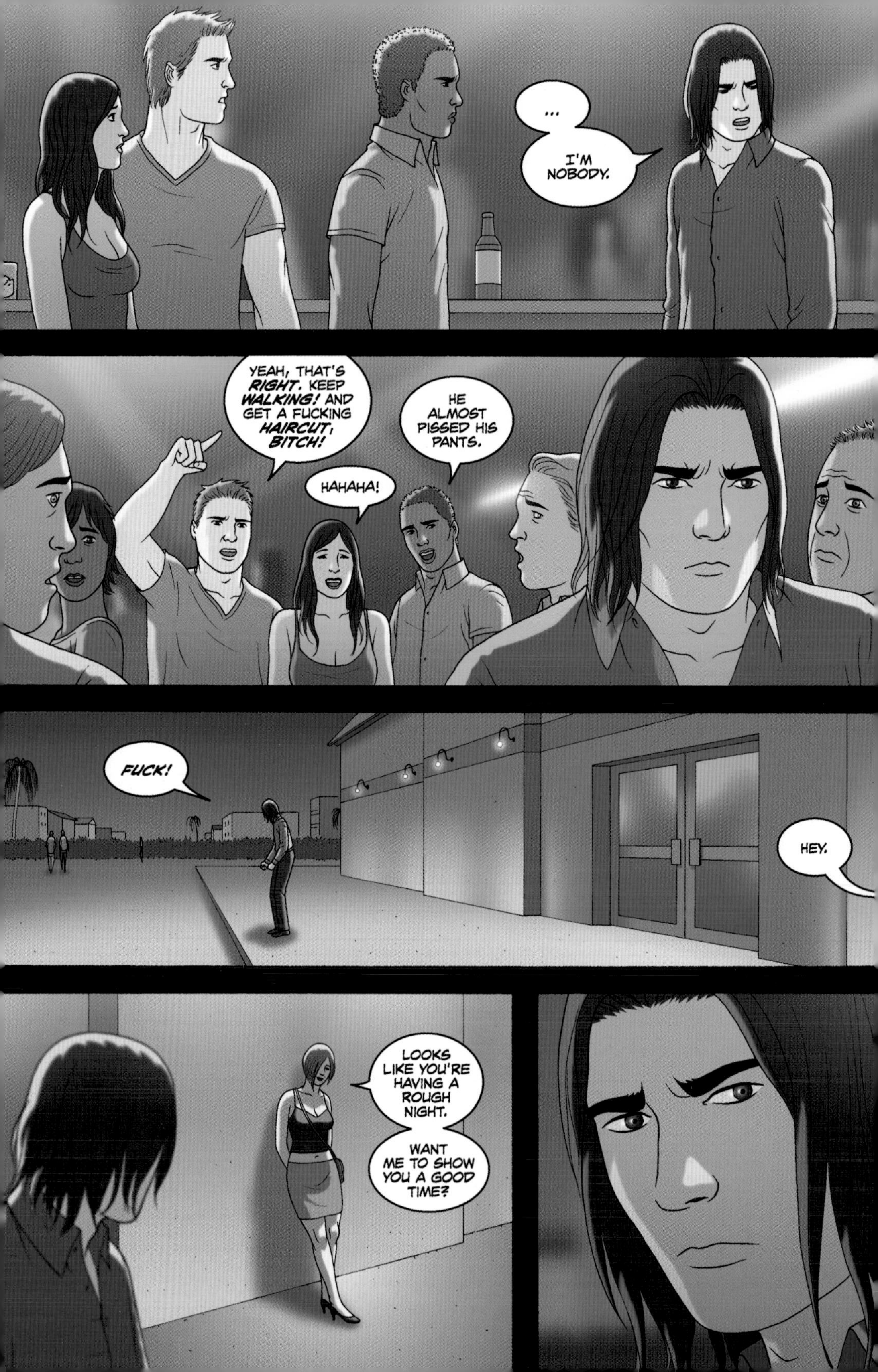
...
I'M NOBODY.
YEAH, THAT'S *RIGHT*. KEEP *WALKING!* AND GET A FUCKING *HAIRCUT*, *BITCH!*
HE ALMOST PISSED HIS PANTS.
HAHAHA!
FUCK!
HEY.
LOOKS LIKE YOU'RE HAVING A ROUGH NIGHT.
WANT ME TO SHOW YOU A GOOD TIME?

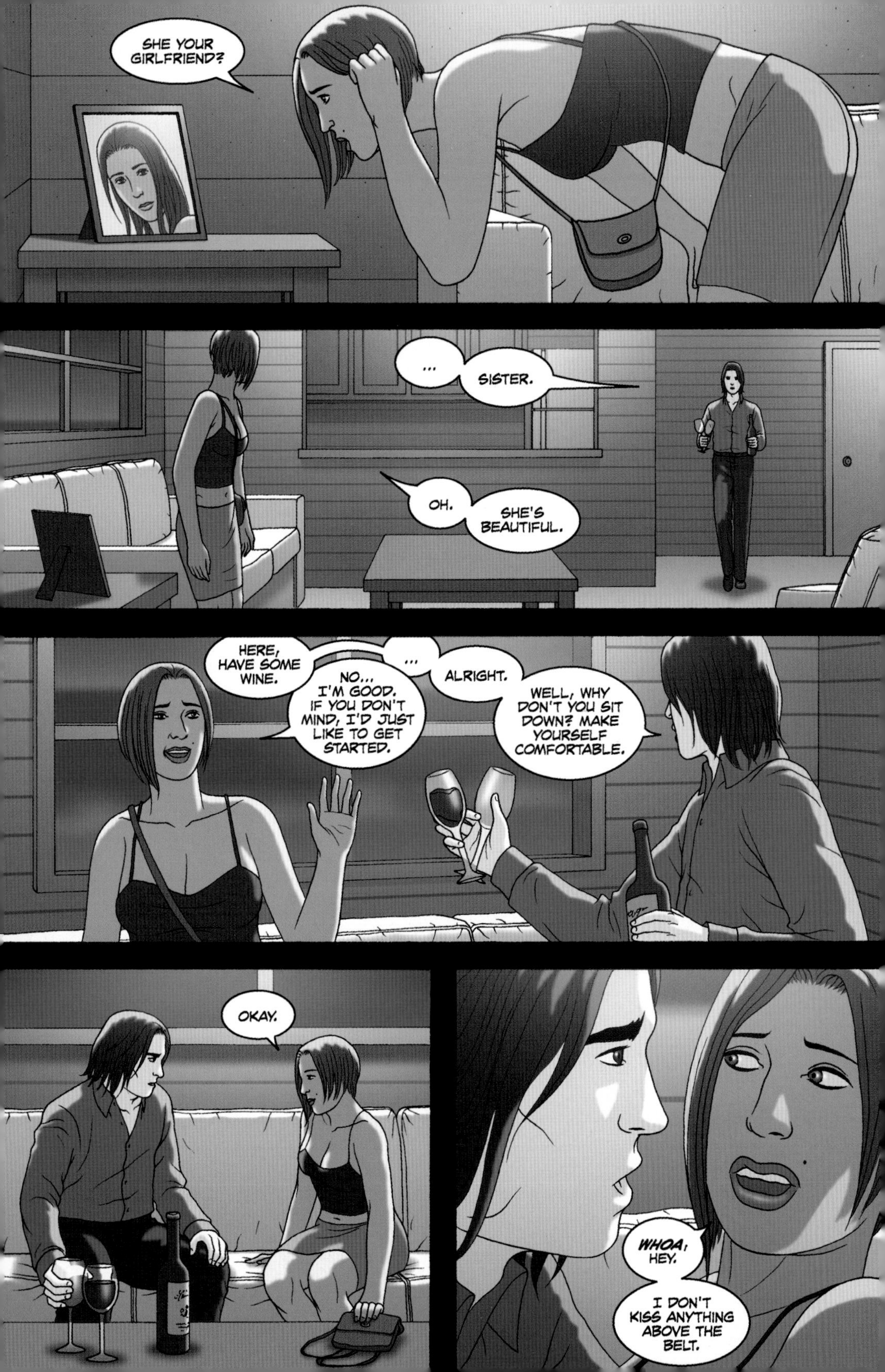

SHE YOUR GIRLFRIEND?
...
SISTER.
OH.
SHE'S BEAUTIFUL.
HERE, HAVE SOME WINE.
NO... I'M GOOD. IF YOU DON'T MIND, I'D JUST LIKE TO GET STARTED.
...
ALRIGHT.
WELL, WHY DON'T YOU SIT DOWN? MAKE YOURSELF COMFORTABLE.
OKAY.
WHOA, HEY.
I DON'T KISS ANYTHING ABOVE THE BELT.

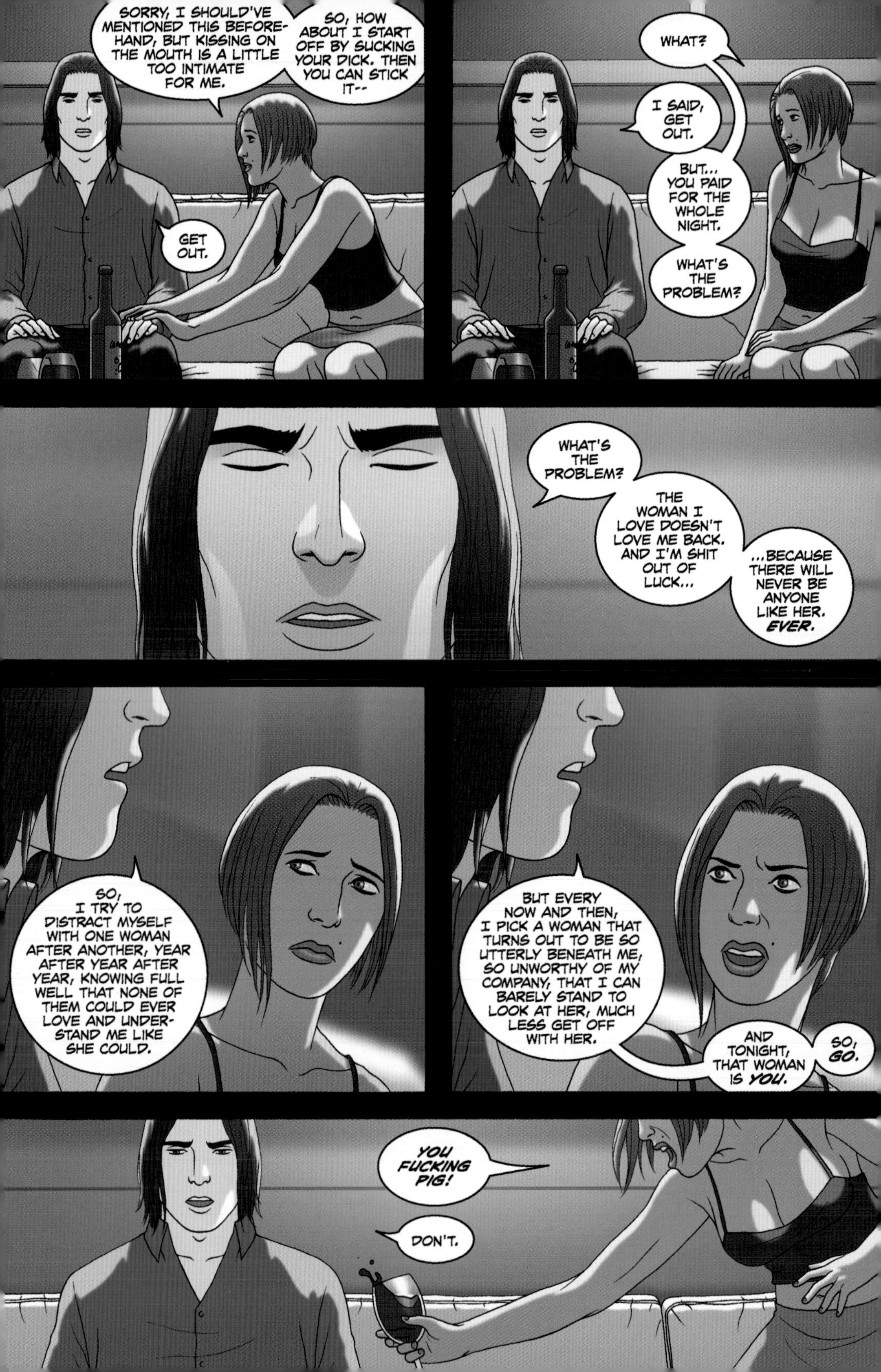
SORRY, I SHOULD'VE MENTIONED THIS BEFORE-HAND, BUT KISSING ON THE MOUTH IS A LITTLE TOO INTIMATE FOR ME.
SO, HOW ABOUT I START OFF BY SUCKING YOUR DICK. THEN YOU CAN STICK IT--
GET OUT.
WHAT?
I SAID, GET OUT.
BUT... YOU PAID FOR THE WHOLE NIGHT.
WHAT'S THE PROBLEM?
WHAT'S THE PROBLEM?
THE WOMAN I LOVE DOESN'T LOVE ME BACK. AND I'M SHIT OUT OF LUCK...
...BECAUSE THERE WILL NEVER BE ANYONE LIKE HER. EVER.
SO, I TRY TO DISTRACT MYSELF WITH ONE WOMAN AFTER ANOTHER, YEAR AFTER YEAR AFTER YEAR, KNOWING FULL WELL THAT NONE OF THEM COULD EVER LOVE AND UNDER-STAND ME LIKE SHE COULD.
BUT EVERY NOW AND THEN, I PICK A WOMAN THAT TURNS OUT TO BE SO UTTERLY BENEATH ME, SO UNWORTHY OF MY COMPANY, THAT I CAN BARELY STAND TO LOOK AT HER, MUCH LESS GET OFF WITH HER.
AND TONIGHT, THAT WOMAN IS YOU.
SO, GO.
YOU FUCKING PIG!
DON'T.

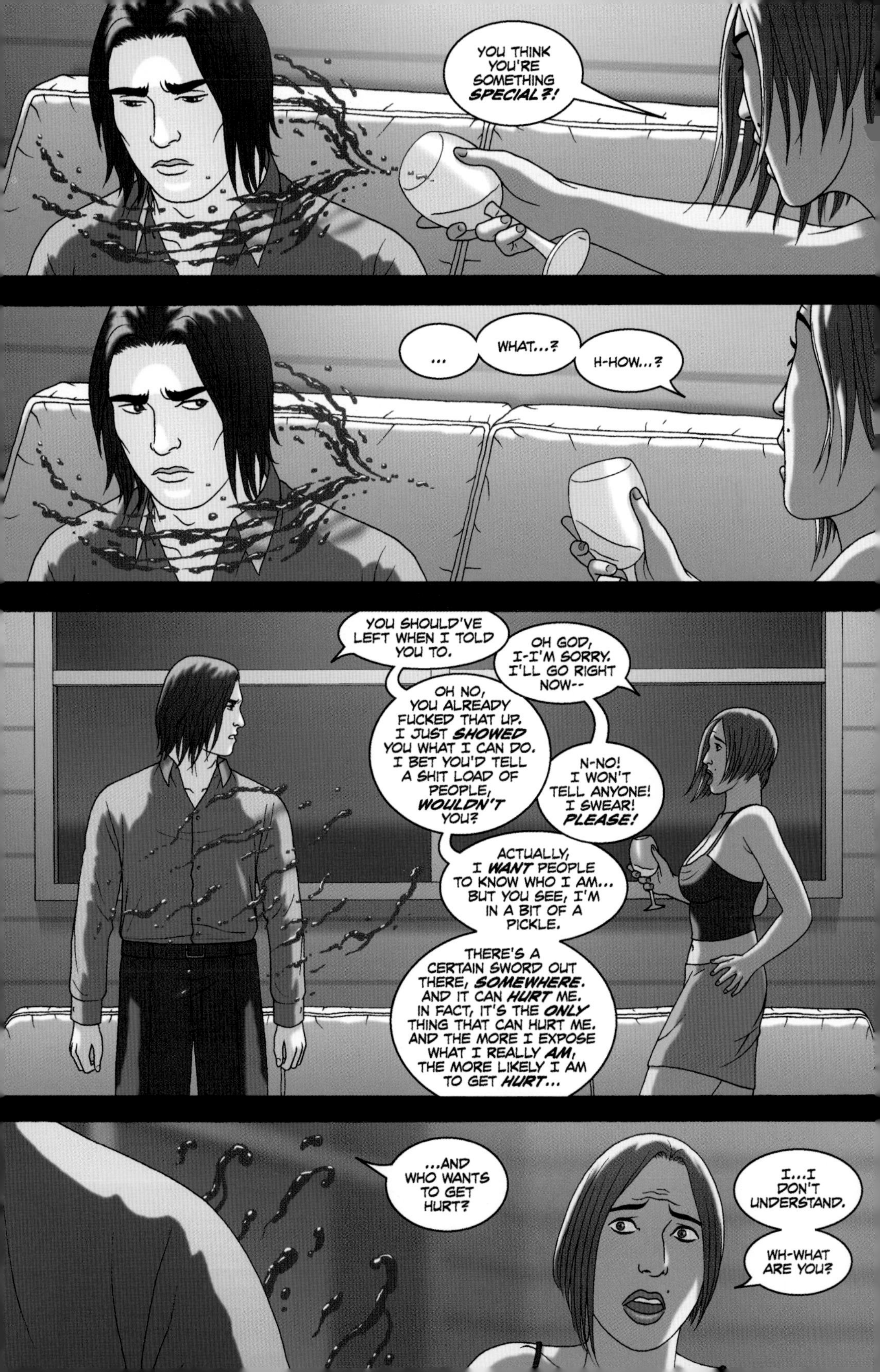
YOU THINK YOU'RE SOMETHING *SPECIAL?!*
...
WHAT...?
H-HOW...?
YOU SHOULD'VE LEFT WHEN I TOLD YOU TO.
OH GOD, I-I'M SORRY. I'LL GO RIGHT NOW--
OH NO, YOU ALREADY FUCKED THAT UP. I JUST *SHOWED* YOU WHAT I CAN DO. I BET YOU'D TELL A SHIT LOAD OF PEOPLE, *WOULDN'T* YOU?
N-NO! I WON'T TELL ANYONE! I SWEAR! *PLEASE!*
ACTUALLY, I *WANT* PEOPLE TO KNOW WHO I AM... BUT YOU SEE, I'M IN A BIT OF A PICKLE.
THERE'S A CERTAIN SWORD OUT THERE, *SOMEWHERE*. AND IT CAN *HURT* ME. IN FACT, IT'S THE *ONLY* THING THAT CAN HURT ME. AND THE MORE I EXPOSE WHAT I REALLY *AM*, THE MORE LIKELY I AM TO GET *HURT*...
...AND WHO WANTS TO GET HURT?
I...I DON'T UNDERSTAND.
WH-WHAT ARE YOU?

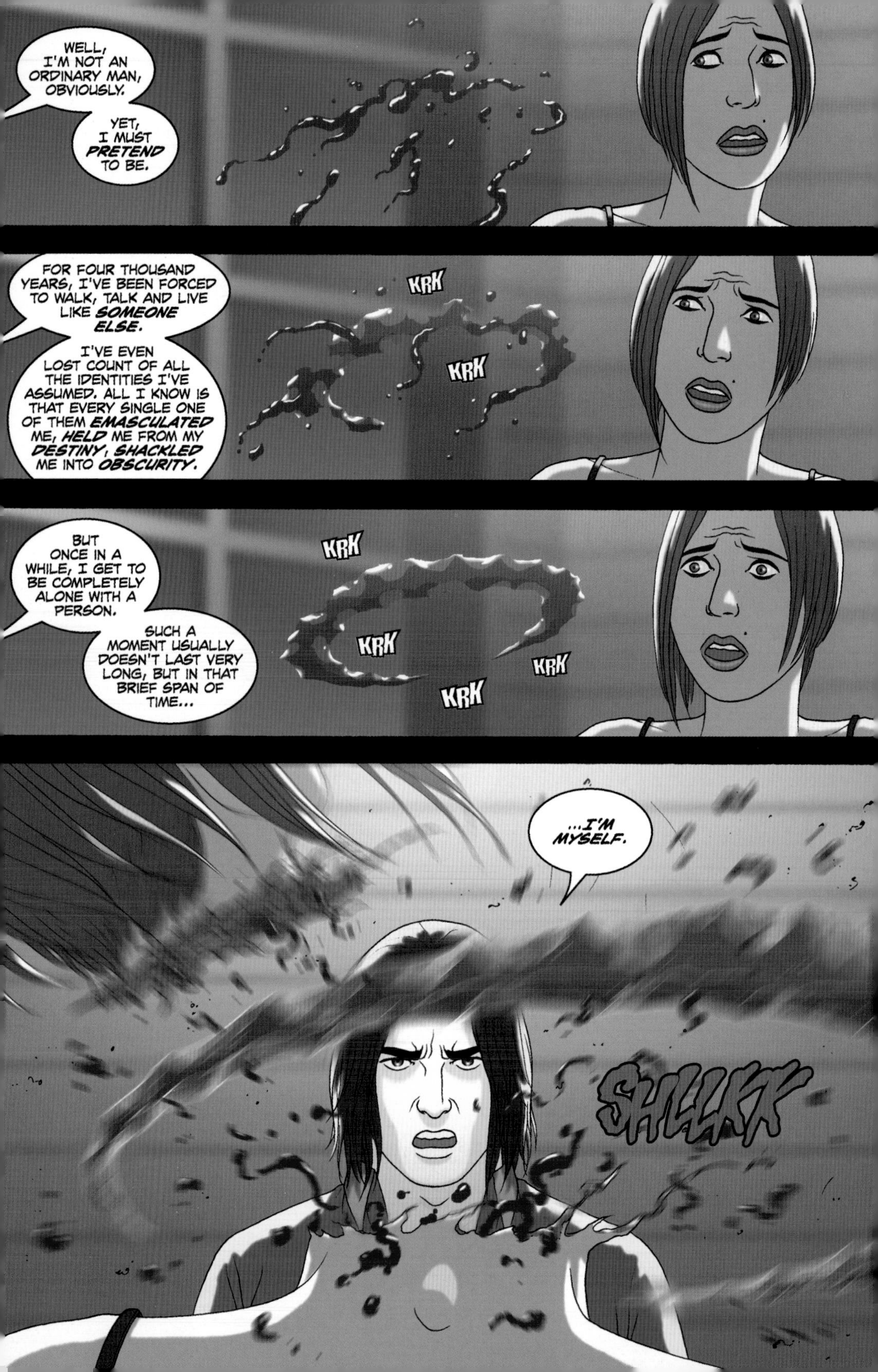
WELL, I'M NOT AN ORDINARY MAN, OBVIOUSLY.
YET, I MUST *PRETEND* TO BE.
FOR FOUR THOUSAND YEARS, I'VE BEEN FORCED TO WALK, TALK AND LIVE LIKE *SOMEONE ELSE*.
I'VE EVEN LOST COUNT OF ALL THE IDENTITIES I'VE ASSUMED. ALL I KNOW IS THAT EVERY SINGLE ONE OF THEM *EMASCULATED* ME, *HELD* ME FROM MY *DESTINY*, *SHACKLED* ME INTO *OBSCURITY*.
KRK
KRK
BUT ONCE IN A WHILE, I GET TO BE COMPLETELY ALONE WITH A PERSON.
SUCH A MOMENT USUALLY DOESN'T LAST VERY LONG, BUT IN THAT BRIEF SPAN OF TIME...
KRK
KRK
KRK
KRK
...*I'M MYSELF*.
SHLLKK

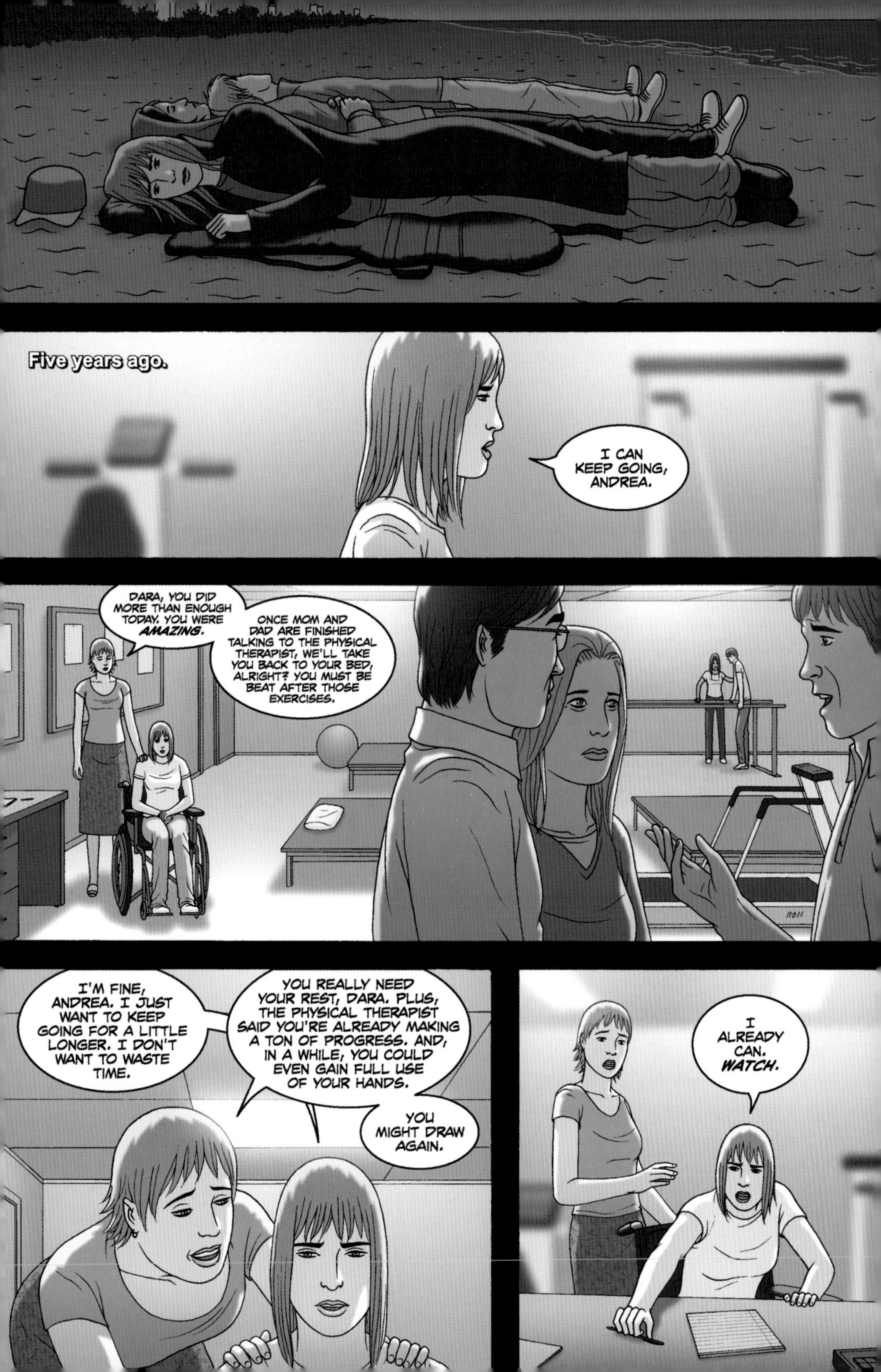
Five years ago.
I CAN KEEP GOING, ANDREA.
DARA, YOU DID MORE THAN ENOUGH TODAY. YOU WERE *AMAZING*.
ONCE MOM AND DAD ARE FINISHED TALKING TO THE PHYSICAL THERAPIST, WE'LL TAKE YOU BACK TO YOUR BED, ALRIGHT? YOU MUST BE BEAT AFTER THOSE EXERCISES.
I'M FINE, ANDREA. I JUST WANT TO KEEP GOING FOR A LITTLE LONGER. I DON'T WANT TO WASTE TIME.
YOU REALLY NEED YOUR REST, DARA. PLUS, THE PHYSICAL THERAPIST SAID YOU'RE ALREADY MAKING A TON OF PROGRESS. AND, IN A WHILE, YOU COULD EVEN GAIN FULL USE OF YOUR HANDS.
YOU MIGHT DRAW AGAIN.
I ALREADY CAN. *WATCH*.

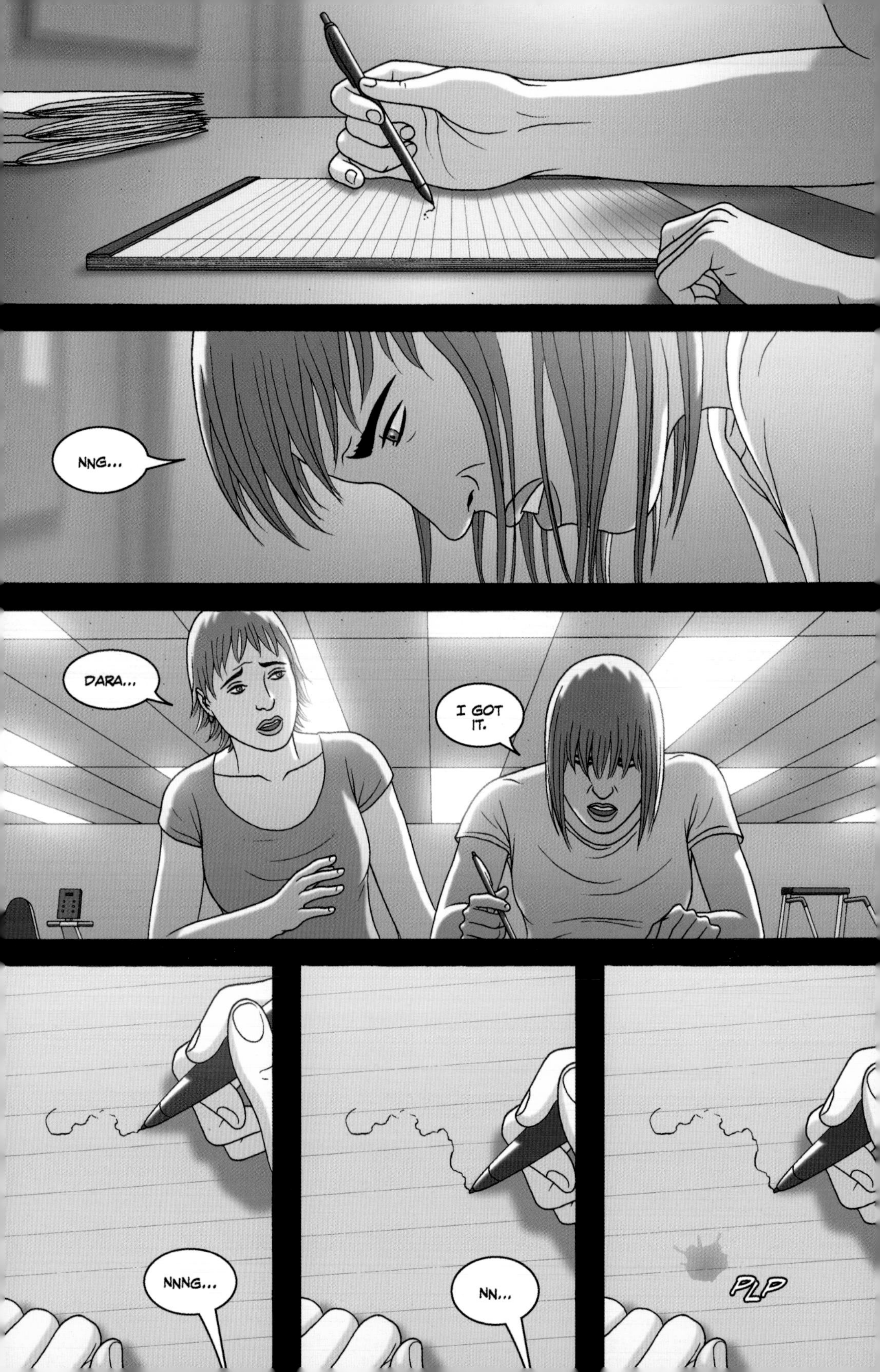
NNG...
DARA...
I GOT IT.
NNNG...
NN...
PLP

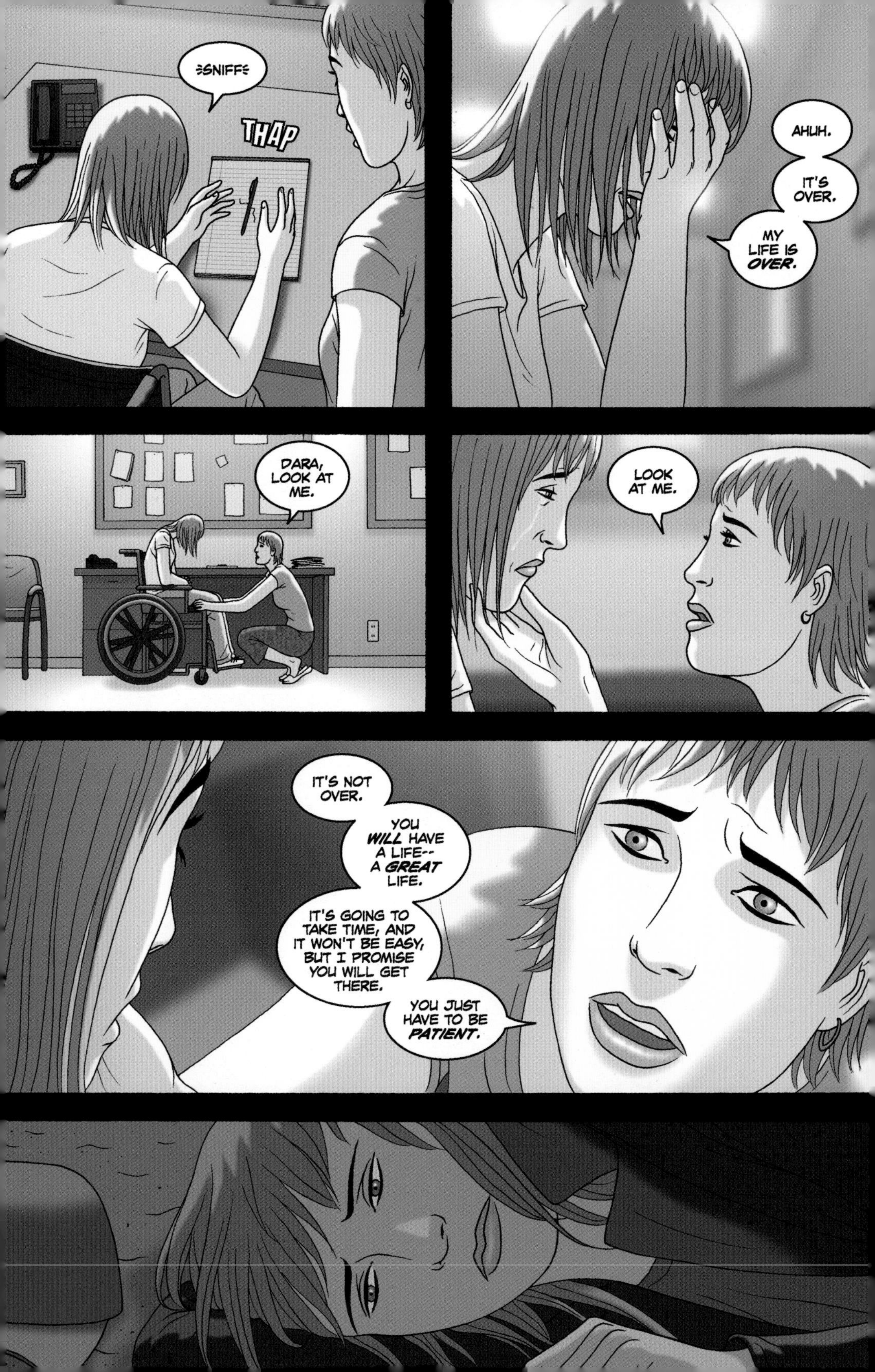

≈SNIFF≈
THAP
AHUH.
IT'S OVER.
MY LIFE IS OVER.
DARA, LOOK AT ME.
LOOK AT ME.
IT'S NOT OVER.
YOU WILL HAVE A LIFE-- A GREAT LIFE.
IT'S GOING TO TAKE TIME, AND IT WON'T BE EASY, BUT I PROMISE YOU WILL GET THERE.
YOU JUST HAVE TO BE PATIENT.

MORNING, SLEEPY-HEADS.

HNN?

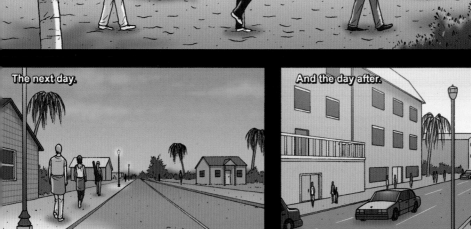

The next day.

And the day after.

HEY, GUYS, CAN WE TAKE A BREAK?

DARA?

HOLD ON.

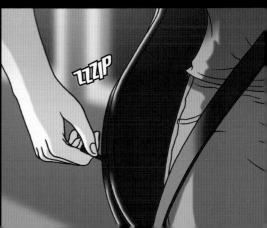

ZZZIP

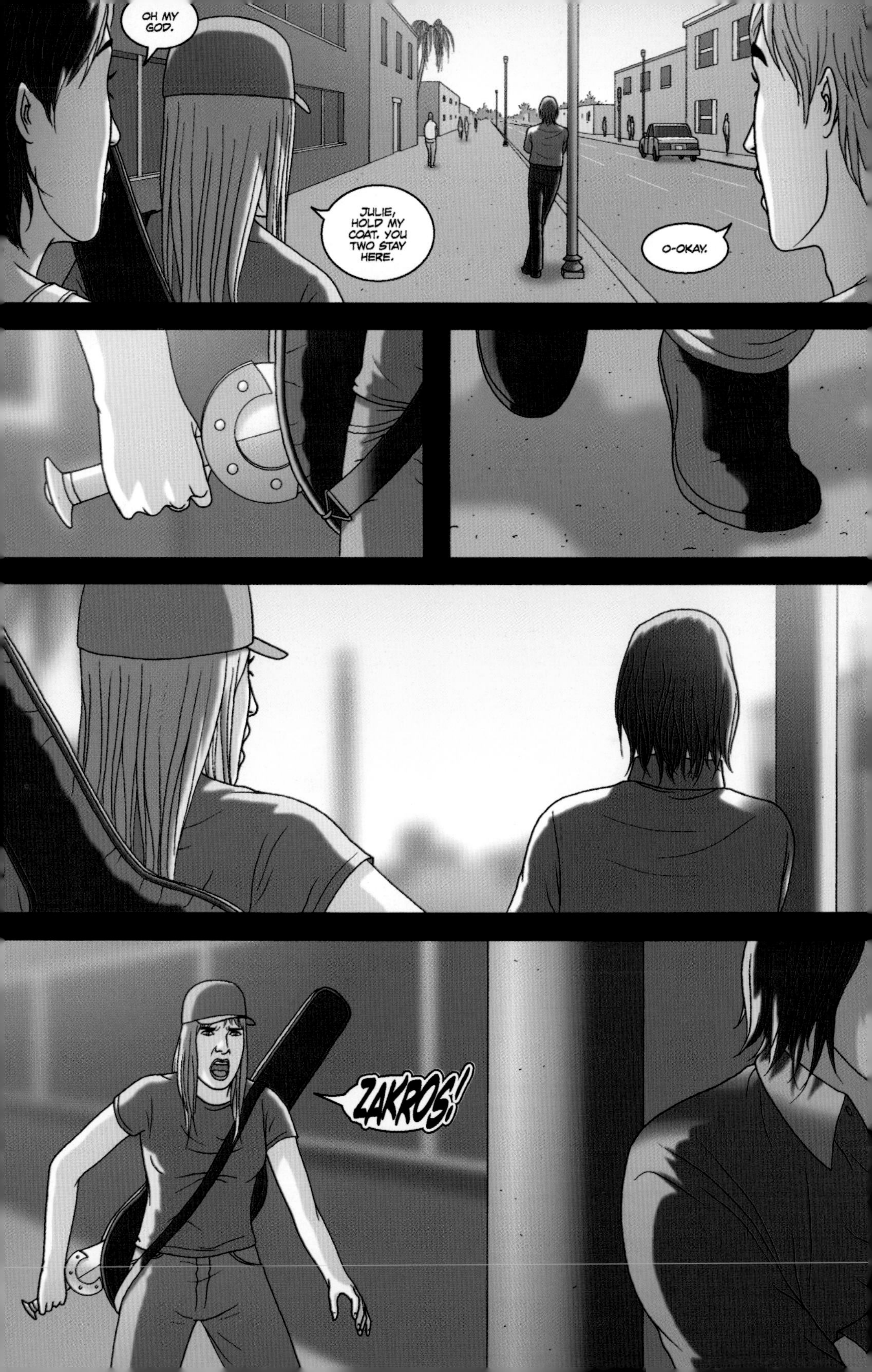
OH MY GOD.
JULIE, HOLD MY COAT. YOU TWO STAY HERE.
O-OKAY.
ZAKROS!

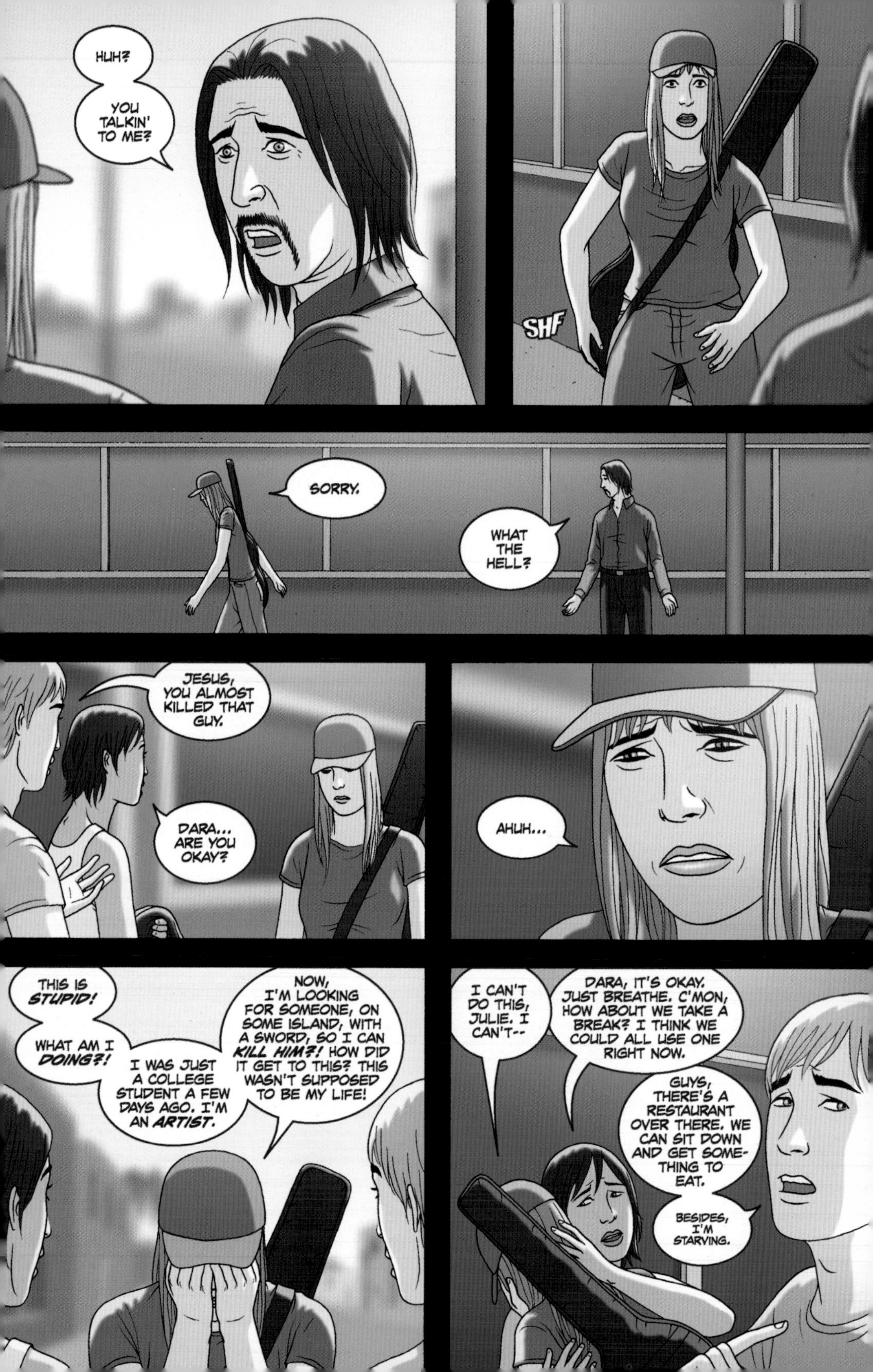
HUH?
YOU TALKIN' TO ME?
SHF
SORRY.
WHAT THE HELL?
JESUS, YOU ALMOST KILLED THAT GUY.
DARA... ARE YOU OKAY?
AHUH...
THIS IS STUPID!
WHAT AM I DOING?!
I WAS JUST A COLLEGE STUDENT A FEW DAYS AGO. I'M AN ARTIST.
NOW, I'M LOOKING FOR SOMEONE, ON SOME ISLAND, WITH A SWORD, SO I CAN KILL HIM?! HOW DID IT GET TO THIS? THIS WASN'T SUPPOSED TO BE MY LIFE!
I CAN'T DO THIS, JULIE. I CAN'T--
DARA, IT'S OKAY. JUST BREATHE. C'MON, HOW ABOUT WE TAKE A BREAK? I THINK WE COULD ALL USE ONE RIGHT NOW.
GUYS, THERE'S A RESTAURANT OVER THERE. WE CAN SIT DOWN AND GET SOME-THING TO EAT.
BESIDES, I'M STARVING.

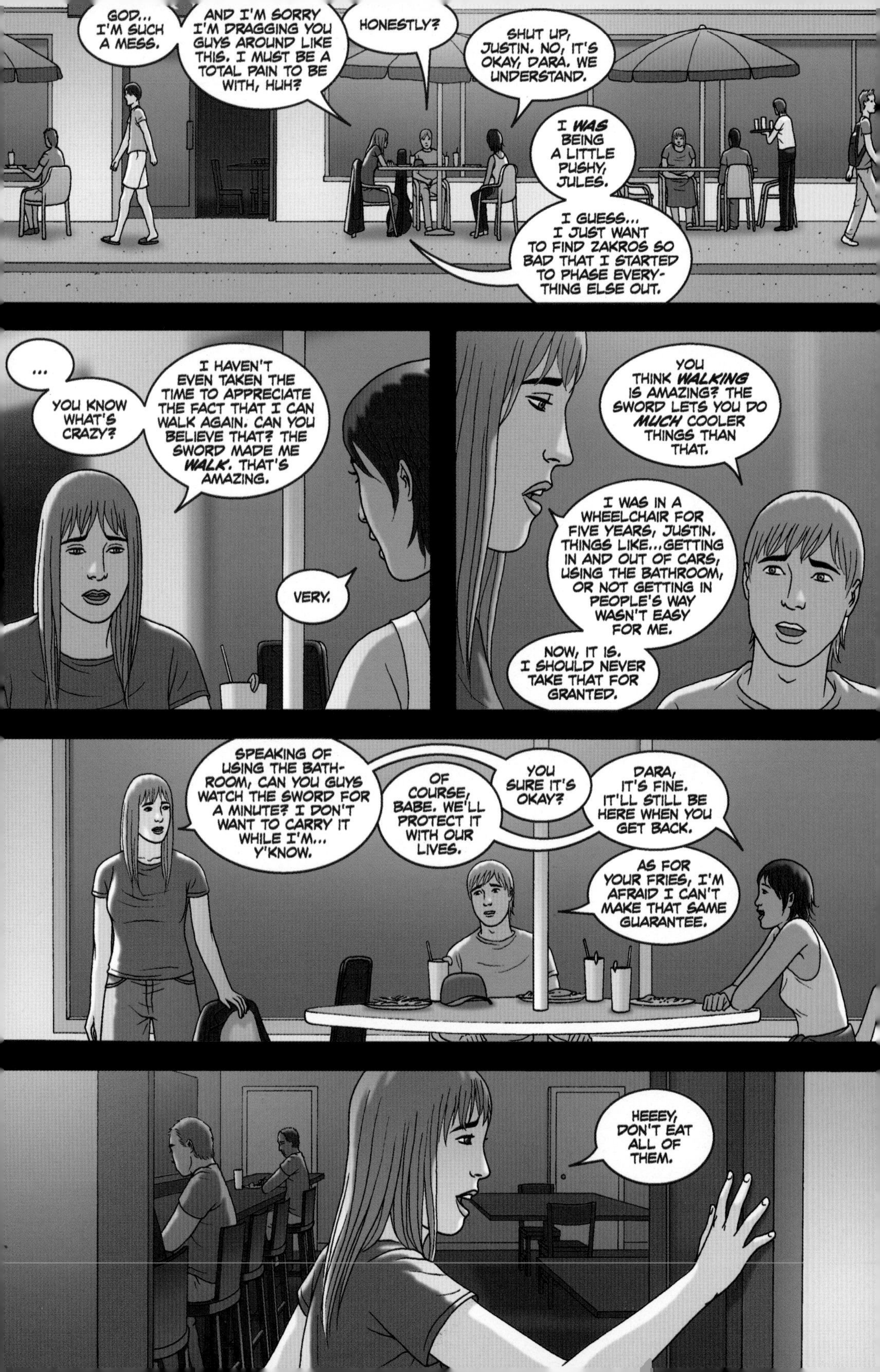
GOD... I'M SUCH A MESS.
AND I'M SORRY I'M DRAGGING YOU GUYS AROUND LIKE THIS. I MUST BE A TOTAL PAIN TO BE WITH, HUH?
HONESTLY?
SHUT UP, JUSTIN. NO, IT'S OKAY, DARA. WE UNDERSTAND.
I WAS BEING A LITTLE PUSHY, JULES.
I GUESS... I JUST WANT TO FIND ZAKROS SO BAD THAT I STARTED TO PHASE EVERY-THING ELSE OUT.
...
YOU KNOW WHAT'S CRAZY?
I HAVEN'T EVEN TAKEN THE TIME TO APPRECIATE THE FACT THAT I CAN WALK AGAIN. CAN YOU BELIEVE THAT? THE SWORD MADE ME WALK. THAT'S AMAZING.
VERY.
YOU THINK WALKING IS AMAZING? THE SWORD LETS YOU DO MUCH COOLER THINGS THAN THAT.
I WAS IN A WHEELCHAIR FOR FIVE YEARS, JUSTIN. THINGS LIKE...GETTING IN AND OUT OF CARS, USING THE BATHROOM, OR NOT GETTING IN PEOPLE'S WAY WASN'T EASY FOR ME.
NOW, IT IS. I SHOULD NEVER TAKE THAT FOR GRANTED.
SPEAKING OF USING THE BATH-ROOM, CAN YOU GUYS WATCH THE SWORD FOR A MINUTE? I DON'T WANT TO CARRY IT WHILE I'M... Y'KNOW.
OF COURSE, BABE. WE'LL PROTECT IT WITH OUR LIVES.
YOU SURE IT'S OKAY?
DARA, IT'S FINE. IT'LL STILL BE HERE WHEN YOU GET BACK.
AS FOR YOUR FRIES, I'M AFRAID I CAN'T MAKE THAT SAME GUARANTEE.
HEEEY, DON'T EAT ALL OF THEM.

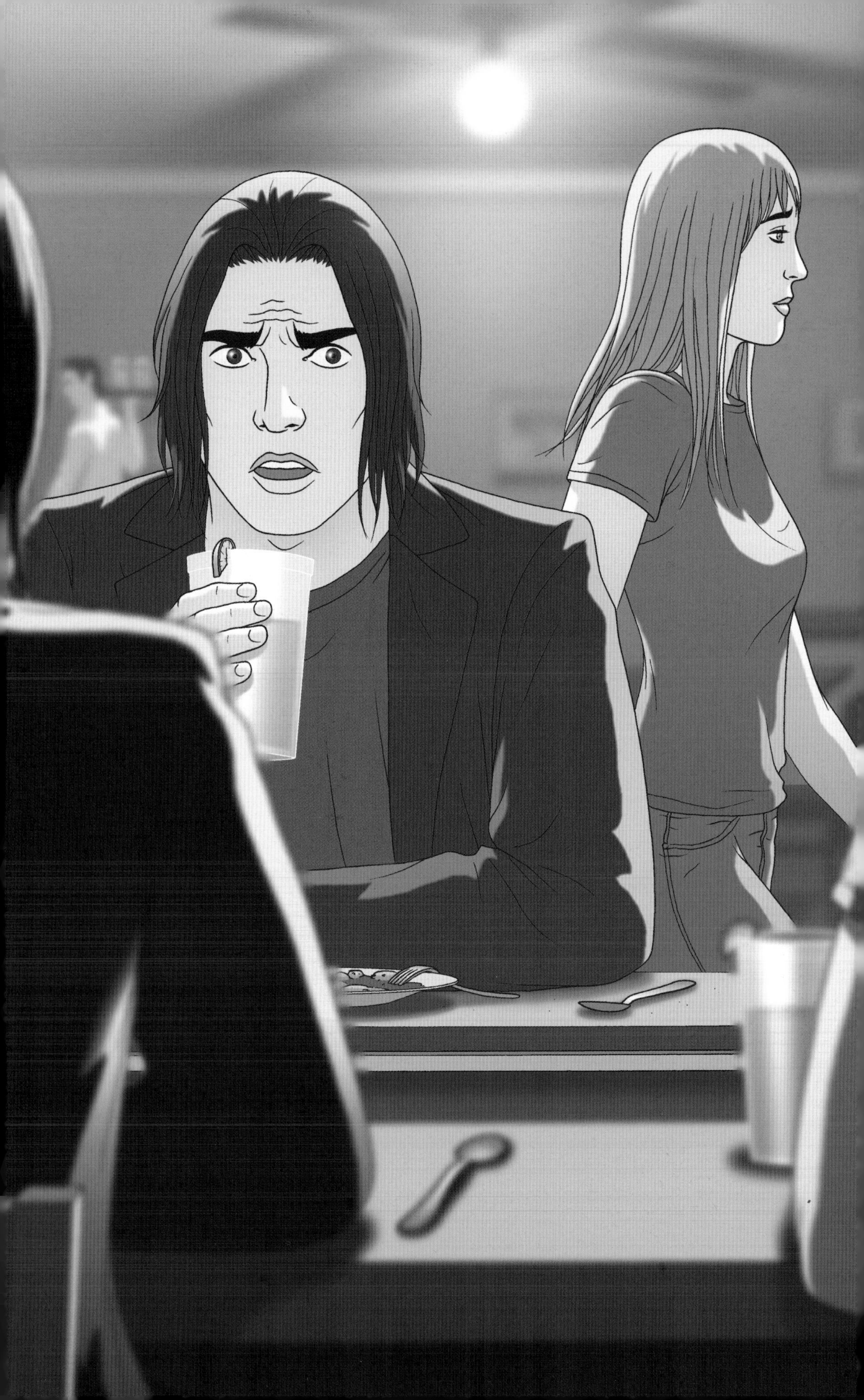

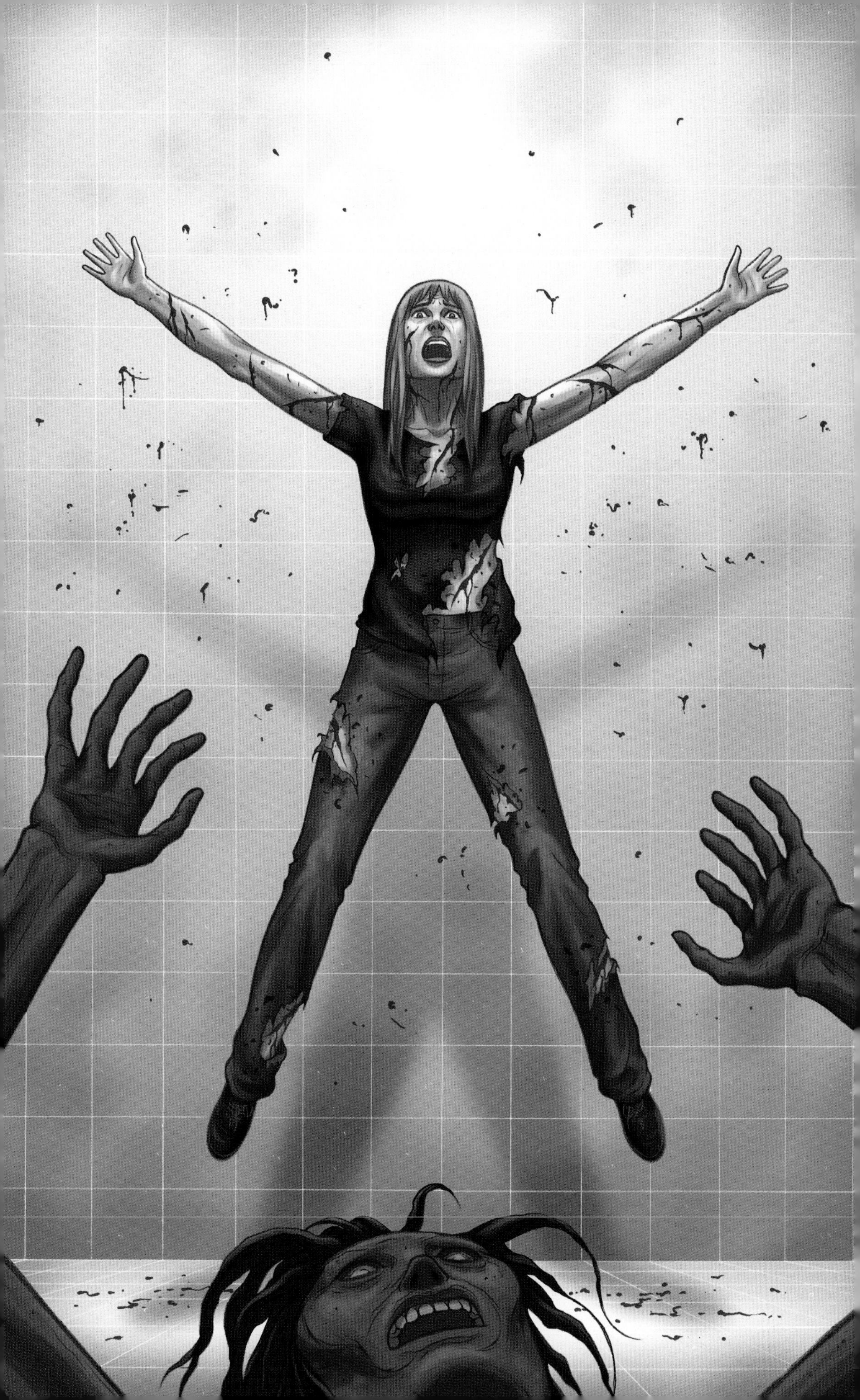

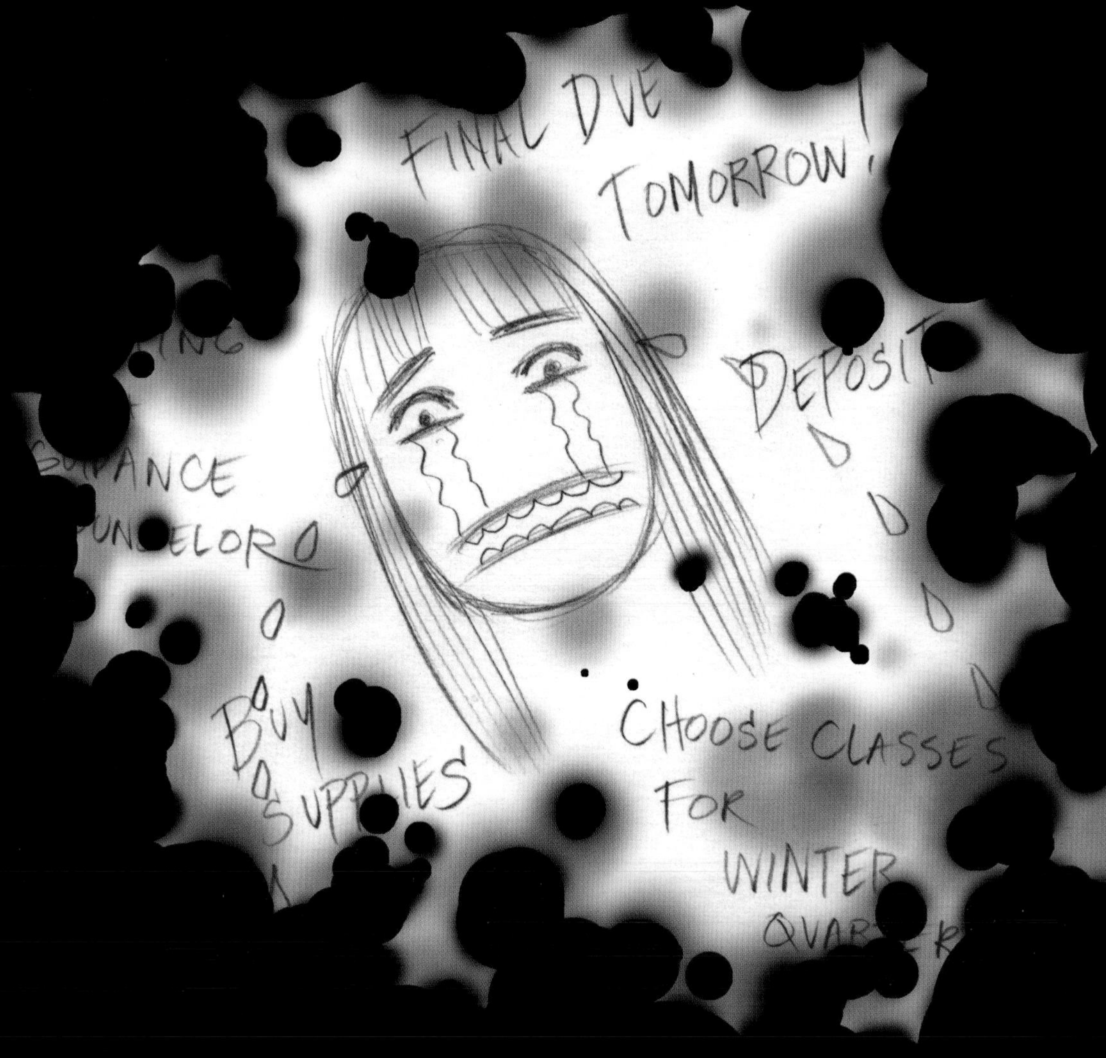
FINAL DUE TOMORROW!
DEPOSIT
BUY SUPPLIES
CHOOSE CLASSES FOR WINTER

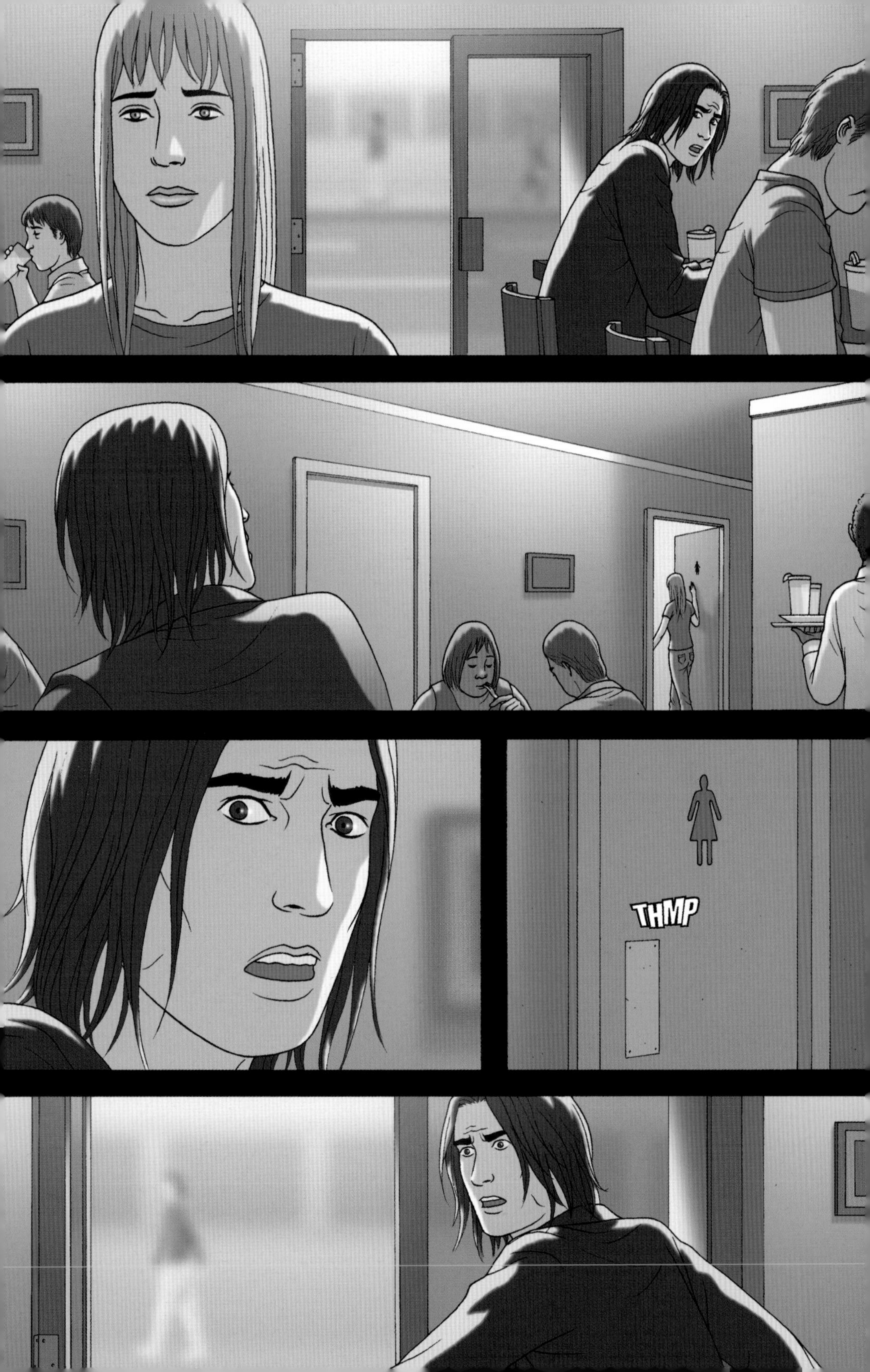
THMP

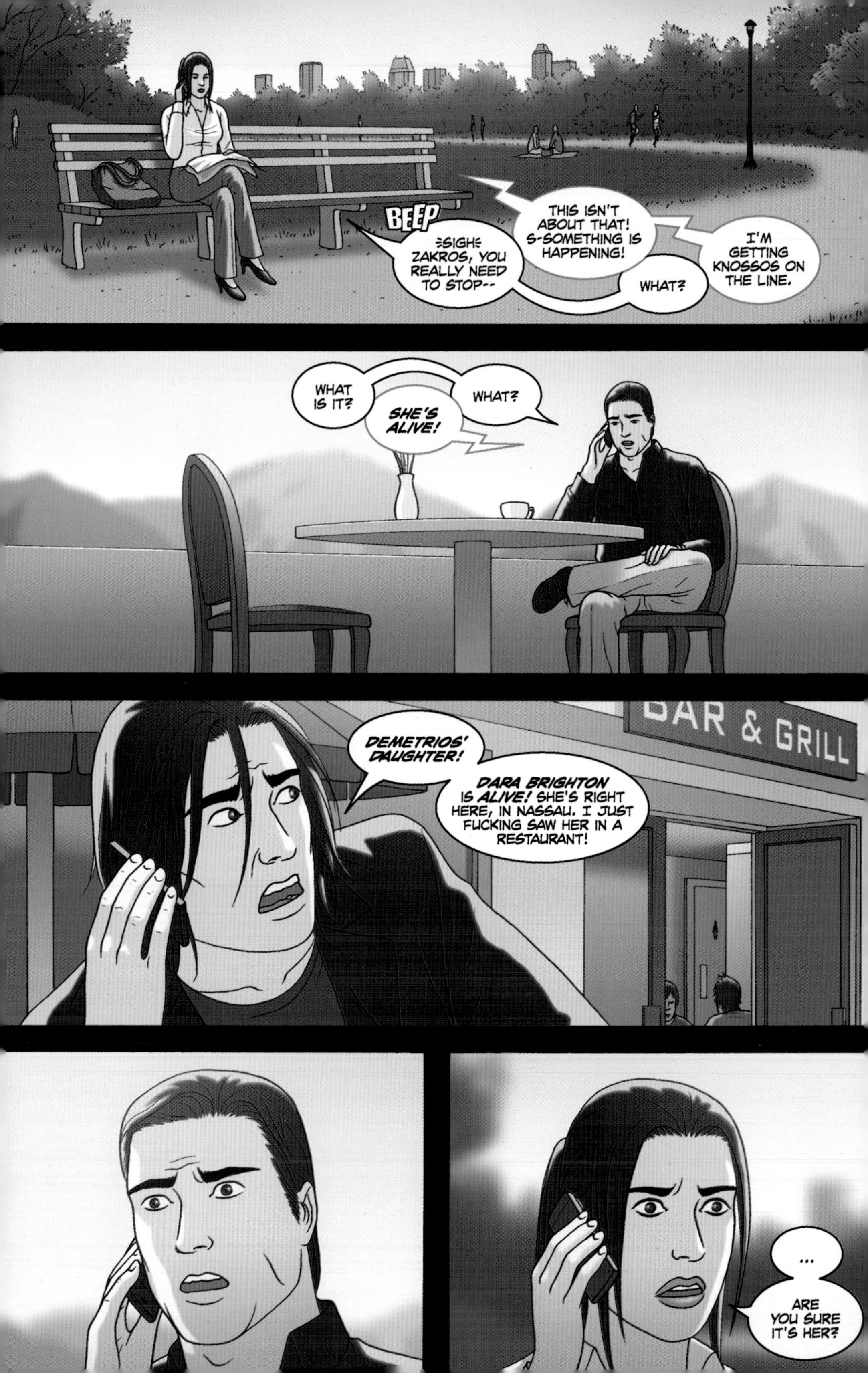
BEEP
≈SIGH≈ ZAKROS, YOU REALLY NEED TO STOP--
THIS ISN'T ABOUT THAT! S-SOMETHING IS HAPPENING!
WHAT?
I'M GETTING KNOSSOS ON THE LINE.
WHAT IS IT?
SHE'S ALIVE!
WHAT?
BAR & GRILL
DEMETRIOS' DAUGHTER!
DARA BRIGHTON IS ALIVE! SHE'S RIGHT HERE, IN NASSAU. I JUST FUCKING SAW HER IN A RESTAURANT!
...
ARE YOU SURE IT'S HER?

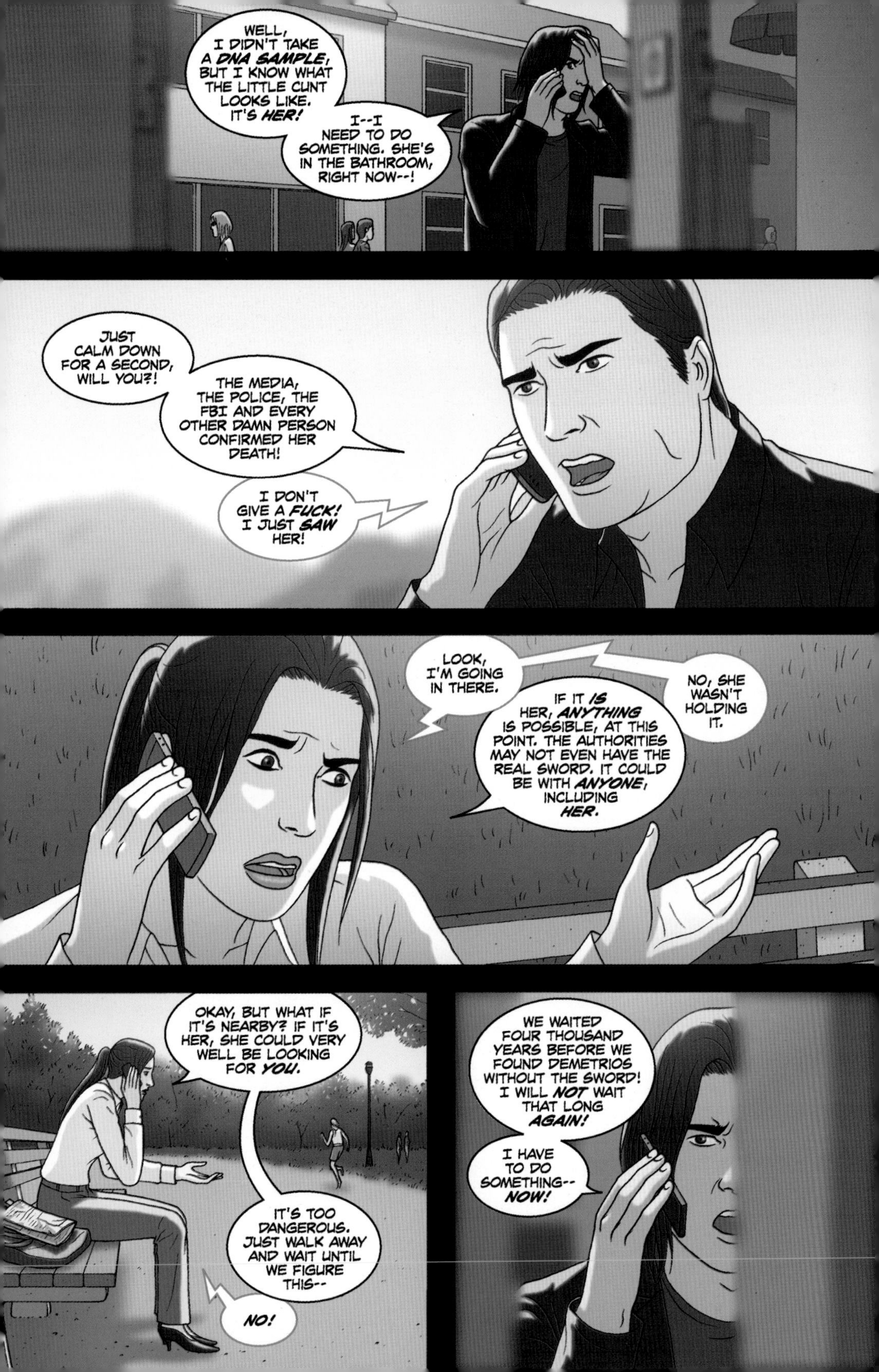
WELL, I DIDN'T TAKE A DNA SAMPLE, BUT I KNOW WHAT THE LITTLE CUNT LOOKS LIKE. IT'S HER!
I--I NEED TO DO SOMETHING. SHE'S IN THE BATHROOM, RIGHT NOW--!
JUST CALM DOWN FOR A SECOND, WILL YOU?!
THE MEDIA, THE POLICE, THE FBI AND EVERY OTHER DAMN PERSON CONFIRMED HER DEATH!
I DON'T GIVE A FUCK! I JUST SAW HER!
LOOK, I'M GOING IN THERE.
IF IT IS HER, ANYTHING IS POSSIBLE, AT THIS POINT. THE AUTHORITIES MAY NOT EVEN HAVE THE REAL SWORD. IT COULD BE WITH ANYONE, INCLUDING HER.
NO, SHE WASN'T HOLDING IT.
OKAY, BUT WHAT IF IT'S NEARBY? IF IT'S HER, SHE COULD VERY WELL BE LOOKING FOR YOU.
IT'S TOO DANGEROUS. JUST WALK AWAY AND WAIT UNTIL WE FIGURE THIS--
NO!
WE WAITED FOUR THOUSAND YEARS BEFORE WE FOUND DEMETRIOS WITHOUT THE SWORD! I WILL NOT WAIT THAT LONG AGAIN!
I HAVE TO DO SOMETHING-- NOW!

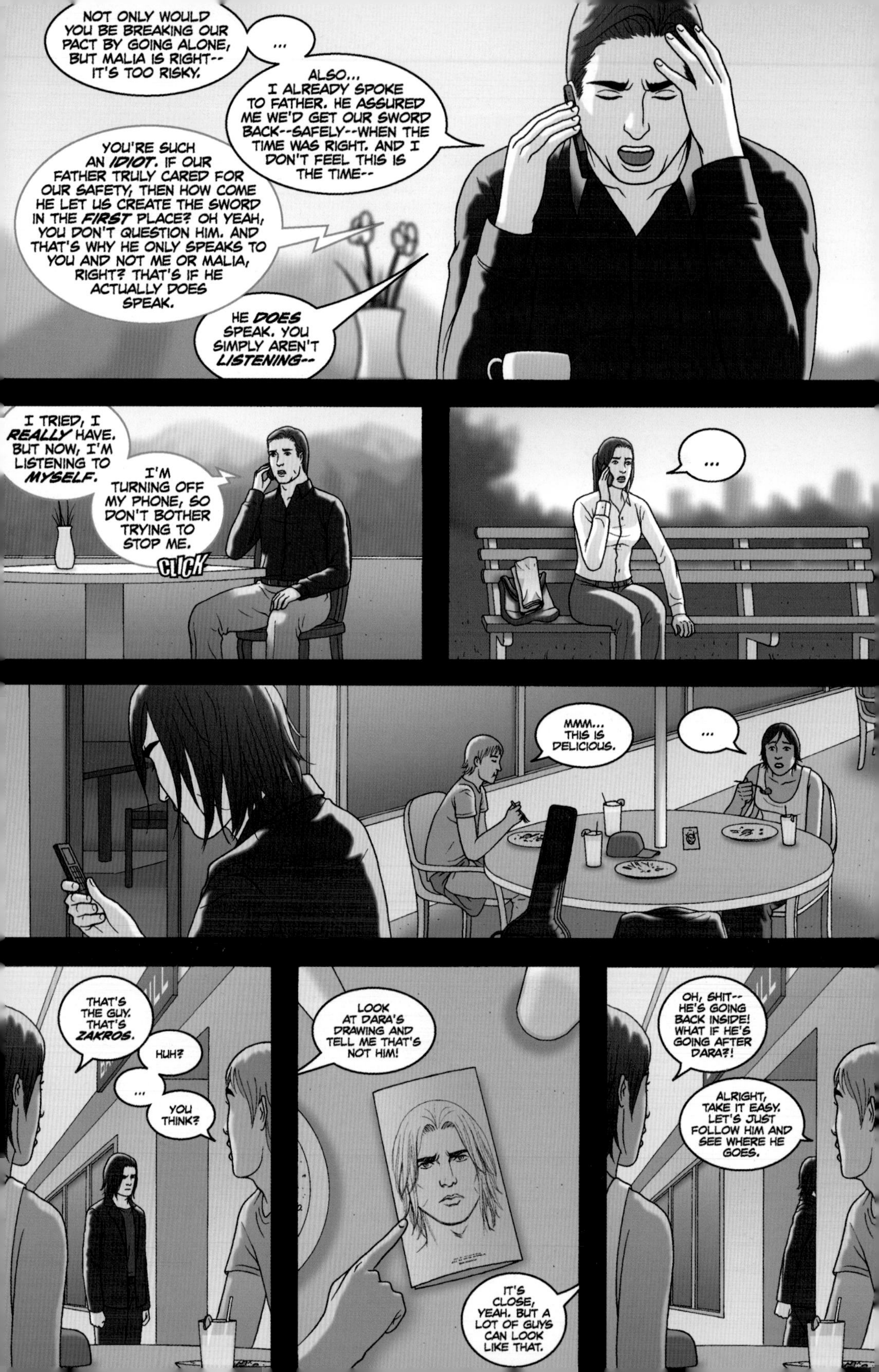
NOT ONLY WOULD YOU BE BREAKING OUR PACT BY GOING ALONE, BUT MALIA IS RIGHT-- IT'S TOO RISKY.
...
ALSO... I ALREADY SPOKE TO FATHER. HE ASSURED ME WE'D GET OUR SWORD BACK--SAFELY--WHEN THE TIME WAS RIGHT. AND I DON'T FEEL THIS IS THE TIME--
YOU'RE SUCH AN IDIOT. IF OUR FATHER TRULY CARED FOR OUR SAFETY, THEN HOW COME HE LET US CREATE THE SWORD IN THE FIRST PLACE? OH YEAH, YOU DON'T QUESTION HIM. AND THAT'S WHY HE ONLY SPEAKS TO YOU AND NOT ME OR MALIA, RIGHT? THAT'S IF HE ACTUALLY DOES SPEAK.
HE DOES SPEAK. YOU SIMPLY AREN'T LISTENING--
I TRIED, I REALLY HAVE. BUT NOW, I'M LISTENING TO MYSELF.
I'M TURNING OFF MY PHONE, SO DON'T BOTHER TRYING TO STOP ME.
CLICK
...
MMM... THIS IS DELICIOUS.
...
THAT'S THE GUY. THAT'S ZAKROS.
HUH?
...
YOU THINK?
LOOK AT DARA'S DRAWING AND TELL ME THAT'S NOT HIM!
IT'S CLOSE, YEAH. BUT A LOT OF GUYS CAN LOOK LIKE THAT.
OH, SHIT-- HE'S GOING BACK INSIDE! WHAT IF HE'S GOING AFTER DARA?!
ALRIGHT, TAKE IT EASY. LET'S JUST FOLLOW HIM AND SEE WHERE HE GOES.

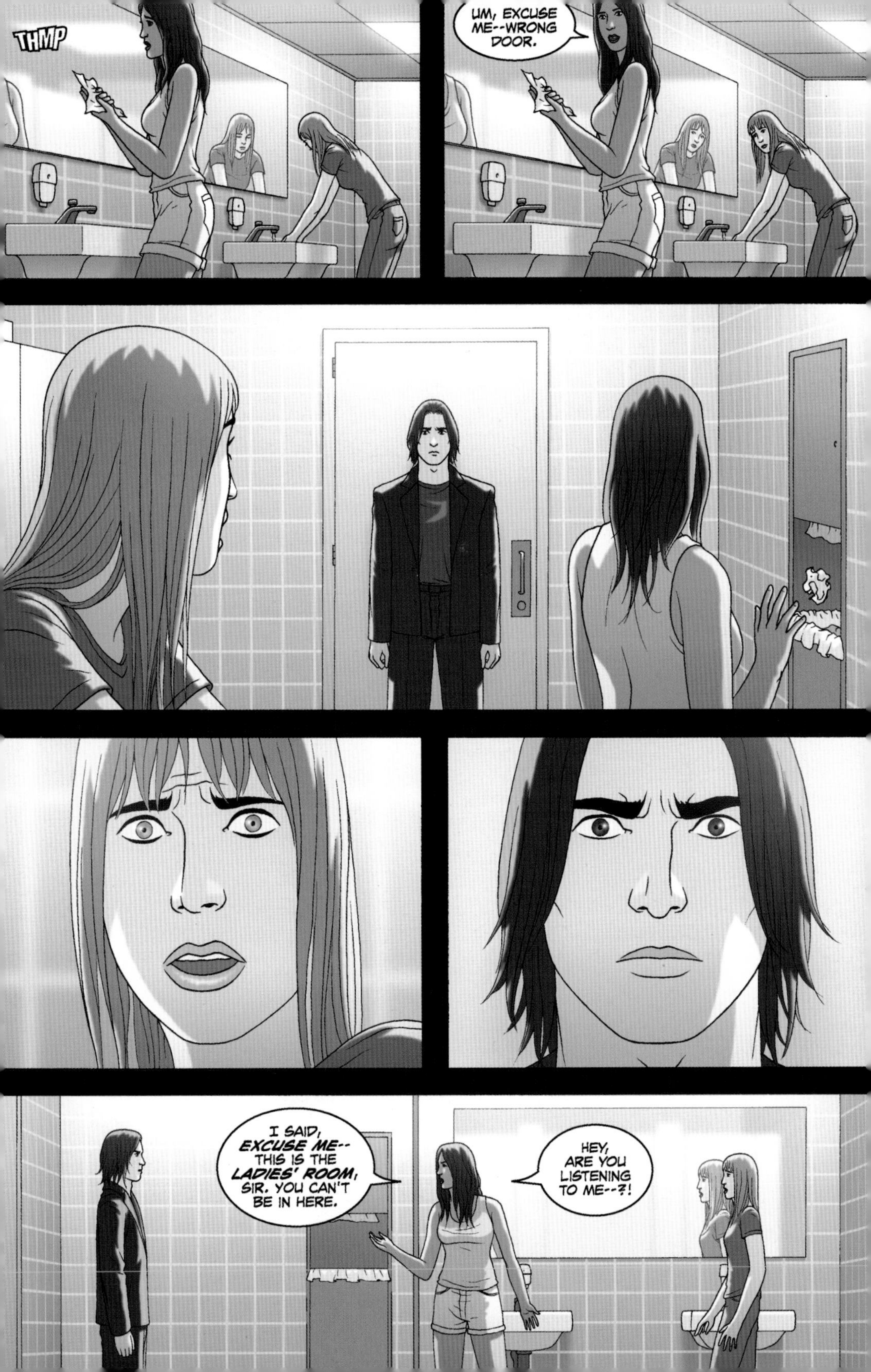
THMP
UM, EXCUSE ME--WRONG DOOR.
I SAID, EXCUSE ME-- THIS IS THE LADIES' ROOM, SIR. YOU CAN'T BE IN HERE.
HEY, ARE YOU LISTENING TO ME--?!

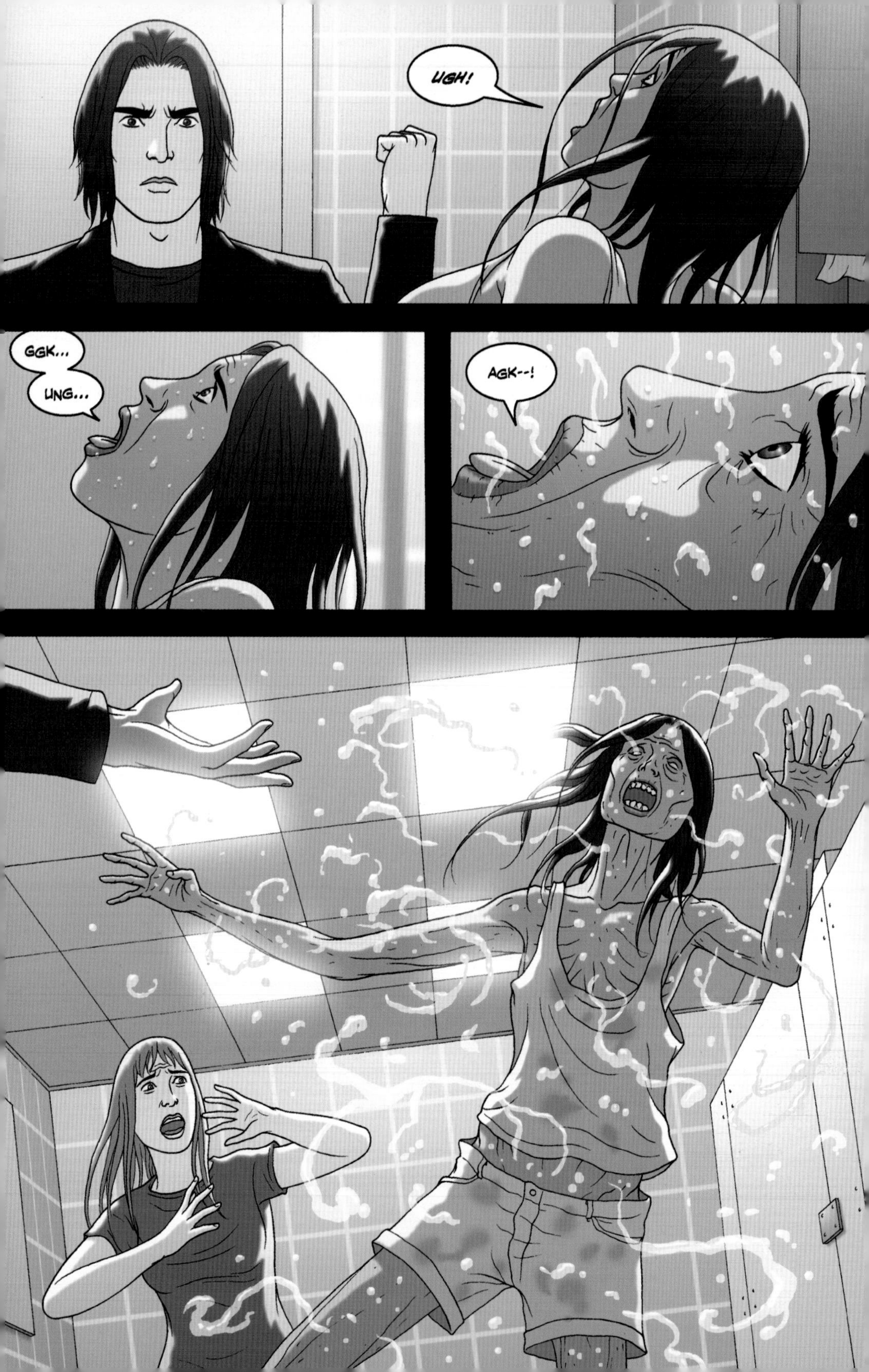
UGH!
GGK...
UNG...
AGK--!

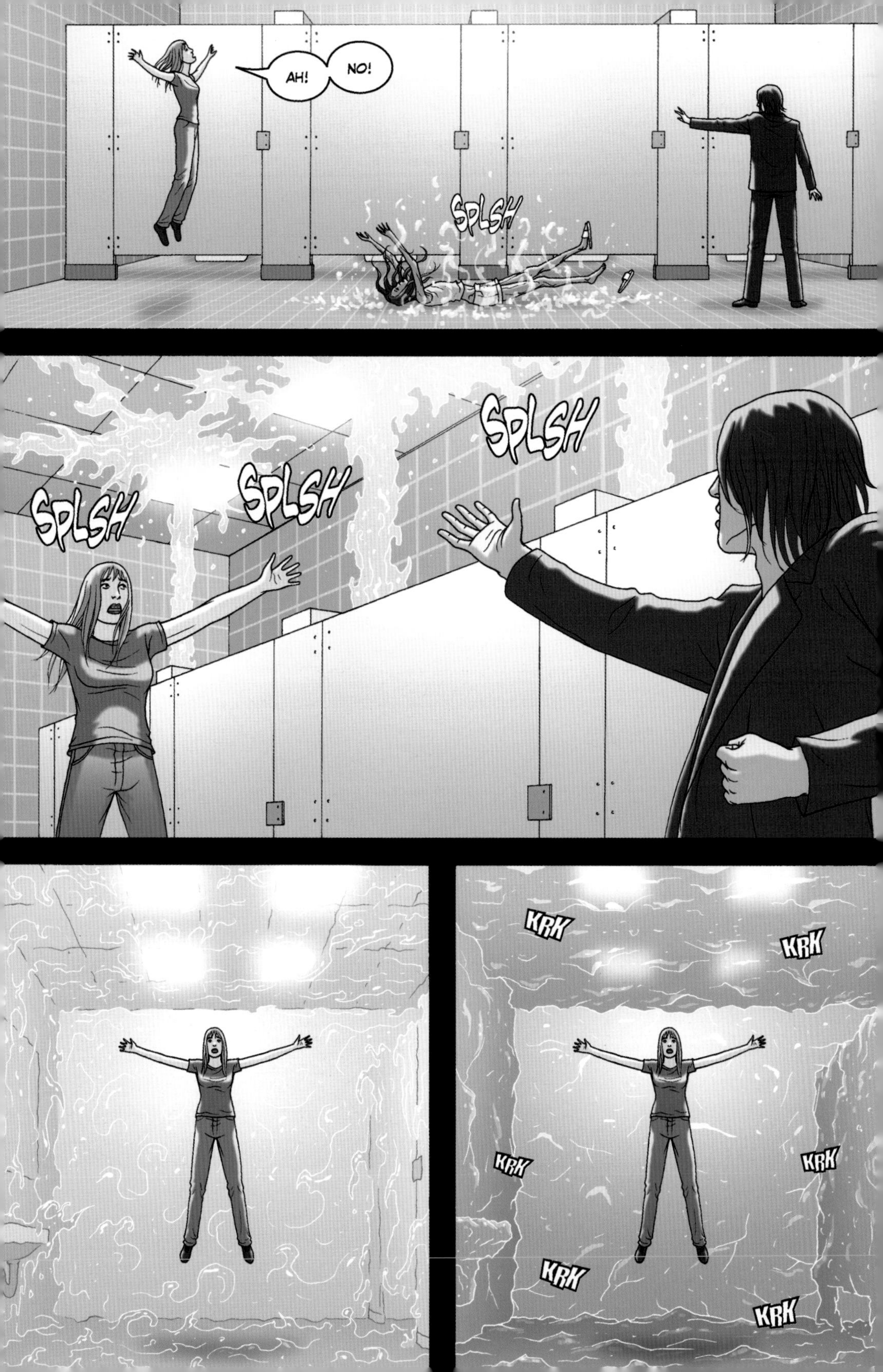
AH!
NO!
SPLSH
SPLSH
SPLSH
SPLSH
KRK
KRK
KRK
KRK
KRK
KRK

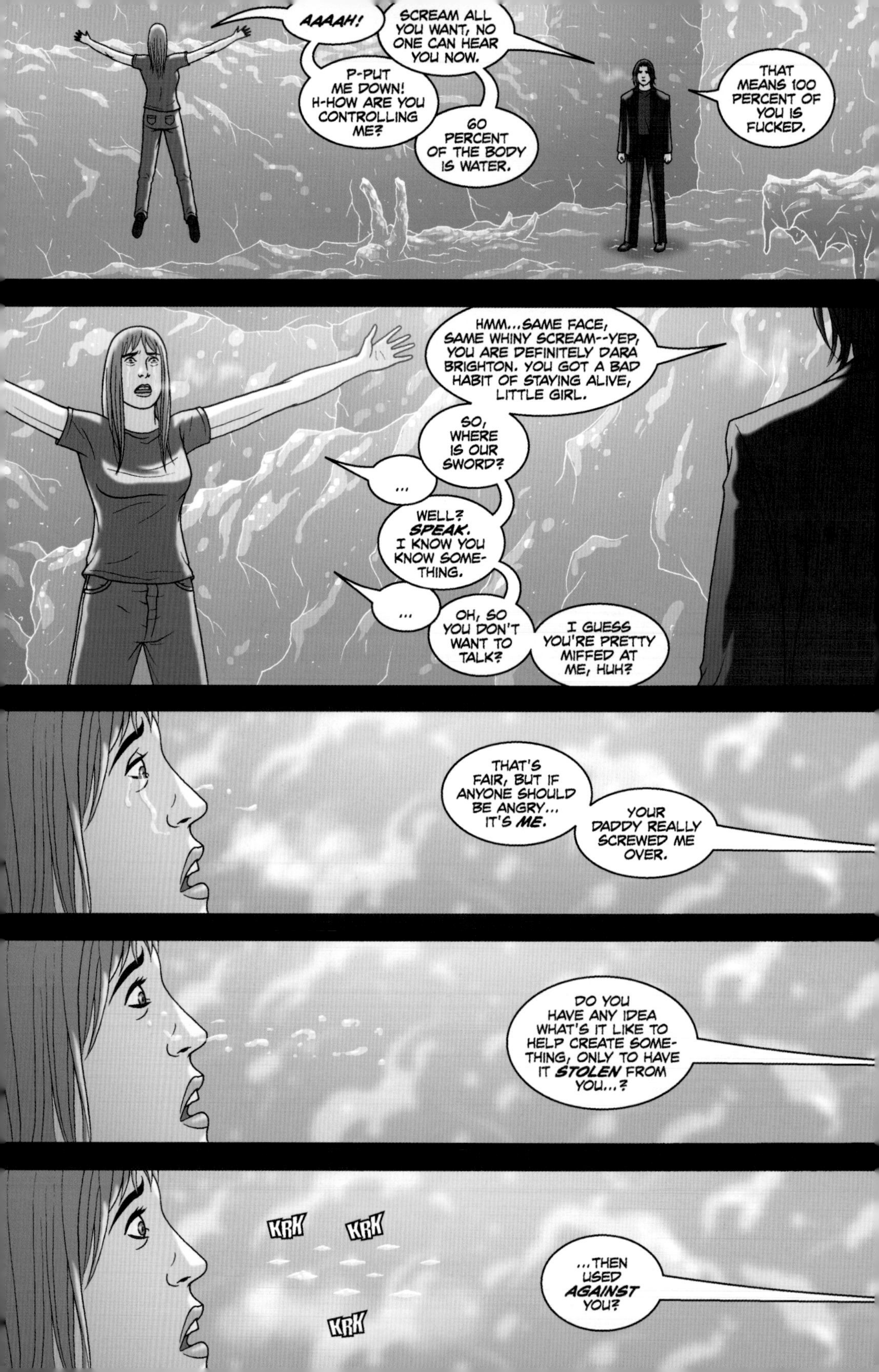
AAAAH!
SCREAM ALL YOU WANT, NO ONE CAN HEAR YOU NOW.
P-PUT ME DOWN! H-HOW ARE YOU CONTROLLING ME?
60 PERCENT OF THE BODY IS WATER.
THAT MEANS 100 PERCENT OF YOU IS FUCKED.
HMM...SAME FACE, SAME WHINY SCREAM--YEP, YOU ARE DEFINITELY DARA BRIGHTON. YOU GOT A BAD HABIT OF STAYING ALIVE, LITTLE GIRL.
SO, WHERE IS OUR SWORD?
...
WELL? SPEAK. I KNOW YOU KNOW SOME-THING.
...
OH, SO YOU DON'T WANT TO TALK?
I GUESS YOU'RE PRETTY MIFFED AT ME, HUH?
THAT'S FAIR, BUT IF ANYONE SHOULD BE ANGRY... IT'S ME.
YOUR DADDY REALLY SCREWED ME OVER.
DO YOU HAVE ANY IDEA WHAT'S IT LIKE TO HELP CREATE SOME-THING, ONLY TO HAVE IT STOLEN FROM YOU...?
KRK
KRK
KRK
...THEN USED AGAINST YOU?

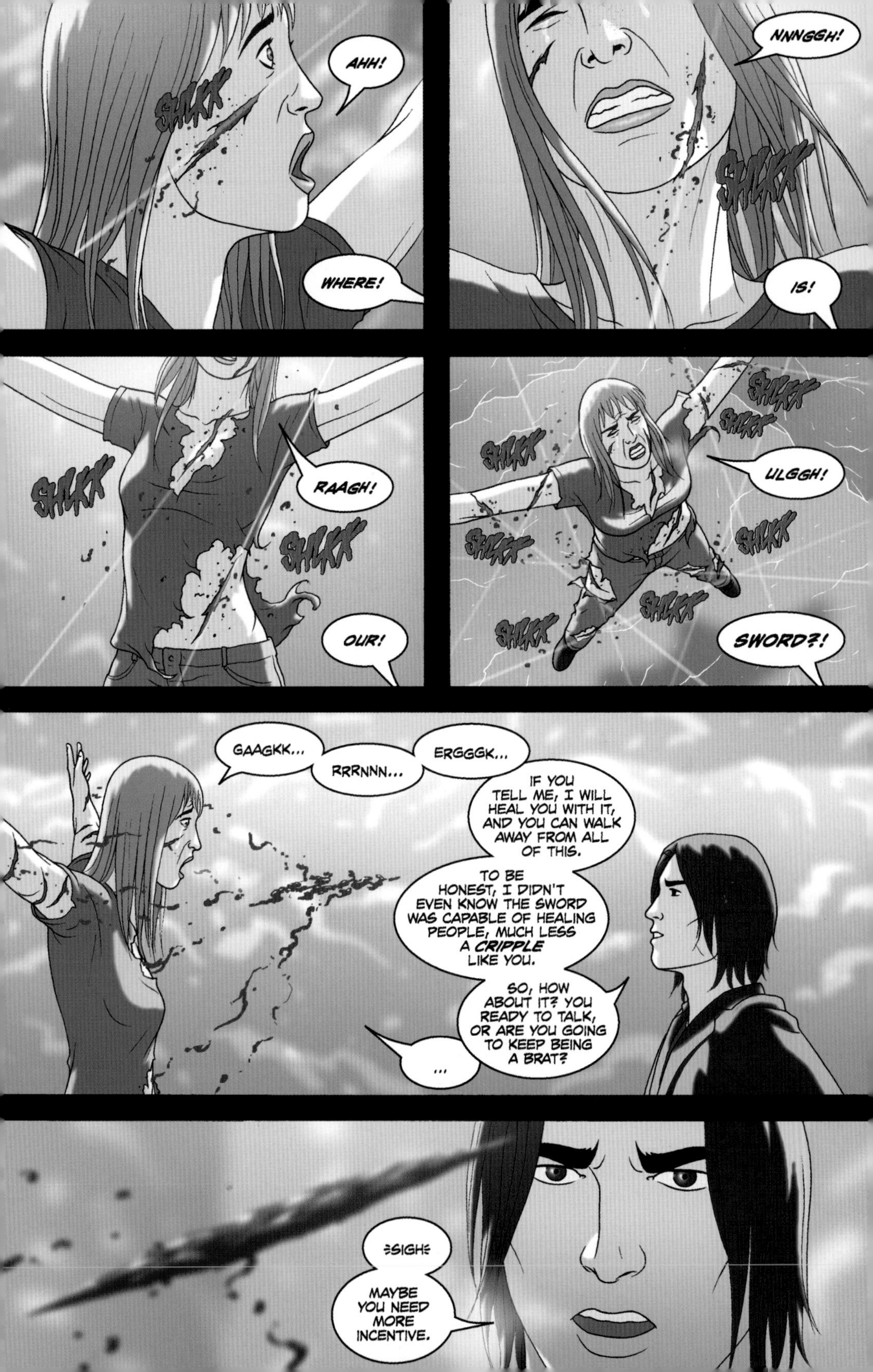
SHLKK
AHH!
WHERE!
NNNGGH!
SHLKK
IS!
SHLKK
RAAGH!
SHLKK
OUR!
SHLKK
SHLKK
SHLKK
ULGGH!
SHLKK
SHLKK
SHLKK
SHLKK
SWORD?!
GAAGKK...
RRRNNN...
ERGGGK...
IF YOU TELL ME, I WILL HEAL YOU WITH IT, AND YOU CAN WALK AWAY FROM ALL OF THIS.
TO BE HONEST, I DIDN'T EVEN KNOW THE SWORD WAS CAPABLE OF HEALING PEOPLE, MUCH LESS A *CRIPPLE* LIKE YOU.
SO, HOW ABOUT IT? YOU READY TO TALK, OR ARE YOU GOING TO KEEP BEING A BRAT?
...
SIGH
MAYBE YOU NEED MORE INCENTIVE.

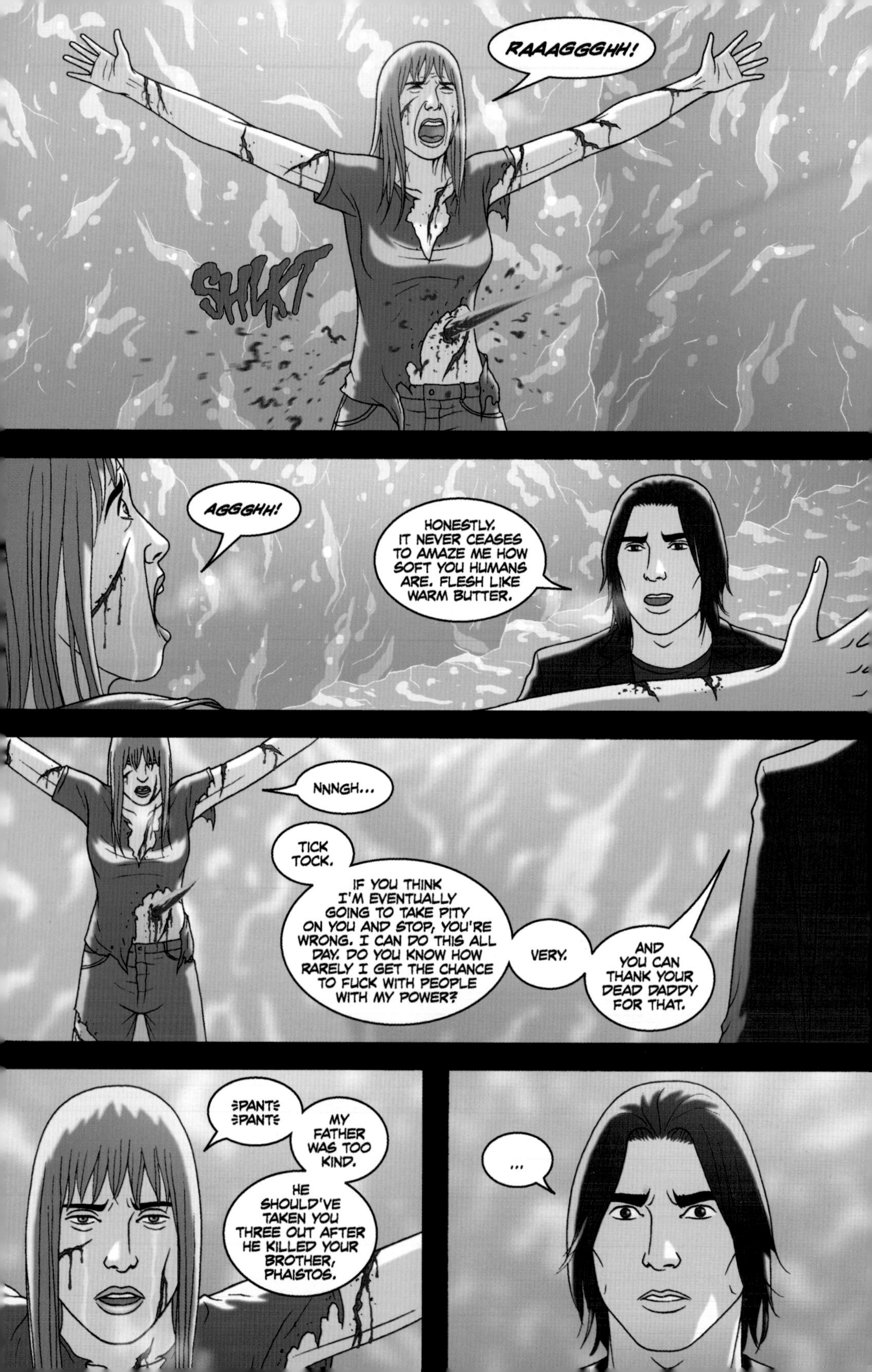

RAAAGGGHH!
SHLKT
AGGGHH!
HONESTLY. IT NEVER CEASES TO AMAZE ME HOW SOFT YOU HUMANS ARE. FLESH LIKE WARM BUTTER.
NNNGH...
TICK TOCK.
IF YOU THINK I'M EVENTUALLY GOING TO TAKE PITY ON YOU AND STOP, YOU'RE WRONG. I CAN DO THIS ALL DAY. DO YOU KNOW HOW RARELY I GET THE CHANCE TO FUCK WITH PEOPLE WITH MY POWER?
VERY.
AND YOU CAN THANK YOUR DEAD DADDY FOR THAT.
=PANT= =PANT=
MY FATHER WAS TOO KIND.
HE SHOULD'VE TAKEN YOU THREE OUT AFTER HE KILLED YOUR BROTHER, PHAISTOS.
...

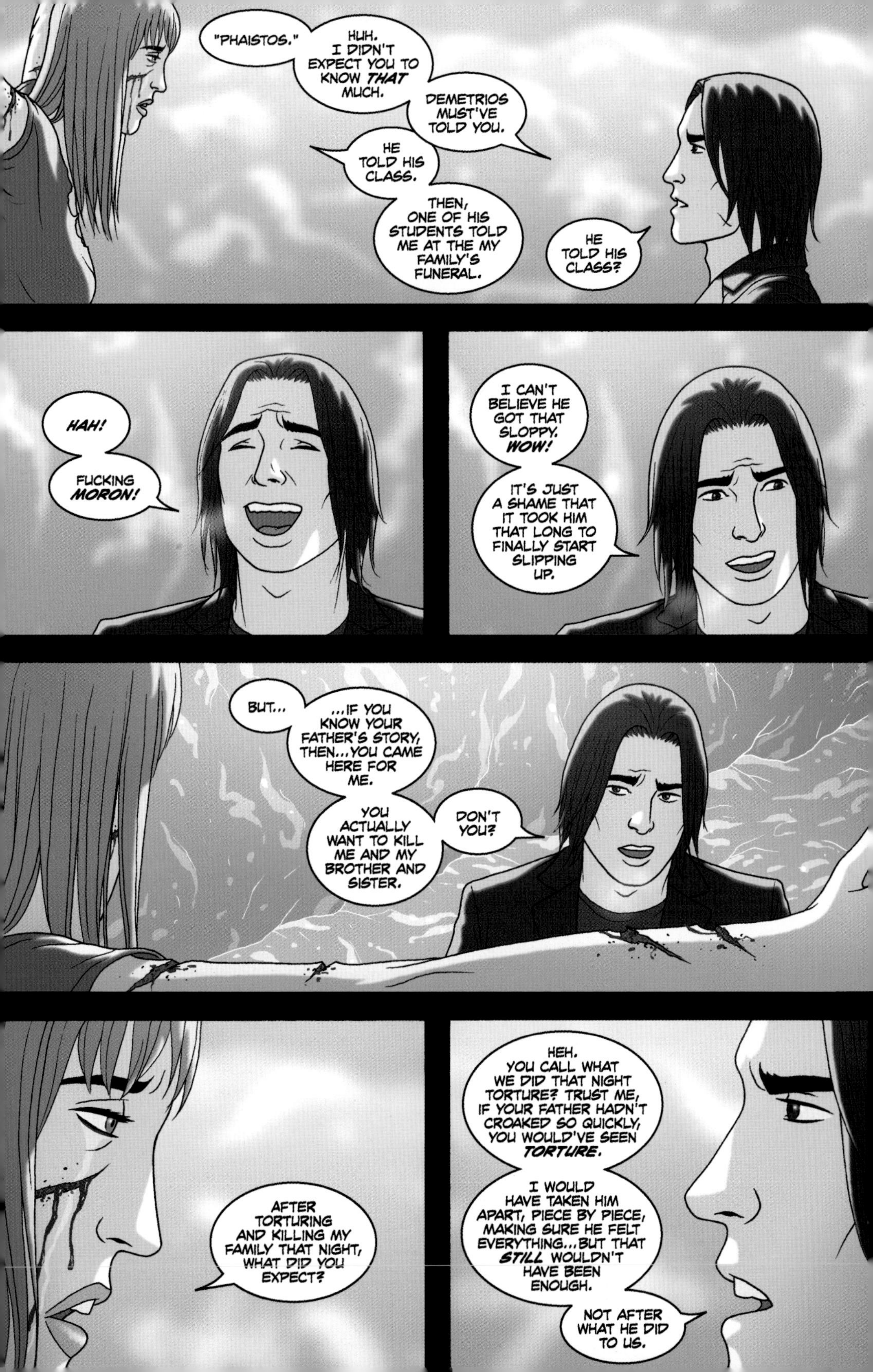
"PHAISTOS."
HUH. I DIDN'T EXPECT YOU TO KNOW *THAT* MUCH.
DEMETRIOS MUST'VE TOLD YOU.
HE TOLD HIS CLASS.
THEN, ONE OF HIS STUDENTS TOLD ME AT THE MY FAMILY'S FUNERAL.
HE TOLD HIS CLASS?
HAH!
FUCKING *MORON!*
I CAN'T BELIEVE HE GOT THAT SLOPPY. *WOW!*
IT'S JUST A SHAME THAT IT TOOK HIM THAT LONG TO FINALLY START SLIPPING UP.
BUT...
...IF YOU KNOW YOUR FATHER'S STORY, THEN...YOU CAME HERE FOR ME.
YOU ACTUALLY WANT TO KILL ME AND MY BROTHER AND SISTER.
DON'T YOU?
AFTER TORTURING AND KILLING MY FAMILY THAT NIGHT, WHAT DID YOU EXPECT?
HEH. YOU CALL WHAT WE DID THAT NIGHT TORTURE? TRUST ME, IF YOUR FATHER HADN'T CROAKED SO QUICKLY, YOU WOULD'VE SEEN *TORTURE*.
I WOULD HAVE TAKEN HIM APART, PIECE BY PIECE, MAKING SURE HE FELT EVERYTHING...BUT THAT *STILL* WOULDN'T HAVE BEEN ENOUGH.
NOT AFTER WHAT HE DID TO US.

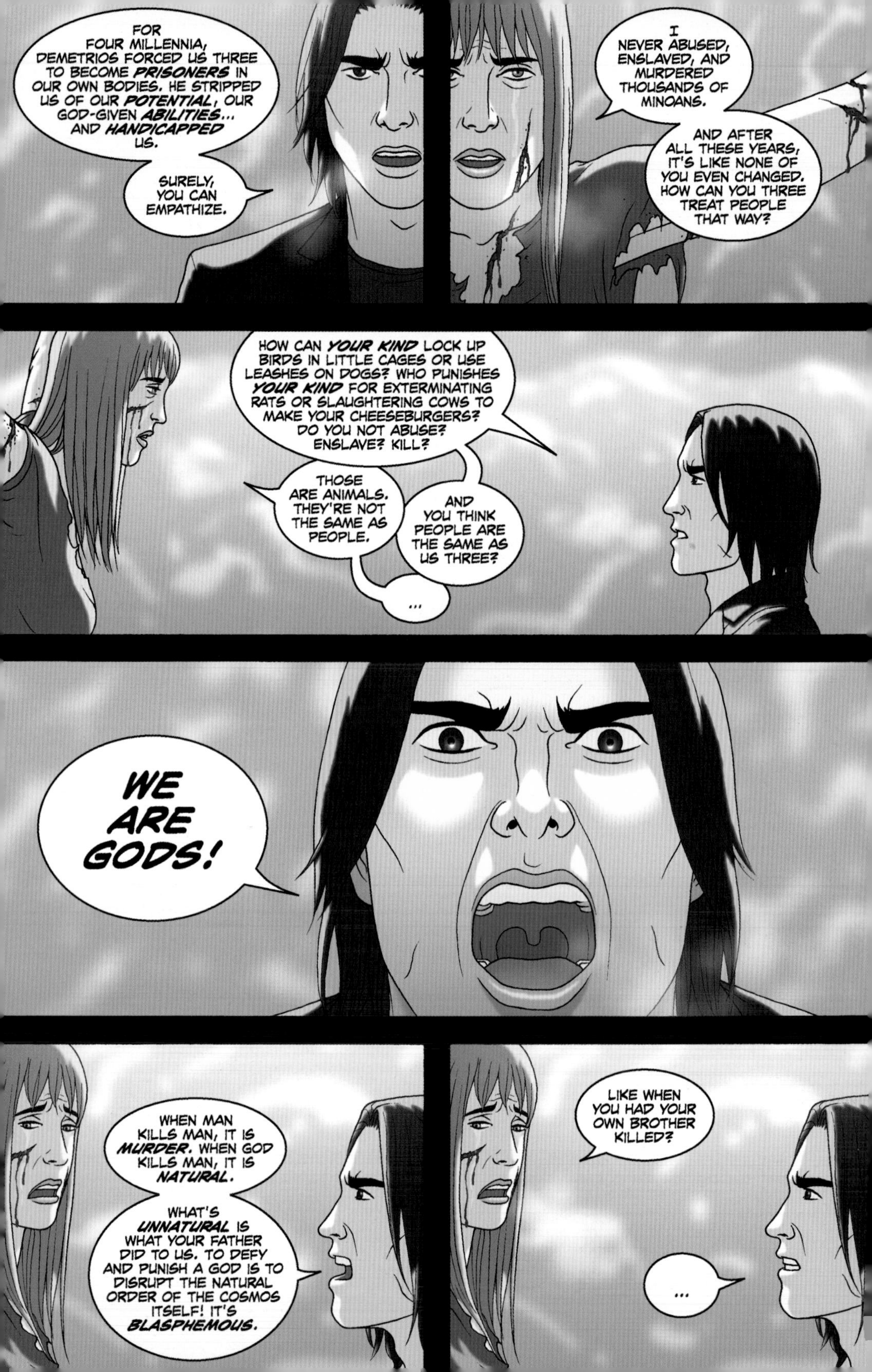
FOR FOUR MILLENNIA, DEMETRIOS FORCED US THREE TO BECOME PRISONERS IN OUR OWN BODIES. HE STRIPPED US OF OUR POTENTIAL, OUR GOD-GIVEN ABILITIES... AND HANDICAPPED US.
SURELY, YOU CAN EMPATHIZE.
I NEVER ABUSED, ENSLAVED, AND MURDERED THOUSANDS OF MINOANS.
AND AFTER ALL THESE YEARS, IT'S LIKE NONE OF YOU EVEN CHANGED. HOW CAN YOU THREE TREAT PEOPLE THAT WAY?
HOW CAN YOUR KIND LOCK UP BIRDS IN LITTLE CAGES OR USE LEASHES ON DOGS? WHO PUNISHES YOUR KIND FOR EXTERMINATING RATS OR SLAUGHTERING COWS TO MAKE YOUR CHEESEBURGERS? DO YOU NOT ABUSE? ENSLAVE? KILL?
THOSE ARE ANIMALS. THEY'RE NOT THE SAME AS PEOPLE.
AND YOU THINK PEOPLE ARE THE SAME AS US THREE?
...
WE ARE GODS!
WHEN MAN KILLS MAN, IT IS MURDER. WHEN GOD KILLS MAN, IT IS NATURAL.
WHAT'S UNNATURAL IS WHAT YOUR FATHER DID TO US. TO DEFY AND PUNISH A GOD IS TO DISRUPT THE NATURAL ORDER OF THE COSMOS ITSELF! IT'S BLASPHEMOUS.
LIKE WHEN YOU HAD YOUR OWN BROTHER KILLED?
...

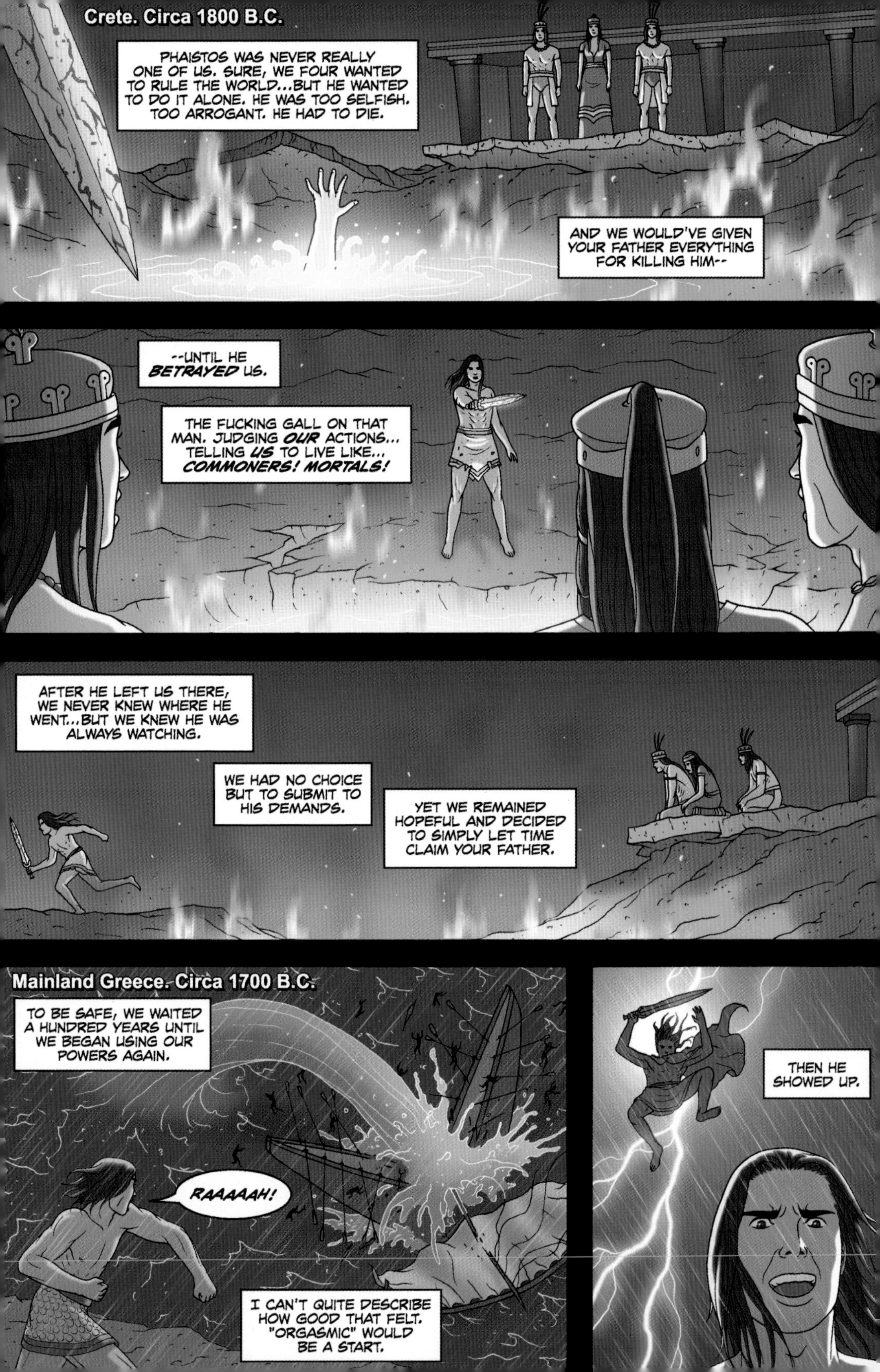
Crete. Circa 1800 B.C.
PHAISTOS WAS NEVER REALLY ONE OF US. SURE, WE FOUR WANTED TO RULE THE WORLD...BUT HE WANTED TO DO IT ALONE. HE WAS TOO SELFISH. TOO ARROGANT. HE HAD TO DIE.
AND WE WOULD'VE GIVEN YOUR FATHER EVERYTHING FOR KILLING HIM--
--UNTIL HE *BETRAYED* US.
THE FUCKING GALL ON THAT MAN. JUDGING *OUR* ACTIONS... TELLING *US* TO LIVE LIKE... *COMMONERS! MORTALS!*
AFTER HE LEFT US THERE, WE NEVER KNEW WHERE HE WENT...BUT WE KNEW HE WAS ALWAYS WATCHING.
WE HAD NO CHOICE BUT TO SUBMIT TO HIS DEMANDS.
YET WE REMAINED HOPEFUL AND DECIDED TO SIMPLY LET TIME CLAIM YOUR FATHER.
Mainland Greece. Circa 1700 B.C.
TO BE SAFE, WE WAITED A HUNDRED YEARS UNTIL WE BEGAN USING OUR POWERS AGAIN.
RAAAAAH!
I CAN'T QUITE DESCRIBE HOW GOOD THAT FELT. "ORGASMIC" WOULD BE A START.
THEN HE SHOWED UP.

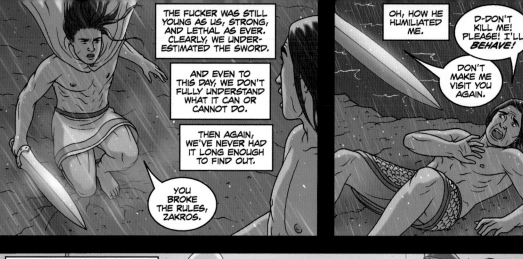

THE FUCKER WAS STILL YOUNG AS US, STRONG, AND LETHAL AS EVER. CLEARLY, WE UNDER-ESTIMATED THE SWORD.

AND EVEN TO THIS DAY, WE DON'T FULLY UNDERSTAND WHAT IT CAN OR CANNOT DO.

THEN AGAIN, WE'VE NEVER HAD IT LONG ENOUGH TO FIND OUT.

YOU BROKE THE RULES, ZAKROS.

OH, HOW HE HUMILIATED ME.

D-DON'T KILL ME! PLEASE! I'LL *BEHAVE!*

DON'T MAKE ME VISIT YOU AGAIN.

THE THOUGHT OF LIVING LIKE A MORTAL FOR ETERNITY NEARLY DROVE ME INSANE...BUT WHAT COULD I HAVE DONE? IT WAS THE ONLY WAY HE *LET* ME LIVE.

THE MORE TIME I SPENT AMONGST HUMANS, THE MORE *INTENSE* AND *SPECIFIC* MY HATRED FOR THEM GREW.

THERE WERE DIFFERENT TYPES.

THE *WEAK*, *DISEASED*, AND *DEFORMED*.

SO FUCKING DISGUSTING.

THE *OBLIVIOUS*, WHO PRAY TO THEIR FALSE GODS WHEN THEY *SHOULD* BE WORSHIPPING ME, MY BROTHER AND SISTER.

THE *HAPPY*, SO CONTENT WITH THEIR MEANINGLESS, FLEETING, LITTLE LIVES.

BUT THOSE TYPES DON'T EVEN TOP MY SHIT LIST. OH NO, THAT SPOT IS DESIGNATED FOR A SPECIAL BREED OF ASSHOLE.

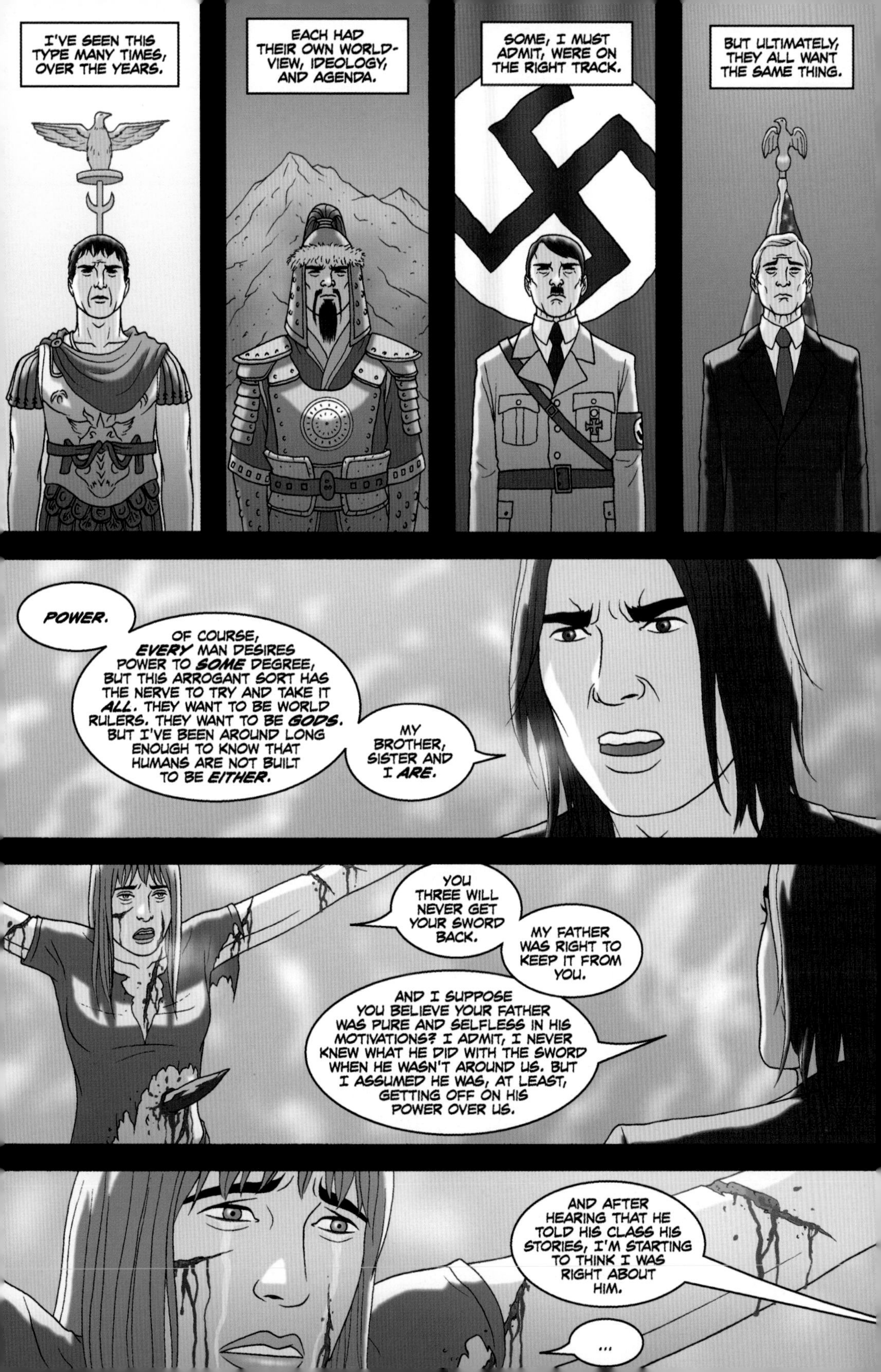
I'VE SEEN THIS TYPE MANY TIMES, OVER THE YEARS.
EACH HAD THEIR OWN WORLD-VIEW, IDEOLOGY, AND AGENDA.
SOME, I MUST ADMIT, WERE ON THE RIGHT TRACK.
BUT ULTIMATELY, THEY ALL WANT THE SAME THING.
POWER.
OF COURSE, EVERY MAN DESIRES POWER TO SOME DEGREE, BUT THIS ARROGANT SORT HAS THE NERVE TO TRY AND TAKE IT ALL. THEY WANT TO BE WORLD RULERS. THEY WANT TO BE GODS. BUT I'VE BEEN AROUND LONG ENOUGH TO KNOW THAT HUMANS ARE NOT BUILT TO BE EITHER.
MY BROTHER, SISTER AND I ARE.
YOU THREE WILL NEVER GET YOUR SWORD BACK.
MY FATHER WAS RIGHT TO KEEP IT FROM YOU.
AND I SUPPOSE YOU BELIEVE YOUR FATHER WAS PURE AND SELFLESS IN HIS MOTIVATIONS? I ADMIT, I NEVER KNEW WHAT HE DID WITH THE SWORD WHEN HE WASN'T AROUND US. BUT I ASSUMED HE WAS, AT LEAST, GETTING OFF ON HIS POWER OVER US.
AND AFTER HEARING THAT HE TOLD HIS CLASS HIS STORIES, I'M STARTING TO THINK I WAS RIGHT ABOUT HIM.
...

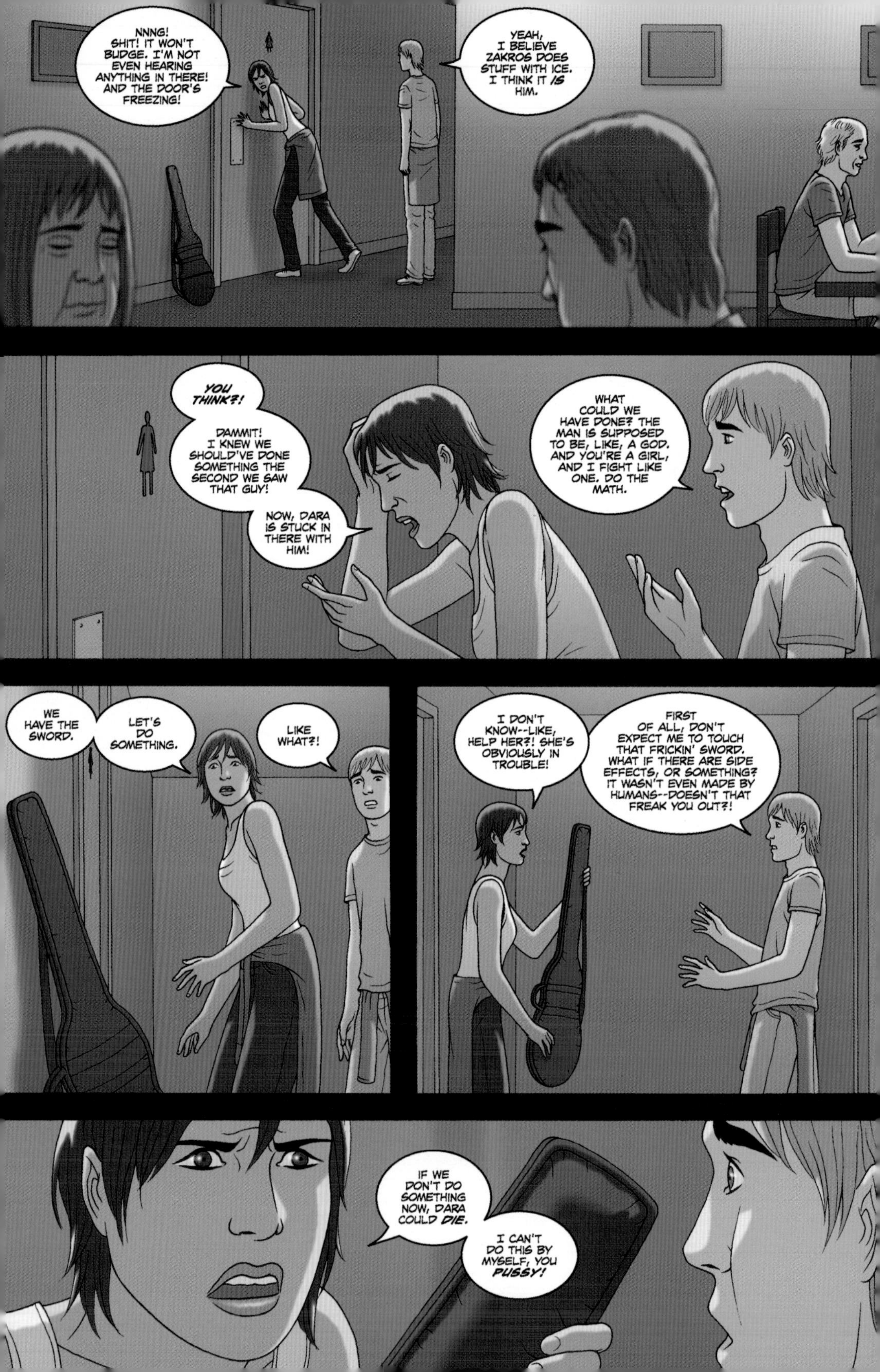
NNNG! SHIT! IT WON'T BUDGE. I'M NOT EVEN HEARING ANYTHING IN THERE! AND THE DOOR'S FREEZING!
YEAH, I BELIEVE ZAKROS DOES STUFF WITH ICE. I THINK IT *IS* HIM.
YOU THINK?!
DAMMIT! I KNEW WE SHOULD'VE DONE SOMETHING THE SECOND WE SAW THAT GUY!
NOW, DARA IS STUCK IN THERE WITH HIM!
WHAT COULD WE HAVE DONE? THE MAN IS SUPPOSED TO BE, LIKE, A GOD. AND YOU'RE A GIRL, AND I FIGHT LIKE ONE. DO THE MATH.
WE HAVE THE SWORD.
LET'S DO SOMETHING.
LIKE WHAT?!
I DON'T KNOW--LIKE, HELP HER?! SHE'S OBVIOUSLY IN TROUBLE!
FIRST OF ALL, DON'T EXPECT ME TO TOUCH THAT FRICKIN' SWORD. WHAT IF THERE ARE SIDE EFFECTS, OR SOMETHING? IT WASN'T EVEN MADE BY HUMANS--DOESN'T THAT FREAK YOU OUT?!
IF WE DON'T DO SOMETHING NOW, DARA COULD *DIE*.
I CAN'T DO THIS BY MYSELF, YOU *PUSSY!*

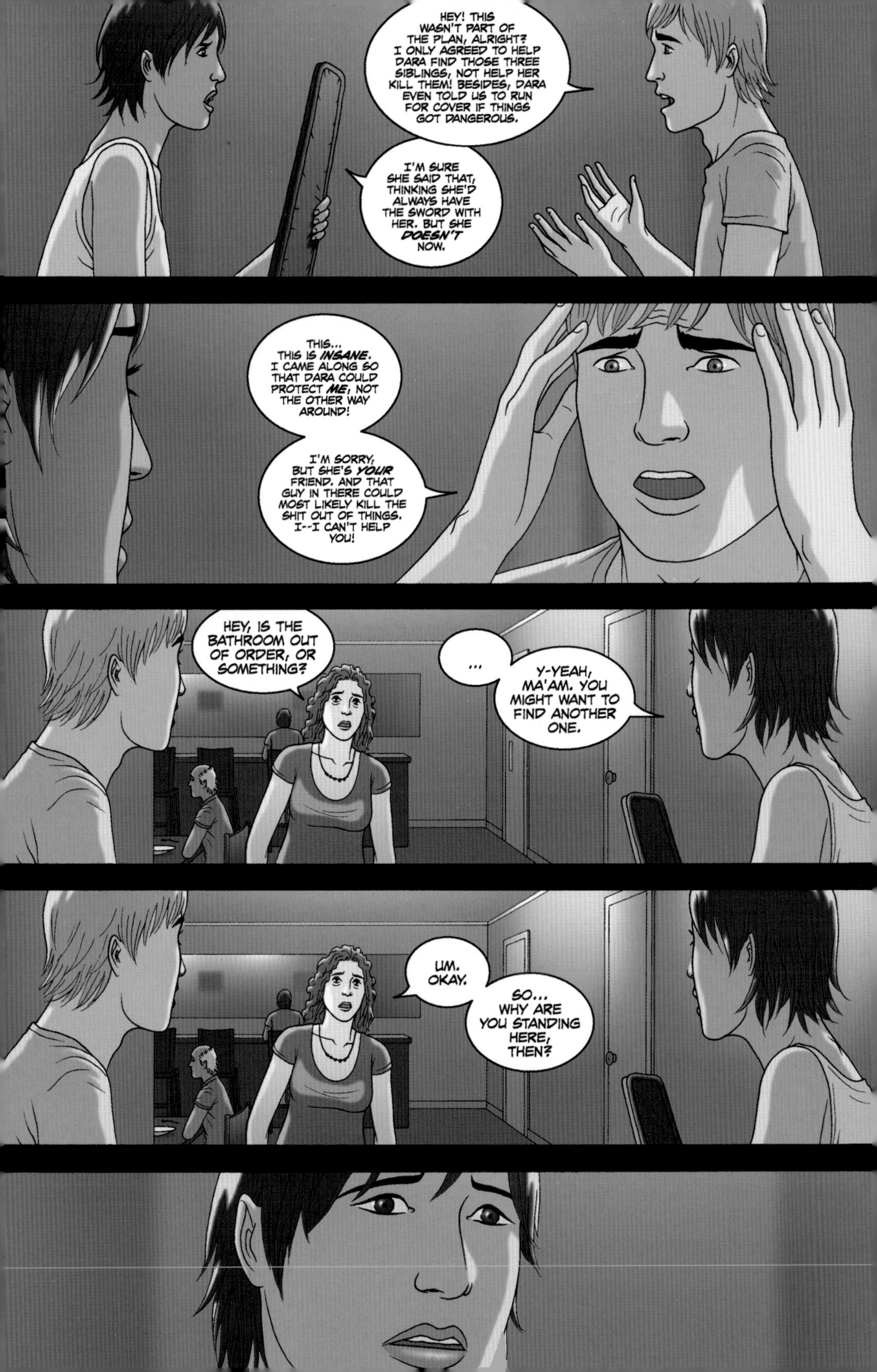
HEY! THIS WASN'T PART OF THE PLAN, ALRIGHT? I ONLY AGREED TO HELP DARA FIND THOSE THREE SIBLINGS, NOT HELP HER KILL THEM! BESIDES, DARA EVEN TOLD US TO RUN FOR COVER IF THINGS GOT DANGEROUS.
I'M SURE SHE SAID THAT, THINKING SHE'D ALWAYS HAVE THE SWORD WITH HER. BUT SHE *DOESN'T* NOW.
THIS... THIS IS *INSANE*. I CAME ALONG SO THAT DARA COULD PROTECT *ME*, NOT THE OTHER WAY AROUND!
I'M SORRY, BUT SHE'S *YOUR* FRIEND. AND THAT GUY IN THERE COULD MOST LIKELY KILL THE SHIT OUT OF THINGS. I--I CAN'T HELP YOU!
HEY, IS THE BATHROOM OUT OF ORDER, OR SOMETHING?
...
Y-YEAH, MA'AM. YOU MIGHT WANT TO FIND ANOTHER ONE.
UM. OKAY.
SO... WHY ARE YOU STANDING HERE, THEN?

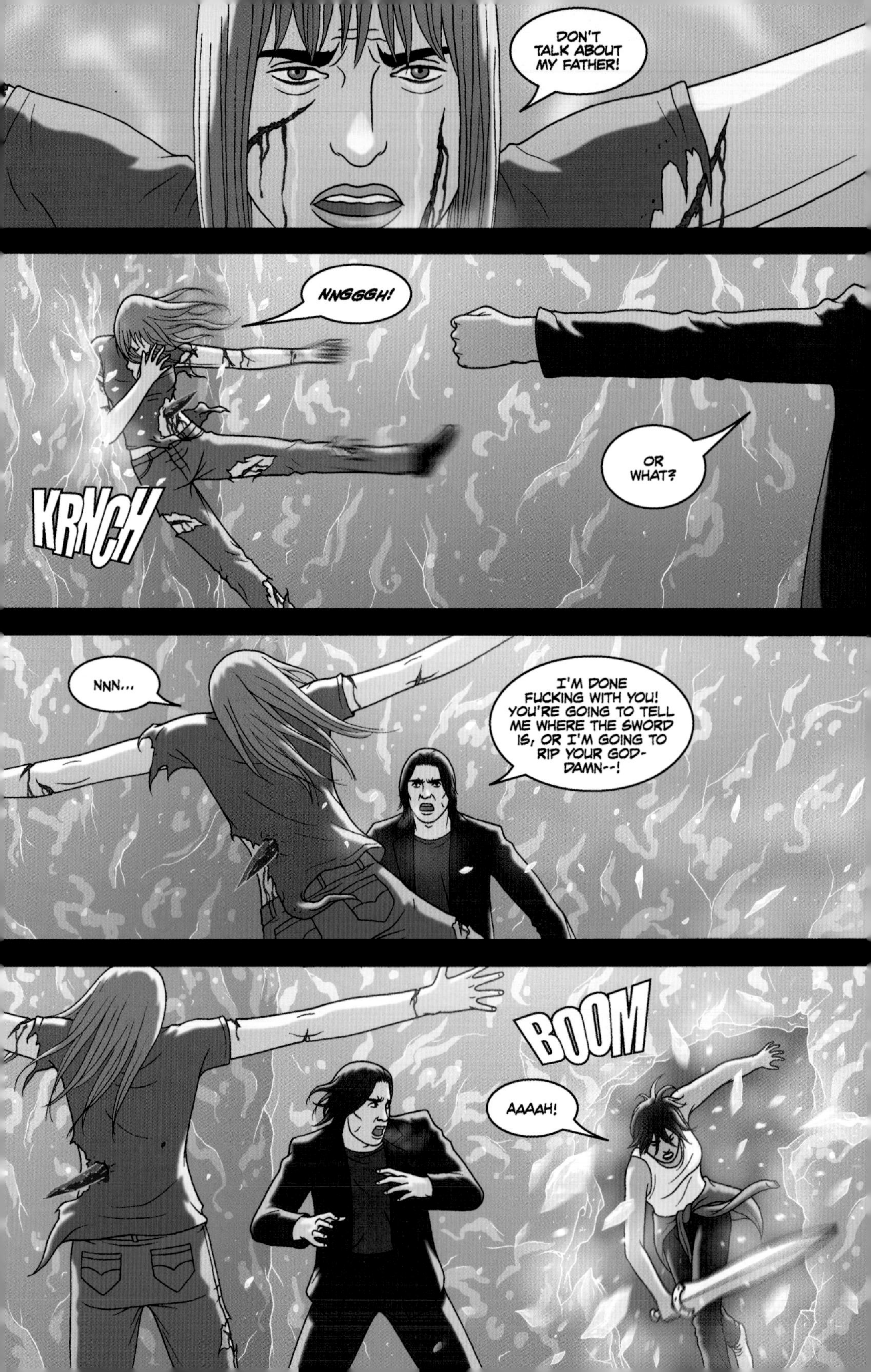
DON'T TALK ABOUT MY FATHER!
NNGGGH!
OR WHAT?
KRNCH
NNN...
I'M DONE FUCKING WITH YOU! YOU'RE GOING TO TELL ME WHERE THE SWORD IS, OR I'M GOING TO RIP YOUR GOD-DAMN--!
BOOM
AAAAH!

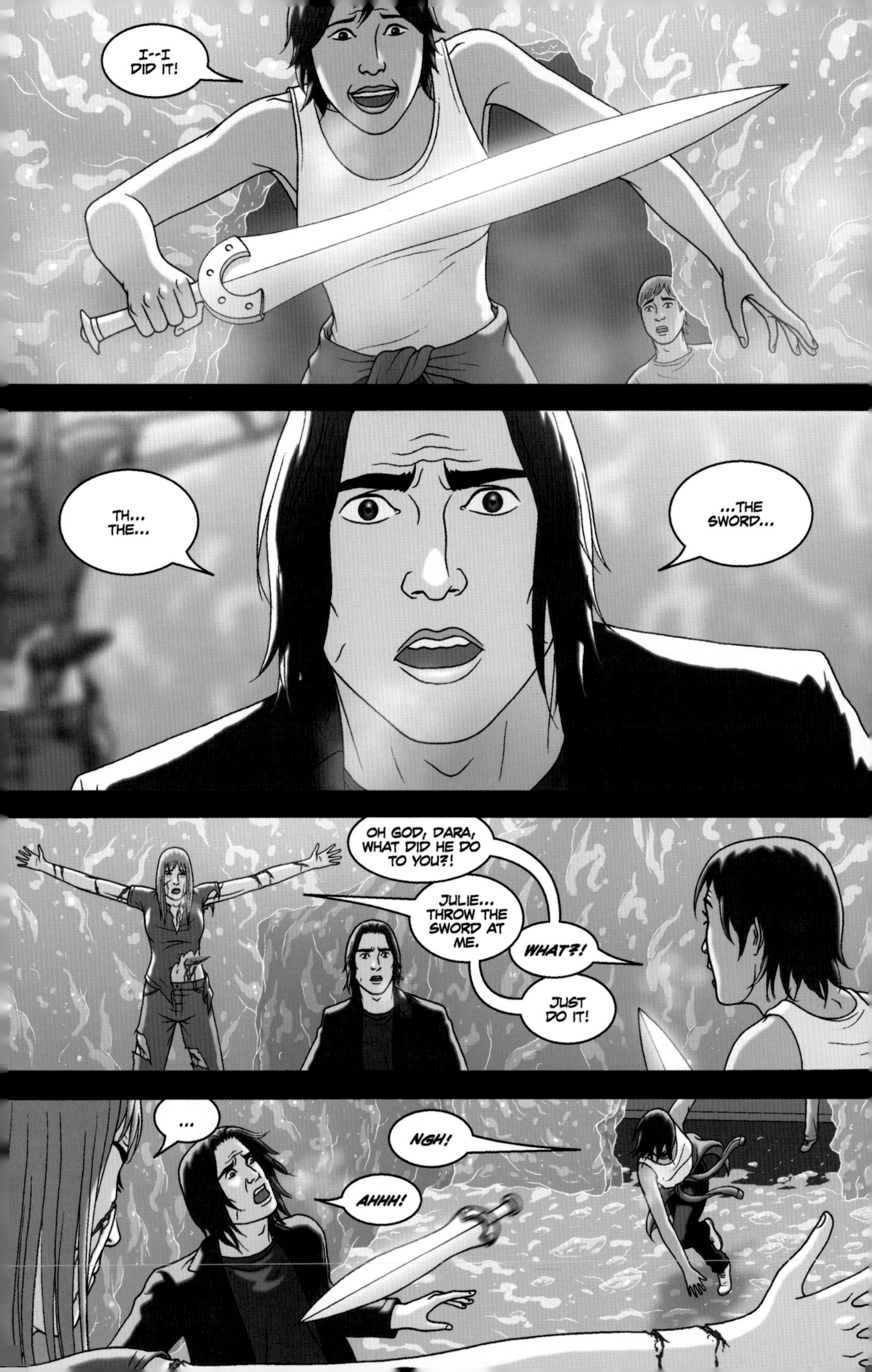
I--I DID IT!
TH... THE...
...THE SWORD...
OH GOD, DARA, WHAT DID HE DO TO YOU?!
JULIE... THROW THE SWORD AT ME.
WHAT?!
JUST DO IT!
...
NGH!
AHHH!

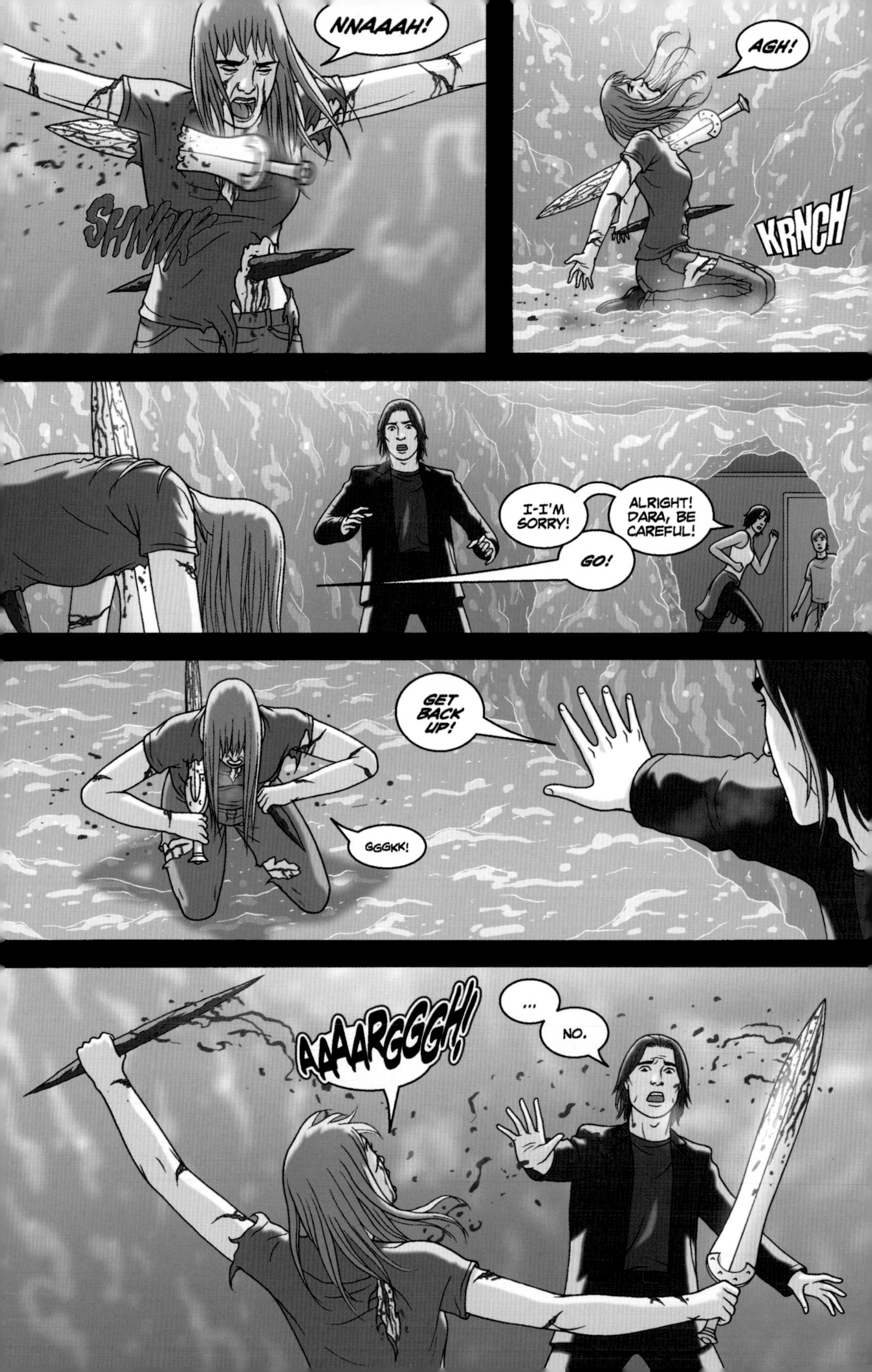

NNAAAAH!
SHNNK
AGH!
KRNCH
I-I'M SORRY!
ALRIGHT! DARA, BE CAREFUL!
GO!
GET BACK UP!
GGGKK!
AAAARGGGH!
...
NO.

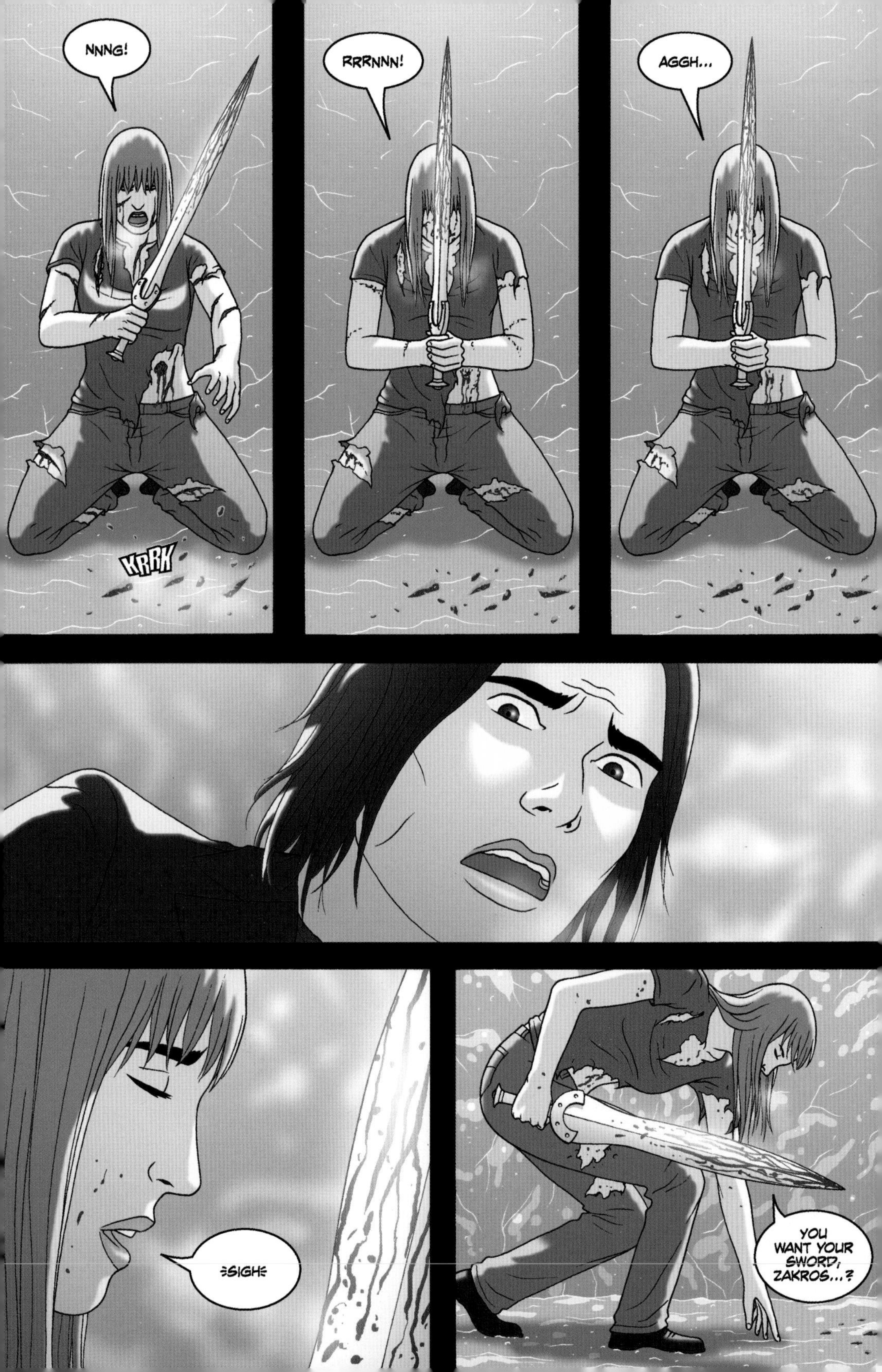
NNNG!
KRRK
RRRNNN!
AGGH...
=SIGH=
YOU WANT YOUR SWORD, ZAKROS...?

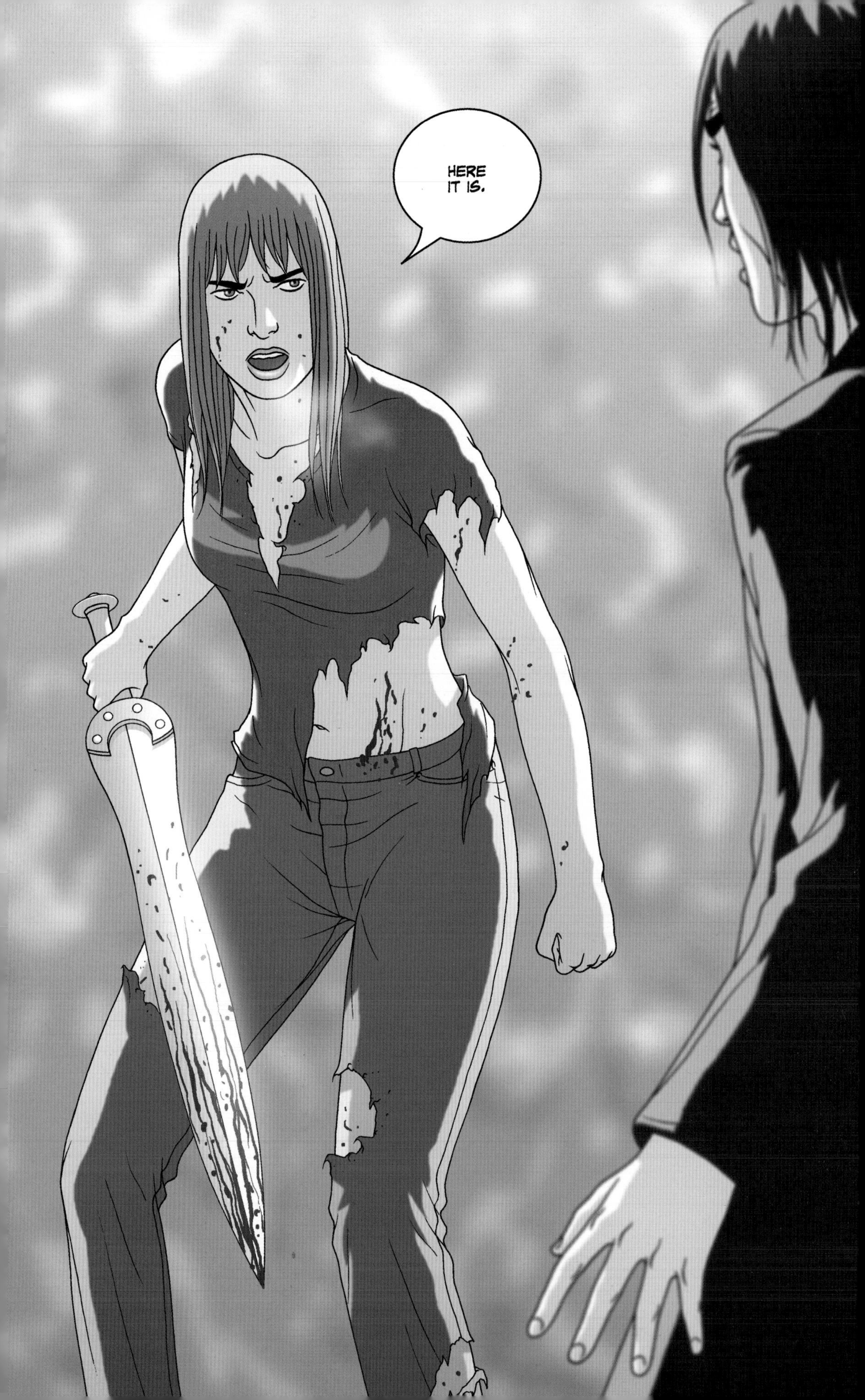
HERE IT IS.

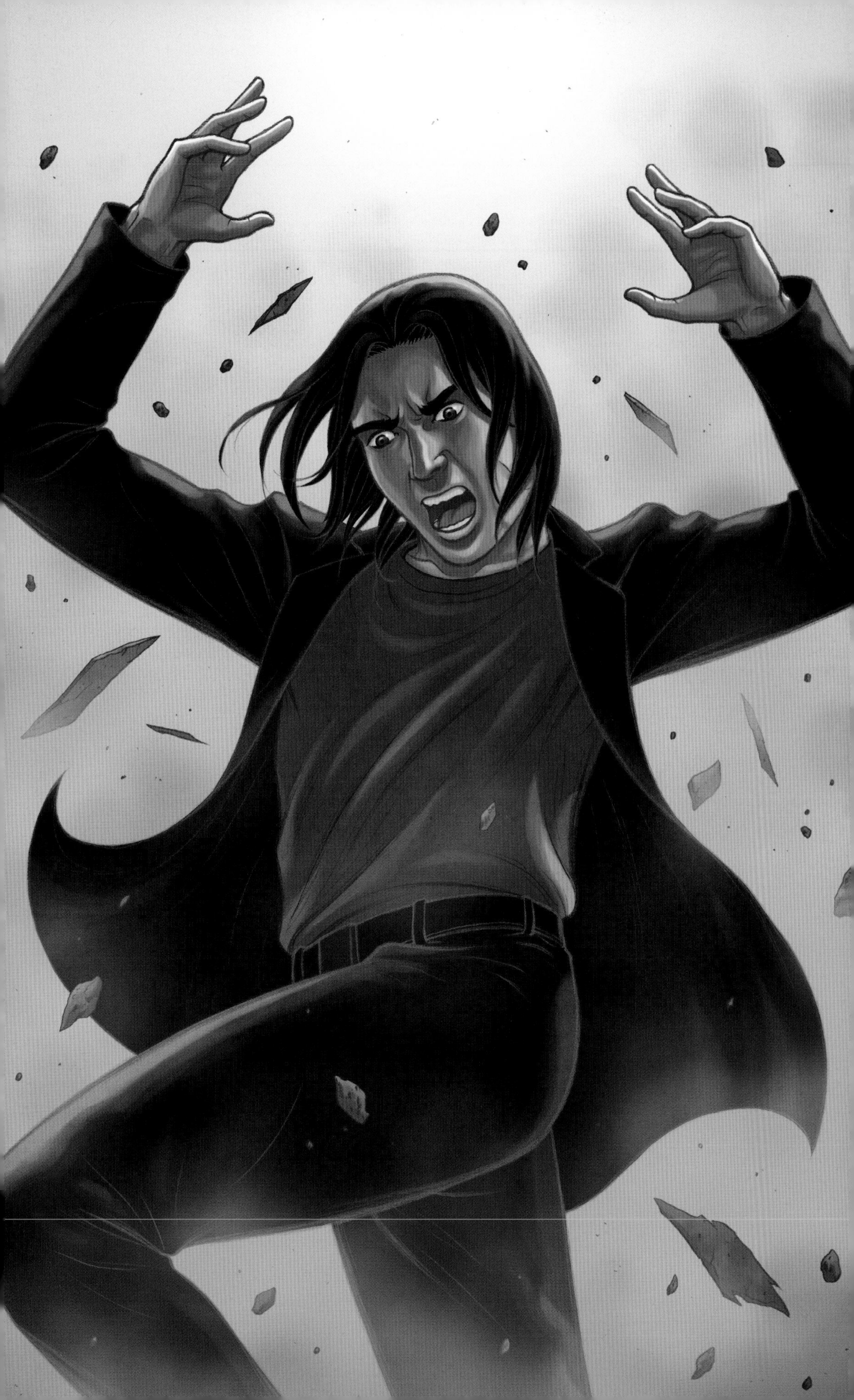

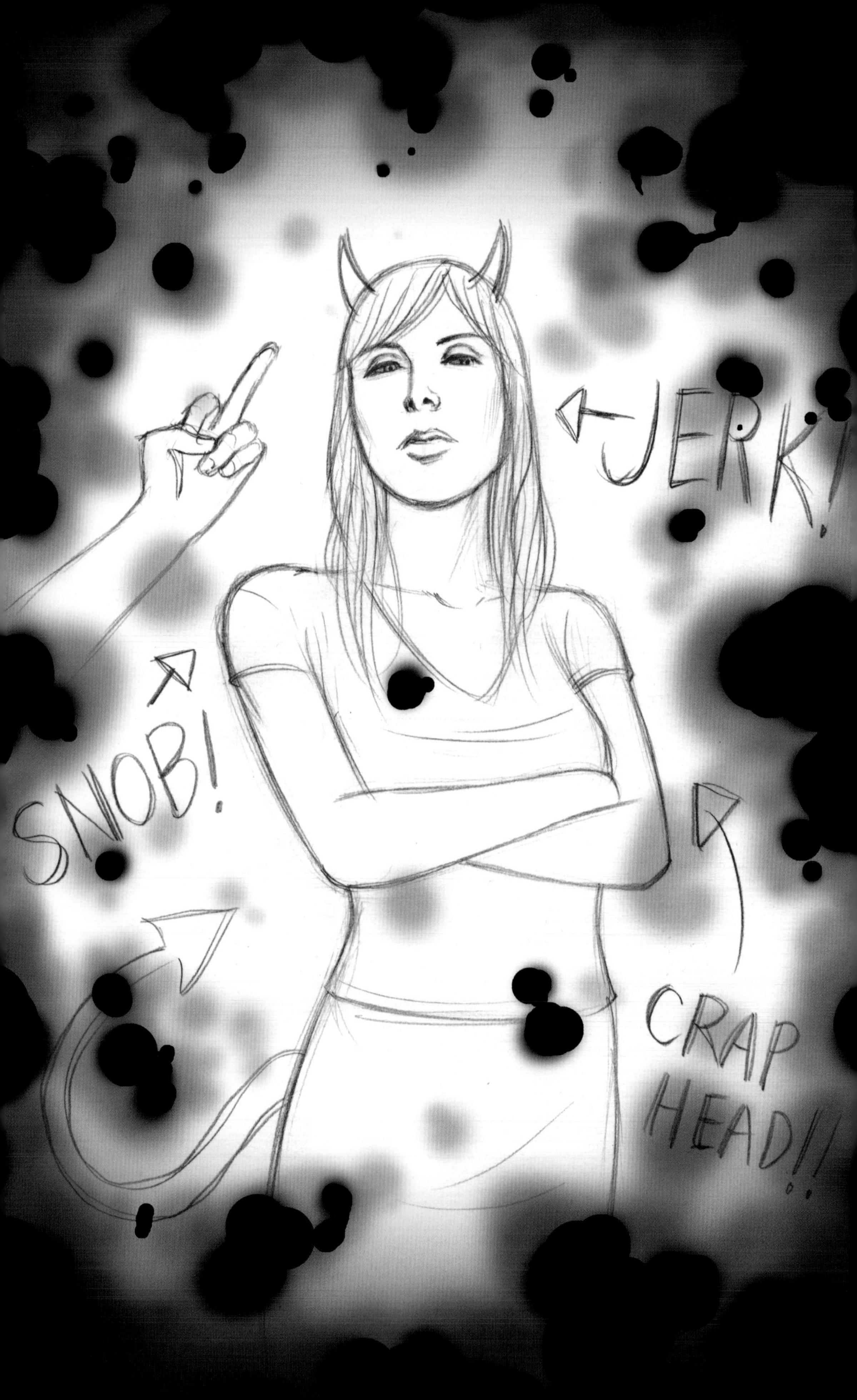
JERK!
SNOB!
CRAP HEAD!!

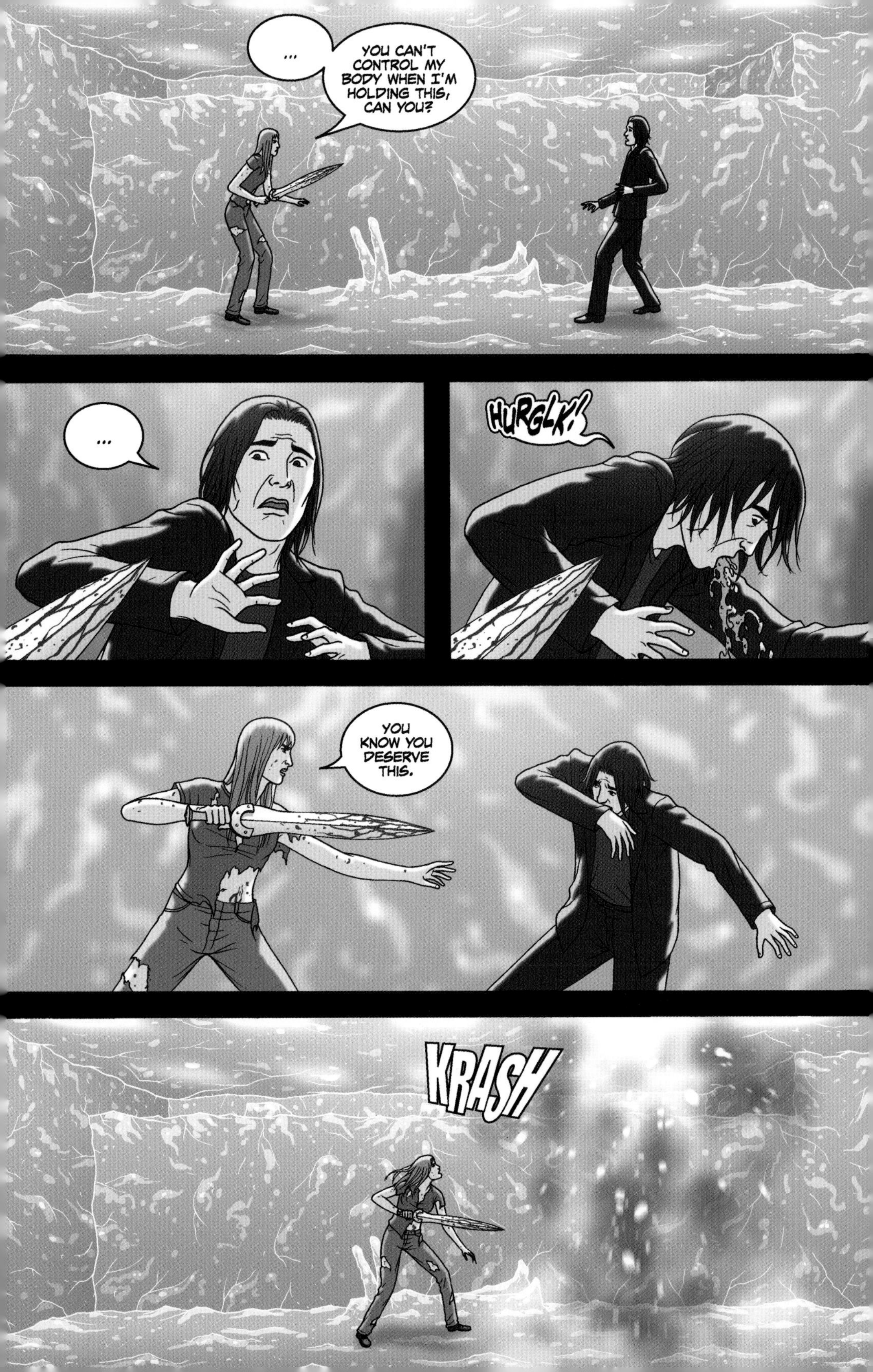
...
YOU CAN'T CONTROL MY BODY WHEN I'M HOLDING THIS, CAN YOU?
...
HURGLK!
YOU KNOW YOU DESERVE THIS.
KRASH

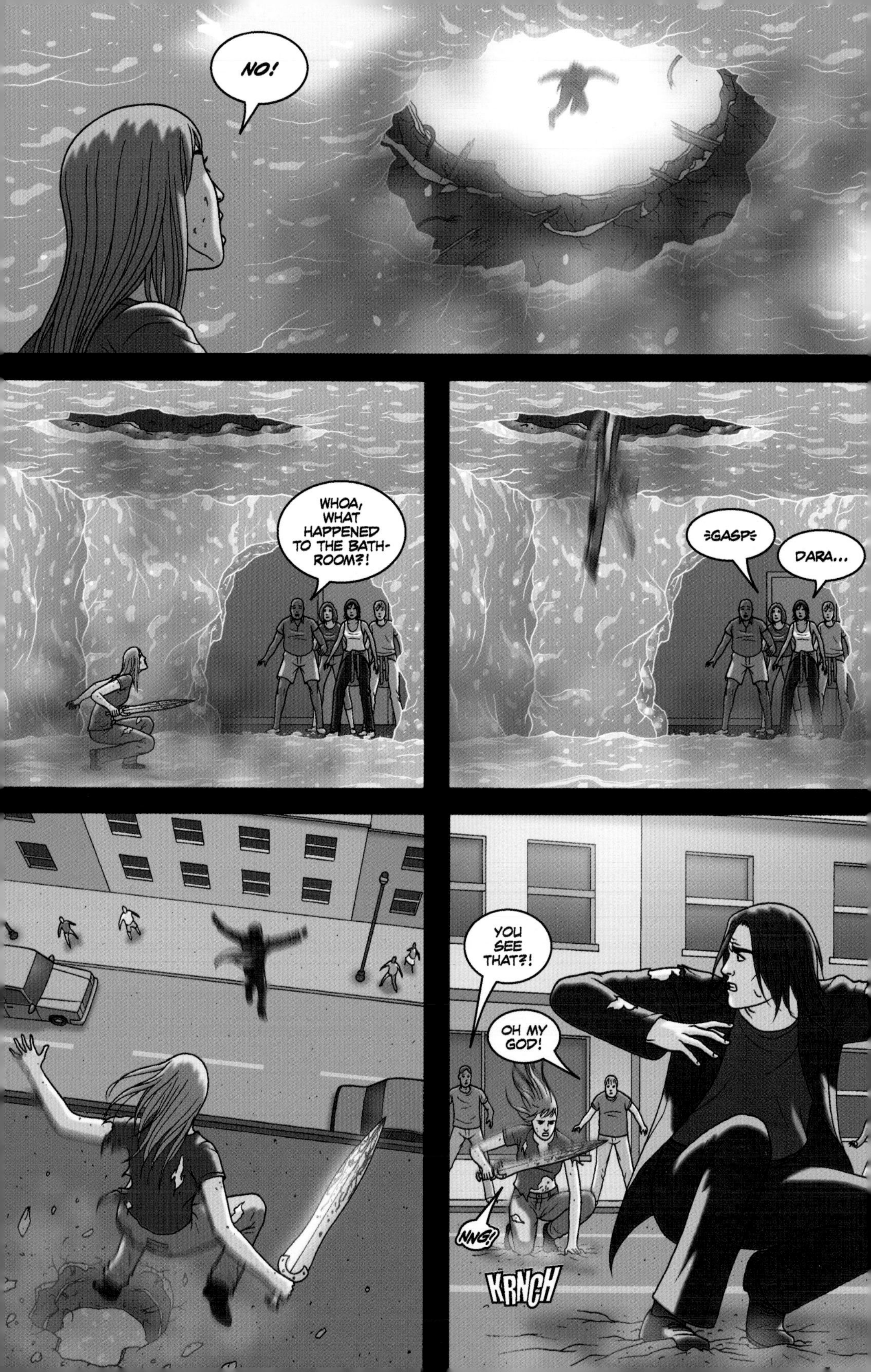
NO!
WHOA, WHAT HAPPENED TO THE BATH-ROOM?!
GASP
DARA...
YOU SEE THAT?!
OH MY GOD!
NNG!
KRNCH

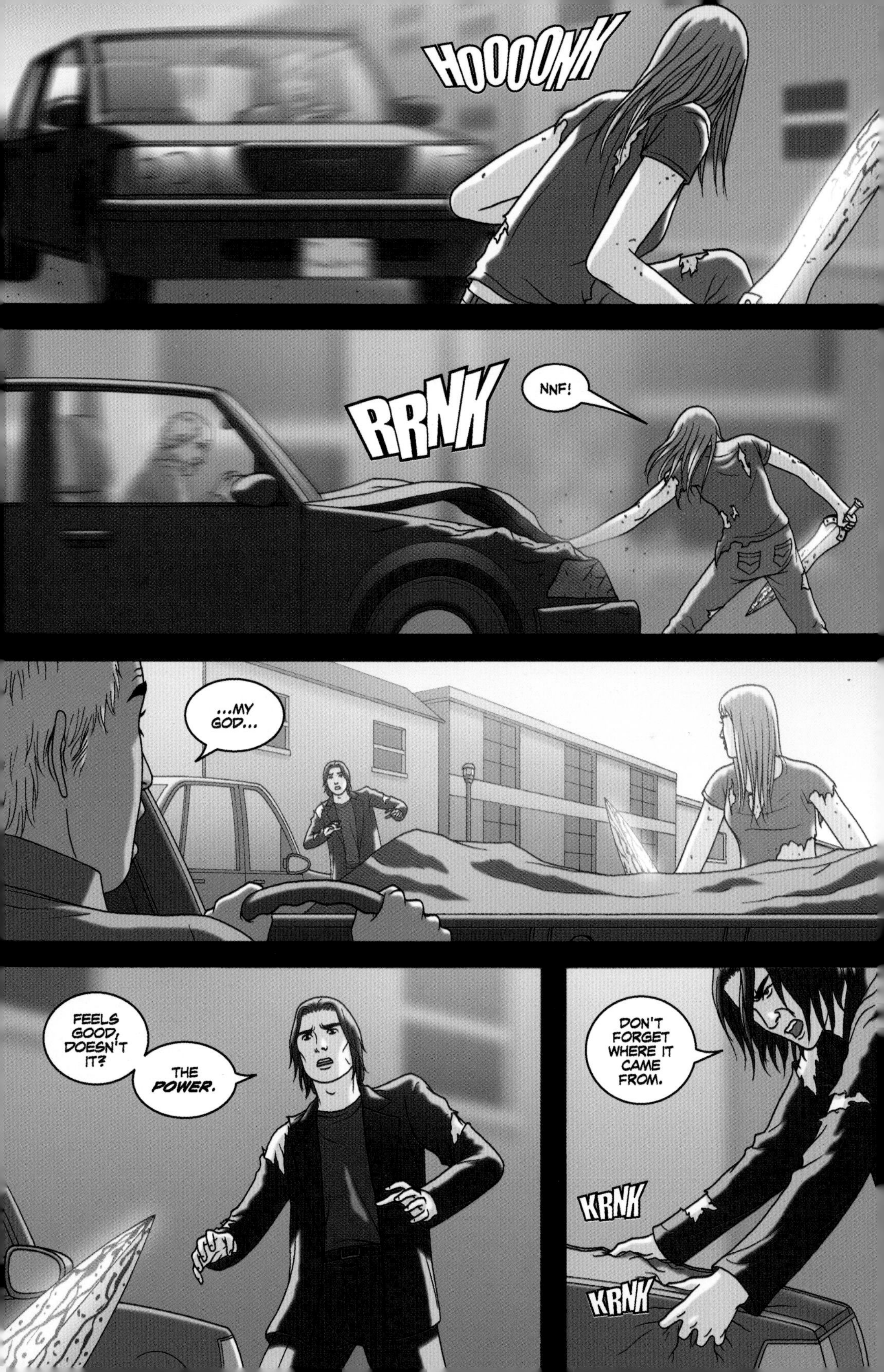
HOOOOONK
RRNK
NNF!
...MY GOD...
FEELS GOOD, DOESN'T IT?
THE *POWER*.
DON'T FORGET WHERE IT CAME FROM.
KRNK
KRNK

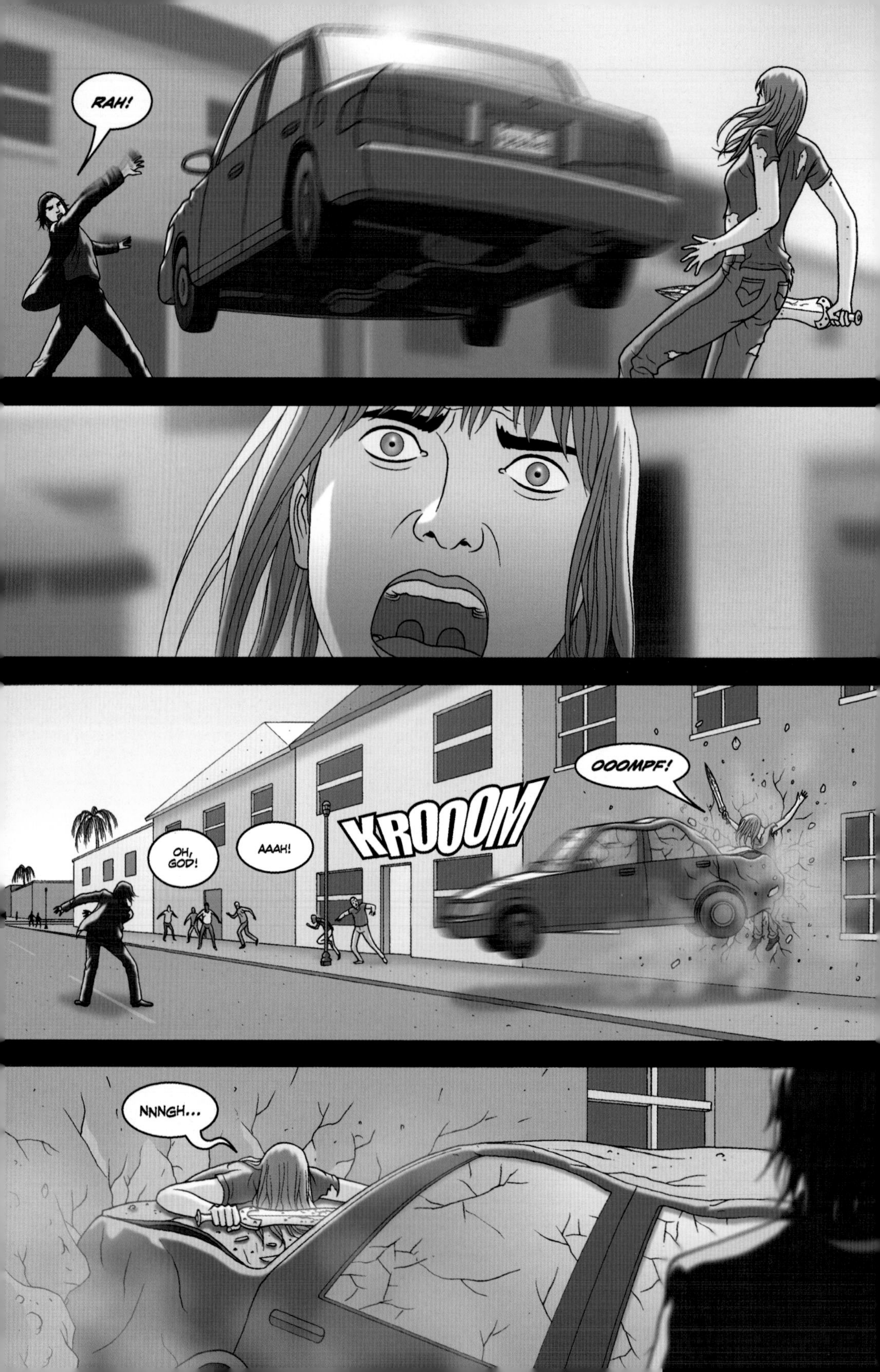
RAH!
OH, GOD!
AAAH!
KROOOM
OOOMPF!
NNNGH...

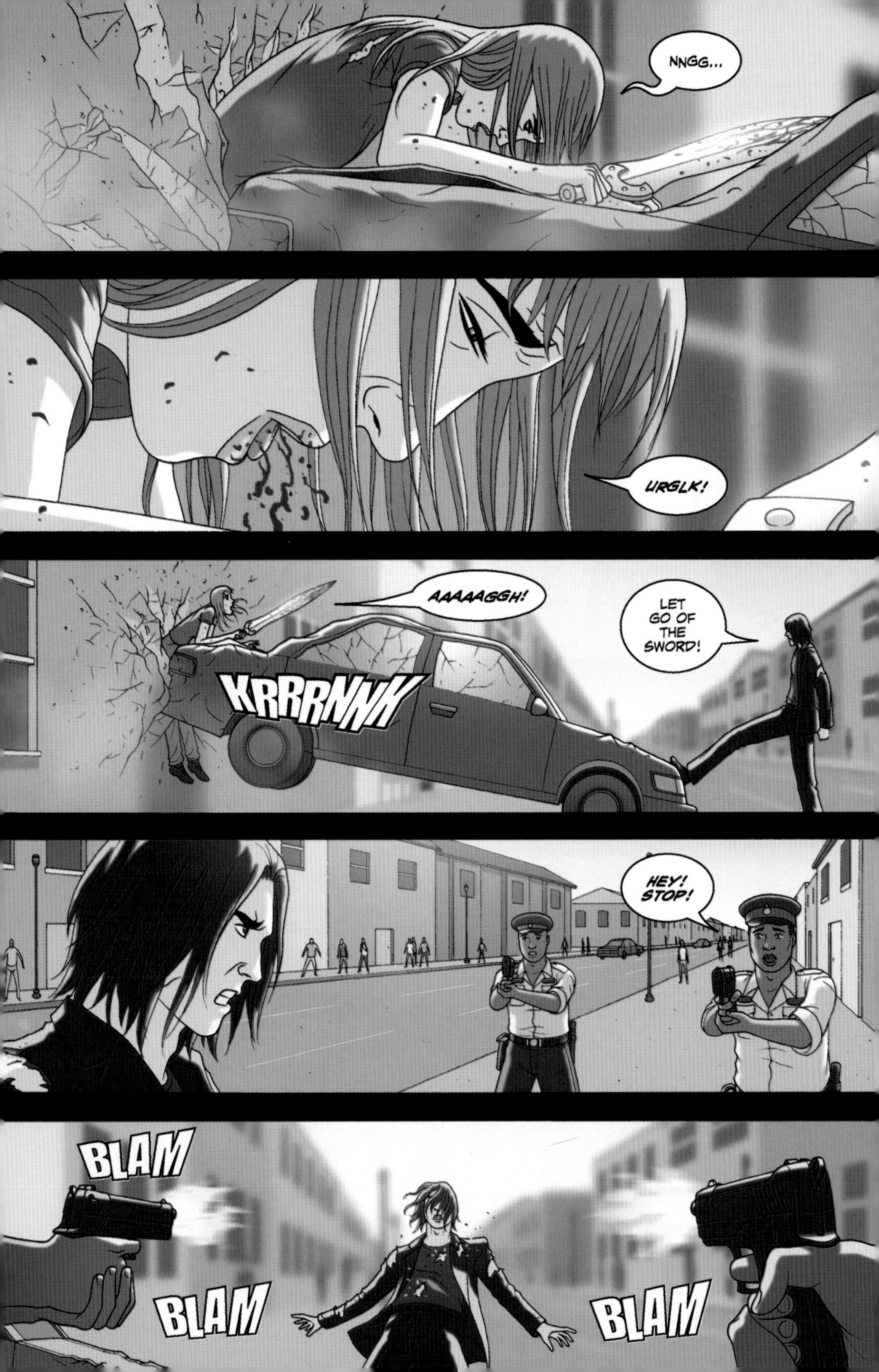
NNGG...
URGLK!
AAAAAGGH!
LET GO OF THE SWORD!
KRRRNNK
HEY! STOP!
BLAM
BLAM
BLAM

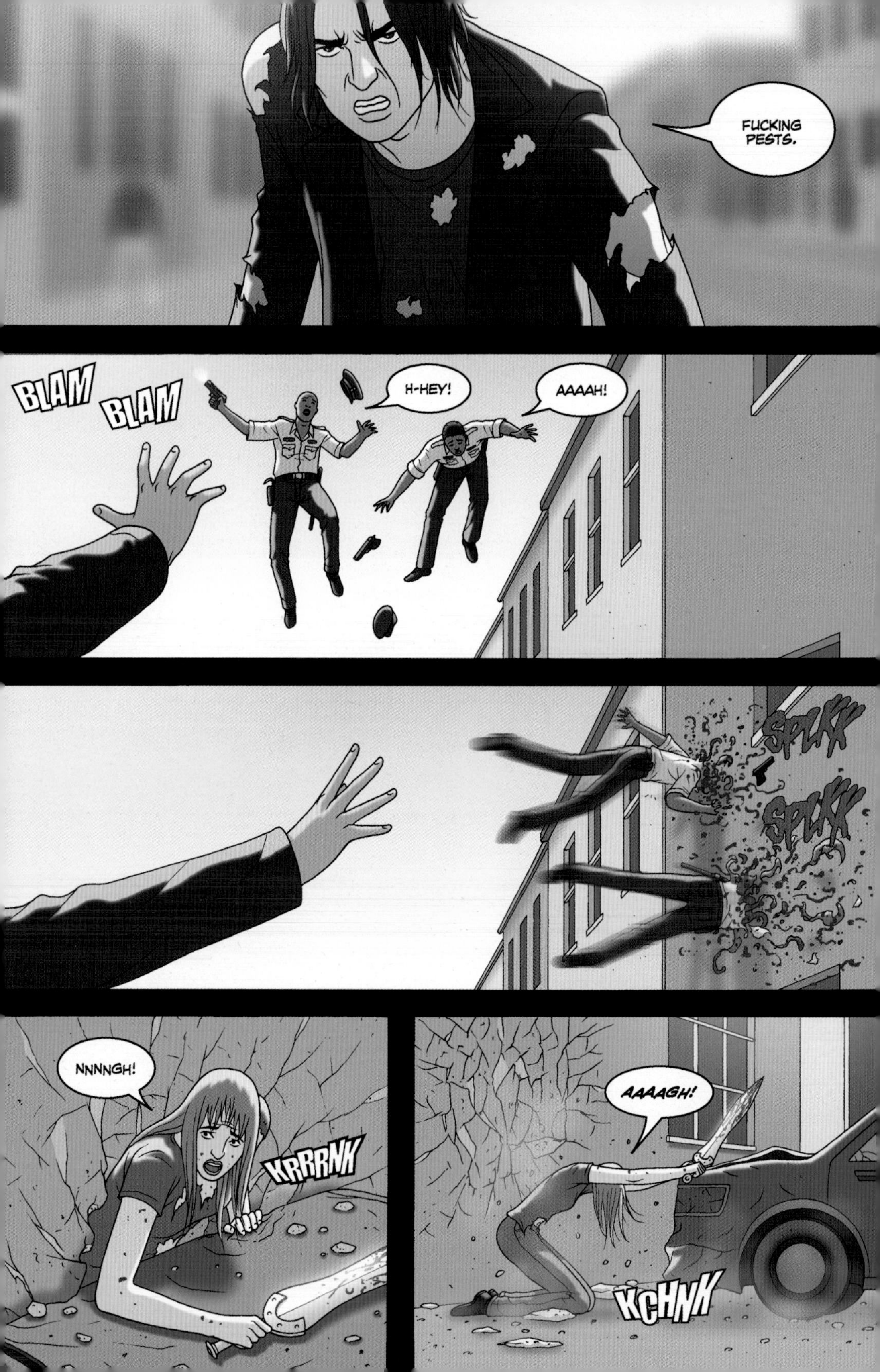
FUCKING PESTS.
BLAM
BLAM
H-HEY!
AAAAH!
SPLKK
SPLKK
NNNNGH!
KRRRNK
AAAAGH!
KCHNK

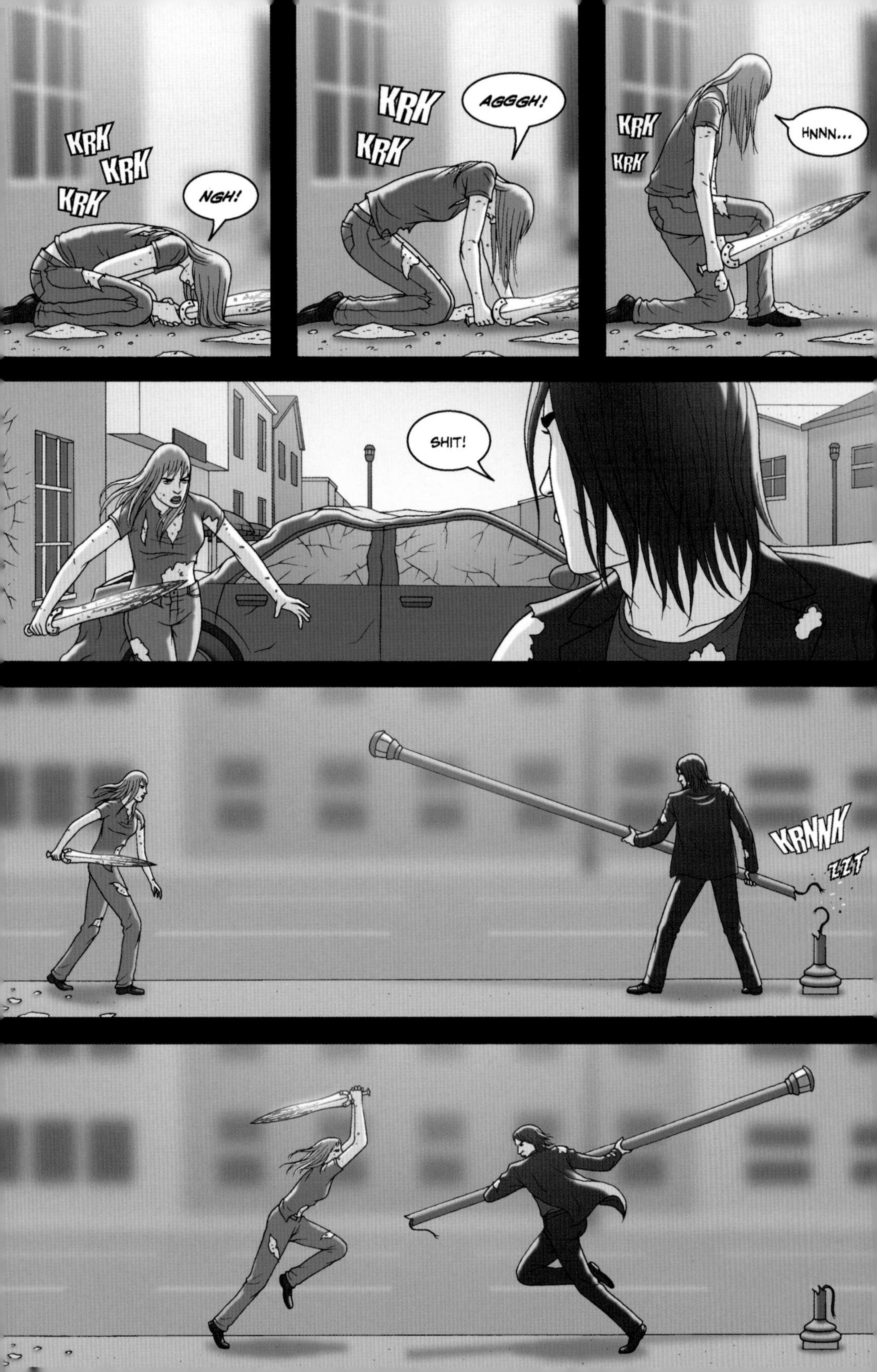
KRK
KRK
KRK
NGH!
KRK
KRK
AGGGH!
KRK
KRK
HNNN...
SHIT!
KRNNK
ZZZT

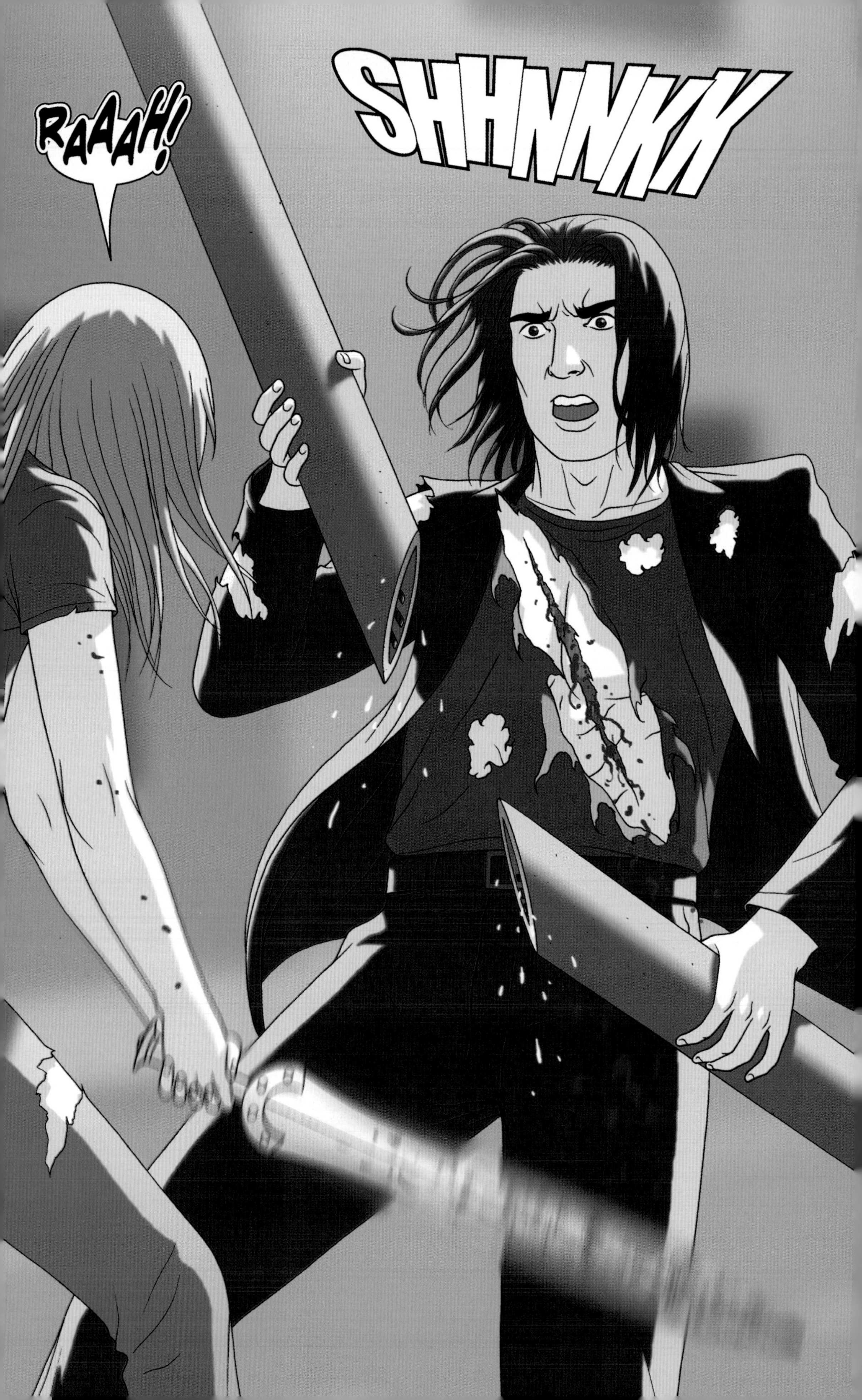
RAAAH!
SHHNNKK

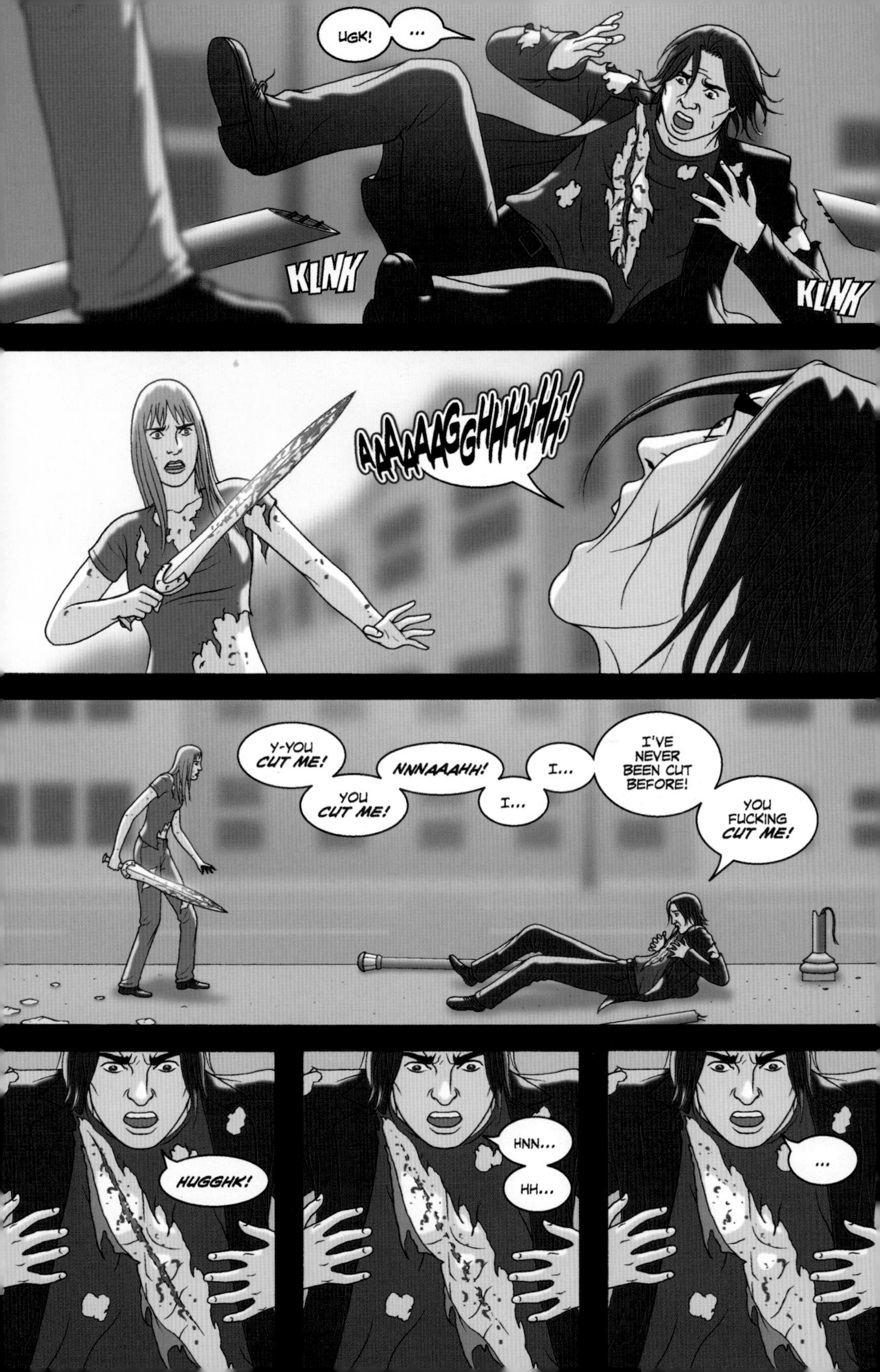
UGK!
...
KLNK
KLNK
AAAAAAGHHHHHH!
Y-YOU CUT ME!
YOU CUT ME!
NNNAAAHH!
I...
I...
I'VE NEVER BEEN CUT BEFORE!
YOU FUCKING CUT ME!
HUGGHK!
HNN...
HH...
...

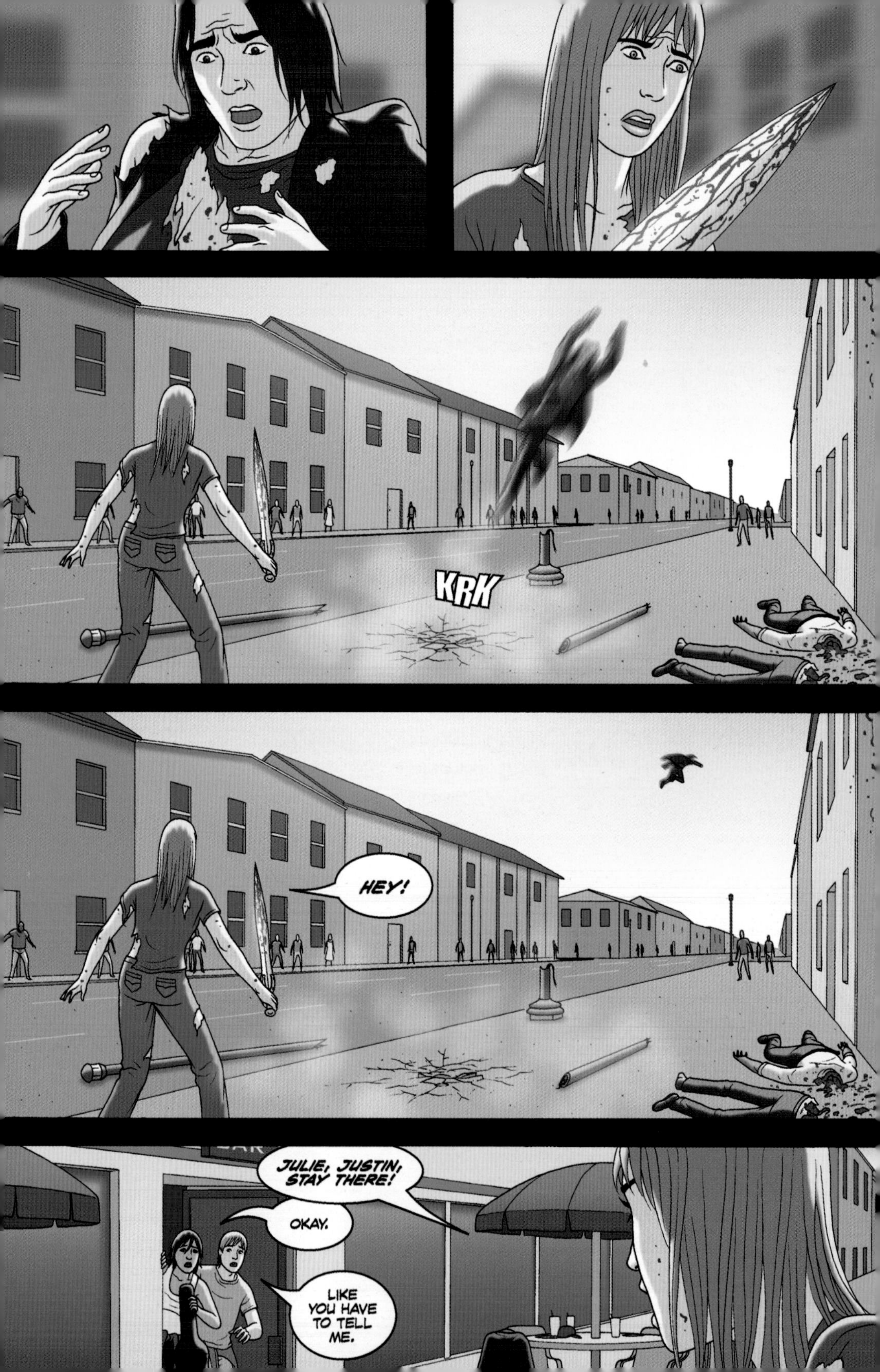
KRK
HEY!
JULIE, JUSTIN, STAY THERE!
OKAY.
LIKE YOU HAVE TO TELL ME.

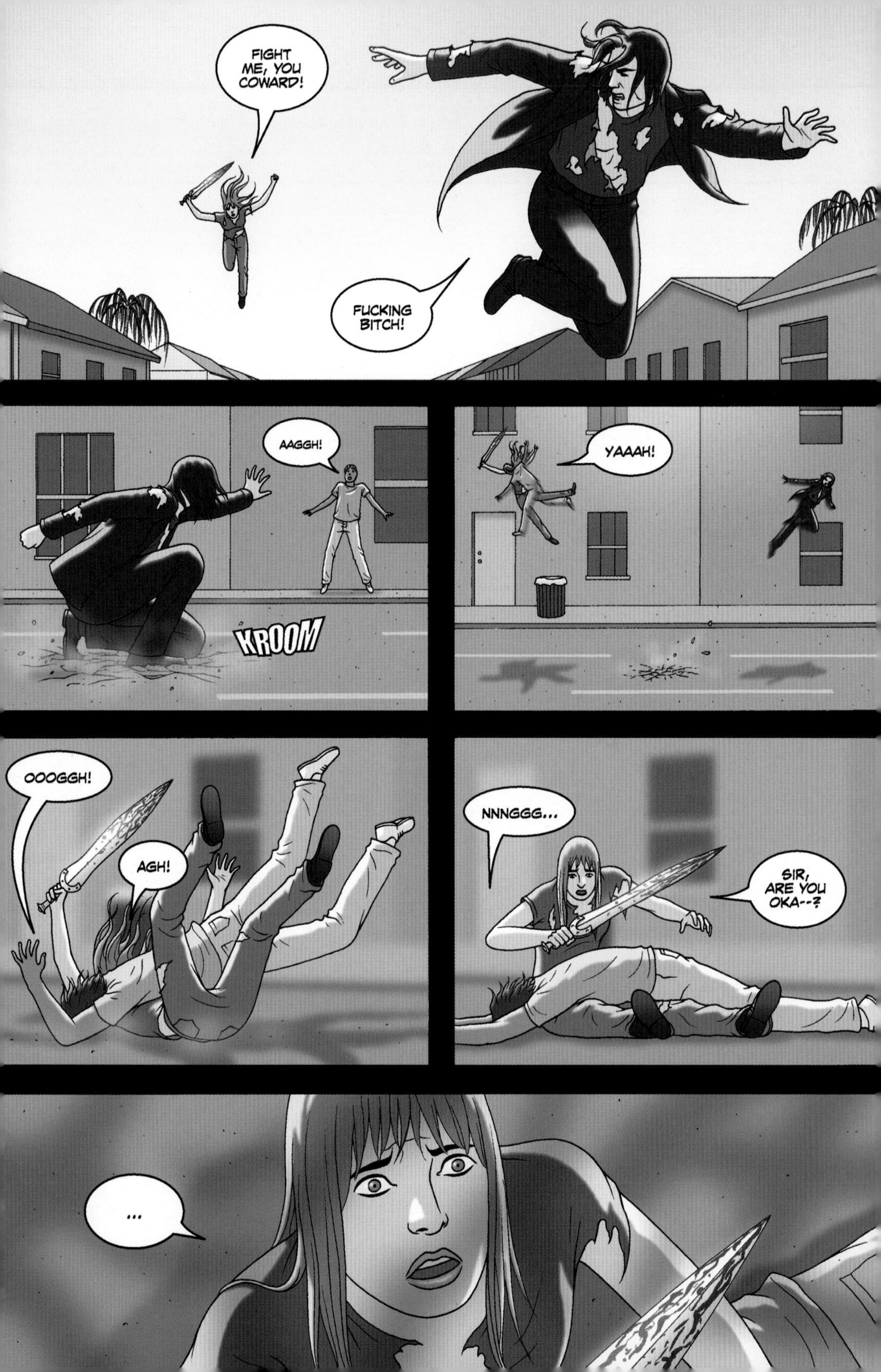
FIGHT ME, YOU COWARD!
FUCKING BITCH!
AAGGH!
KROOM
YAAAH!
OOOGGH!
AGH!
NNNGGG...
SIR, ARE YOU OKA--?
...

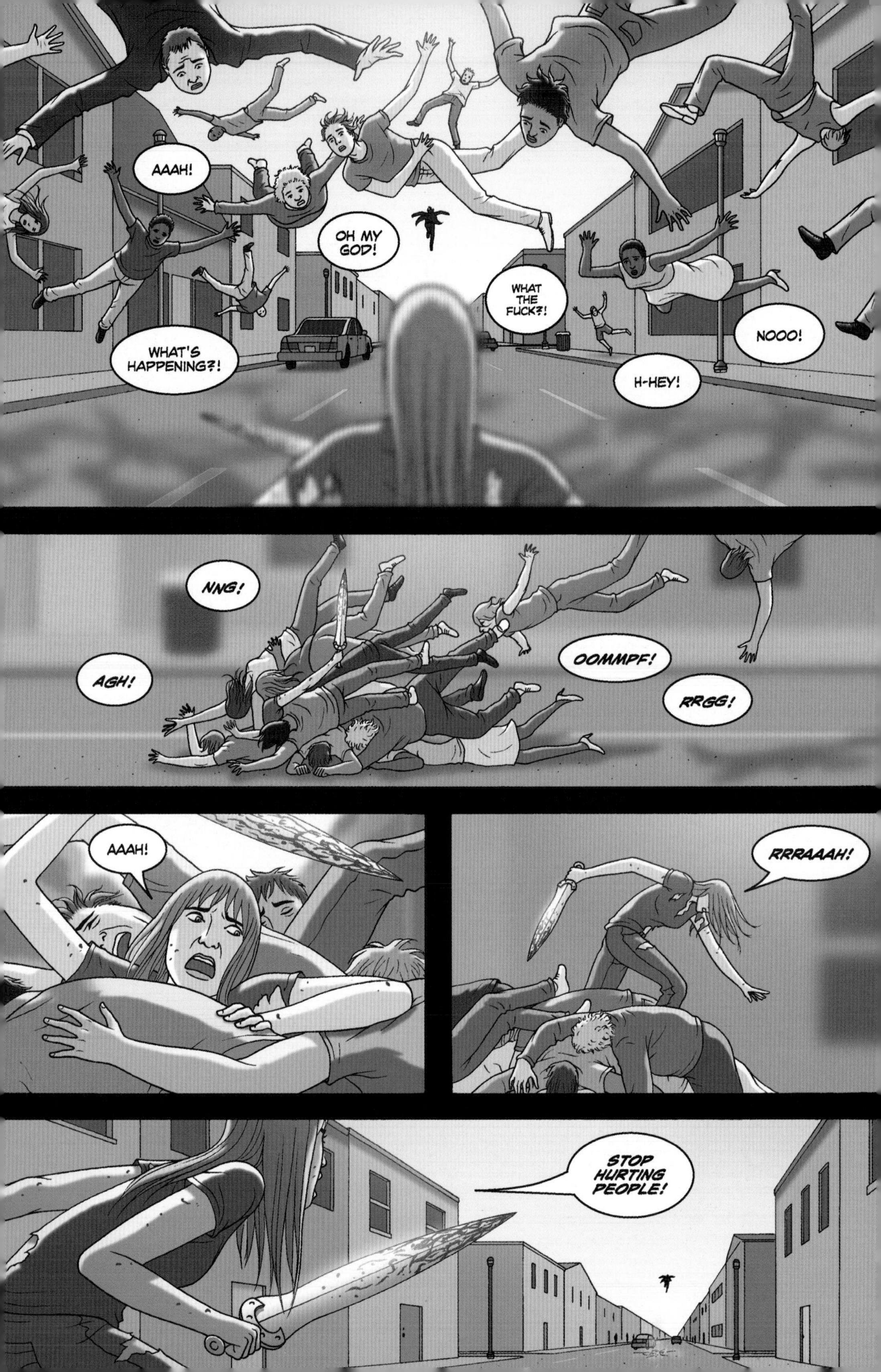
AAAH!
OH MY GOD!
WHAT THE FUCK?!
WHAT'S HAPPENING?!
NOOO!
H-HEY!
NNG!
AGH!
OOMMPF!
RRGG!
AAAH!
RRRAAAH!
STOP HURTING PEOPLE!

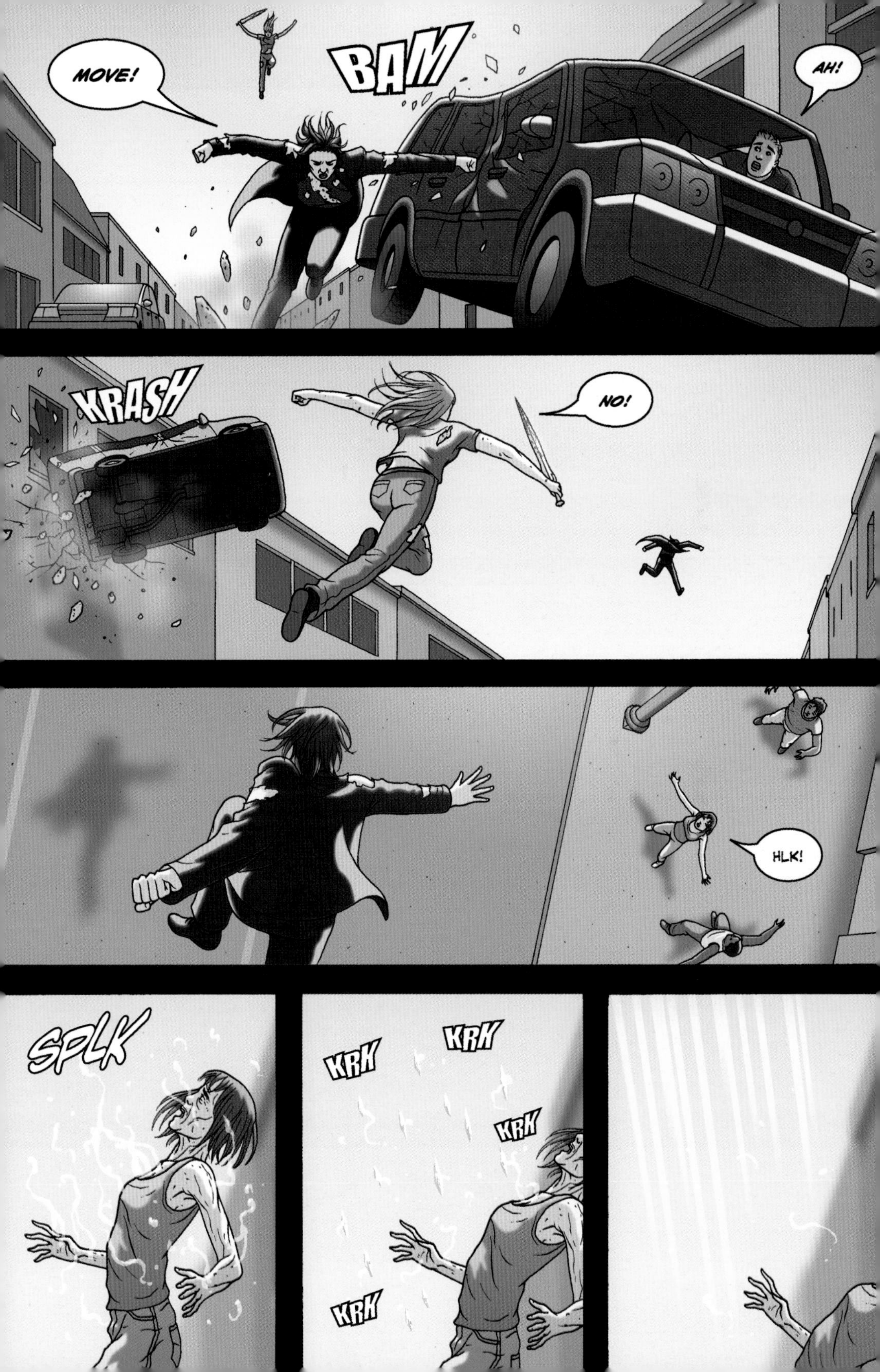
MOVE!
BAM
AH!
KRASH
NO!
HLK!
SPLK
KRK
KRK
KRK
KRK

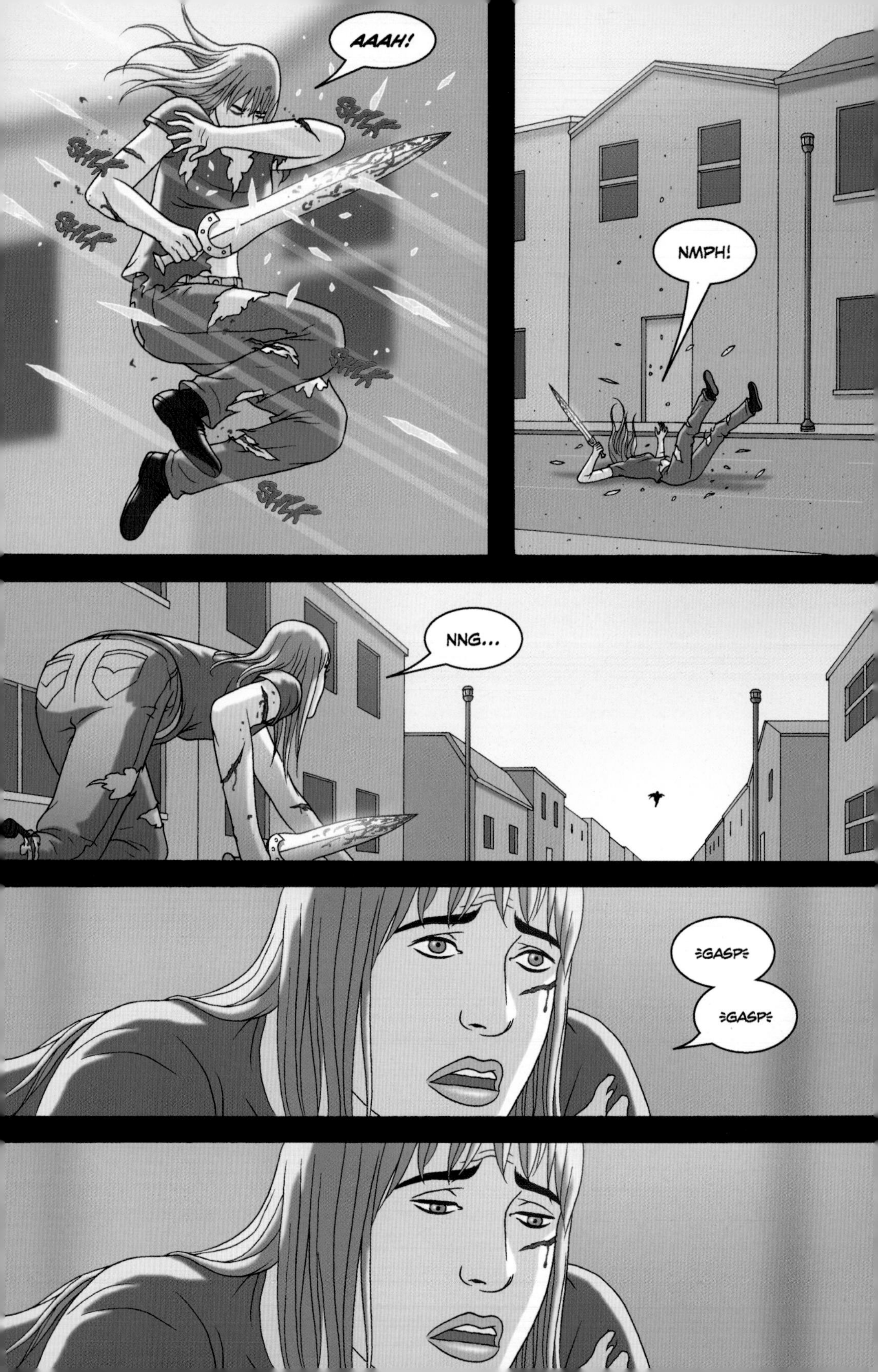
AAAH!
SHLK
SHLK
SHLK
SHLK
SHLK
NMPH!
NNG...
GASP
GASP

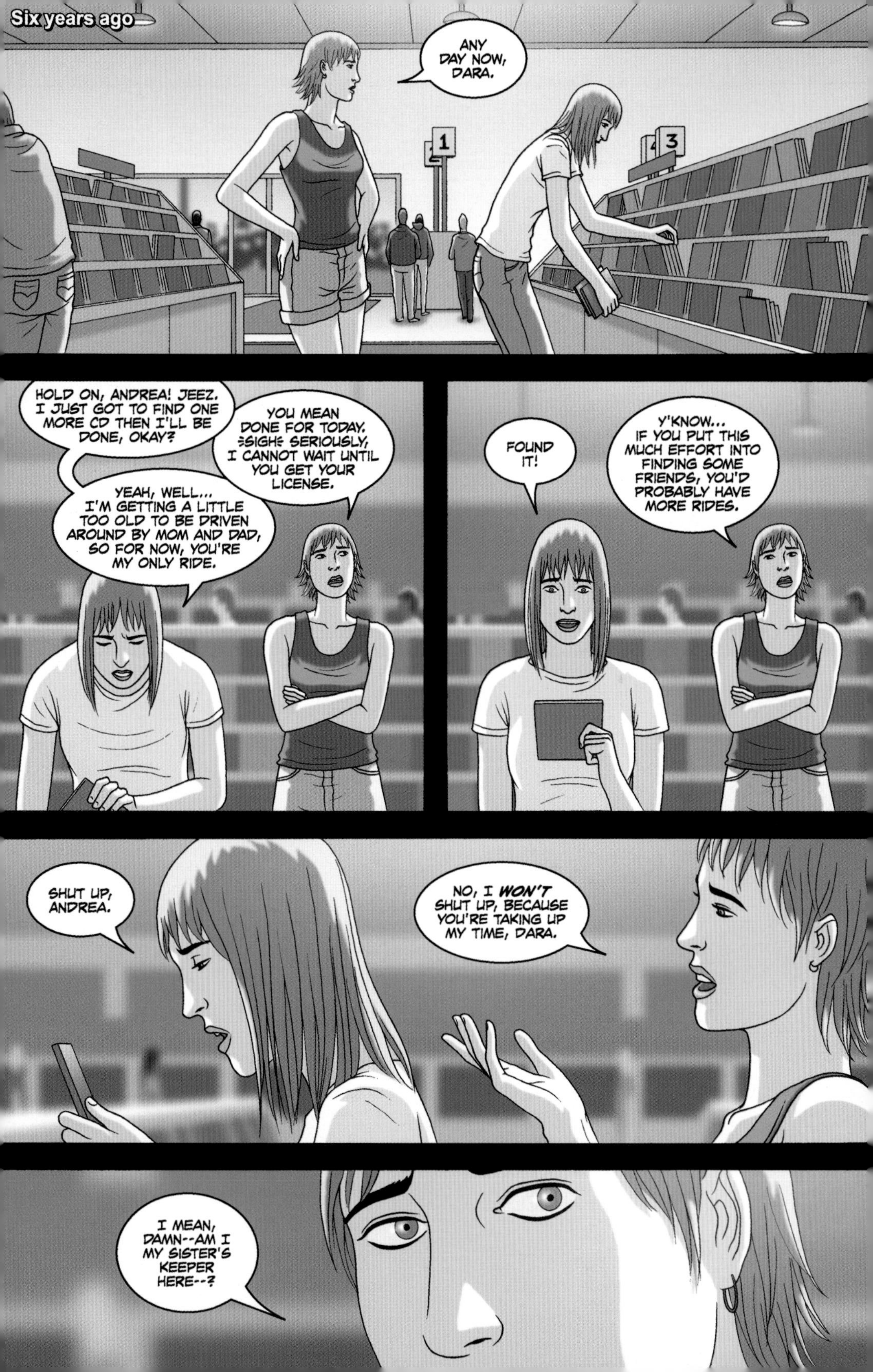
Six years ago
ANY DAY NOW, DARA.
HOLD ON, ANDREA! JEEZ. I JUST GOT TO FIND ONE MORE CD THEN I'LL BE DONE, OKAY?
YOU MEAN DONE FOR TODAY. ⁼SIGH⁼ SERIOUSLY, I CANNOT WAIT UNTIL YOU GET YOUR LICENSE.
YEAH, WELL... I'M GETTING A LITTLE TOO OLD TO BE DRIVEN AROUND BY MOM AND DAD, SO FOR NOW, YOU'RE MY ONLY RIDE.
FOUND IT!
Y'KNOW... IF YOU PUT THIS MUCH EFFORT INTO FINDING SOME FRIENDS, YOU'D PROBABLY HAVE MORE RIDES.
SHUT UP, ANDREA.
NO, I *WON'T* SHUT UP, BECAUSE YOU'RE TAKING UP MY TIME, DARA.
I MEAN, DAMN--AM I MY SISTER'S KEEPER HERE--?

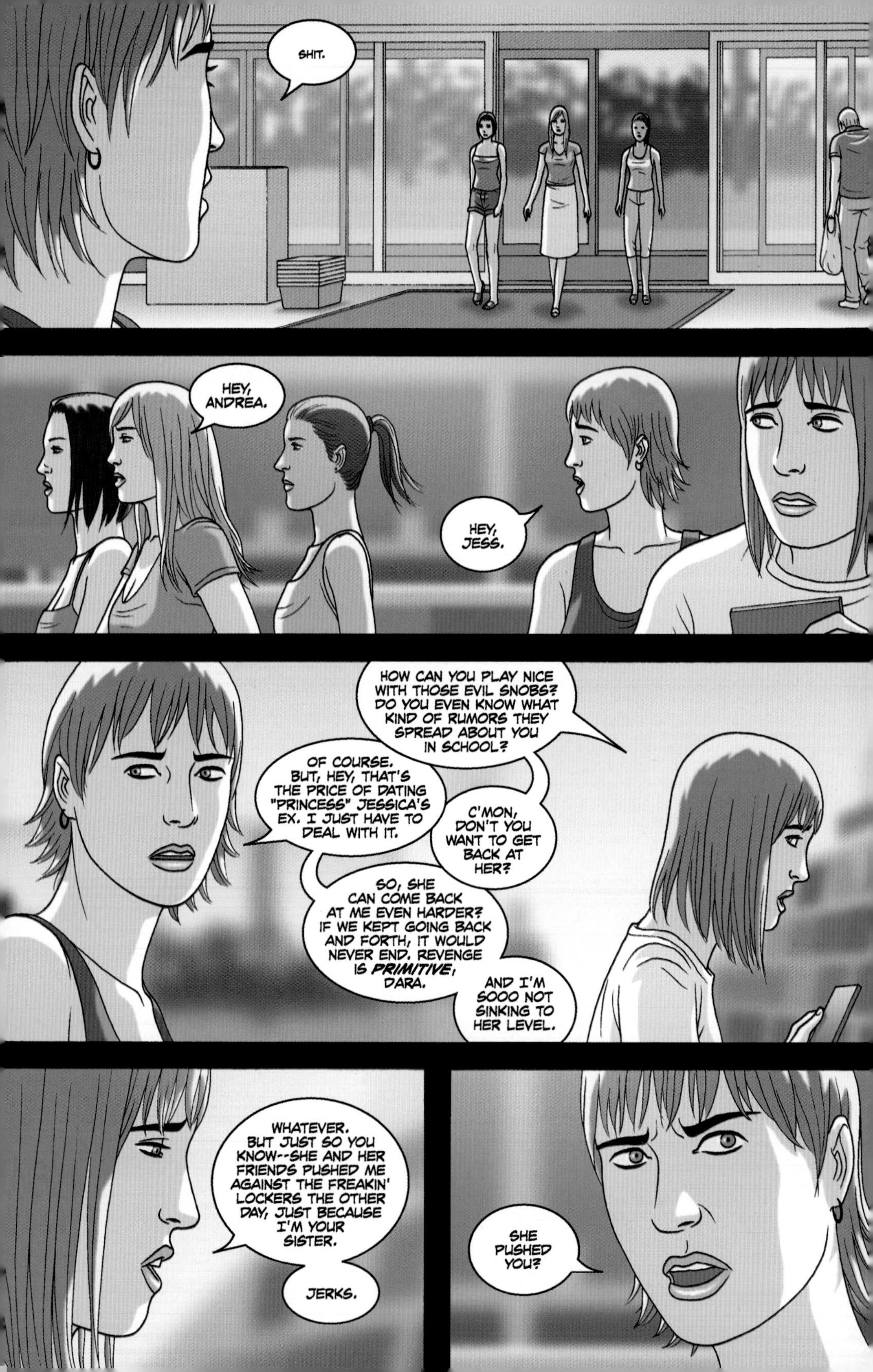
SHIT.
HEY, ANDREA.
HEY, JESS.
HOW CAN YOU PLAY NICE WITH THOSE EVIL SNOBS? DO YOU EVEN KNOW WHAT KIND OF RUMORS THEY SPREAD ABOUT YOU IN SCHOOL?
OF COURSE. BUT, HEY, THAT'S THE PRICE OF DATING "PRINCESS" JESSICA'S EX. I JUST HAVE TO DEAL WITH IT.
C'MON, DON'T YOU WANT TO GET BACK AT HER?
SO, SHE CAN COME BACK AT ME EVEN HARDER? IF WE KEPT GOING BACK AND FORTH, IT WOULD NEVER END. REVENGE IS *PRIMITIVE*, DARA.
AND I'M SOOO NOT SINKING TO HER LEVEL.
WHATEVER. BUT JUST SO YOU KNOW--SHE AND HER FRIENDS PUSHED ME AGAINST THE FREAKIN' LOCKERS THE OTHER DAY, JUST BECAUSE I'M YOUR SISTER.
JERKS.
SHE PUSHED YOU?

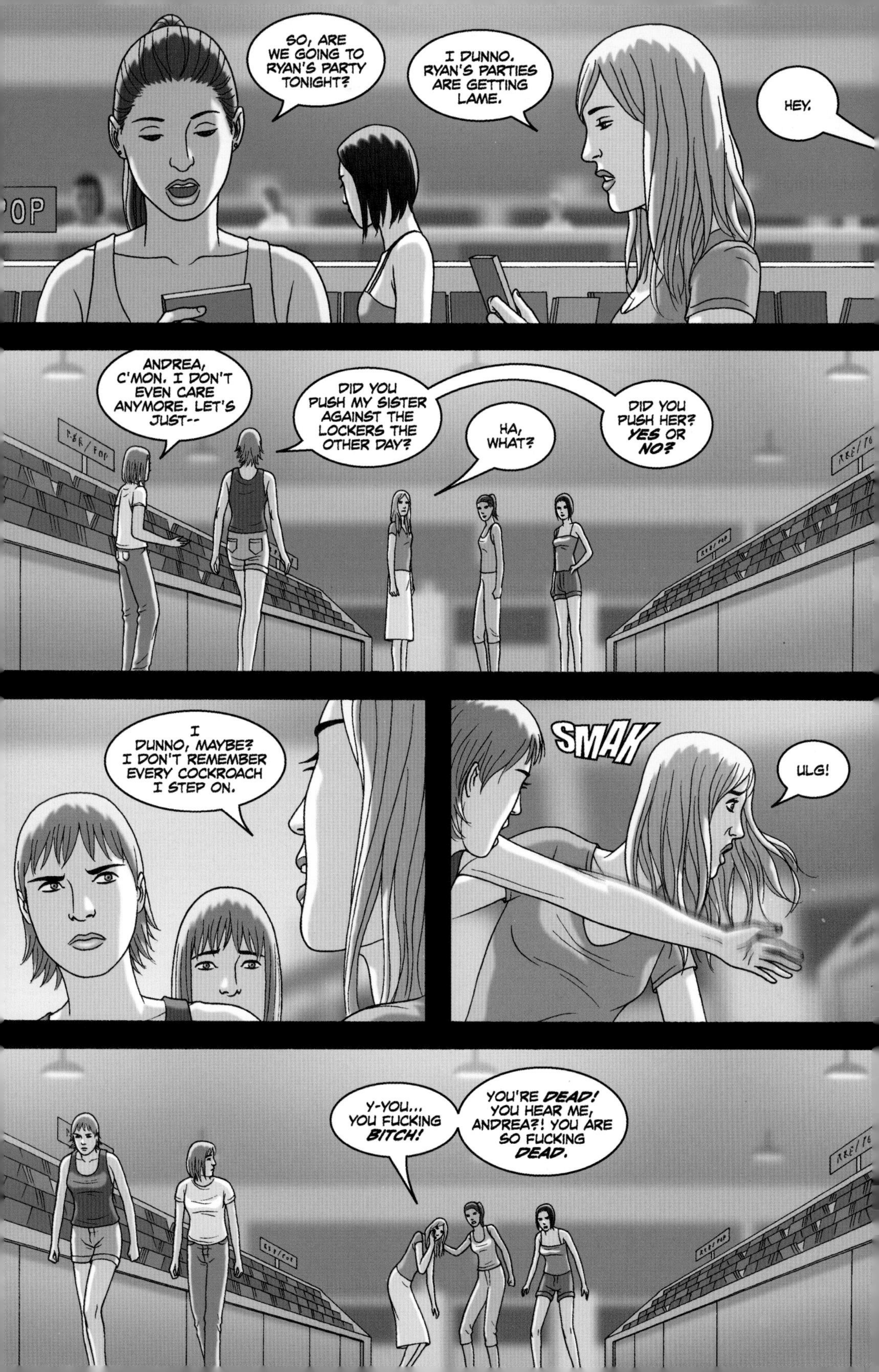
POP
SO, ARE WE GOING TO RYAN'S PARTY TONIGHT?
I DUNNO. RYAN'S PARTIES ARE GETTING LAME.
HEY.
ANDREA, C'MON. I DON'T EVEN CARE ANYMORE. LET'S JUST--
DID YOU PUSH MY SISTER AGAINST THE LOCKERS THE OTHER DAY?
HA, WHAT?
DID YOU PUSH HER? YES OR NO?
I DUNNO, MAYBE? I DON'T REMEMBER EVERY COCKROACH I STEP ON.
SMAK
ULG!
Y-YOU... YOU FUCKING BITCH!
YOU'RE DEAD! YOU HEAR ME, ANDREA?! YOU ARE SO FUCKING DEAD.

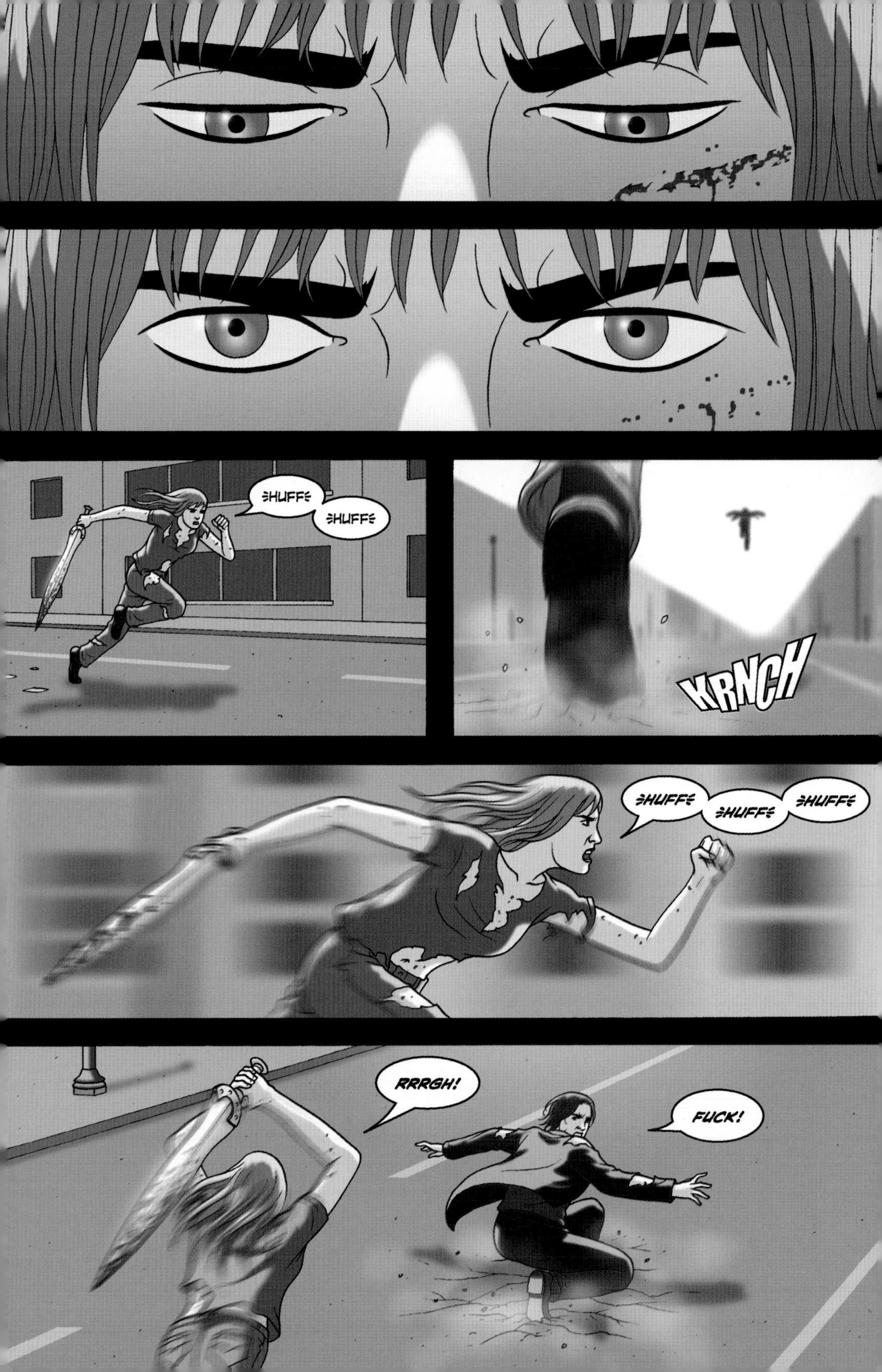

HUFF
HUFF
KRNCH
HUFF
HUFF
HUFF
RRRGH!
FUCK!

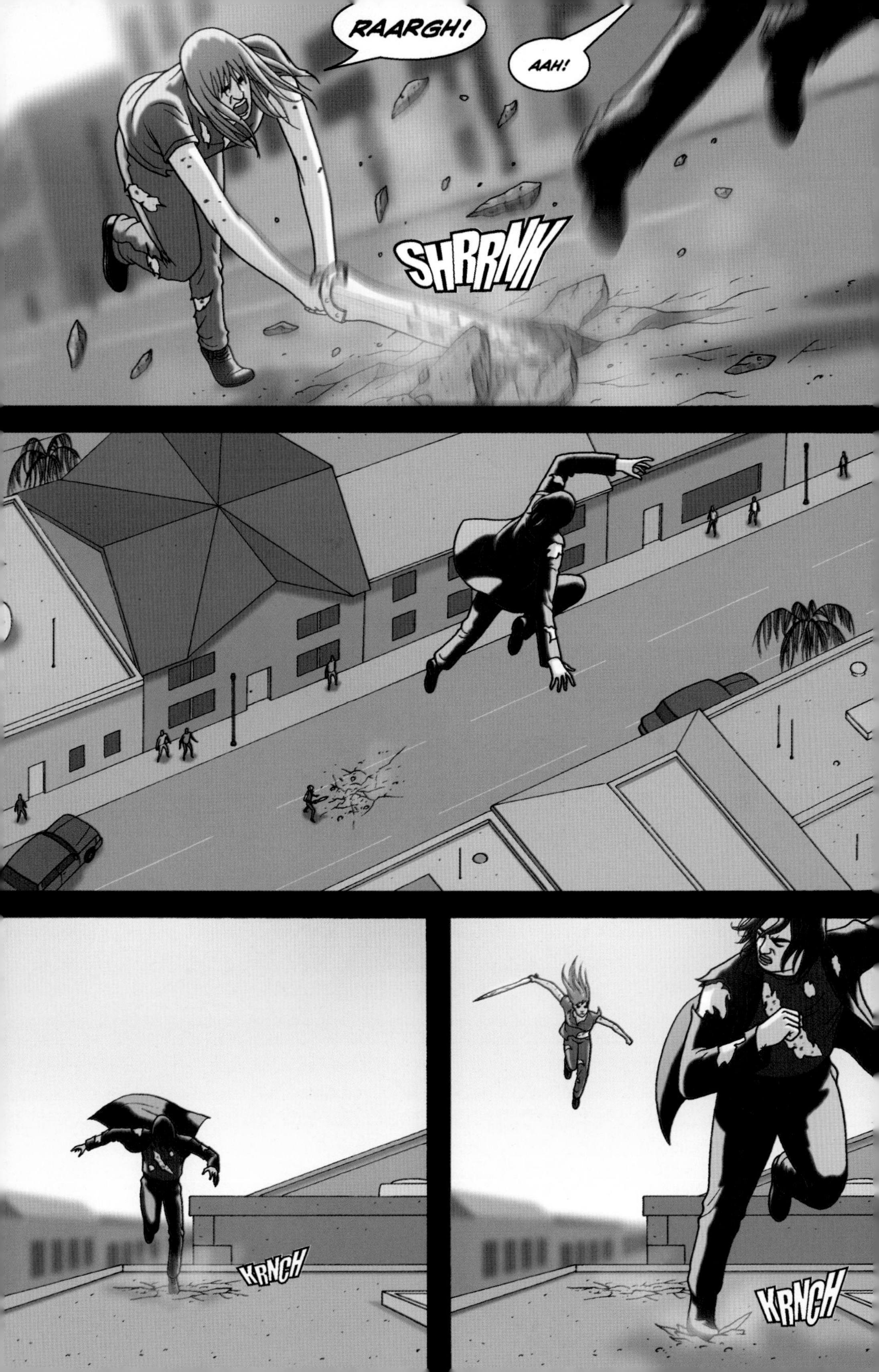
RAARGH!
AAH!
SHRRNK
KRNCH
KRNCH

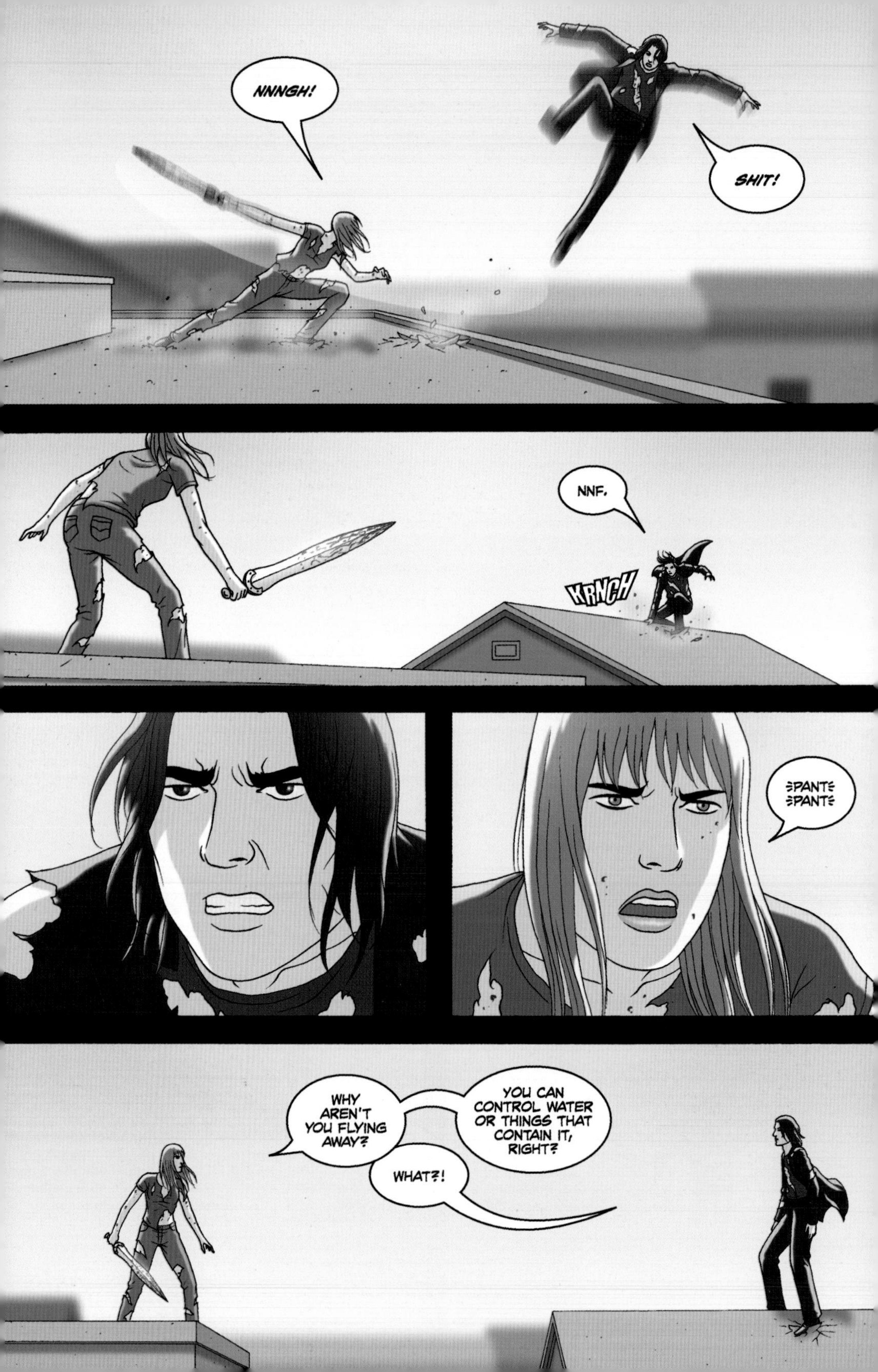
NNNGH!
SHIT!
NNF.
KRNCH
PANT
PANT
WHY AREN'T YOU FLYING AWAY?
WHAT?!
YOU CAN CONTROL WATER OR THINGS THAT CONTAIN IT, RIGHT?

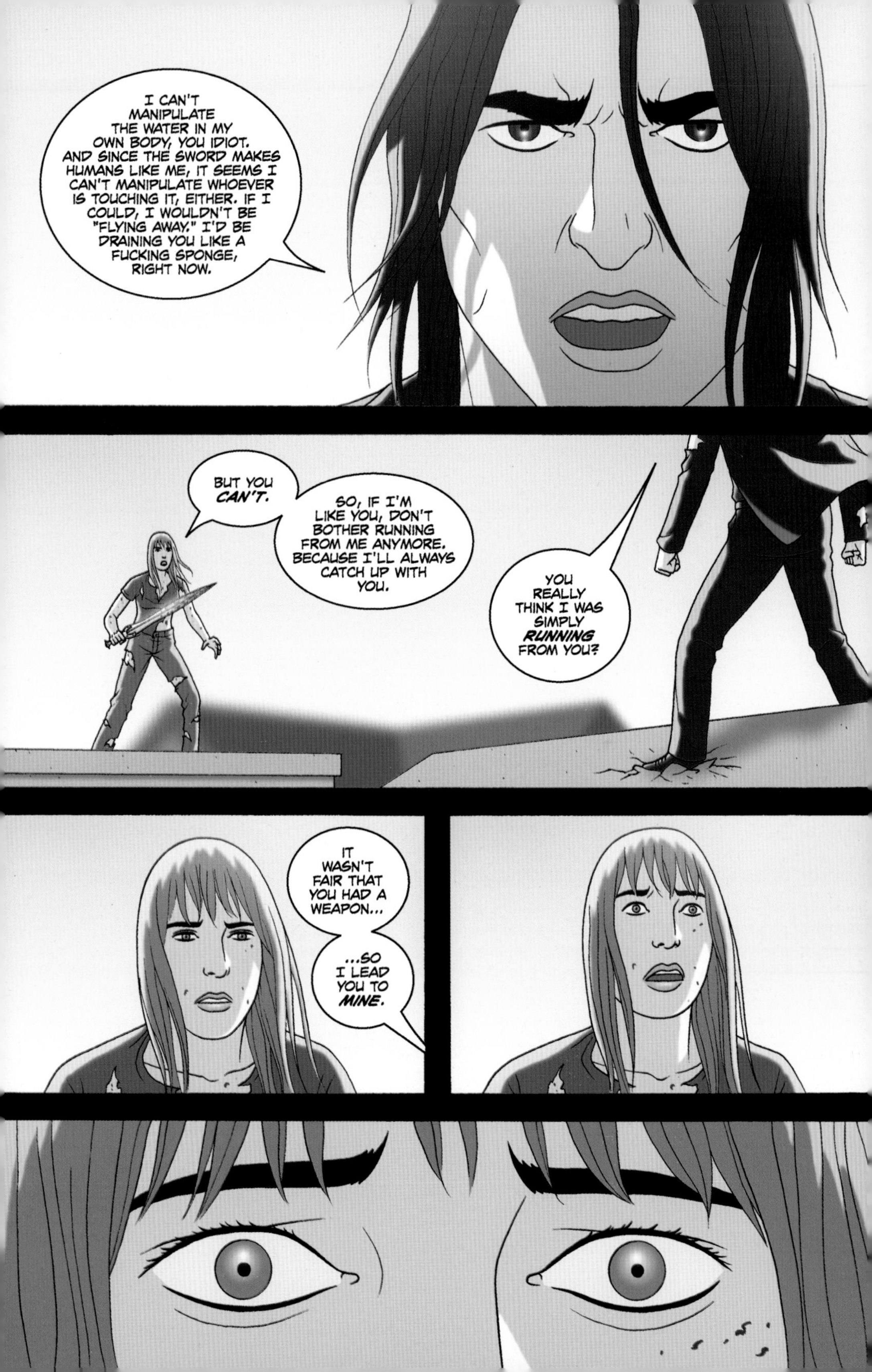
I CAN'T MANIPULATE THE WATER IN MY OWN BODY, YOU IDIOT. AND SINCE THE SWORD MAKES HUMANS LIKE ME, IT SEEMS I CAN'T MANIPULATE WHOEVER IS TOUCHING IT, EITHER. IF I COULD, I WOULDN'T BE "FLYING AWAY." I'D BE DRAINING YOU LIKE A FUCKING SPONGE, RIGHT NOW.
BUT YOU *CAN'T*.
SO, IF I'M LIKE YOU, DON'T BOTHER RUNNING FROM ME ANYMORE. BECAUSE I'LL ALWAYS CATCH UP WITH YOU.
YOU REALLY THINK I WAS SIMPLY ***RUNNING*** FROM YOU?
IT WASN'T FAIR THAT YOU HAD A WEAPON...
...SO I LEAD YOU TO ***MINE***.

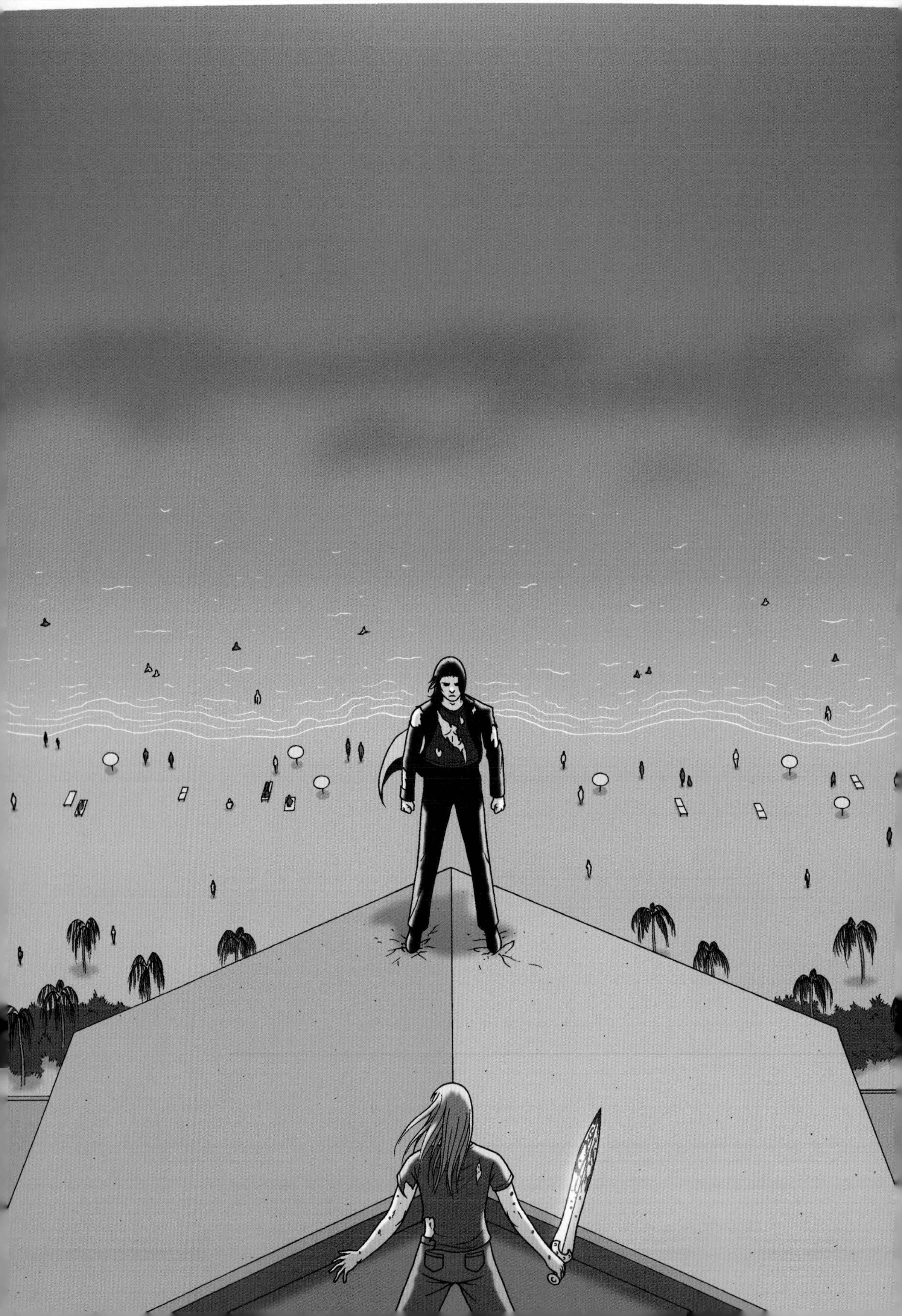

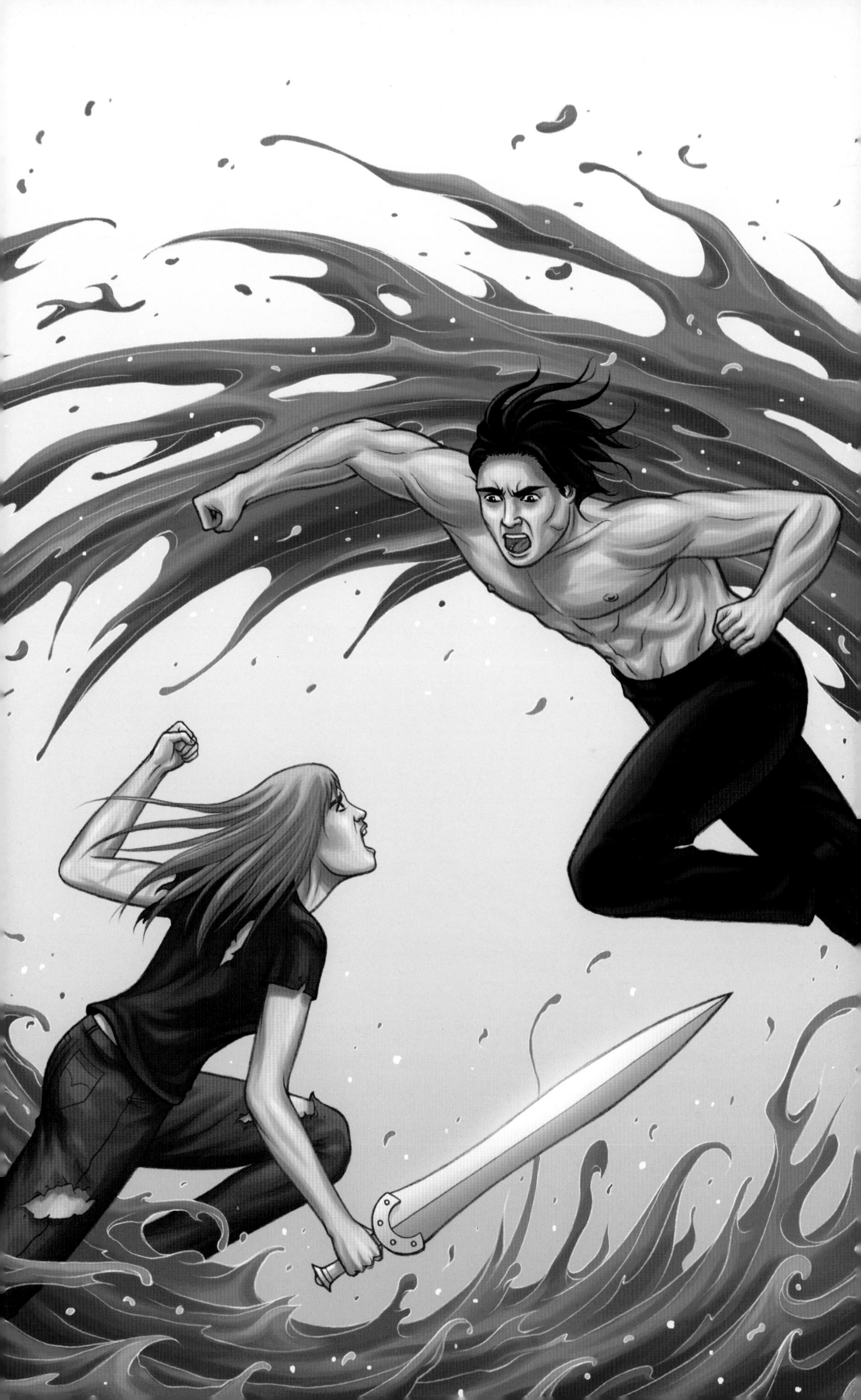

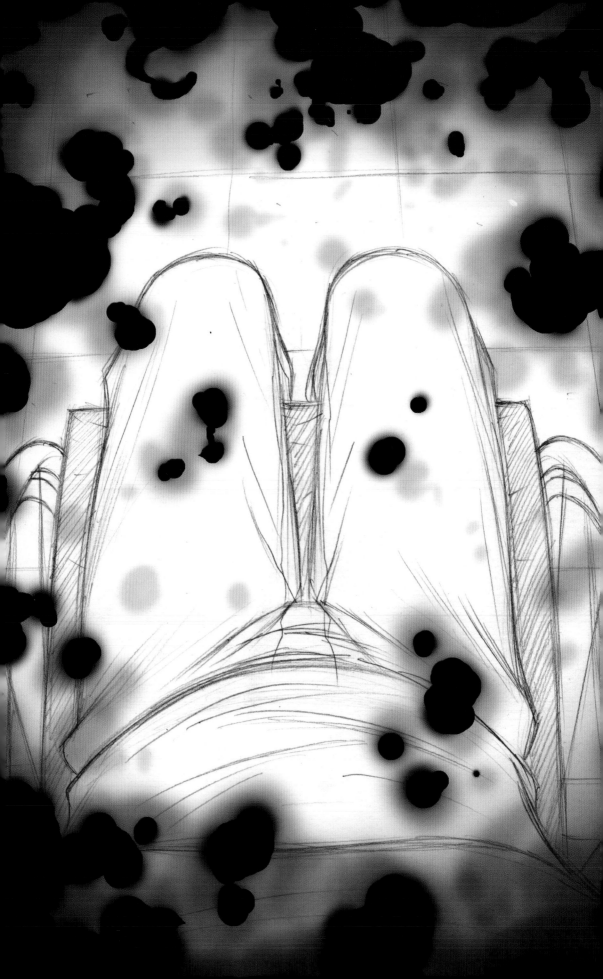

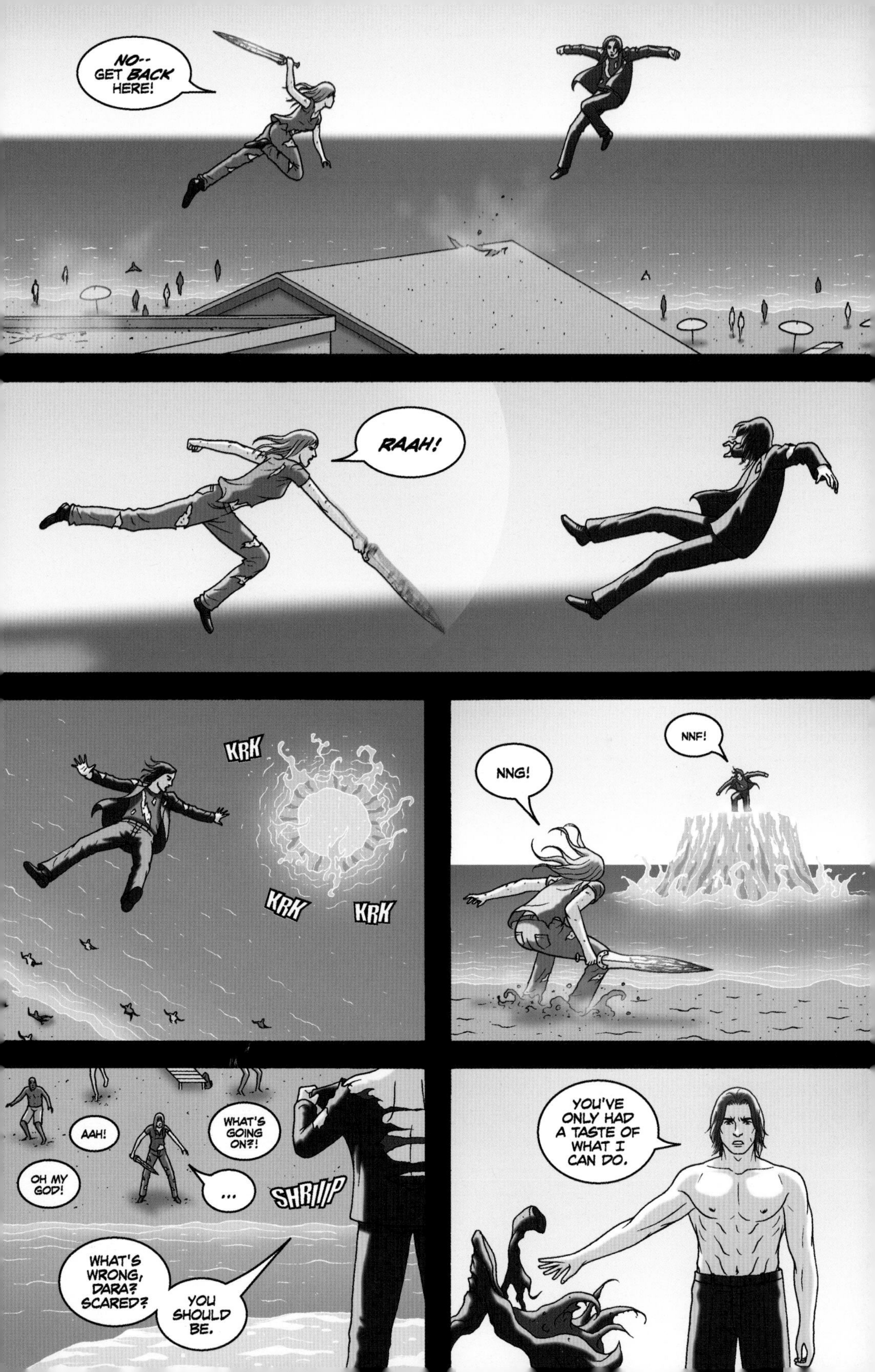
NO-- GET BACK HERE!
RAAH!
KRK
KRK
KRK
NNG!
NNF!
AAH!
WHAT'S GOING ON?!
OH MY GOD!
...
SHRIIIP
WHAT'S WRONG, DARA? SCARED?
YOU SHOULD BE.
YOU'VE ONLY HAD A TASTE OF WHAT I CAN DO.

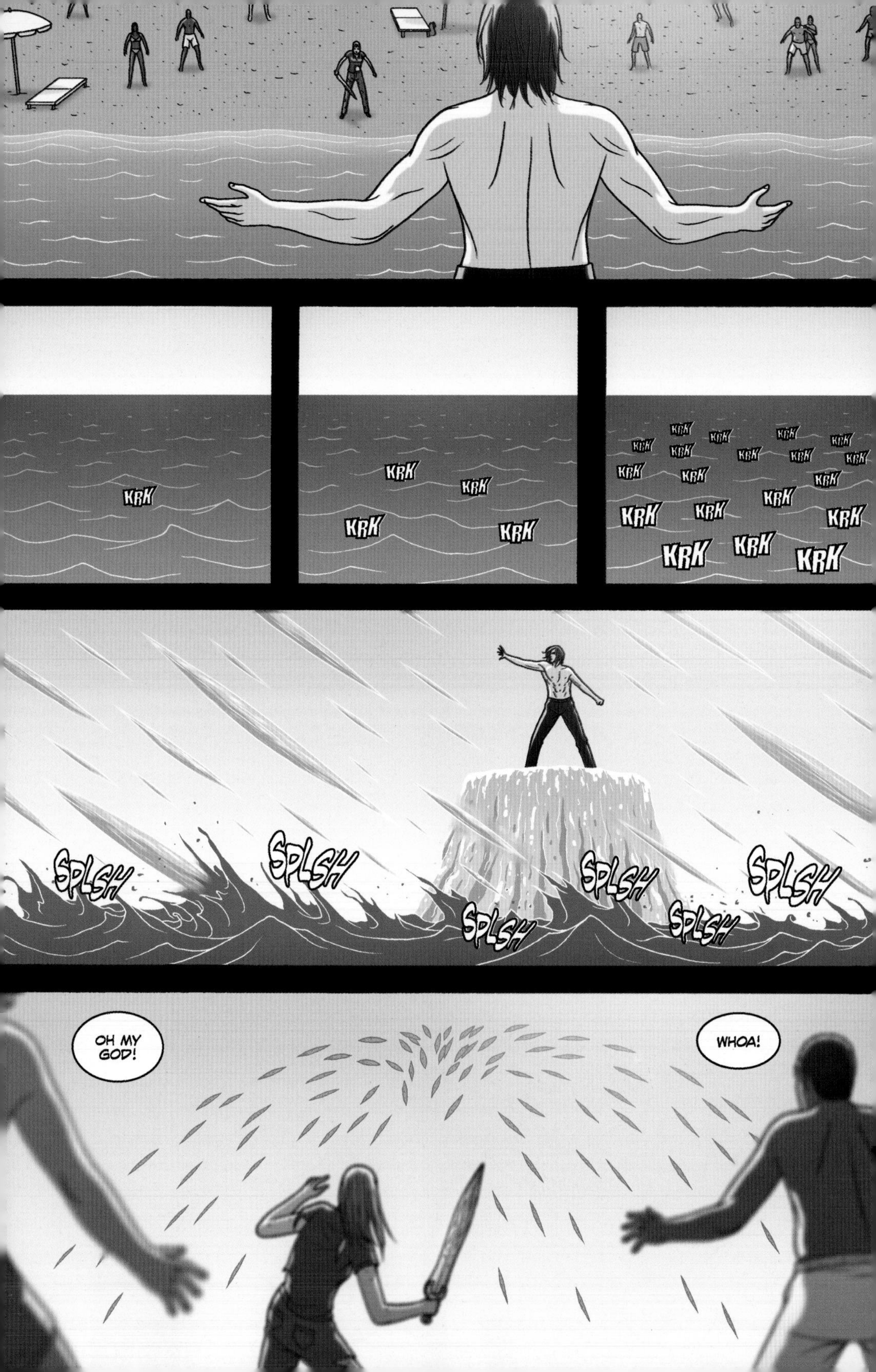
KRK
KRK
KRK
KRK
KRK
KRK KRK KRK KRK KRK KRK KRK KRK KRK KRK KRK KRK KRK KRK KRK KRK KRK KRK KRK
SPLSH
SPLSH
SPLSH
SPLSH
SPLSH
SPLSH
OH MY GOD!
WHOA!

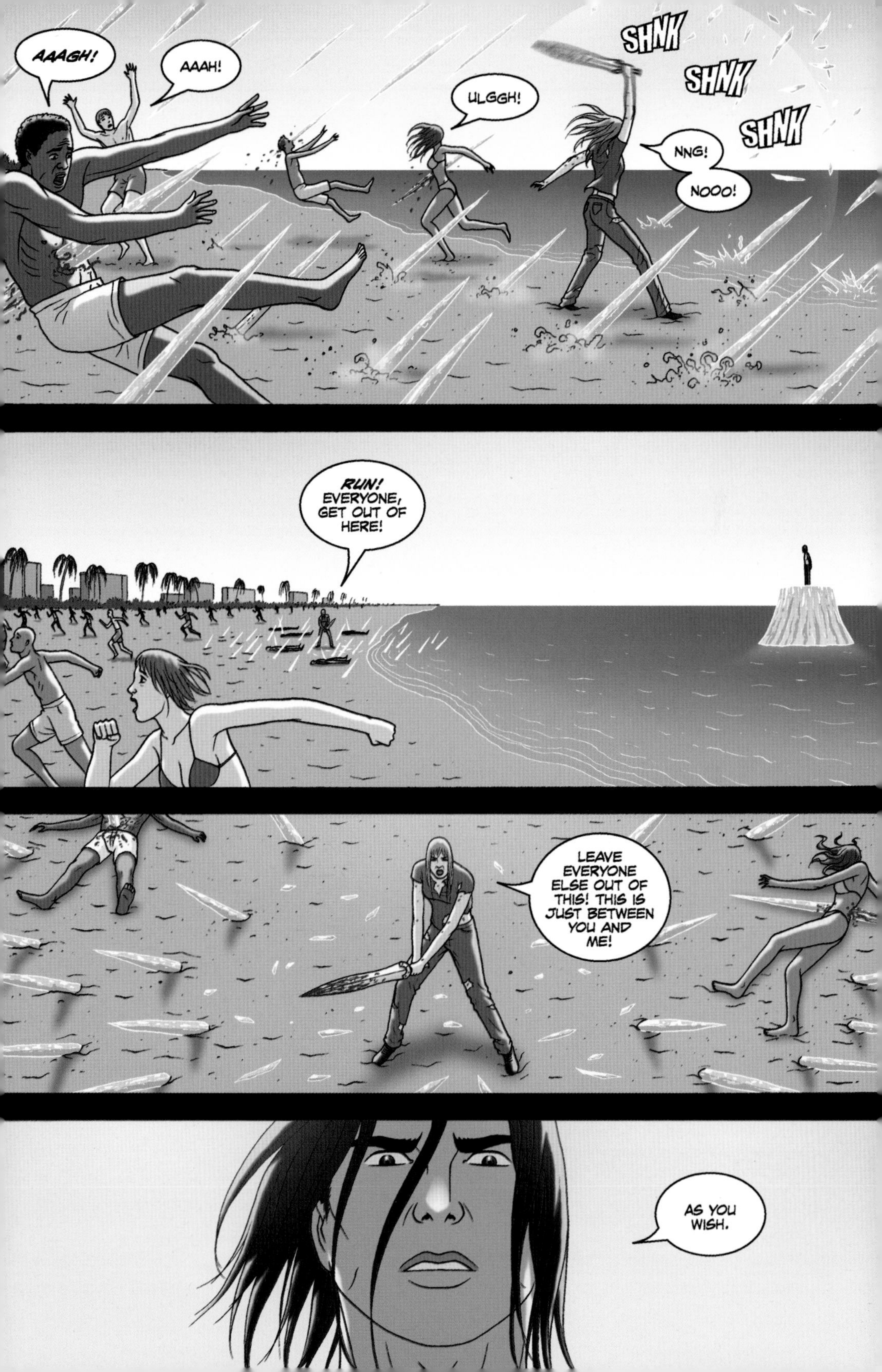
AAAGH!
AAAH!
ULGGH!
SHNK
SHNK
SHNK
NNG!
NOOO!
RUN! EVERYONE, GET OUT OF HERE!
LEAVE EVERYONE ELSE OUT OF THIS! THIS IS JUST BETWEEN YOU AND ME!
AS YOU WISH.

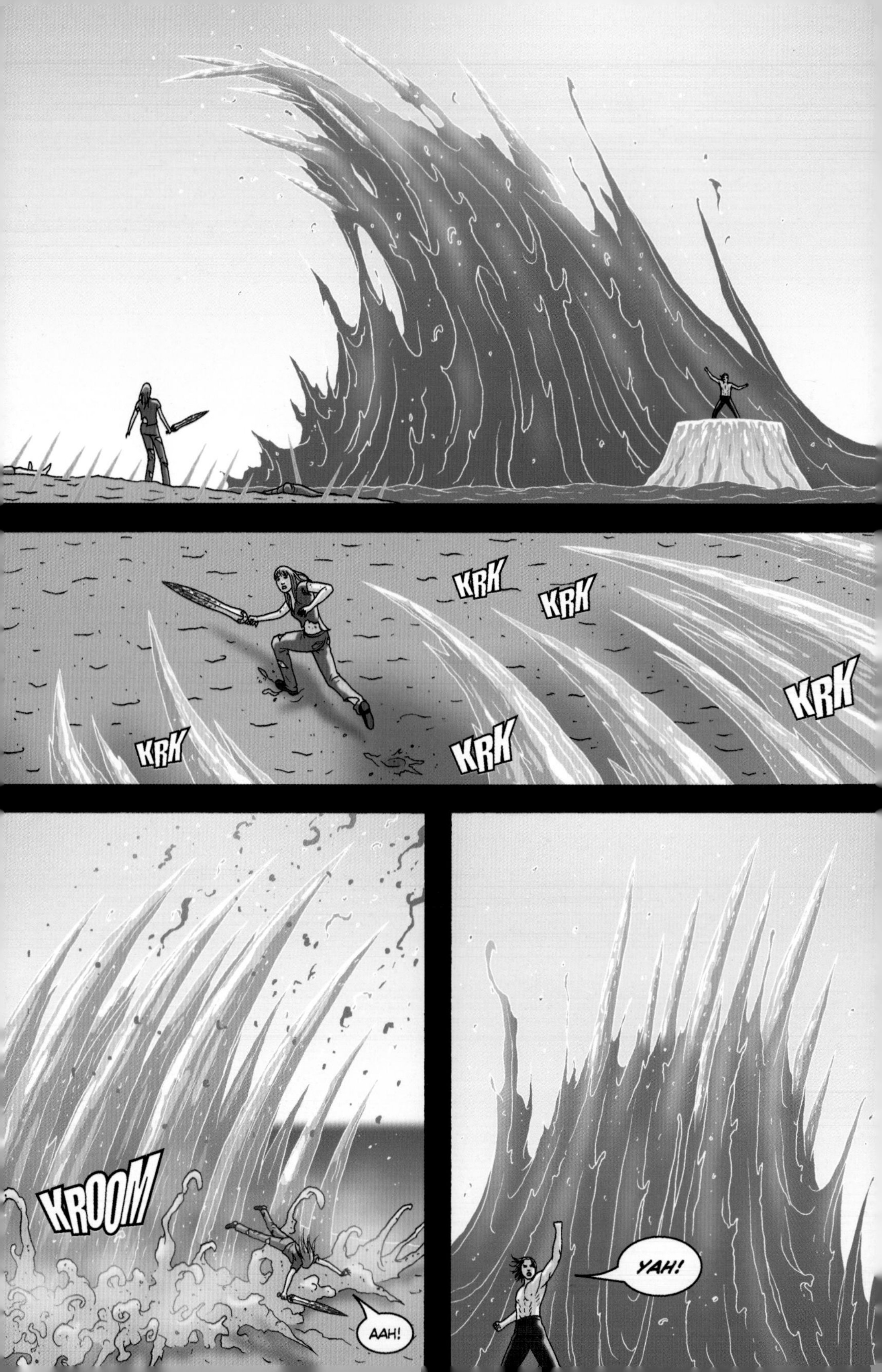
KRK
KRK
KRK
KRK
KRK
KROOM
AAH!
YAH!

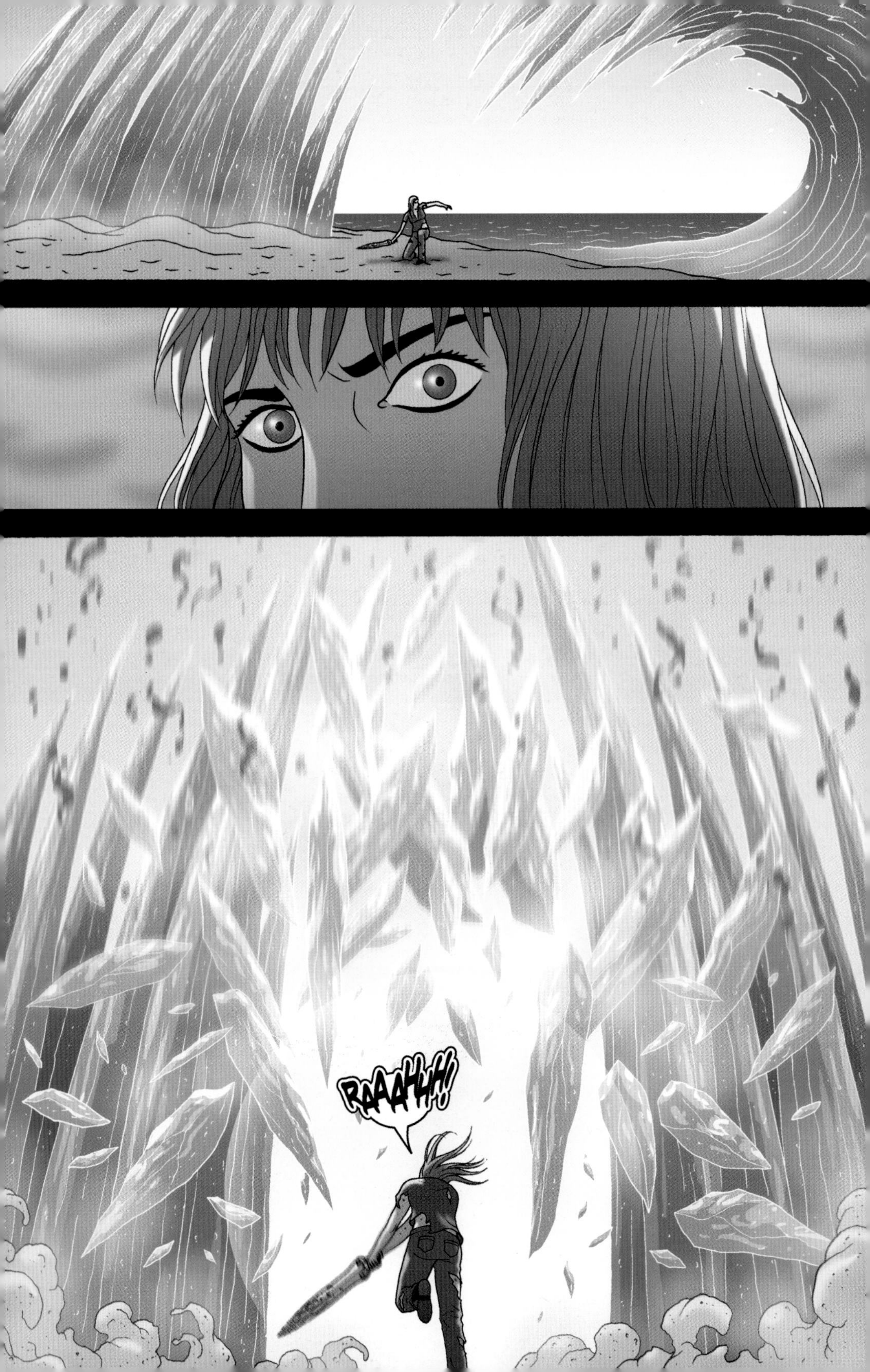
RAAAHHH!

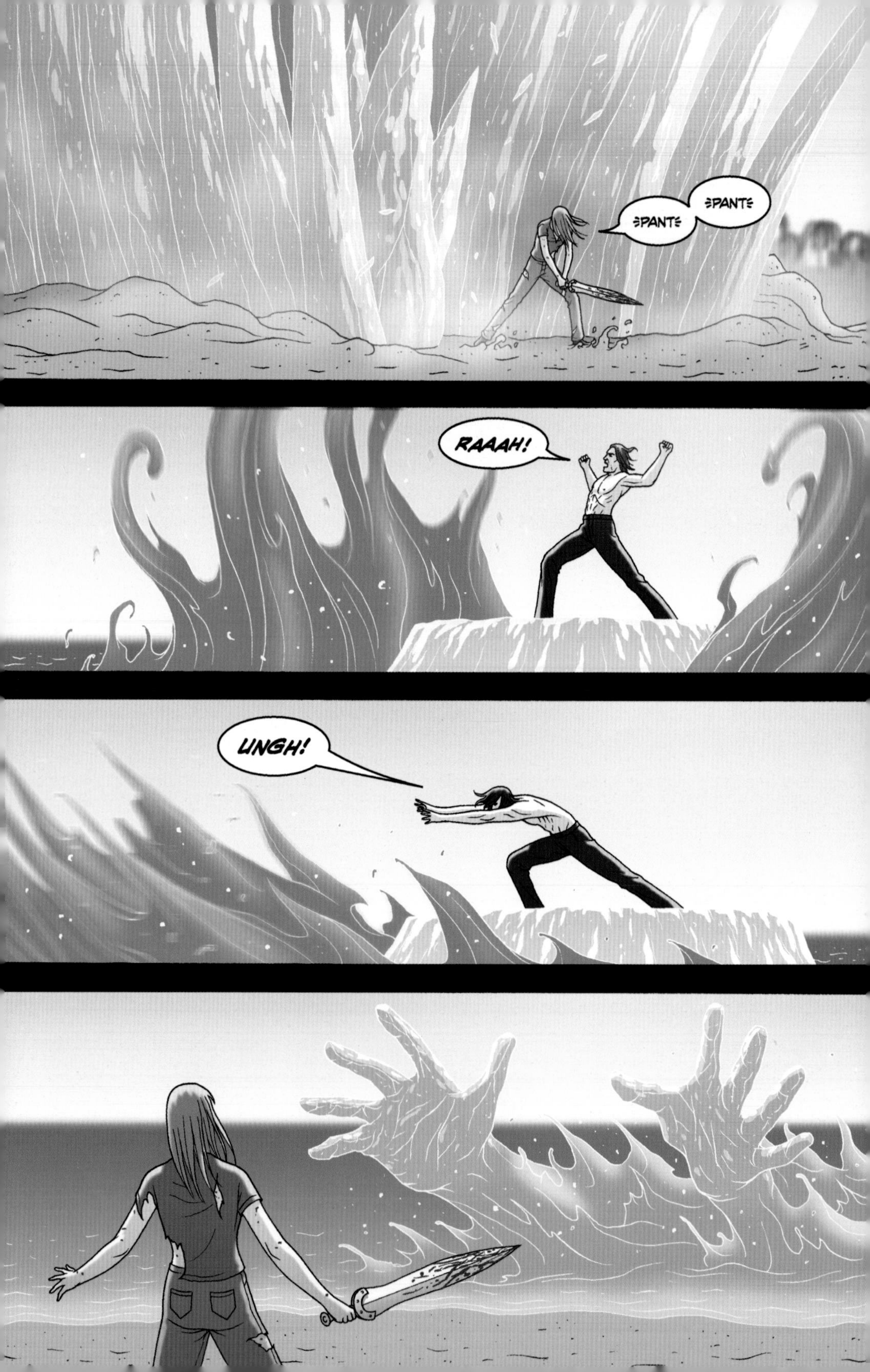
PANT
PANT
RAAAH!
UNGH!

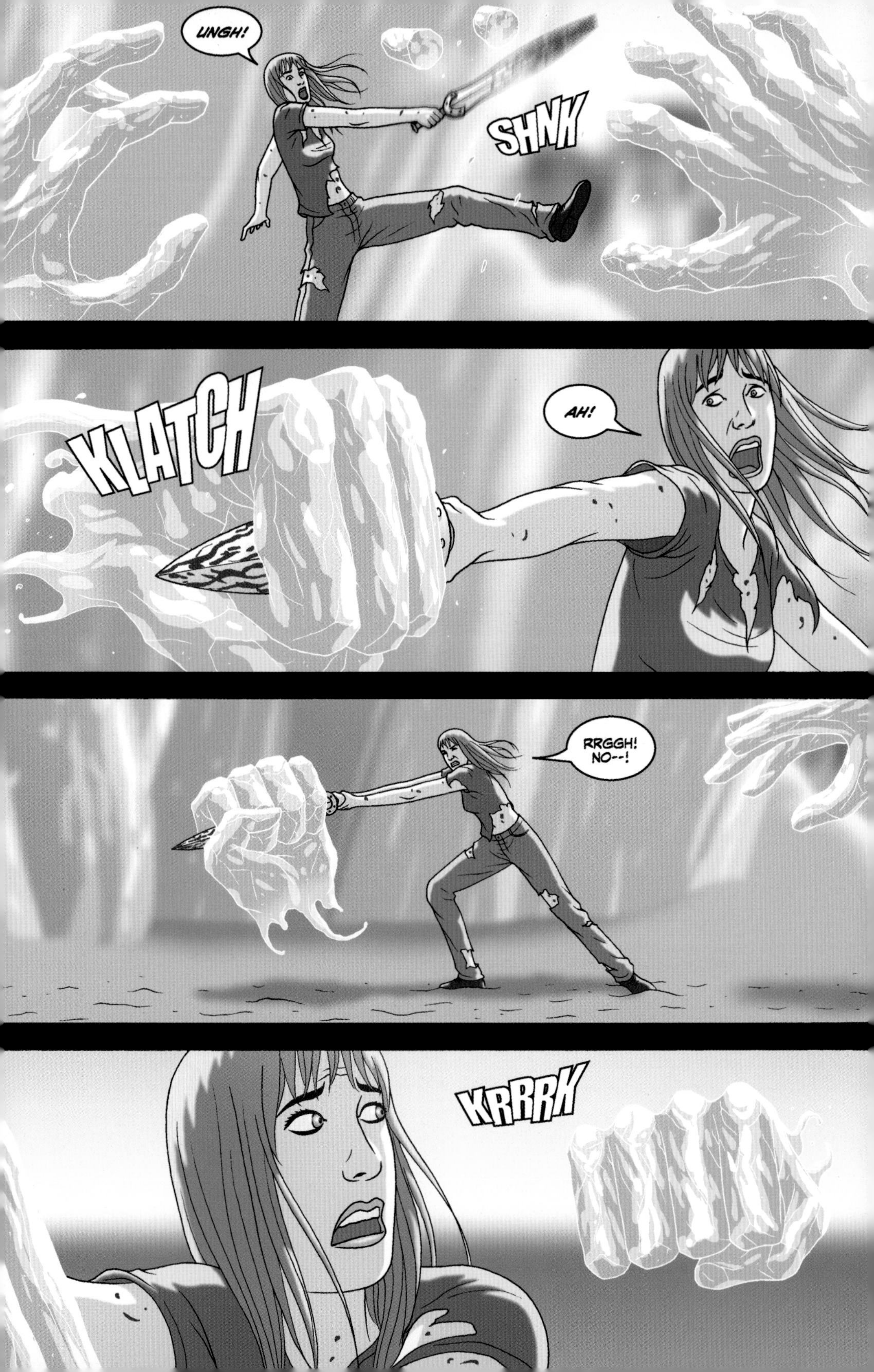
UNGH!
SHNK
KLATCH
AH!
RRGGH! NO--!
KRRRK

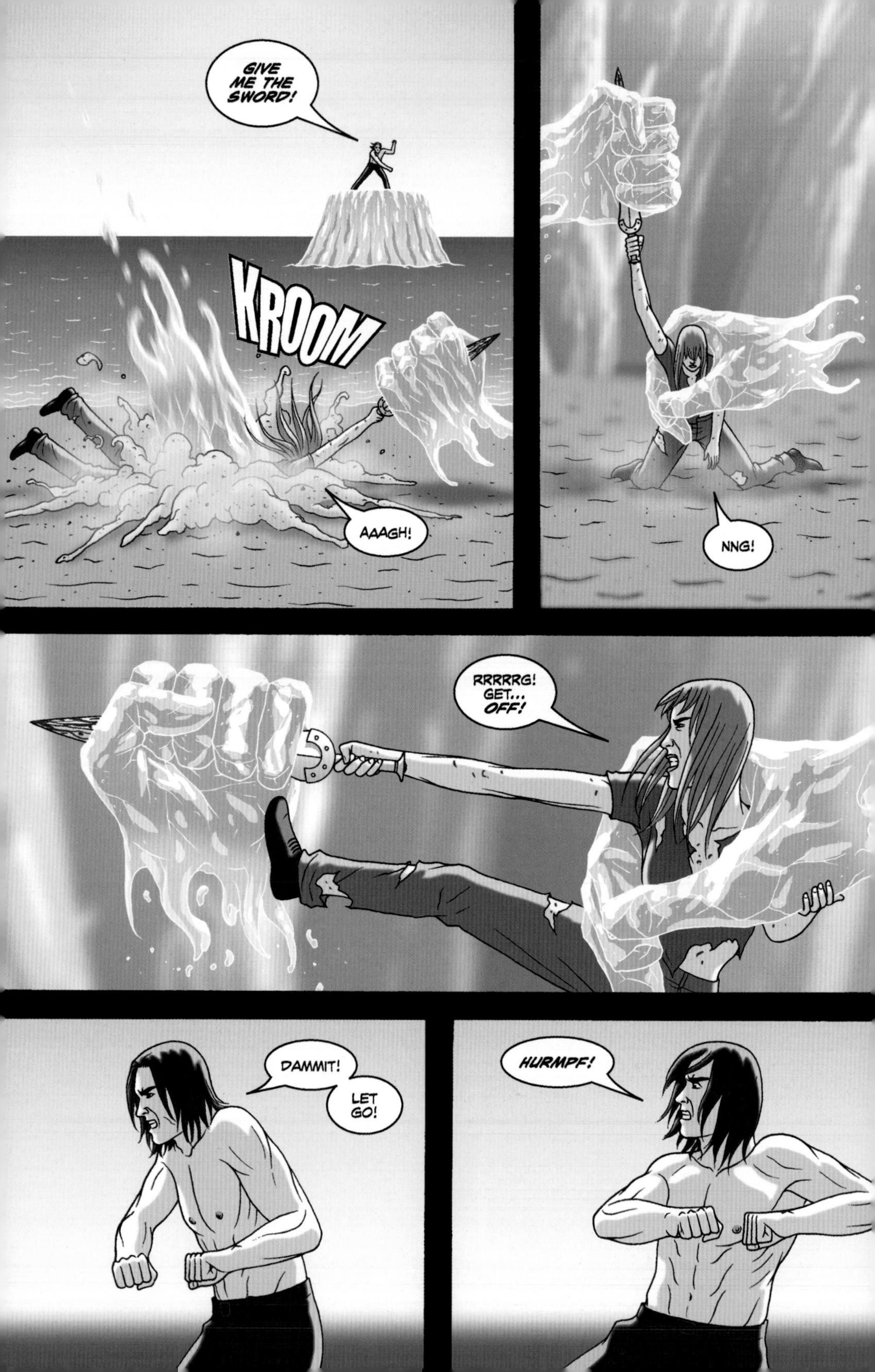
GIVE ME THE SWORD!
KROOM
AAAGH!
NNG!
RRRRRG! GET... OFF!
DAMMIT!
LET GO!
HURMPF!

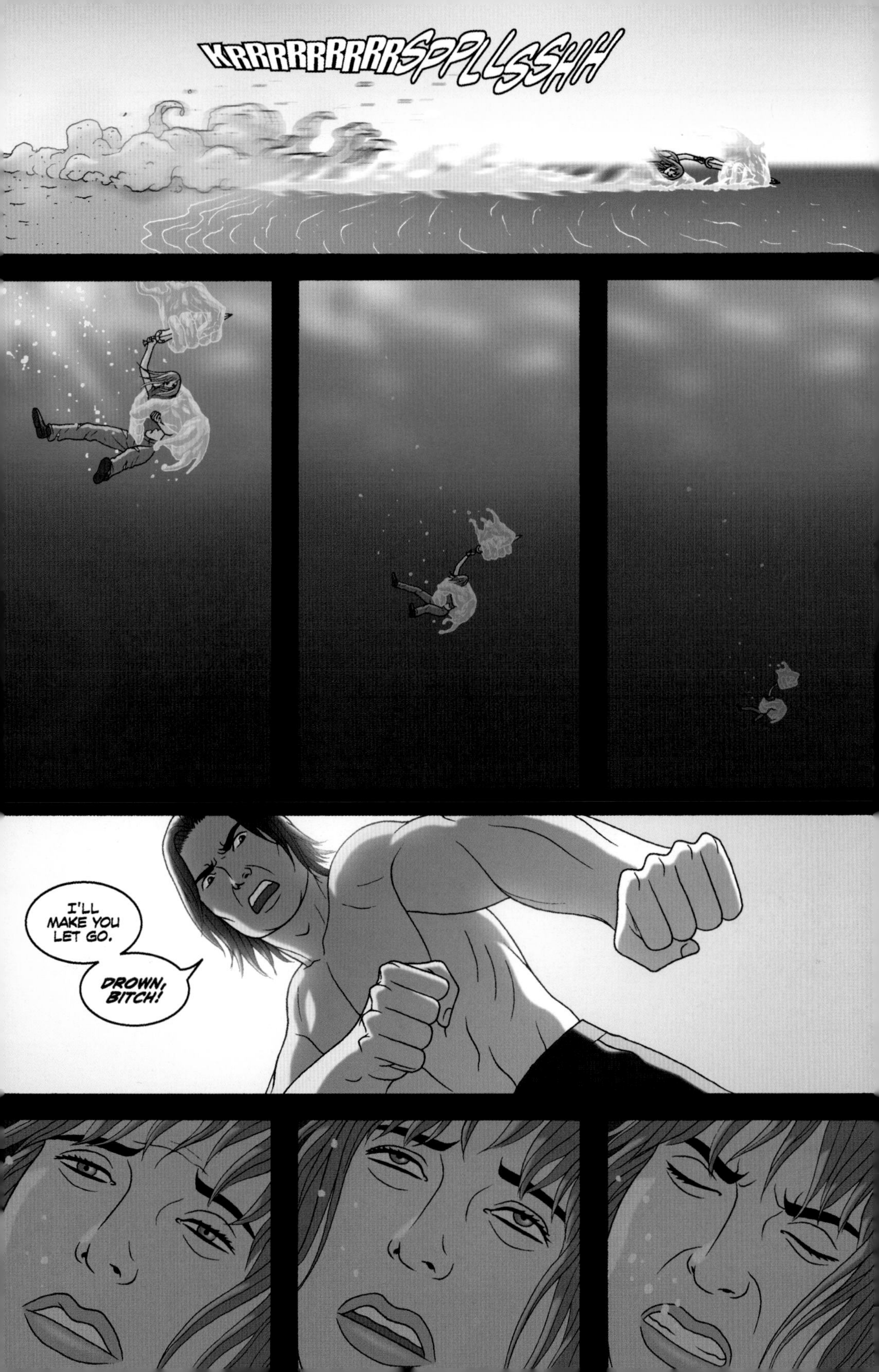
KRRRRRRRRRSPPLLSSHH
I'LL MAKE YOU LET GO.
DROWN, BITCH!

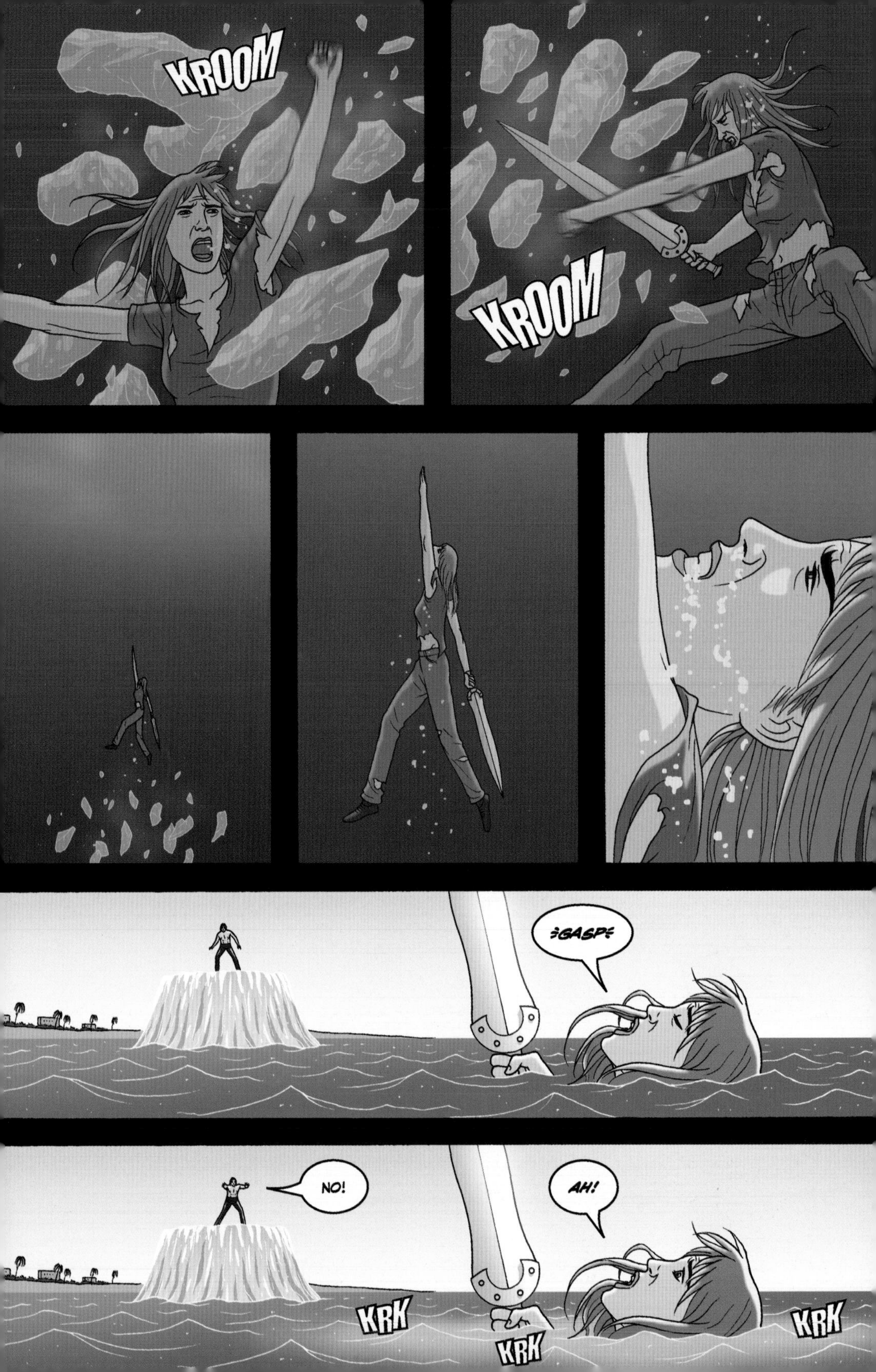
KROOM
KROOM
GASP
NO!
AH!
KRK
KRK
KRK

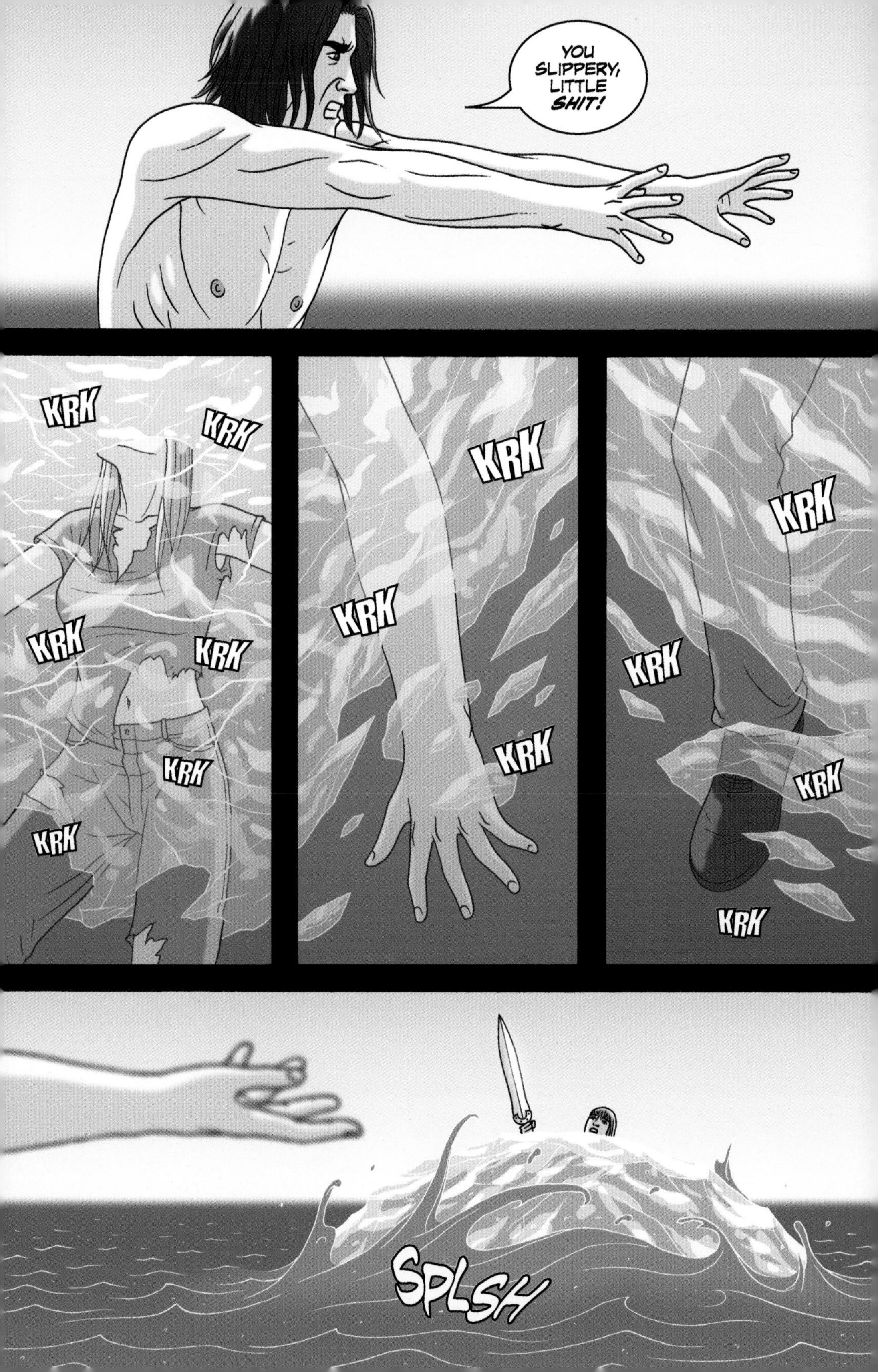

YOU SLIPPERY, LITTLE SHIT!
KRK
KRK
KRK
KRK
KRK
KRK
KRK
KRK
KRK
KRK
KRK
KRK
KRK
SPLSH

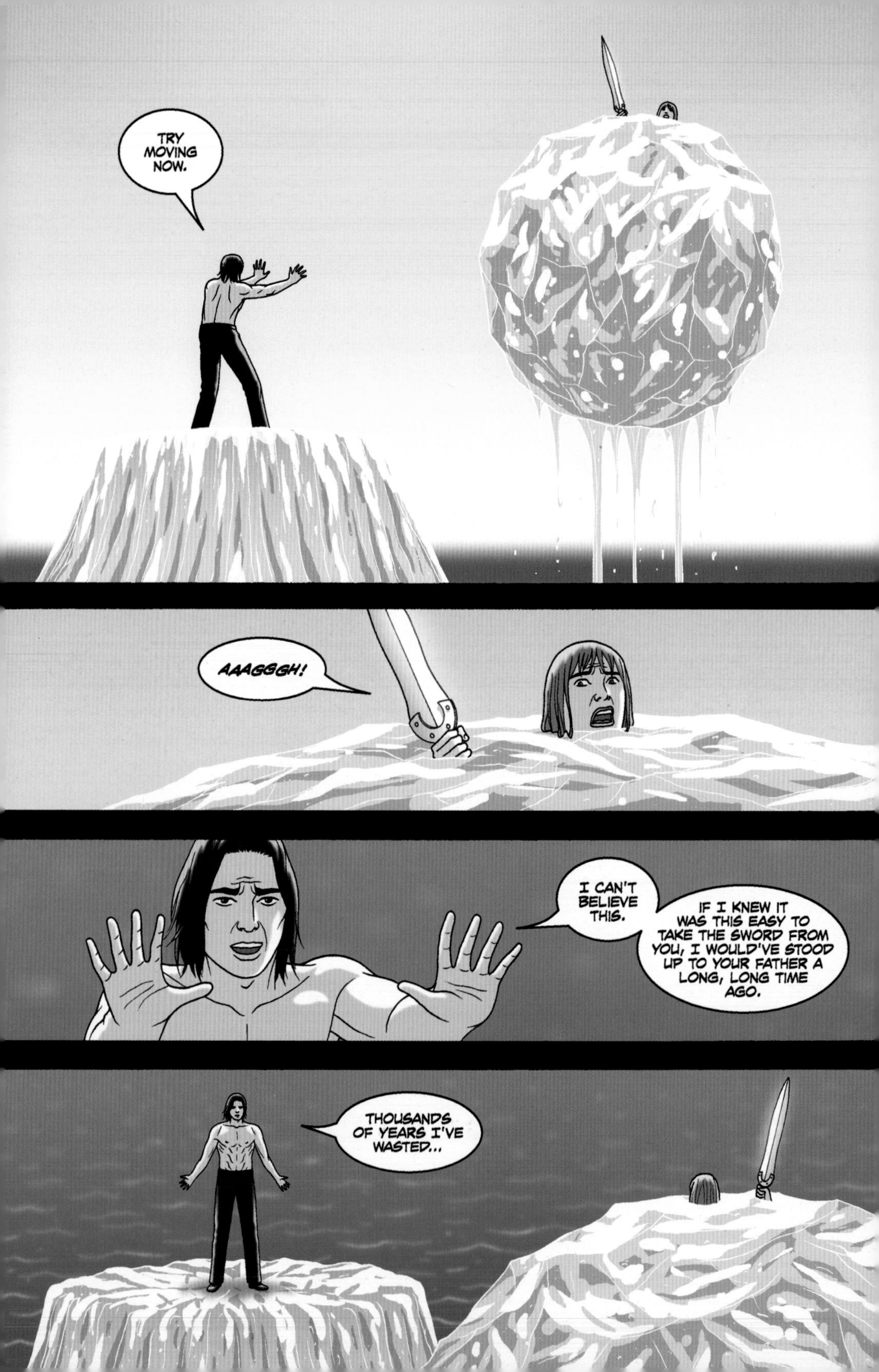
TRY MOVING NOW.
AAAGGGH!
I CAN'T BELIEVE THIS.
IF I KNEW IT WAS THIS EASY TO TAKE THE SWORD FROM YOU, I WOULD'VE STOOD UP TO YOUR FATHER A LONG, LONG TIME AGO.
THOUSANDS OF YEARS I'VE WASTED...

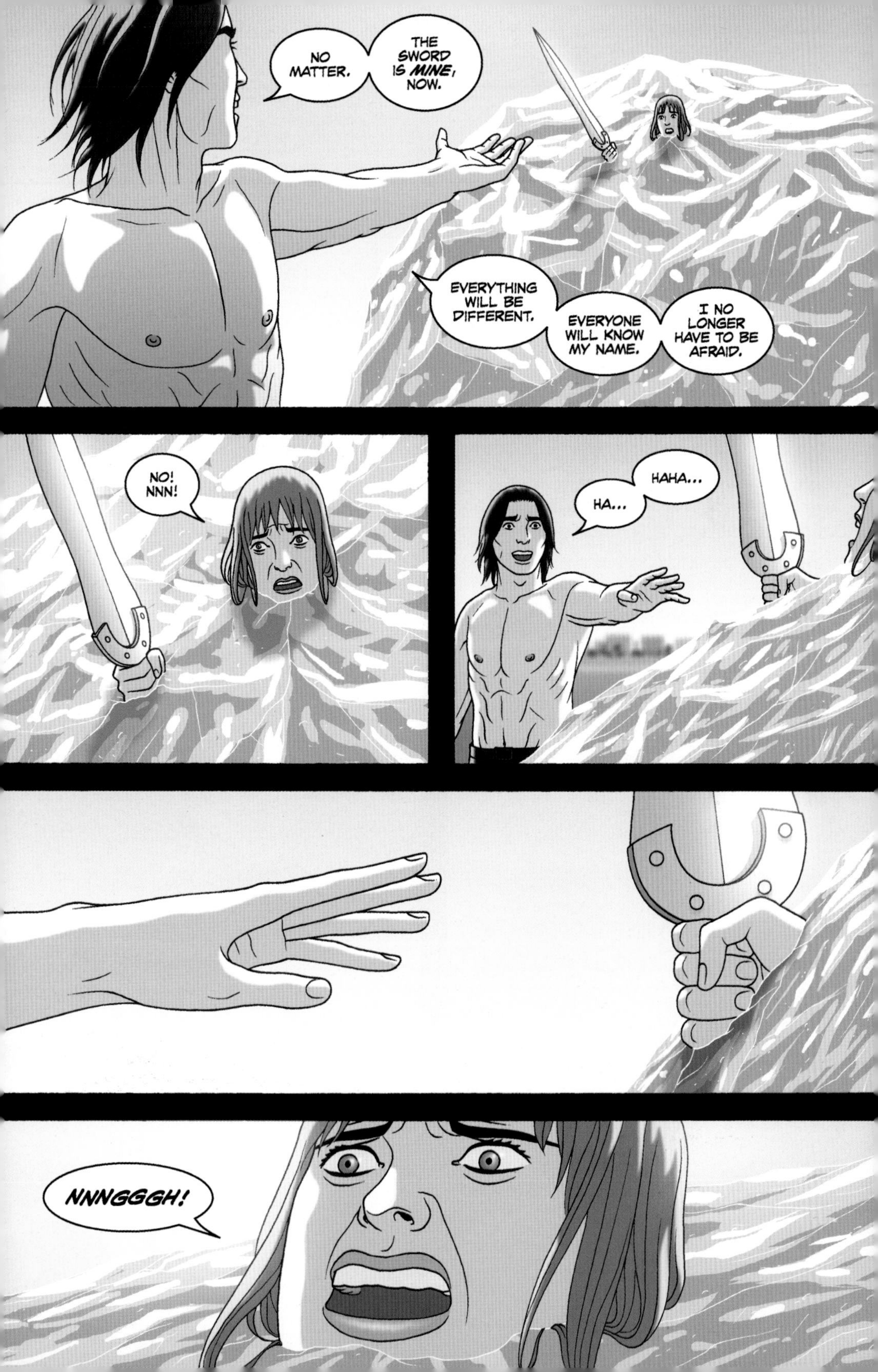
NO MATTER.
THE SWORD IS *MINE*, NOW.
EVERYTHING WILL BE DIFFERENT.
EVERYONE WILL KNOW MY NAME.
I NO LONGER HAVE TO BE AFRAID.
NO! NNN!
HA...
HAHA...
NNNGGGH!

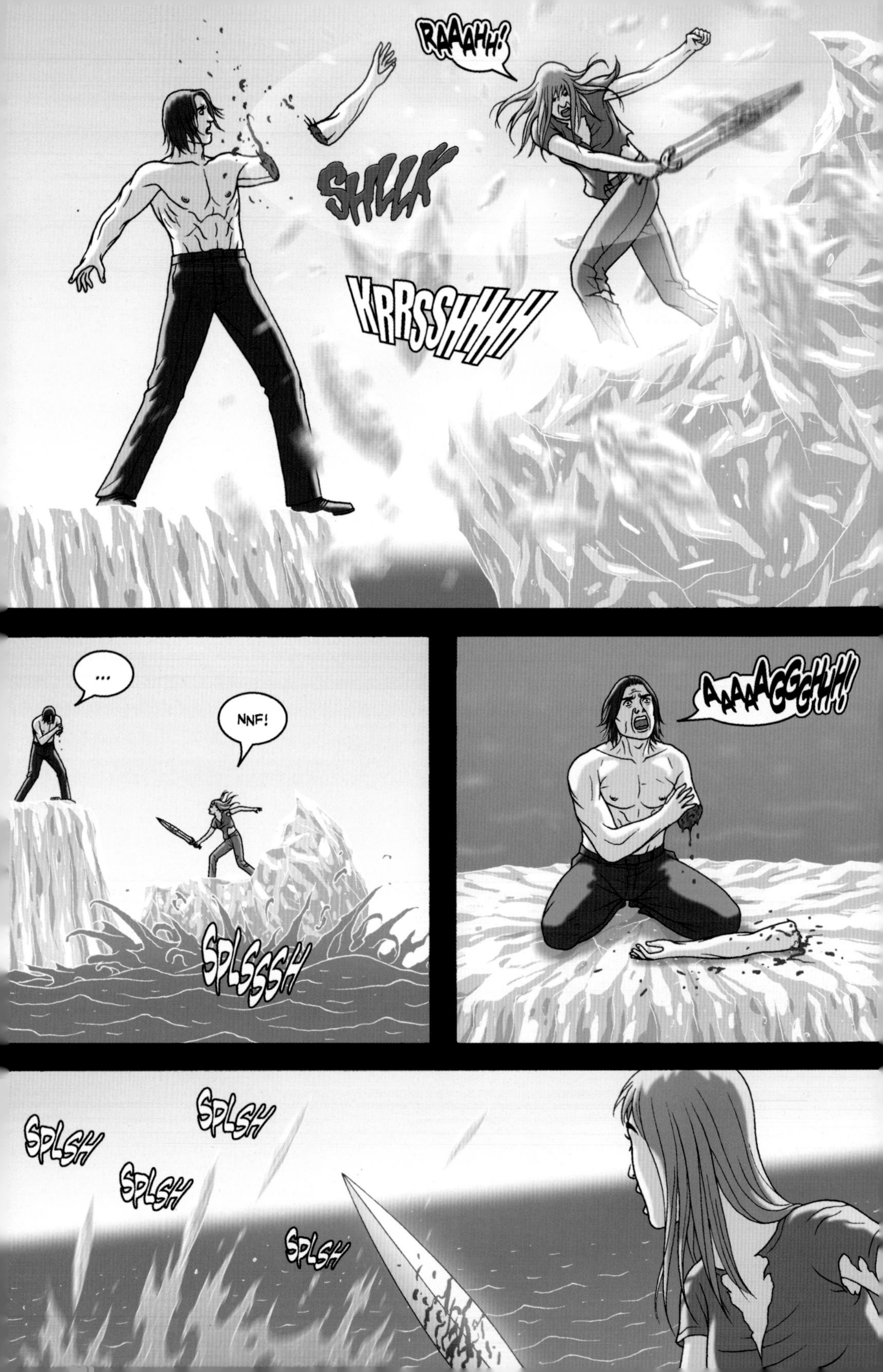
RAAAHH!
SHLLK
KRRSSHHHH
...
NNF!
SPLSSSH
AAAAAGGGHHH!
SPLSH
SPLSH
SPLSH
SPLSH

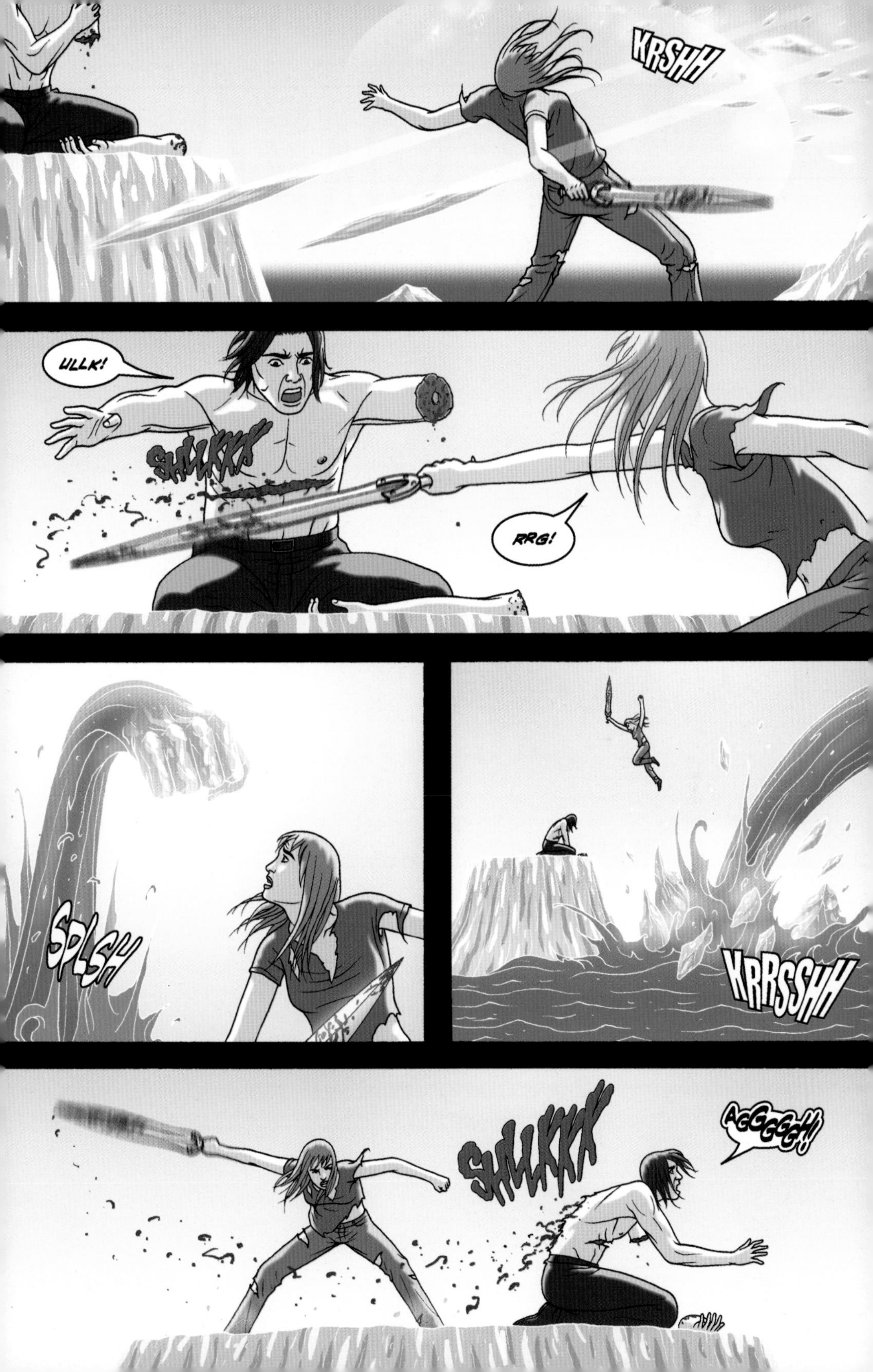
KRSHH
ULLK!
SHLKKK
RRG!
SPLSH
KRRSSHH
SHLKKK
AGGGGGH!

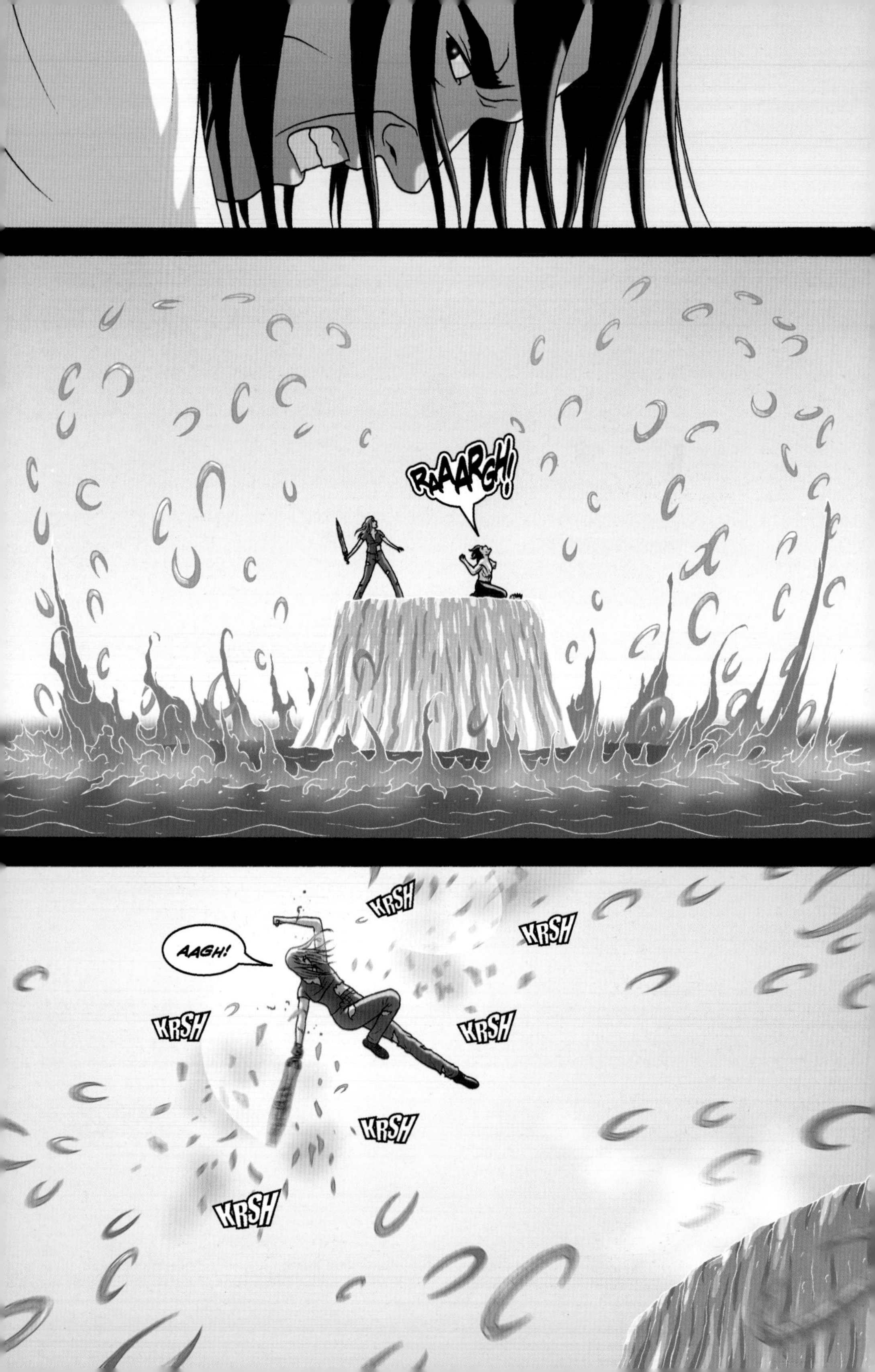
RAAARGH!
KRSH
KRSH
AAGH!
KRSH
KRSH
KRSH
KRSH

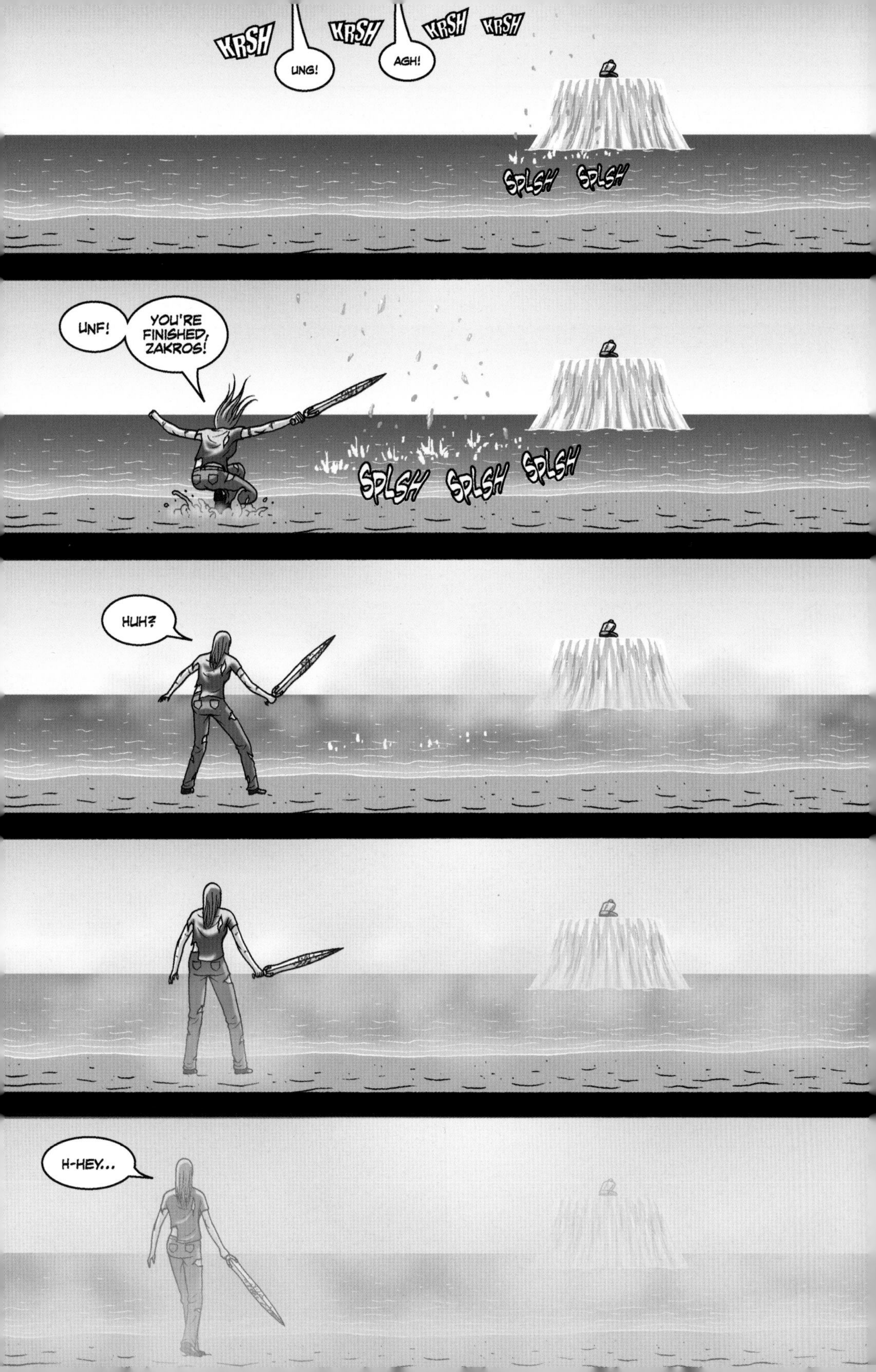
KRSH
UNG!
KRSH
AGH!
KRSH
KRSH
SPLSH
SPLSH
UNF!
YOU'RE FINISHED, ZAKROS!
SPLSH
SPLSH
SPLSH
HUH?
H-HEY...

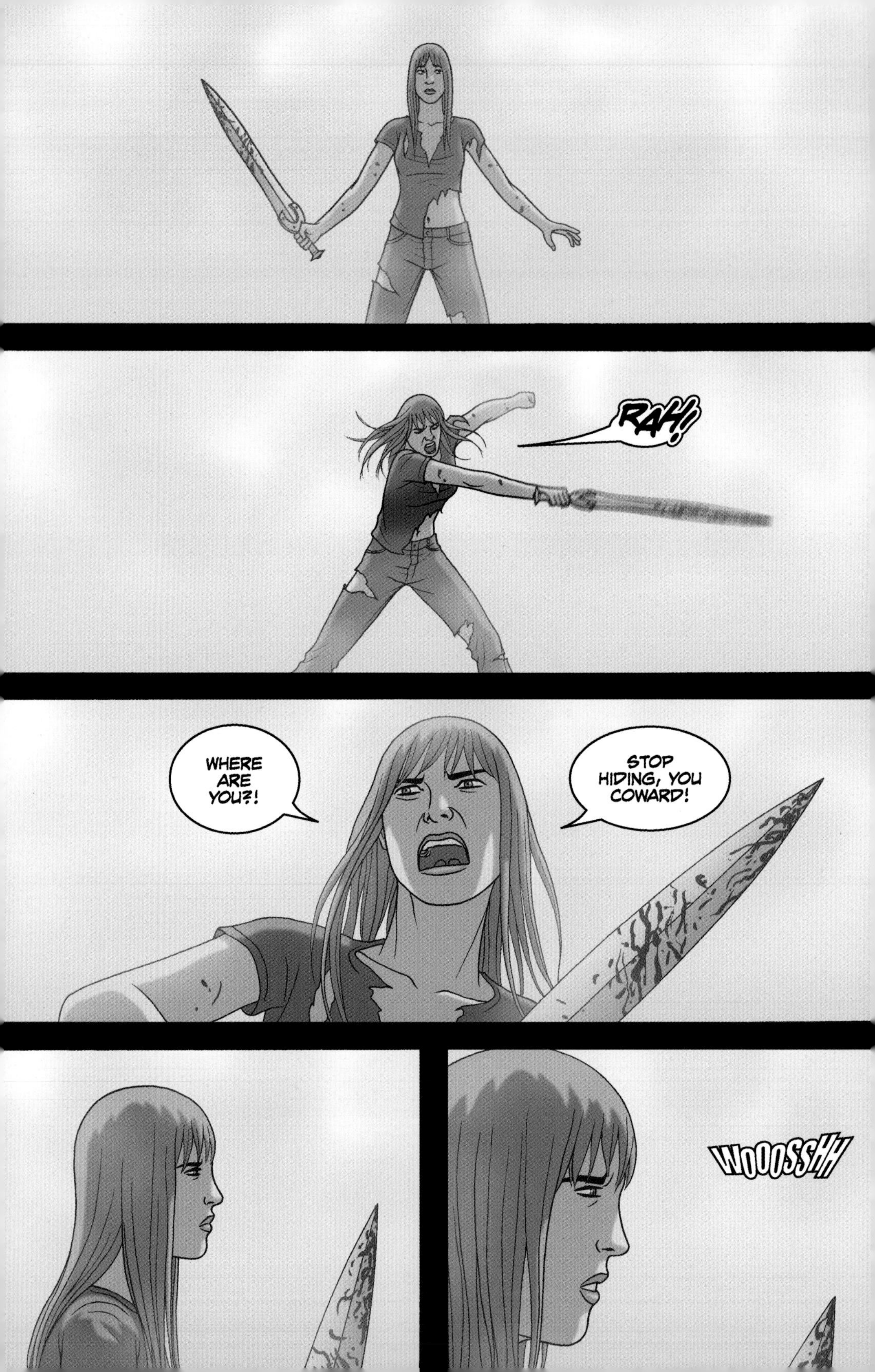
RAH!
WHERE ARE YOU?!
STOP HIDING, YOU COWARD!
WOOOSSHH

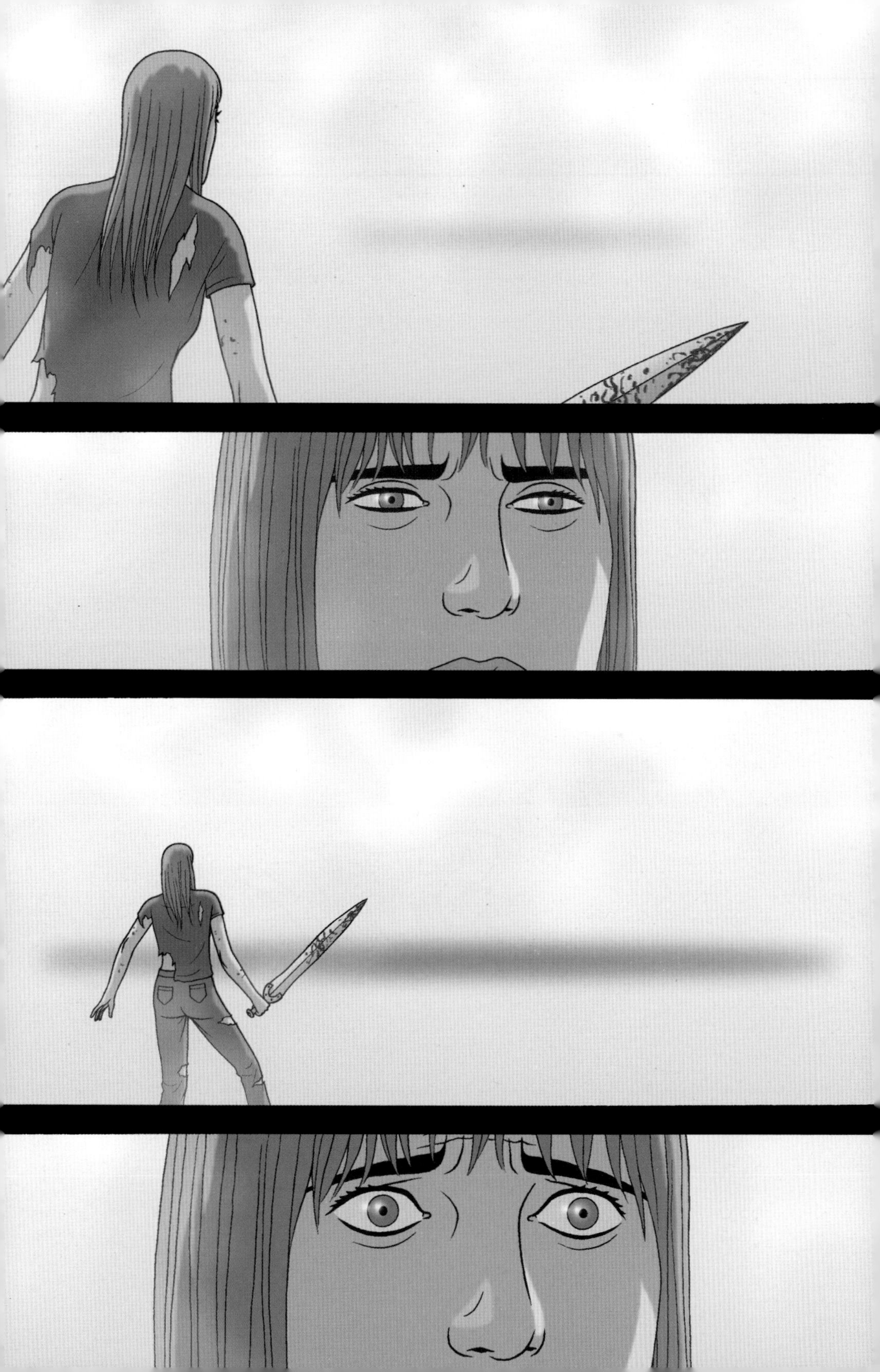

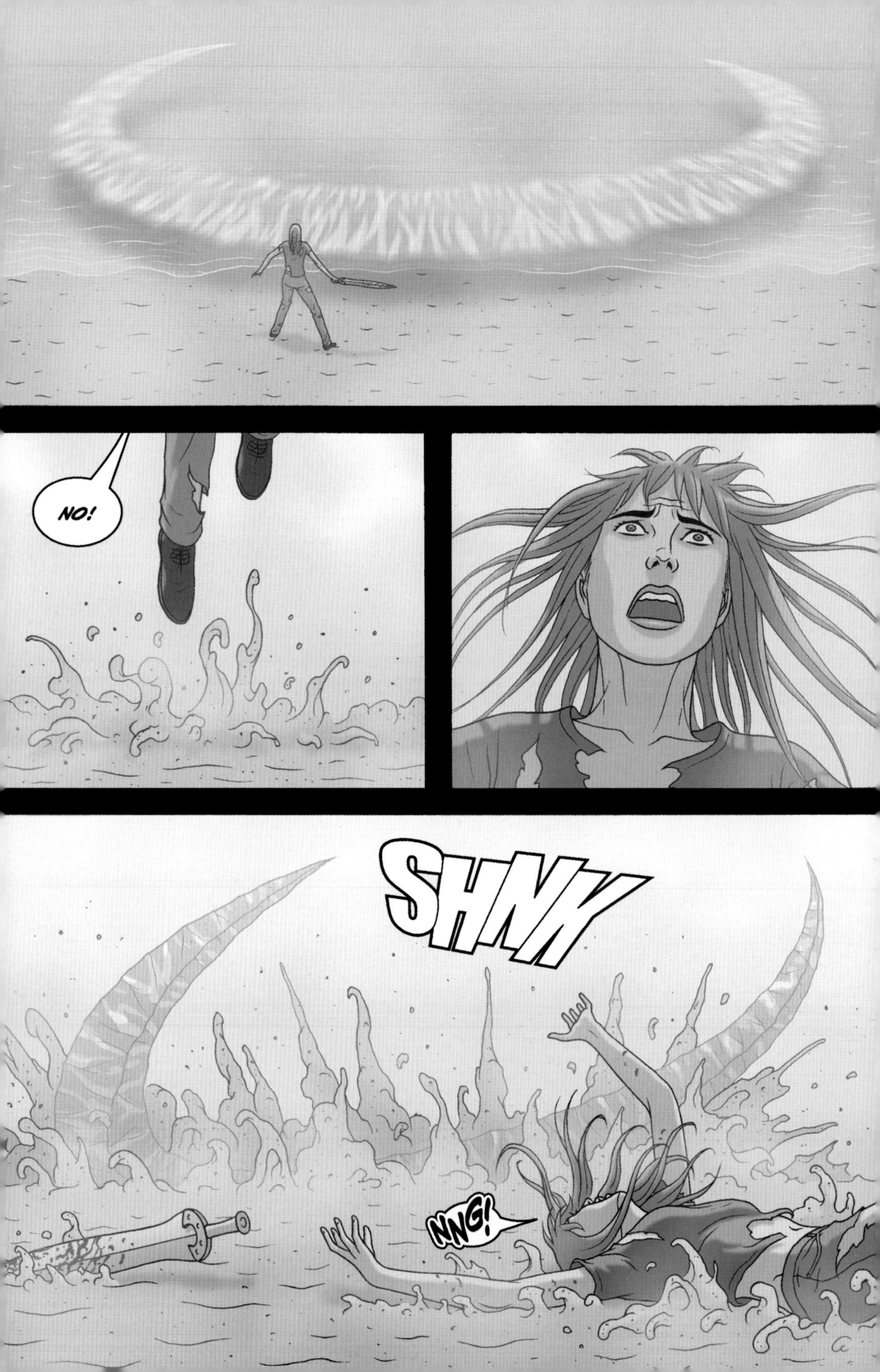
NO!
SHNK
NNG!

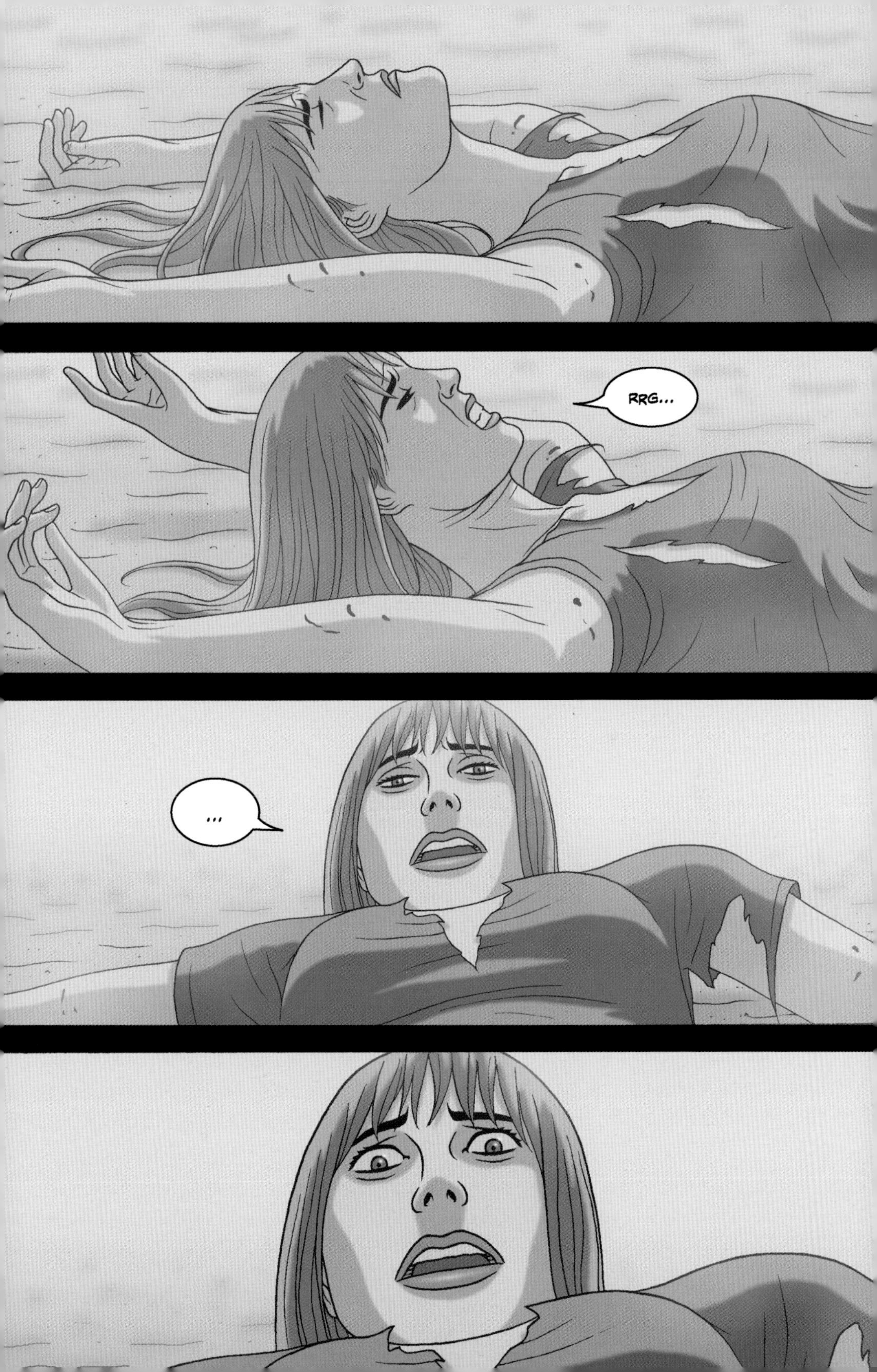
RRG...
...

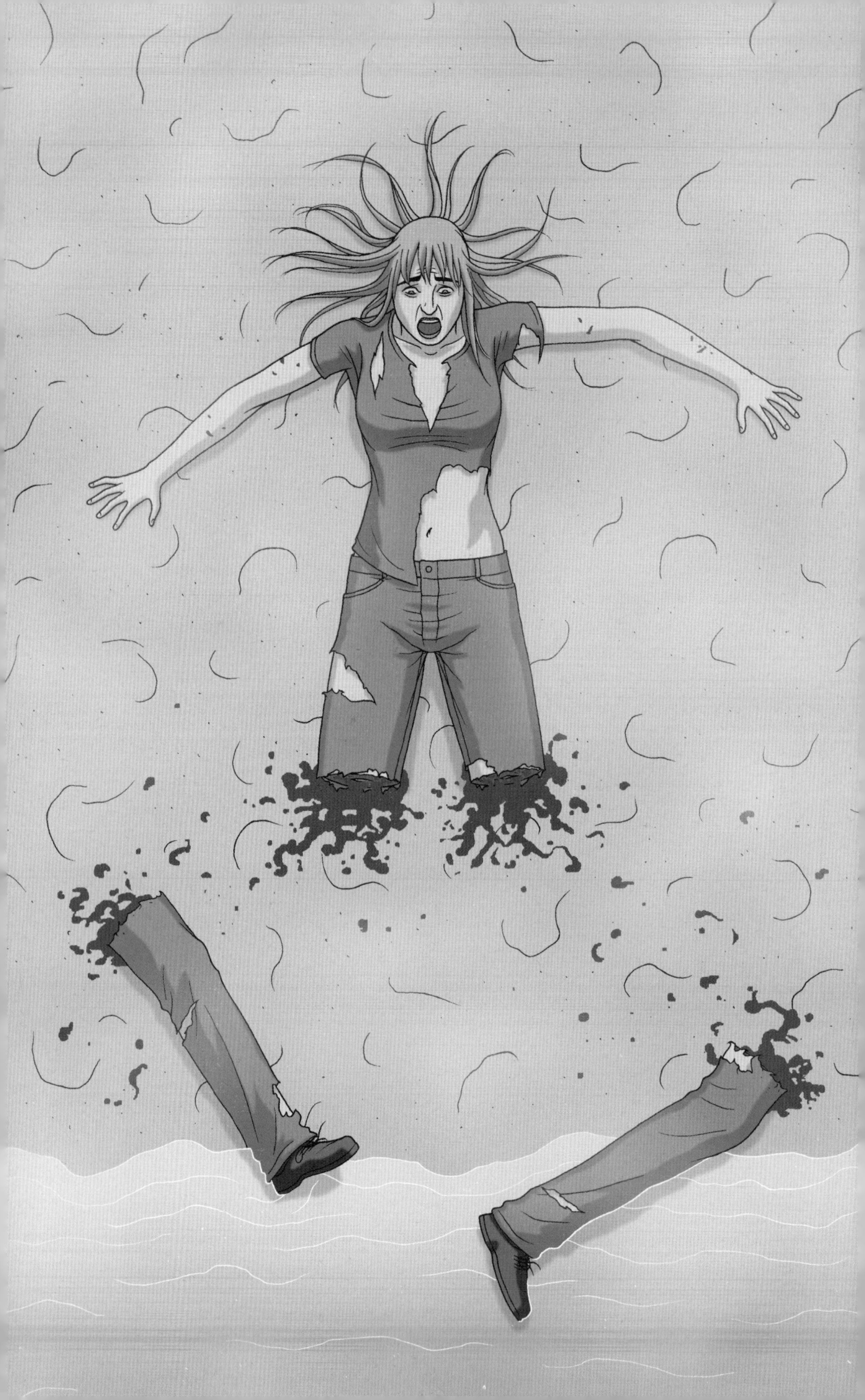

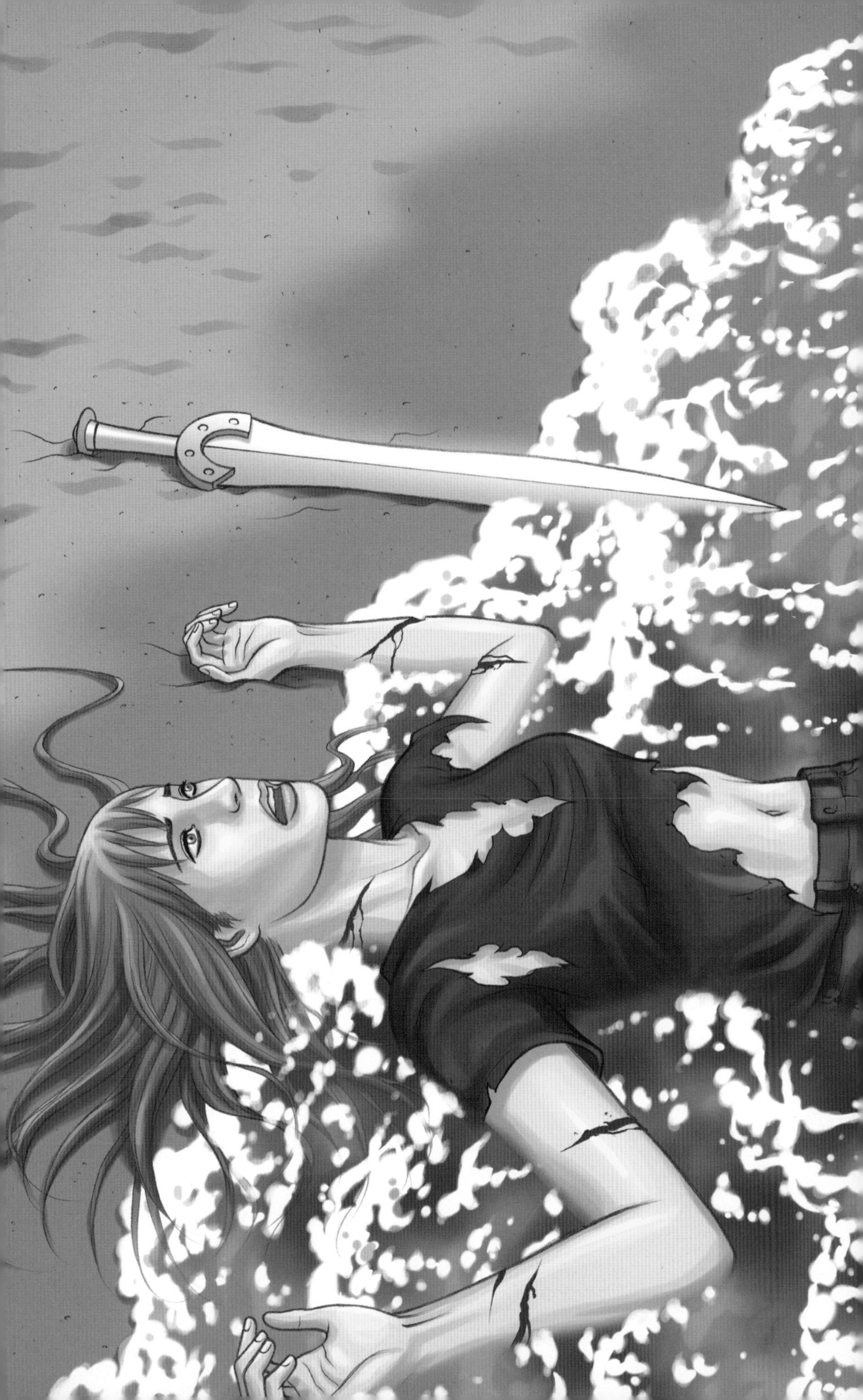

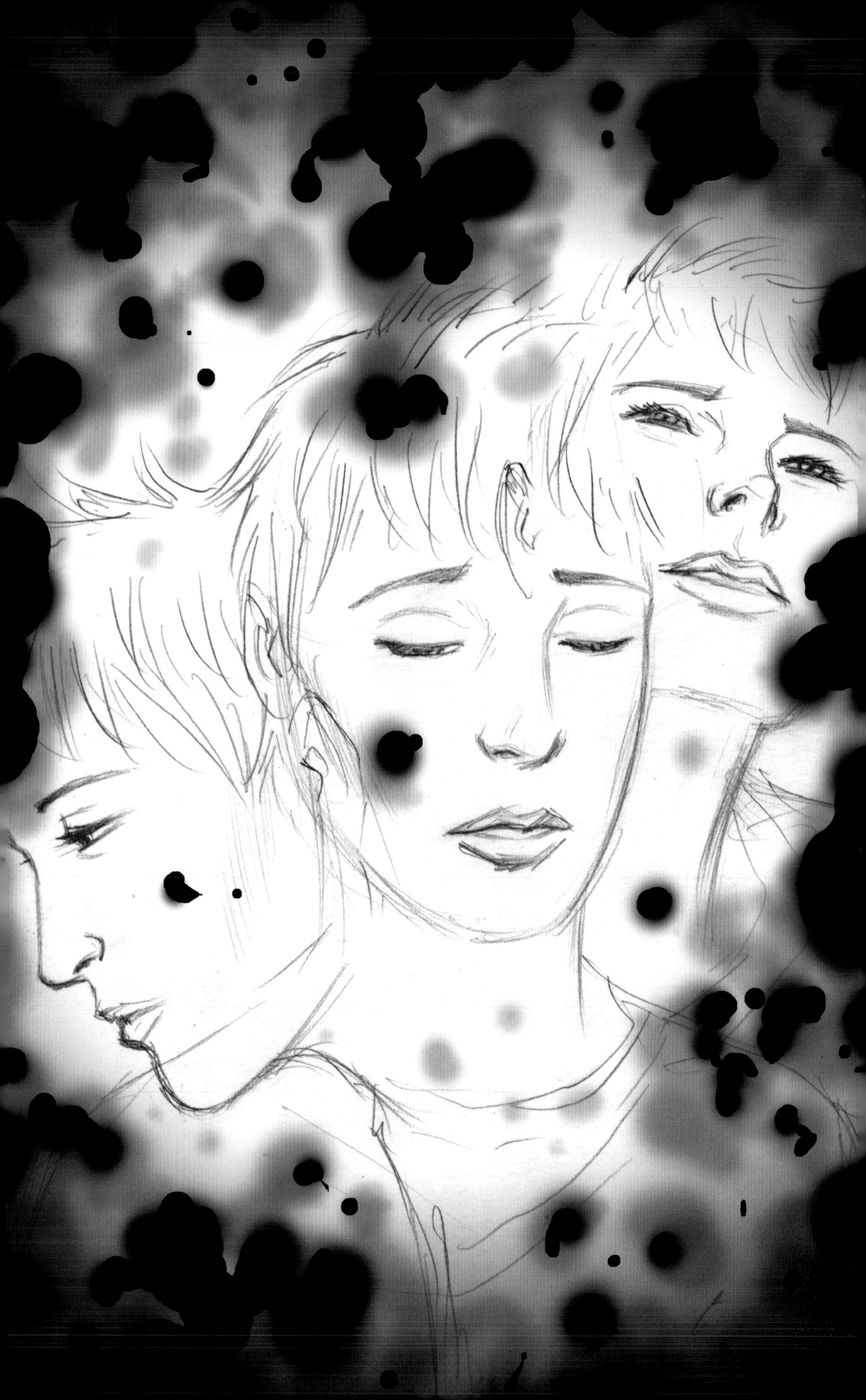

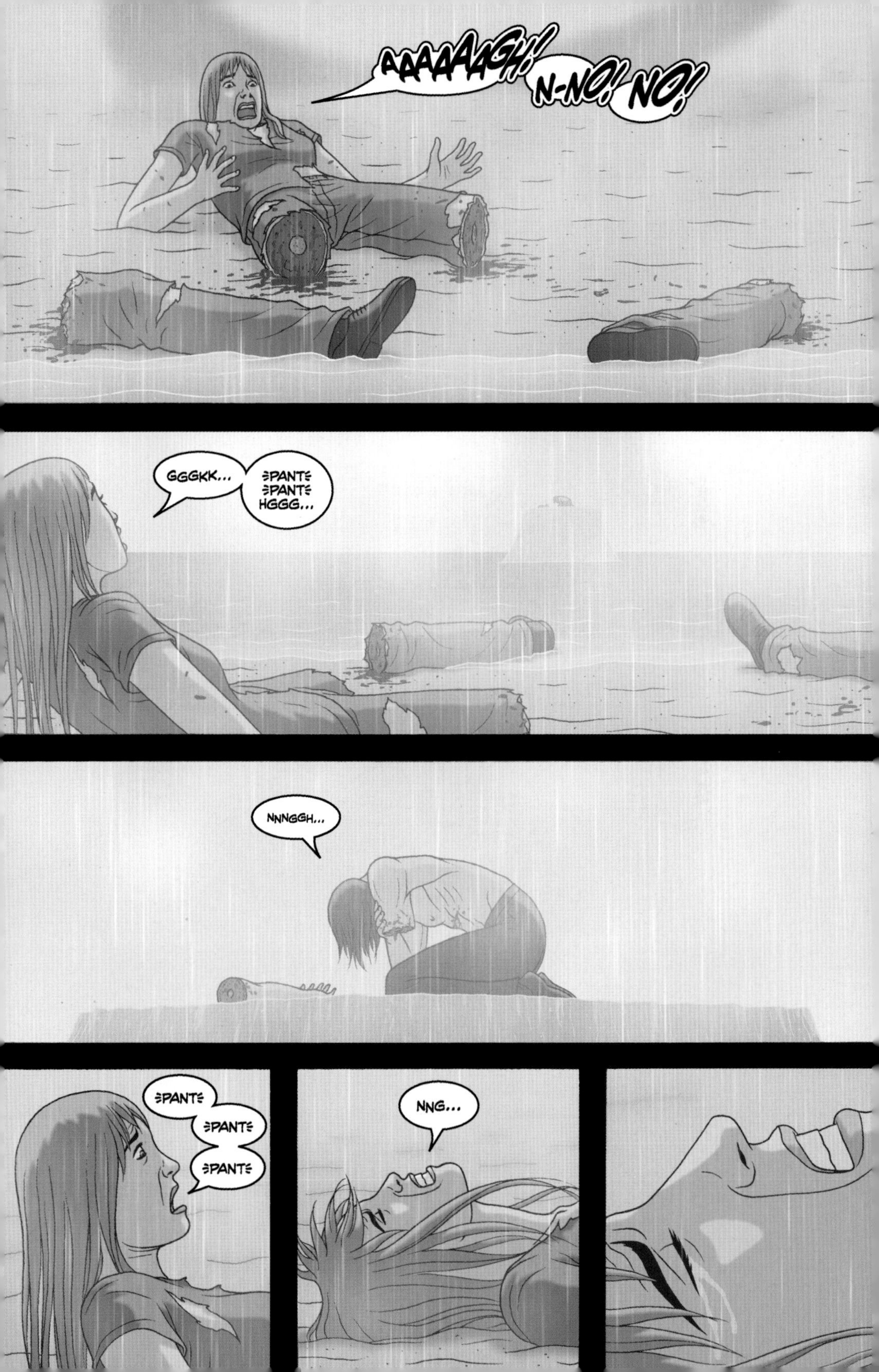
AAAAAAGH!
N-NO! NO!
GGGKK...
=PANT=
=PANT=
HGGG...
NNNGGH...
=PANT=
=PANT=
=PANT=
NNG...

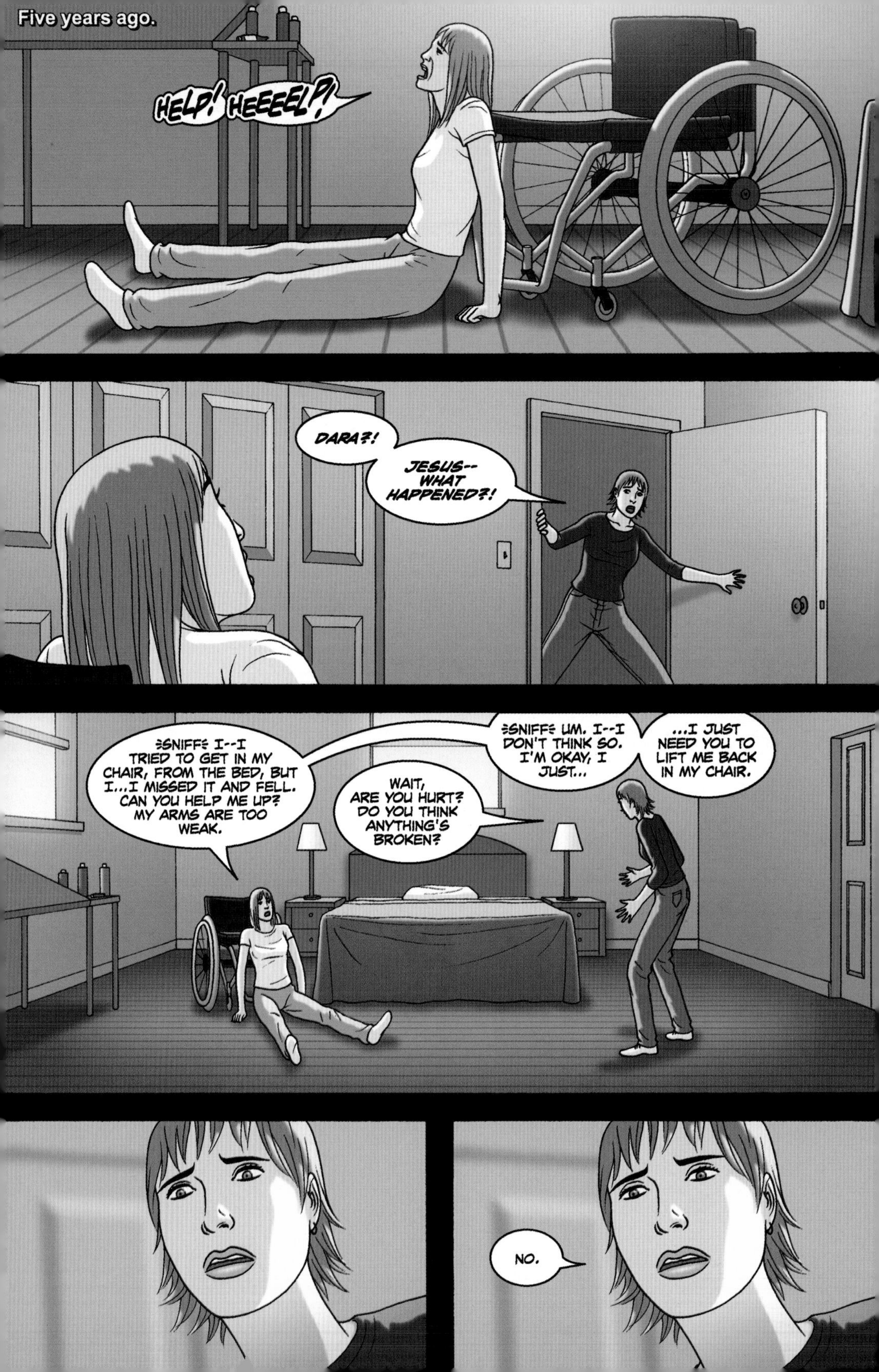
Five years ago.
HELP! HEEEEELP!
DARA?!
JESUS-- WHAT HAPPENED?!
SNIFF I--I TRIED TO GET IN MY CHAIR, FROM THE BED, BUT I...I MISSED IT AND FELL. CAN YOU HELP ME UP? MY ARMS ARE TOO WEAK.
WAIT, ARE YOU HURT? DO YOU THINK ANYTHING'S BROKEN?
SNIFF UM. I--I DON'T THINK SO. I'M OKAY, I JUST...
...I JUST NEED YOU TO LIFT ME BACK IN MY CHAIR.
NO.

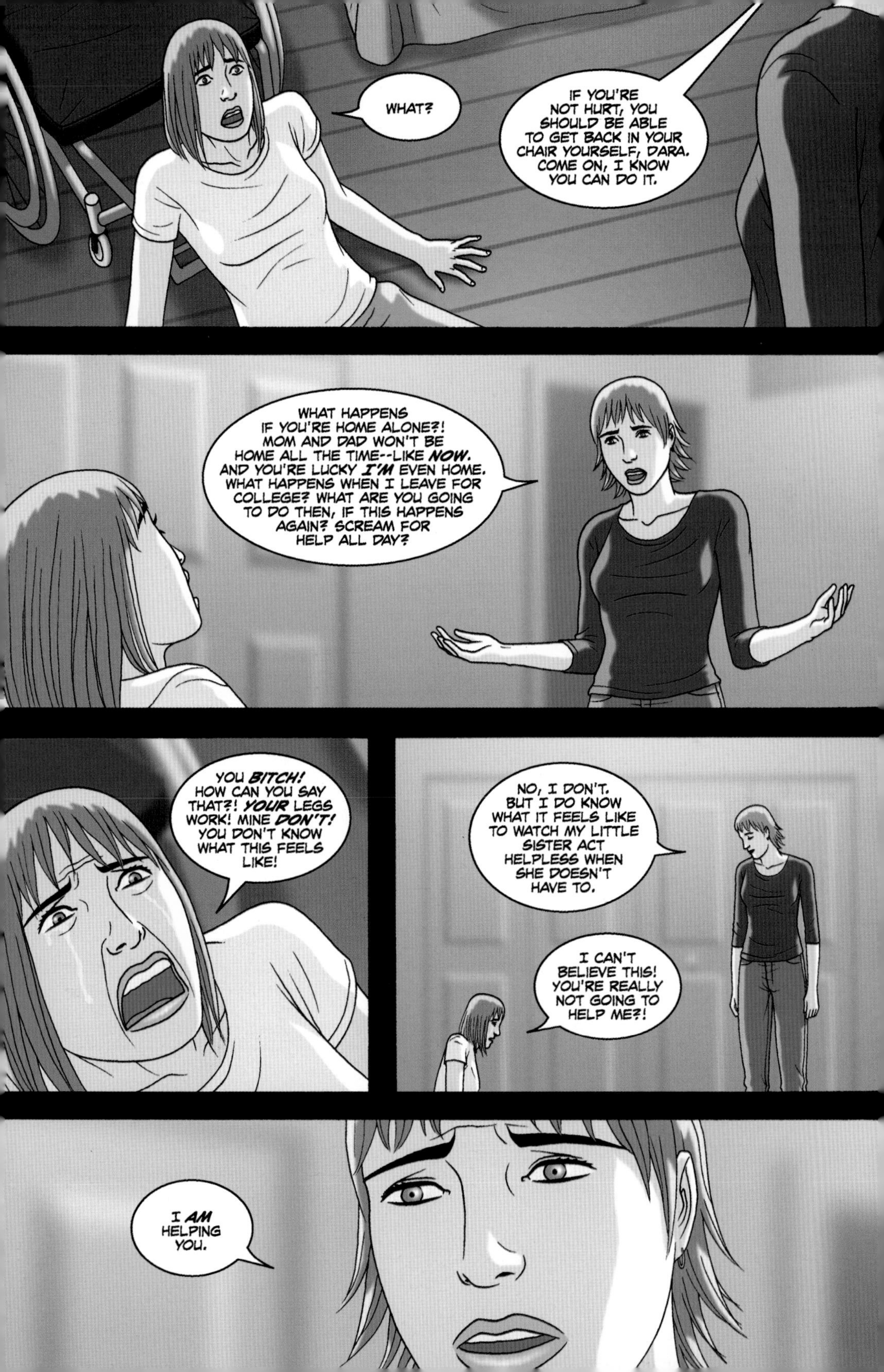
WHAT?
IF YOU'RE NOT HURT, YOU SHOULD BE ABLE TO GET BACK IN YOUR CHAIR YOURSELF, DARA. COME ON, I KNOW YOU CAN DO IT.
WHAT HAPPENS IF YOU'RE HOME ALONE?! MOM AND DAD WON'T BE HOME ALL THE TIME--LIKE NOW. AND YOU'RE LUCKY I'M EVEN HOME. WHAT HAPPENS WHEN I LEAVE FOR COLLEGE? WHAT ARE YOU GOING TO DO THEN, IF THIS HAPPENS AGAIN? SCREAM FOR HELP ALL DAY?
YOU BITCH! HOW CAN YOU SAY THAT?! YOUR LEGS WORK! MINE DON'T! YOU DON'T KNOW WHAT THIS FEELS LIKE!
NO, I DON'T. BUT I DO KNOW WHAT IT FEELS LIKE TO WATCH MY LITTLE SISTER ACT HELPLESS WHEN SHE DOESN'T HAVE TO.
I CAN'T BELIEVE THIS! YOU'RE REALLY NOT GOING TO HELP ME?!
I AM HELPING YOU.

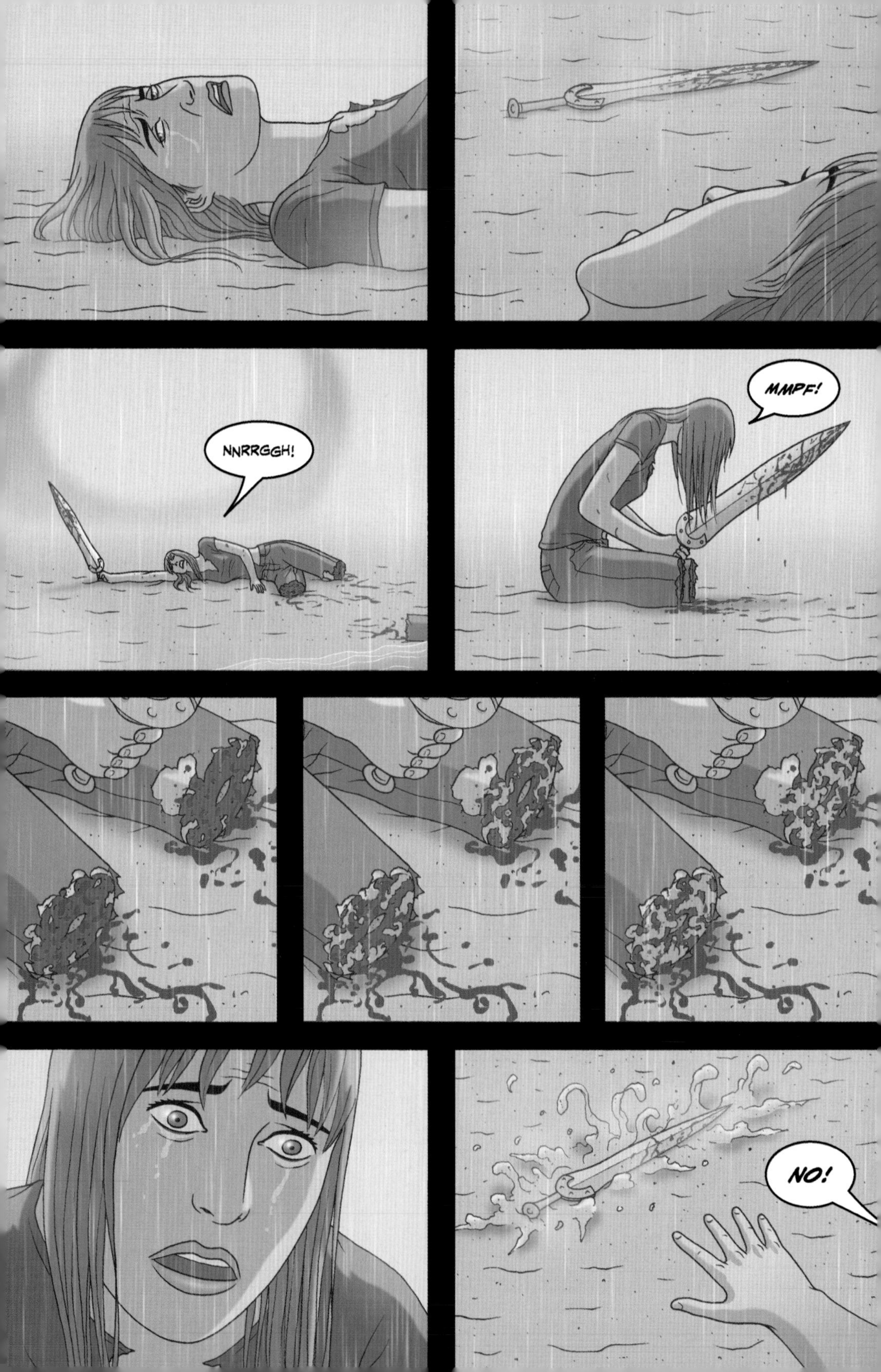
NNRRGGH!
MMPF!
NO!

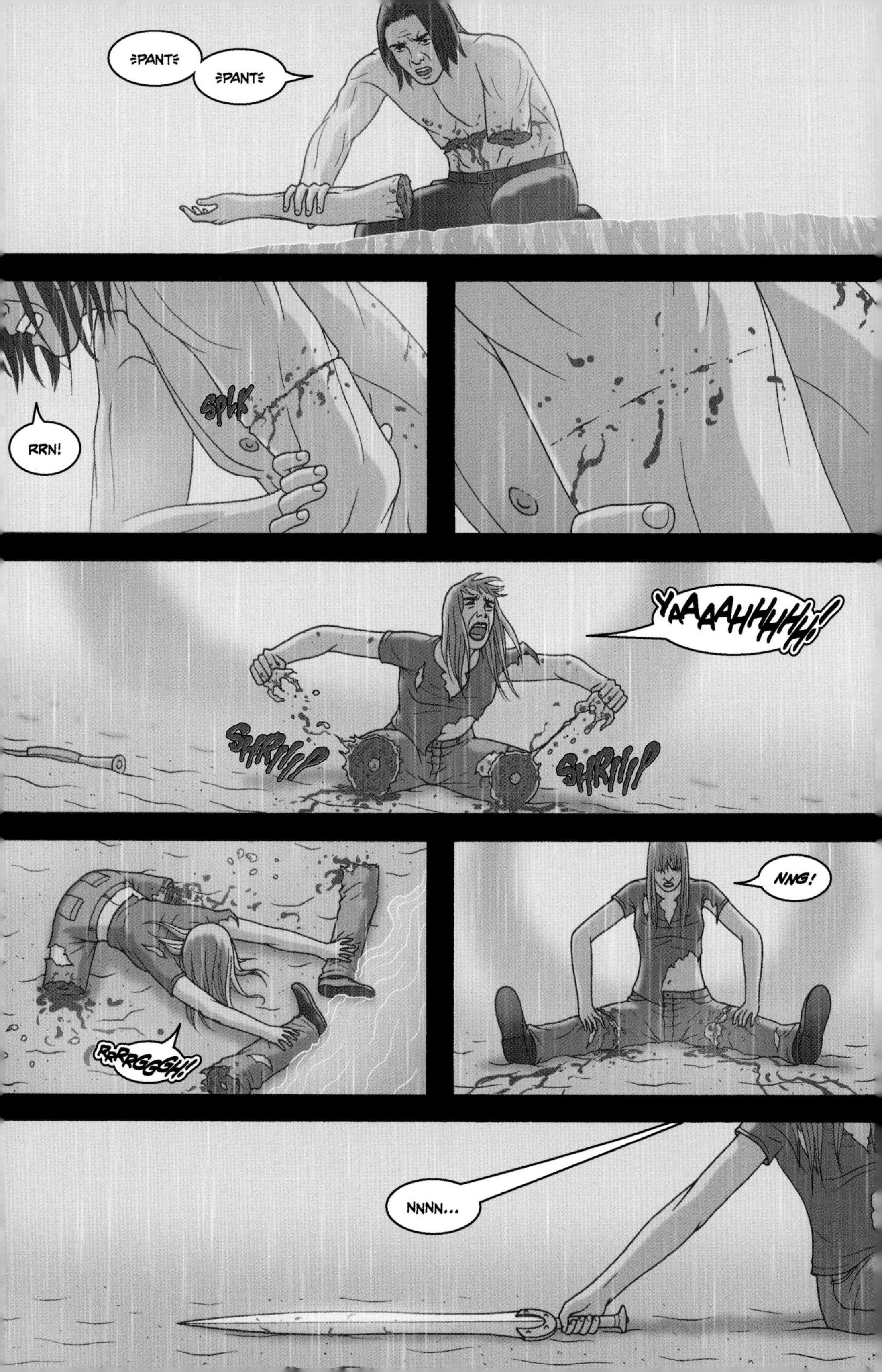

PANT
PANT
RRN!
SPLK
YAAAAHHHHH!
SHRIIII!
SHRIIII!
RRRRGGGH!!
NNG!
NNNN...

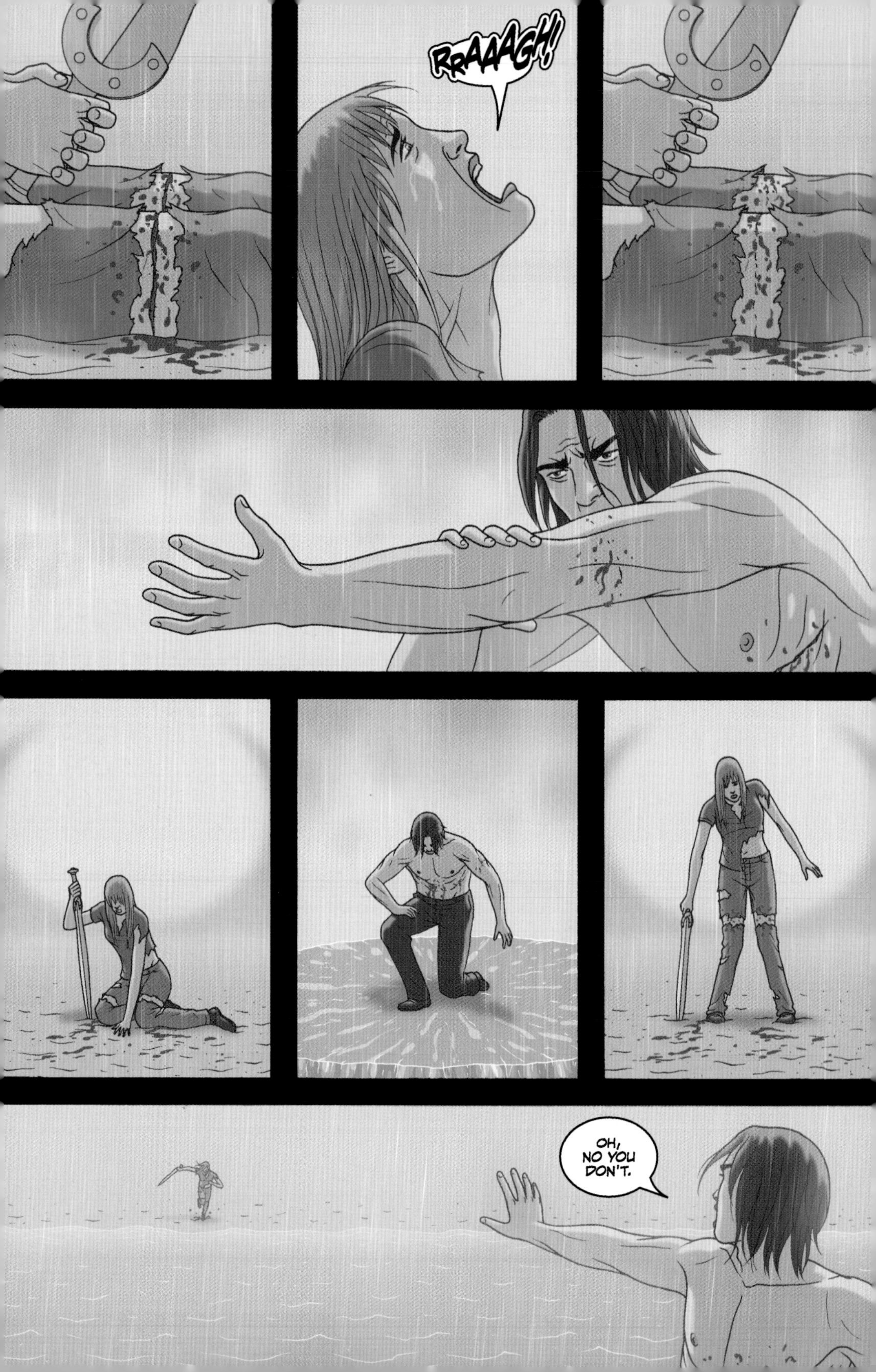
RRAAAGH!
OH, NO YOU DON'T.

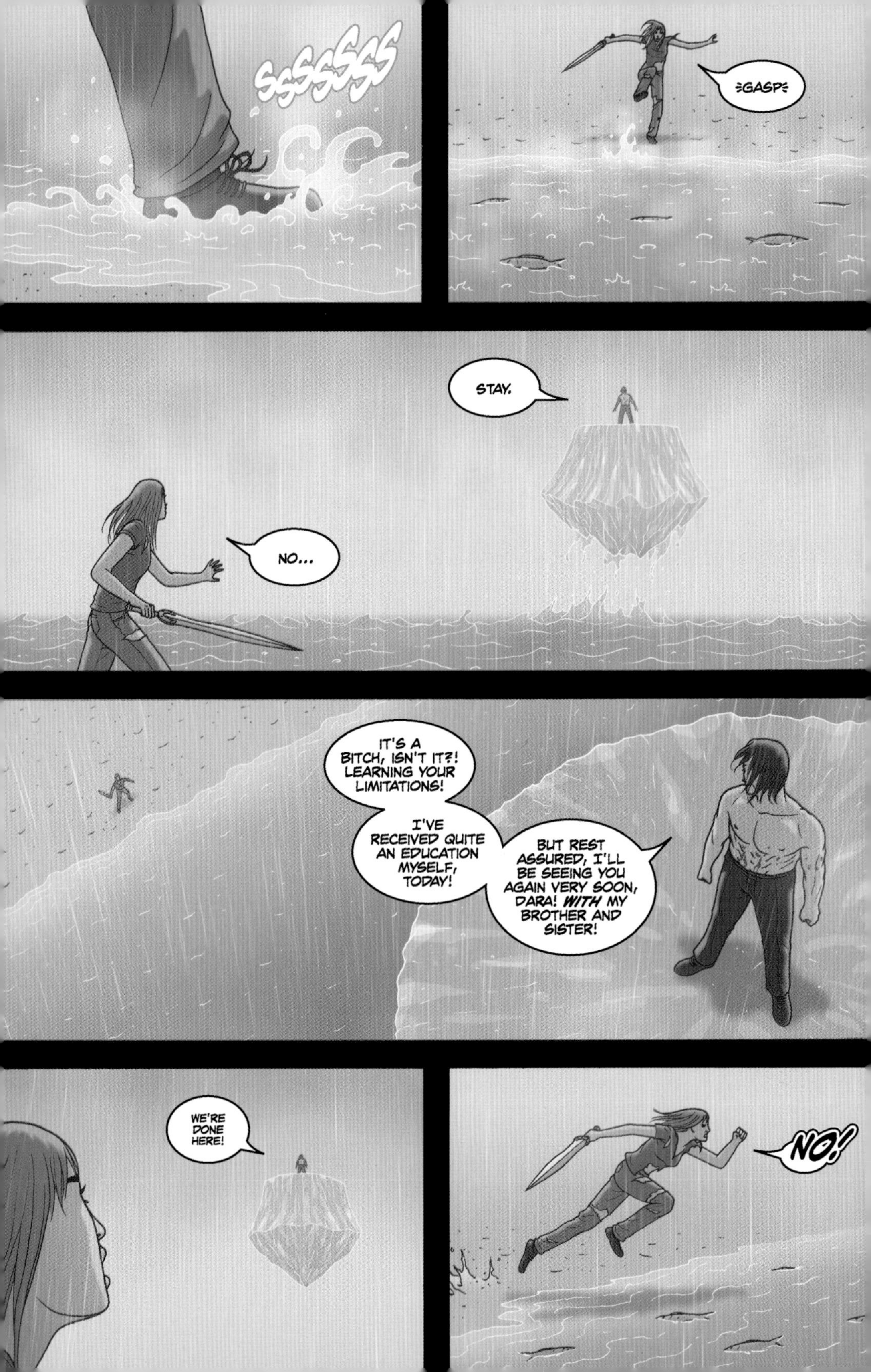
SSSSSSS
≈GASP≈
STAY.
NO...
IT'S A BITCH, ISN'T IT?! LEARNING YOUR LIMITATIONS!
I'VE RECEIVED QUITE AN EDUCATION MYSELF, TODAY!
BUT REST ASSURED, I'LL BE SEEING YOU AGAIN VERY SOON, DARA! *WITH* MY BROTHER AND SISTER!
WE'RE DONE HERE!
NO!

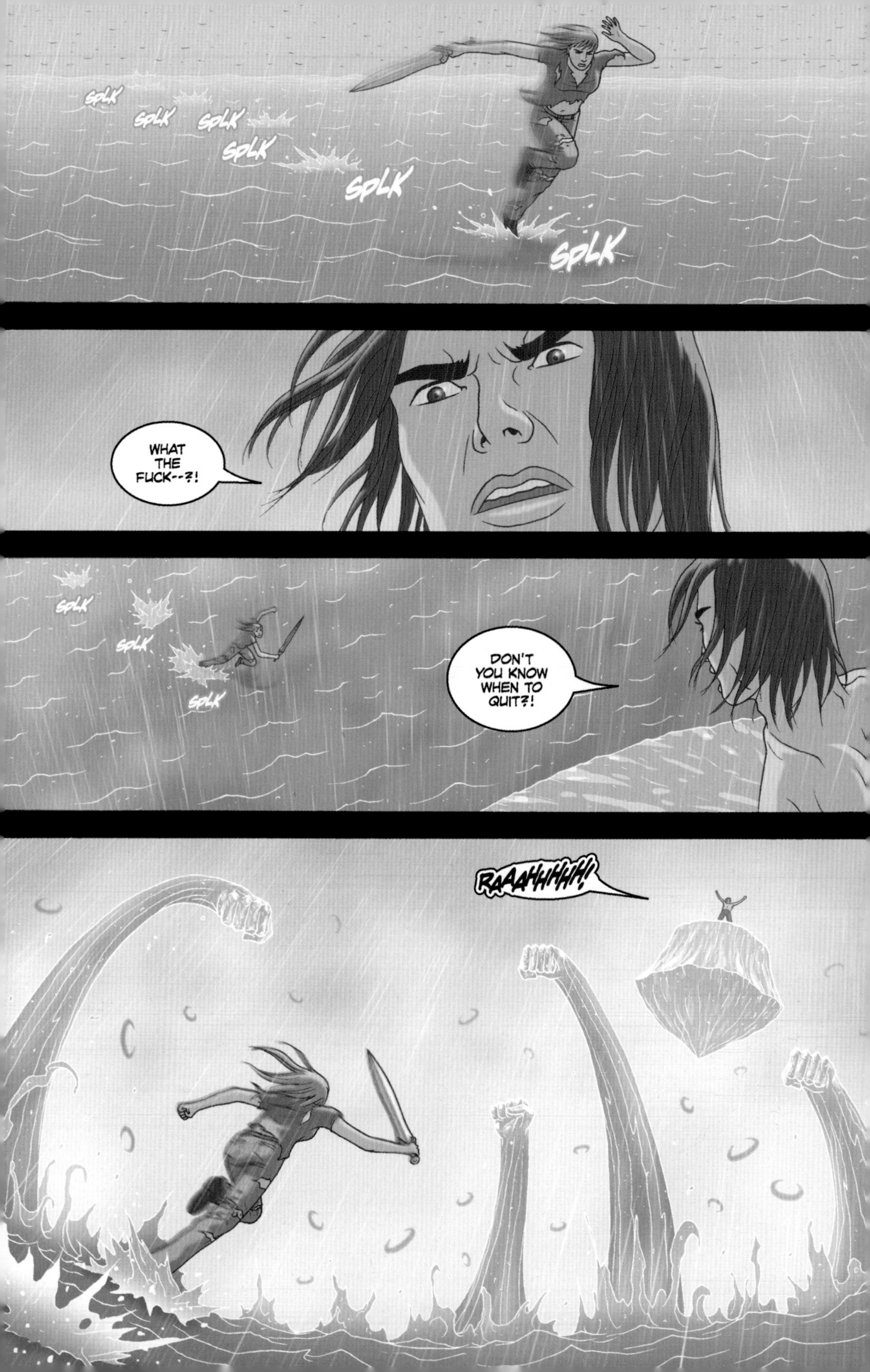
SPLK
SPLK
SPLK
SPLK
SPLK
SPLK
WHAT THE FUCK--?!
SPLK
SPLK
SPLK
DON'T YOU KNOW WHEN TO QUIT?!
RAAAHHHHH!

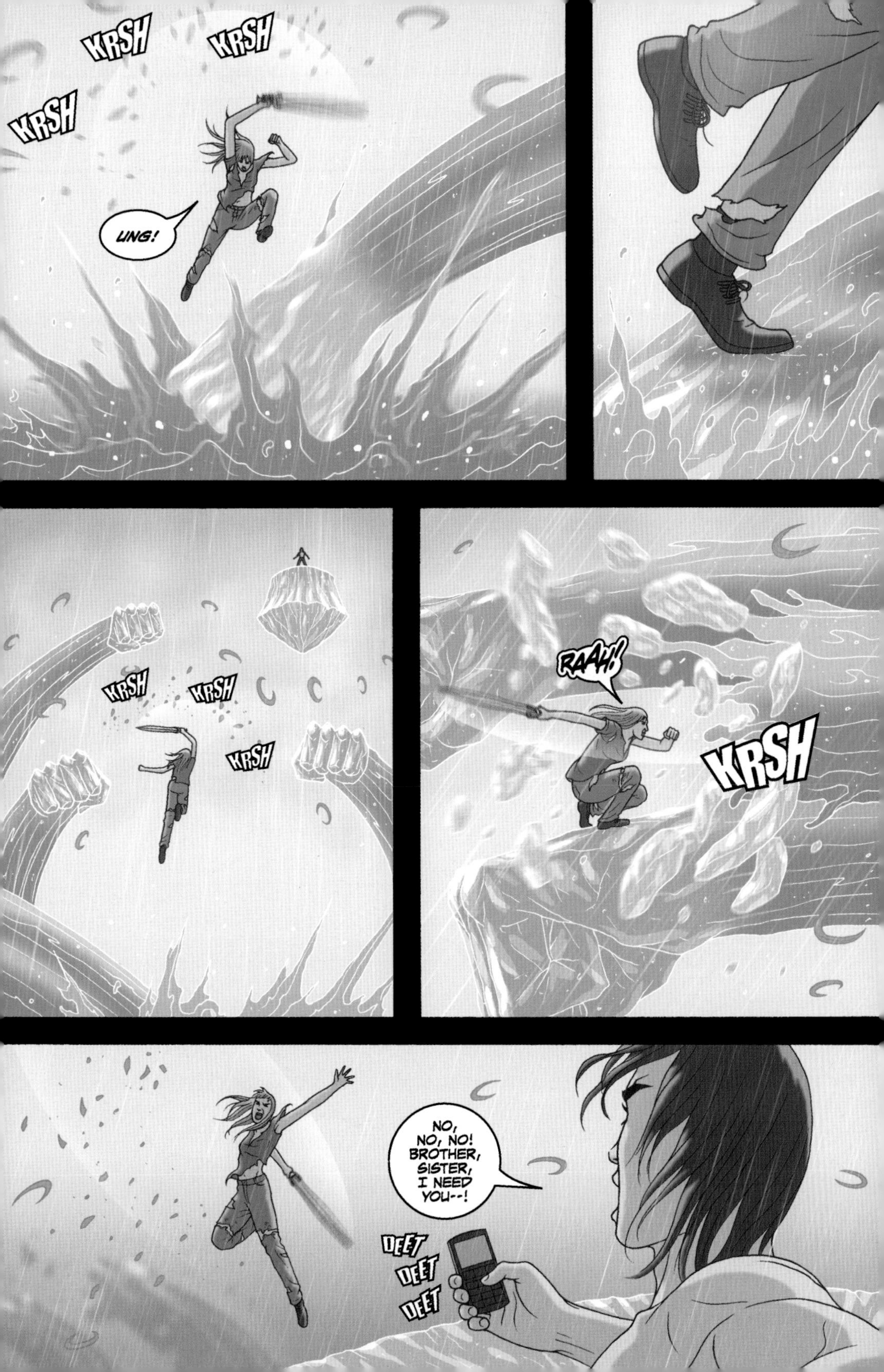
KRSH
KRSH
KRSH
UNG!
KRSH
KRSH
KRSH
RAAH!
KRSH
NO, NO, NO! BROTHER, SISTER, I NEED YOU--!
DEET
DEET
DEET

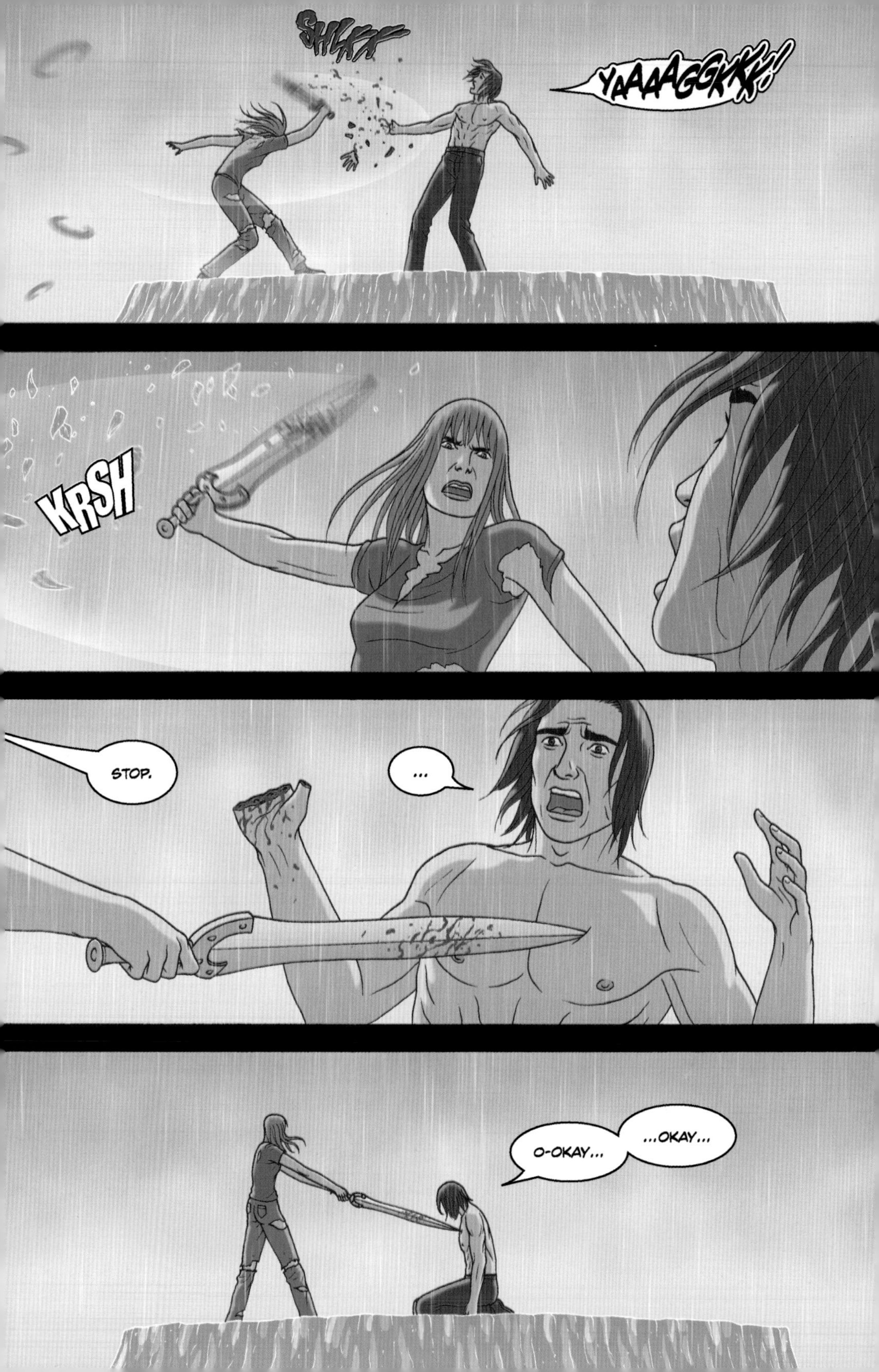
SHLKK
YAAAAGGKKK!
KRSH
STOP.
...
O-OKAY...
...OKAY...

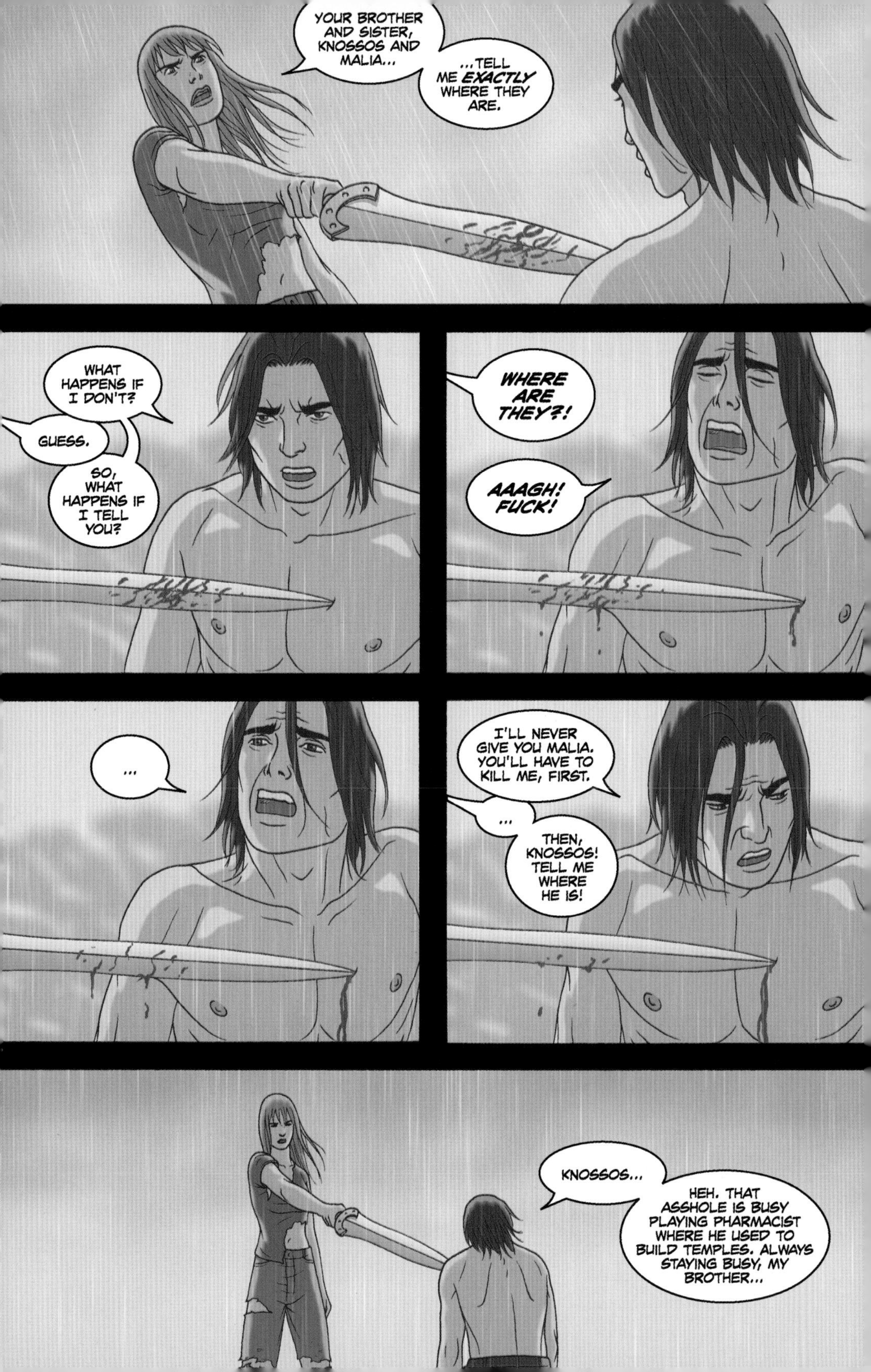
YOUR BROTHER AND SISTER, KNOSSOS AND MALIA...
...TELL ME *EXACTLY* WHERE THEY ARE.
WHAT HAPPENS IF I DON'T?
GUESS.
SO, WHAT HAPPENS IF I TELL YOU?
WHERE ARE THEY?!
AAAGH! FUCK!
...
I'LL NEVER GIVE YOU MALIA. YOU'LL HAVE TO KILL ME, FIRST.
...
THEN, KNOSSOS! TELL ME WHERE HE IS!
KNOSSOS...
HEH. THAT ASSHOLE IS BUSY PLAYING PHARMACIST WHERE HE USED TO BUILD TEMPLES. ALWAYS STAYING BUSY, MY BROTHER...

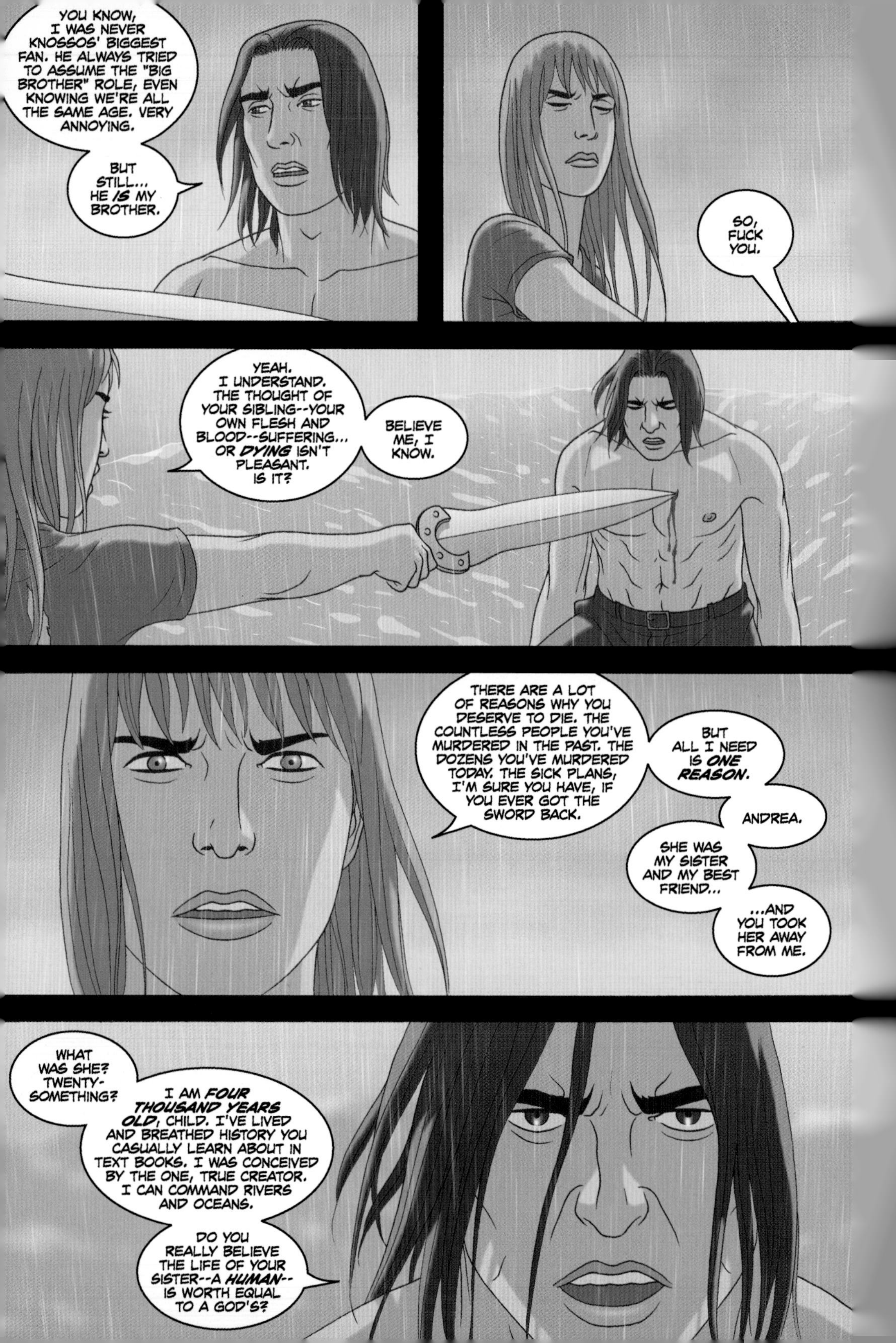
YOU KNOW, I WAS NEVER KNOSSOS' BIGGEST FAN. HE ALWAYS TRIED TO ASSUME THE "BIG BROTHER" ROLE, EVEN KNOWING WE'RE ALL THE SAME AGE. VERY ANNOYING.
BUT STILL... HE *IS* MY BROTHER.
SO, FUCK YOU.
YEAH. I UNDERSTAND. THE THOUGHT OF YOUR SIBLING--YOUR OWN FLESH AND BLOOD--SUFFERING... OR *DYING* ISN'T PLEASANT. IS IT?
BELIEVE ME, I KNOW.
THERE ARE A LOT OF REASONS WHY YOU DESERVE TO DIE. THE COUNTLESS PEOPLE YOU'VE MURDERED IN THE PAST. THE DOZENS YOU'VE MURDERED TODAY. THE SICK PLANS, I'M SURE YOU HAVE, IF YOU EVER GOT THE SWORD BACK.
BUT ALL I NEED IS *ONE REASON*.
ANDREA.
SHE WAS MY SISTER AND MY BEST FRIEND...
...AND YOU TOOK HER AWAY FROM ME.
WHAT WAS SHE? TWENTY-SOMETHING?
I AM *FOUR THOUSAND YEARS OLD*, CHILD. I'VE LIVED AND BREATHED HISTORY YOU CASUALLY LEARN ABOUT IN TEXT BOOKS. I WAS CONCEIVED BY THE ONE, TRUE CREATOR. I CAN COMMAND RIVERS AND OCEANS.
DO YOU REALLY BELIEVE THE LIFE OF YOUR SISTER--A *HUMAN*--IS WORTH EQUAL TO A GOD'S?

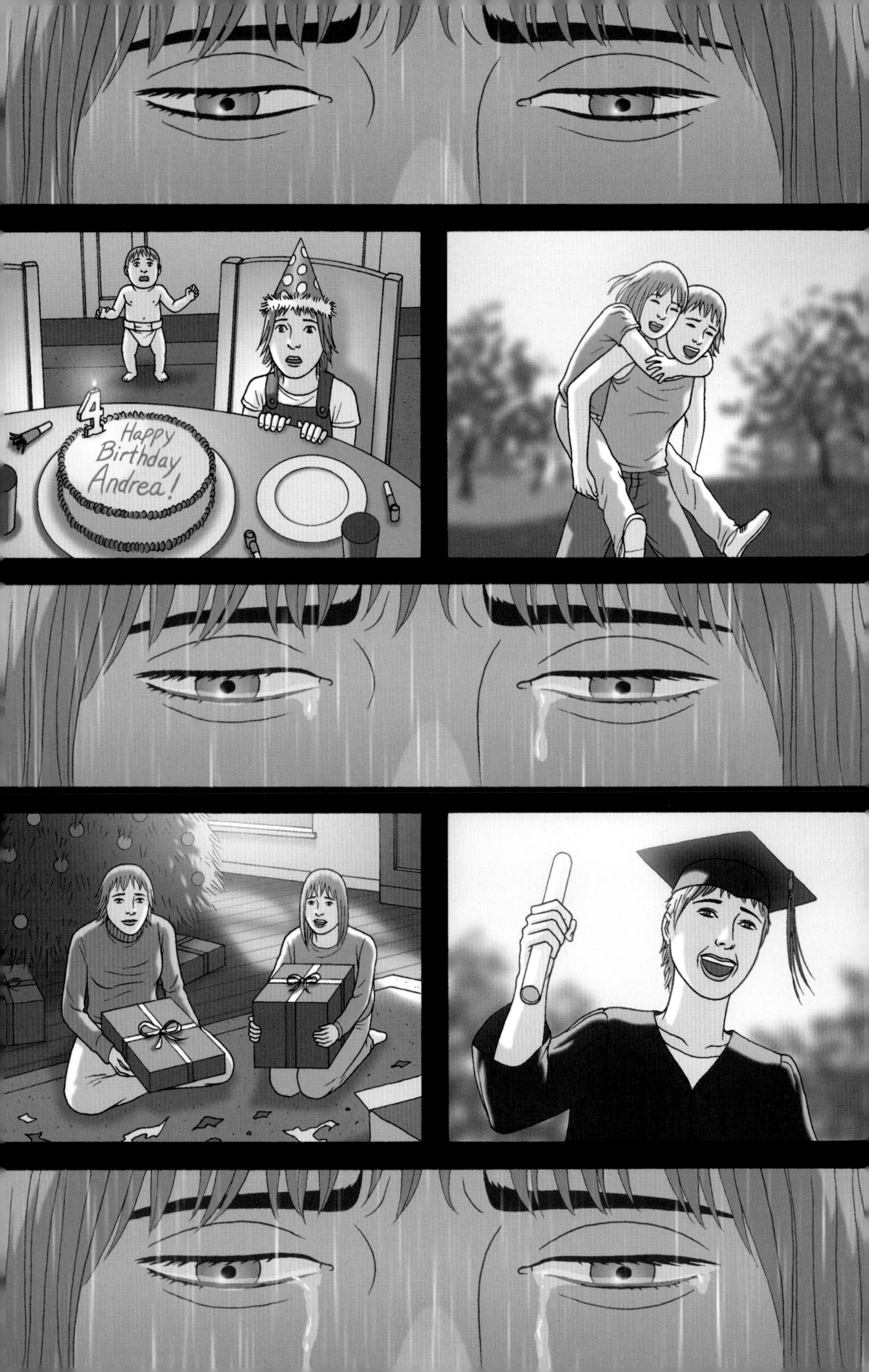
4
Happy Birthday Andrea!

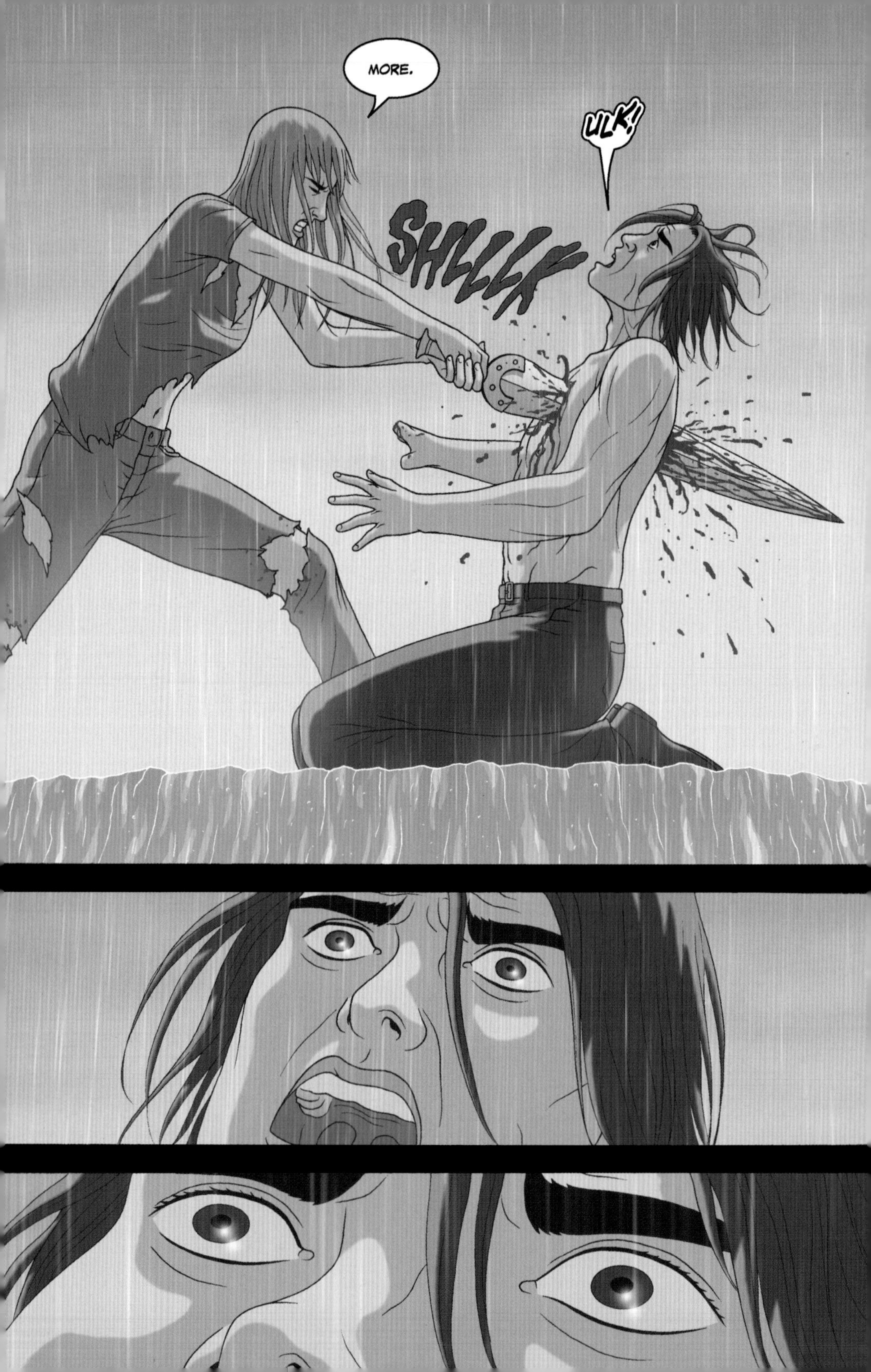
MORE.
ULK!
SHLLLK

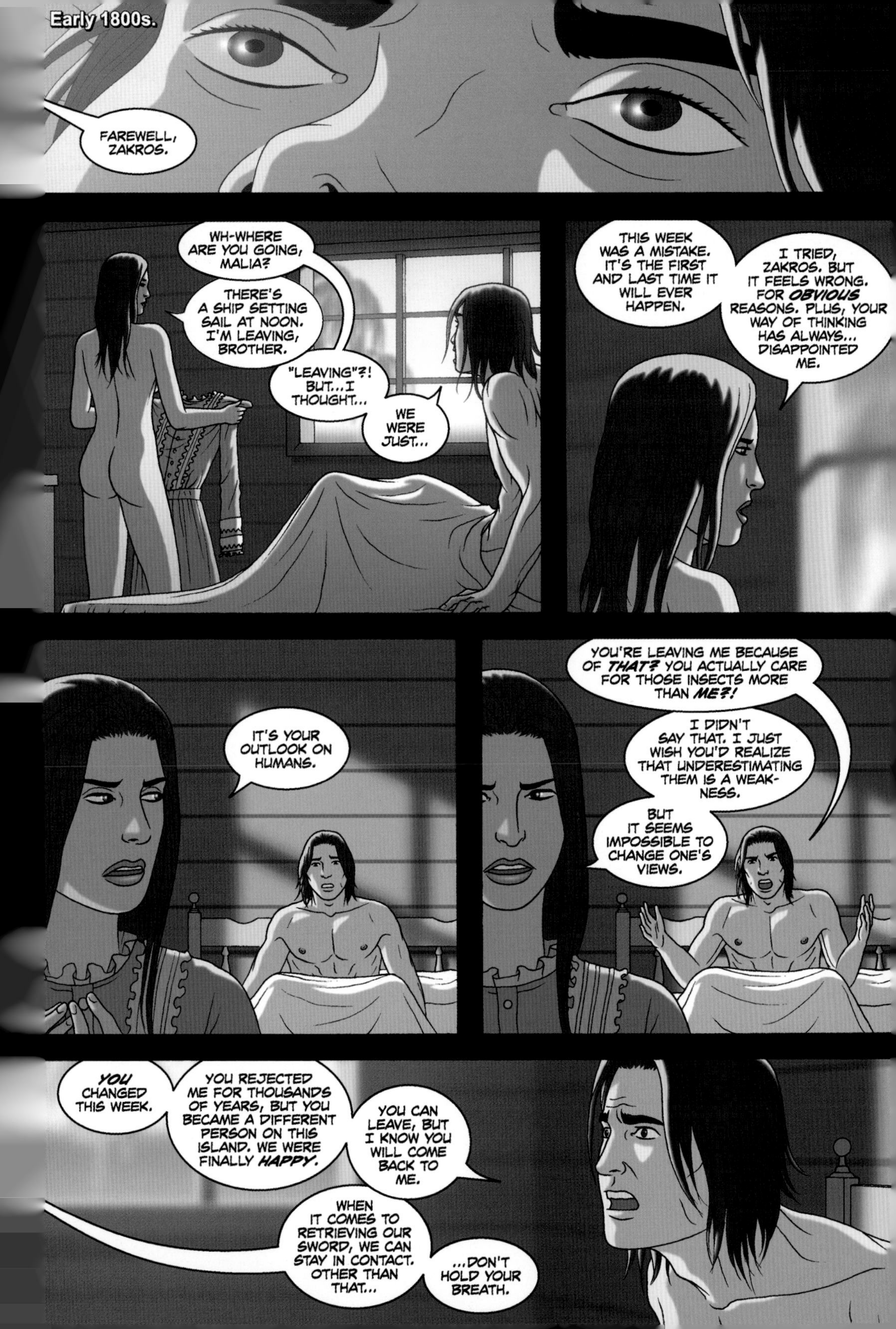
Early 1800s.
FAREWELL, ZAKROS.
WH-WHERE ARE YOU GOING, MALIA?
THERE'S A SHIP SETTING SAIL AT NOON. I'M LEAVING, BROTHER.
"LEAVING"?! BUT... I THOUGHT...
WE WERE JUST...
THIS WEEK WAS A MISTAKE. IT'S THE FIRST AND LAST TIME IT WILL EVER HAPPEN.
I TRIED, ZAKROS. BUT IT FEELS WRONG. FOR OBVIOUS REASONS. PLUS, YOUR WAY OF THINKING HAS ALWAYS... DISAPPOINTED ME.
IT'S YOUR OUTLOOK ON HUMANS.
YOU'RE LEAVING ME BECAUSE OF THAT? YOU ACTUALLY CARE FOR THOSE INSECTS MORE THAN ME?!
I DIDN'T SAY THAT. I JUST WISH YOU'D REALIZE THAT UNDERESTIMATING THEM IS A WEAK-NESS.
BUT IT SEEMS IMPOSSIBLE TO CHANGE ONE'S VIEWS.
YOU CHANGED THIS WEEK.
YOU REJECTED ME FOR THOUSANDS OF YEARS, BUT YOU BECAME A DIFFERENT PERSON ON THIS ISLAND. WE WERE FINALLY HAPPY.
YOU CAN LEAVE, BUT I KNOW YOU WILL COME BACK TO ME.
WHEN IT COMES TO RETRIEVING OUR SWORD, WE CAN STAY IN CONTACT. OTHER THAN THAT...
...DON'T HOLD YOUR BREATH.

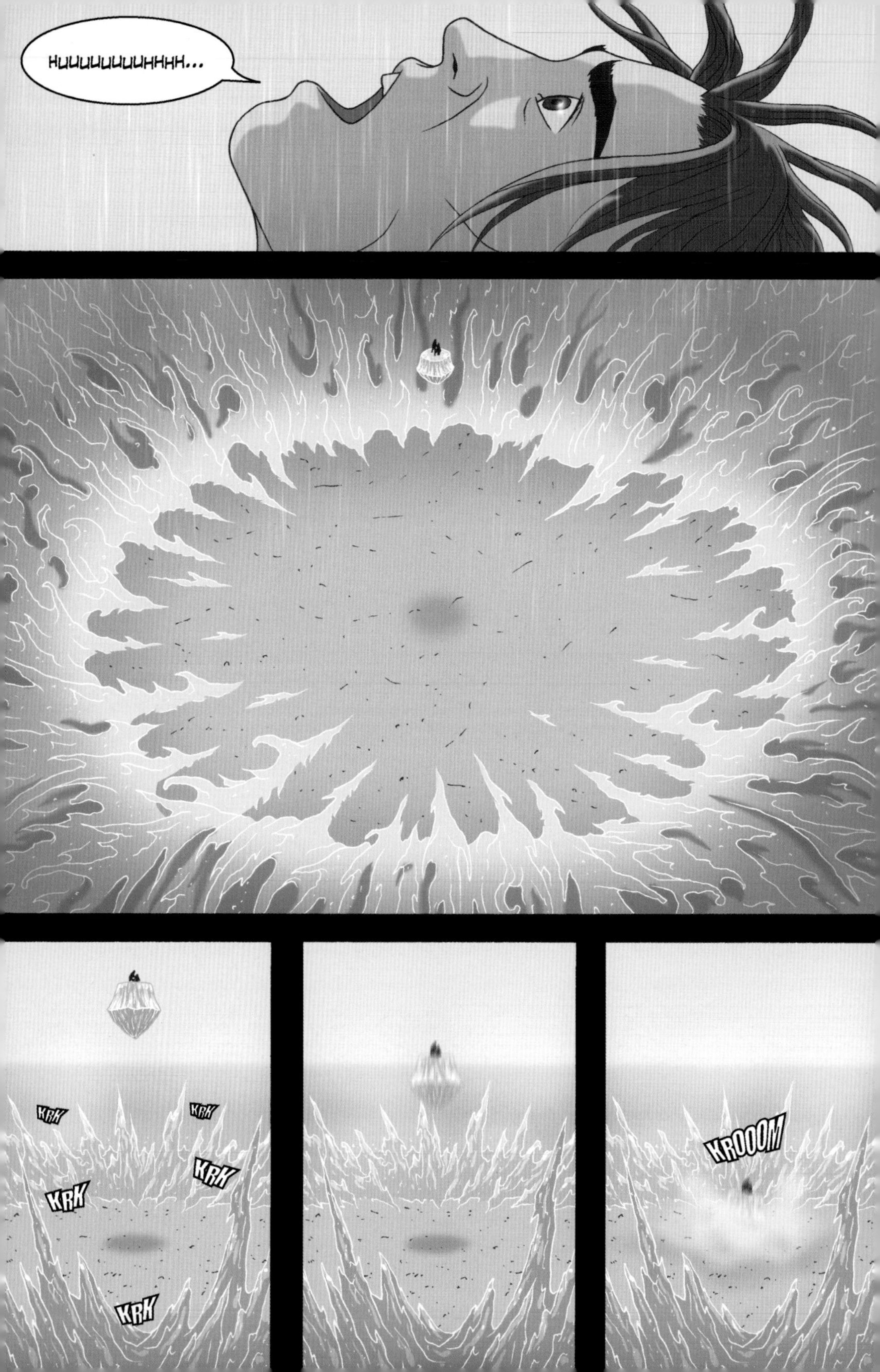
HUUUUUUUUHHHH...
KRK
KRK
KRK
KRK
KRK
KROOOM

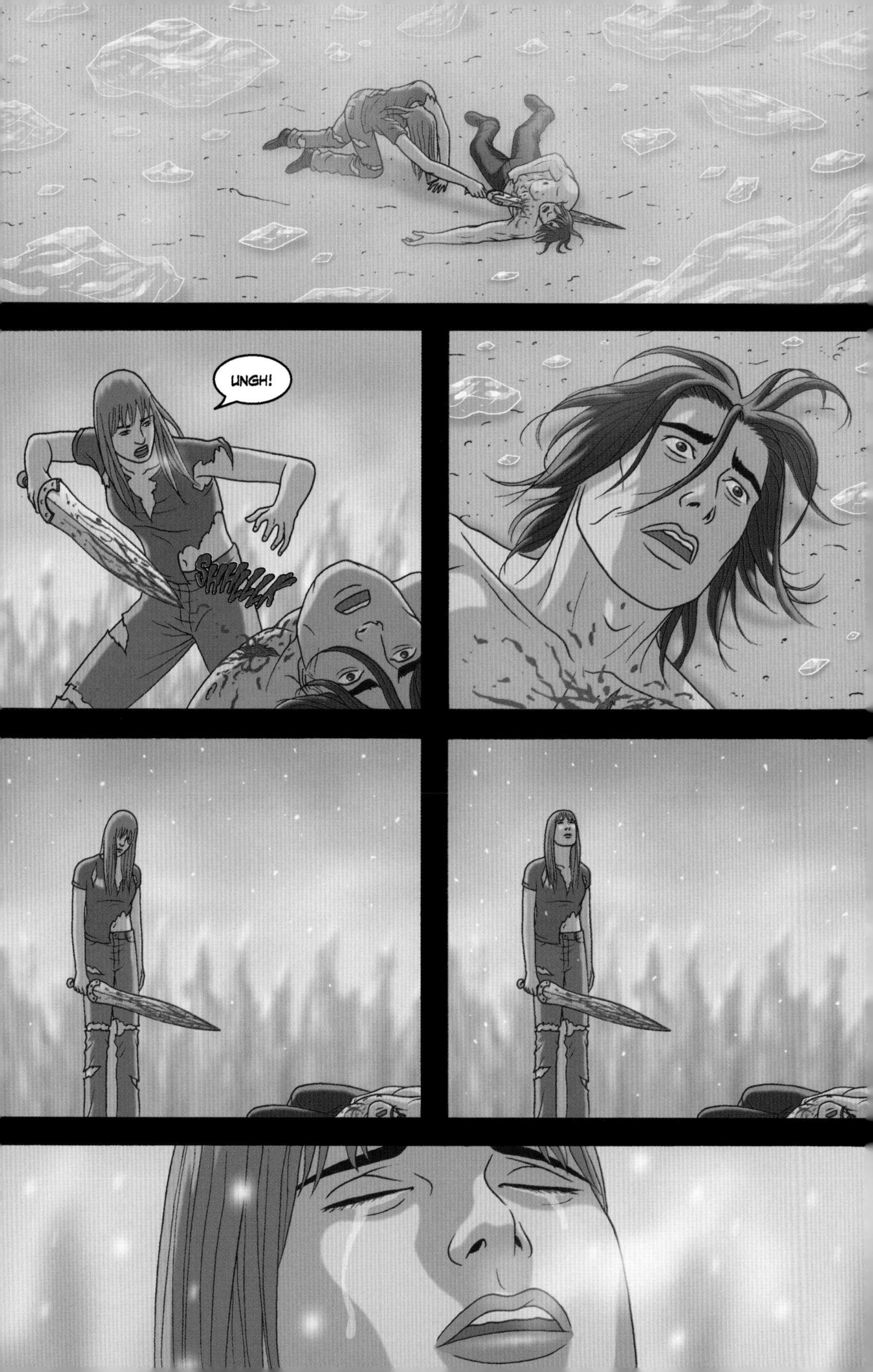
UNGH!
SHHLLLK

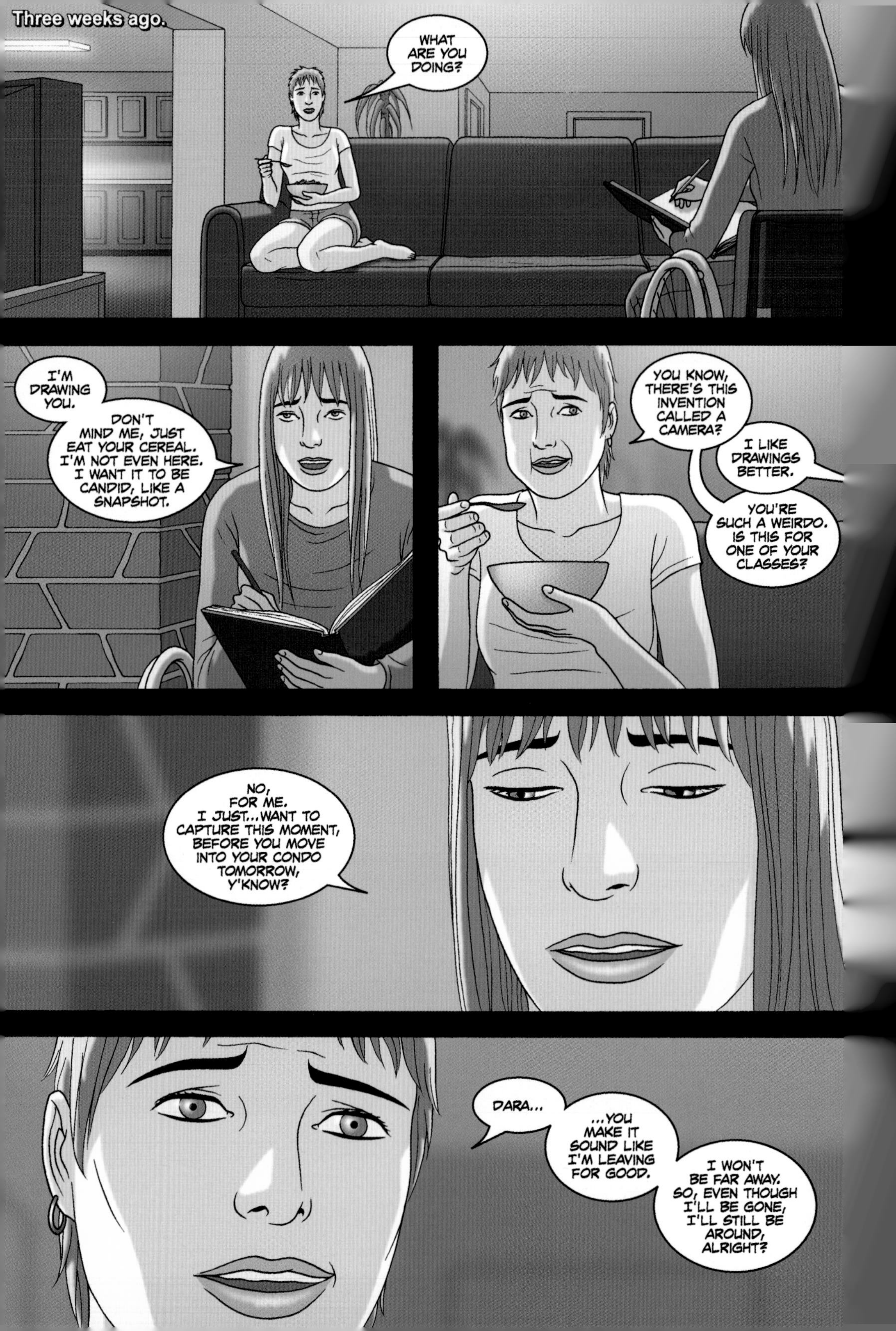
Three weeks ago.
WHAT ARE YOU DOING?
I'M DRAWING YOU.
DON'T MIND ME, JUST EAT YOUR CEREAL. I'M NOT EVEN HERE. I WANT IT TO BE CANDID, LIKE A SNAPSHOT.
YOU KNOW, THERE'S THIS INVENTION CALLED A CAMERA?
I LIKE DRAWINGS BETTER.
YOU'RE SUCH A WEIRDO. IS THIS FOR ONE OF YOUR CLASSES?
NO, FOR ME. I JUST...WANT TO CAPTURE THIS MOMENT, BEFORE YOU MOVE INTO YOUR CONDO TOMORROW, Y'KNOW?
DARA...
...YOU MAKE IT SOUND LIKE I'M LEAVING FOR GOOD.
I WON'T BE FAR AWAY. SO, EVEN THOUGH I'LL BE GONE, I'LL STILL BE AROUND, ALRIGHT?

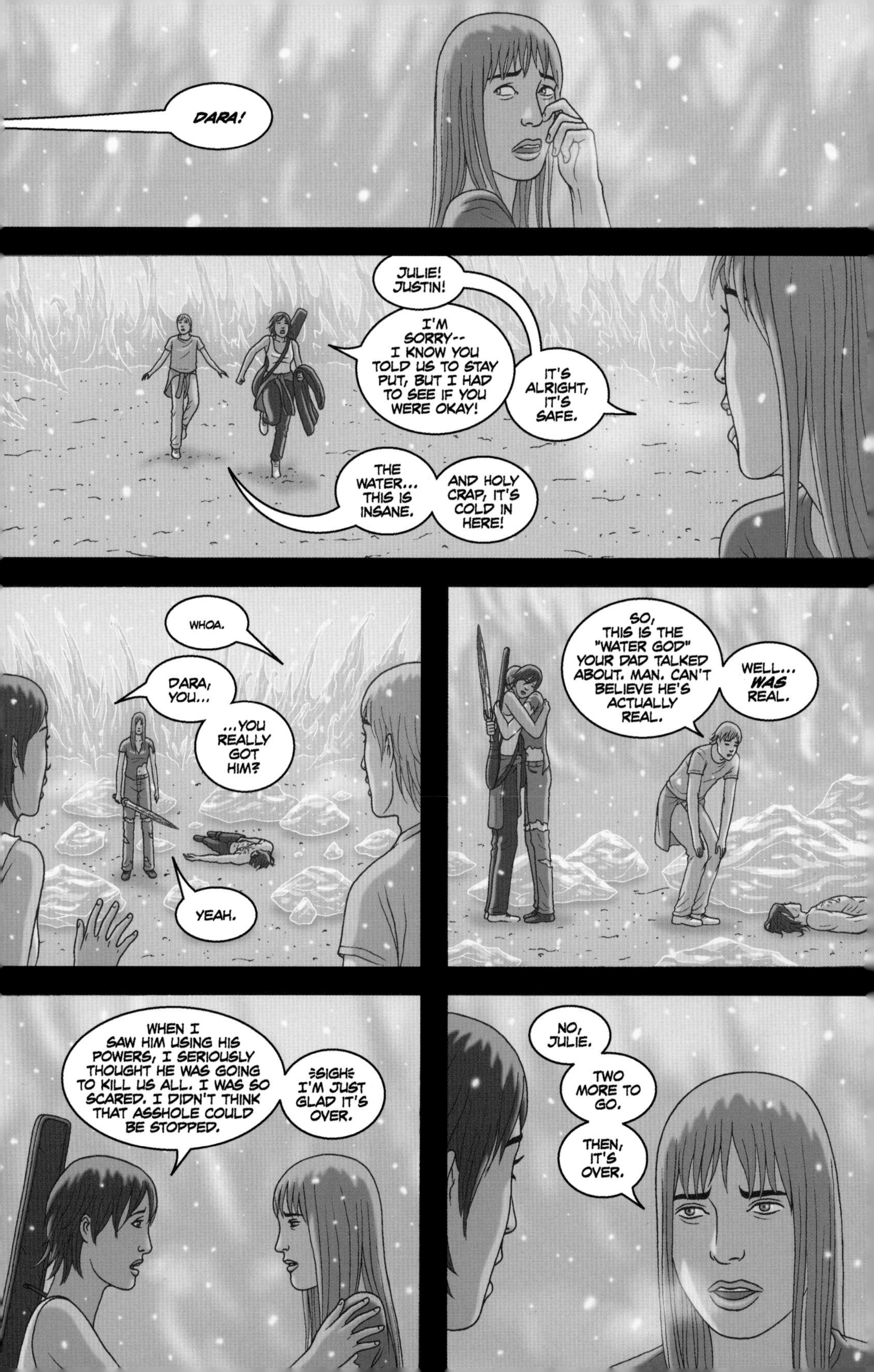
DARA!
JULIE! JUSTIN!
I'M SORRY-- I KNOW YOU TOLD US TO STAY PUT, BUT I HAD TO SEE IF YOU WERE OKAY!
IT'S ALRIGHT, IT'S SAFE.
THE WATER... THIS IS INSANE.
AND HOLY CRAP, IT'S COLD IN HERE!
WHOA.
DARA, YOU...
...YOU REALLY GOT HIM?
YEAH.
SO, THIS IS THE "WATER GOD" YOUR DAD TALKED ABOUT. MAN. CAN'T BELIEVE HE'S ACTUALLY REAL.
WELL... *WAS* REAL.
WHEN I SAW HIM USING HIS POWERS, I SERIOUSLY THOUGHT HE WAS GOING TO KILL US ALL. I WAS SO SCARED. I DIDN'T THINK THAT ASSHOLE COULD BE STOPPED.
≠SIGH≠ I'M JUST GLAD IT'S OVER.
NO, JULIE.
TWO MORE TO GO.
THEN, IT'S OVER.

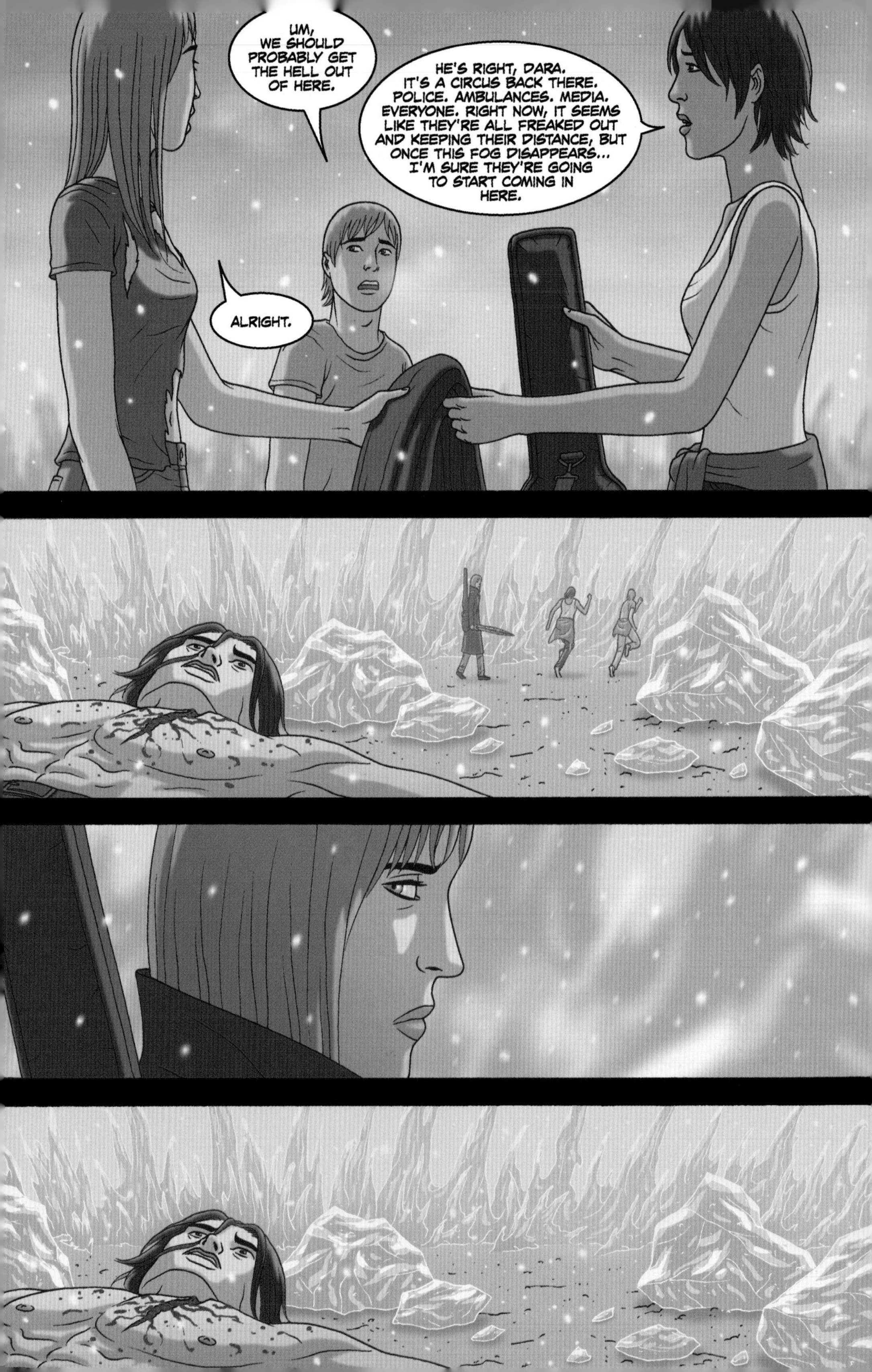
UM, WE SHOULD PROBABLY GET THE HELL OUT OF HERE.
HE'S RIGHT, DARA. IT'S A CIRCUS BACK THERE. POLICE. AMBULANCES. MEDIA. EVERYONE. RIGHT NOW, IT SEEMS LIKE THEY'RE ALL FREAKED OUT AND KEEPING THEIR DISTANCE, BUT ONCE THIS FOG DISAPPEARS... I'M SURE THEY'RE GOING TO START COMING IN HERE.
ALRIGHT.

...WHAT YOU ARE SEEING NOW IS AN INCREDIBLY BAFFLING AND DISTURBING LIVE SHOT HERE IN CABLE BEACH, IN THE NORTH END OF THE ISLAND OF NEW PROVIDENCE...

UNEXPLAINABLE DISASTER | CNB

JUST FROM LOOKING AT THESE MASSIVE, INEXPLICABLE ICE-STRUCTURES AND THE SNOW FALL HERE IN THE BAHAMAS, CLEARLY, SOMETHING ABNORMAL HAS HAPPENED.

UNEXPLAINABLE DISASTER | CNB

THE DENSE FOG, WHICH COMPLETELY ENGULFED THIS BEACH AREA AT AN ALARMING RATE AND CAUSED MASS PANDEMONIUM, IS FINALLY SUBSIDING...

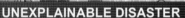

UNEXPLAINABLE DISASTER | CNB

...RIGHT NOW, VERY LITTLE IS KNOWN ABOUT THIS UNIDENTIFIED MALE, WHOM EYE-WITNESSES CLAIM WAS ACTUALLY THE CAUSE OF THE ABNORMAL ACTIVITY AND, AT LEAST, SEVEN DEATHS AND THIRTY TO FORTY MORE INJURED...

UNEXPLAINABLE DISASTER | CNB

...IF THIS INCIDENT WASN'T STRANGE ENOUGH, THE MAN WAS SEEN FIGHTING A WOMAN WHO HAS BEEN IDENTIFIED AS DARA BRIGHTON, THE SWORD-WIELDING, SUPERHUMAN WOMAN WHO WAS SUSPECTED FOR THE MURDER OF HER FAMILY AND THOUGHT TO BE DEAD...

UNEXPLAINABLE DISASTER | CNB

...IT IS STILL UNCLEAR HOW DARA BRIGHTON IS STILL ALIVE OR WHY SHE TRAVELED TO THE BAHAMAS AND ATTACKED AND ALLEGEDLY MURDERED THIS UNIDENTIFIED MALE. BUT WHAT'S EVEN MORE CRITICAL, IS WHERE SHE IS NOW--

UNEXPLAINABLE DISASTER | CNB

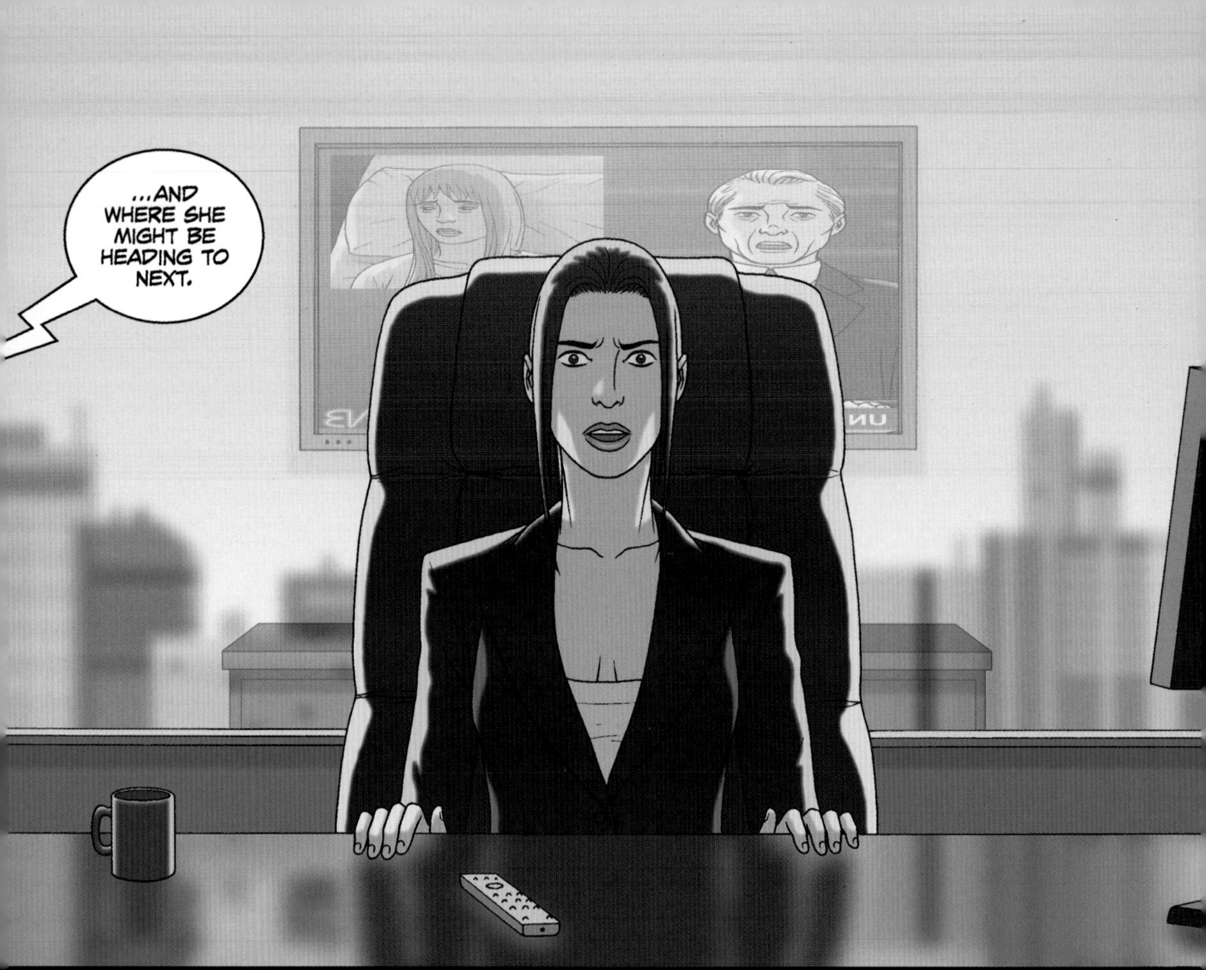
...AND WHERE SHE MIGHT BE HEADING TO NEXT.

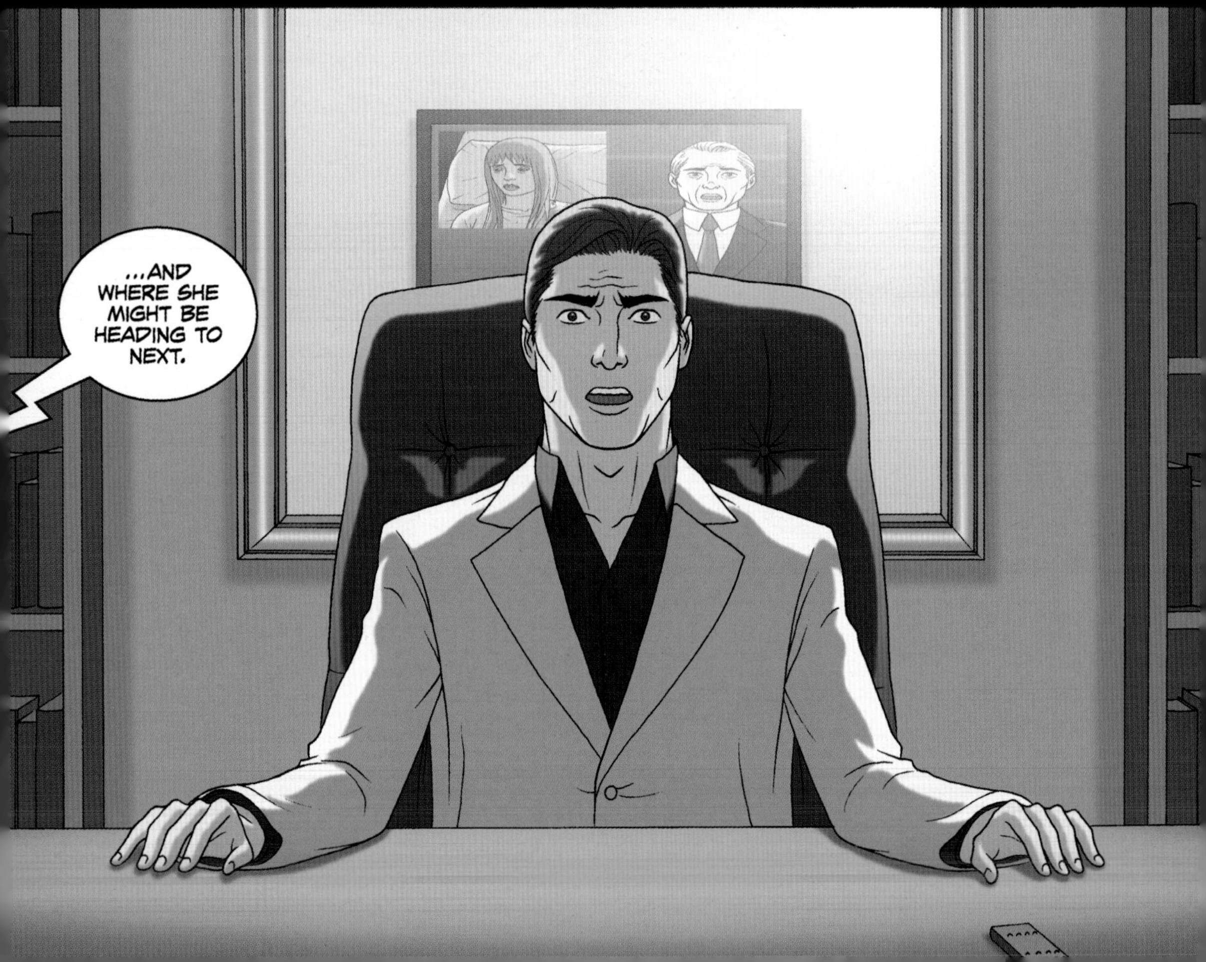
...AND WHERE SHE MIGHT BE HEADING TO NEXT.

TO BE CONTINUED...

MORE GREAT IMAGE BOOKS FROM

THE LUNA BROTHERS

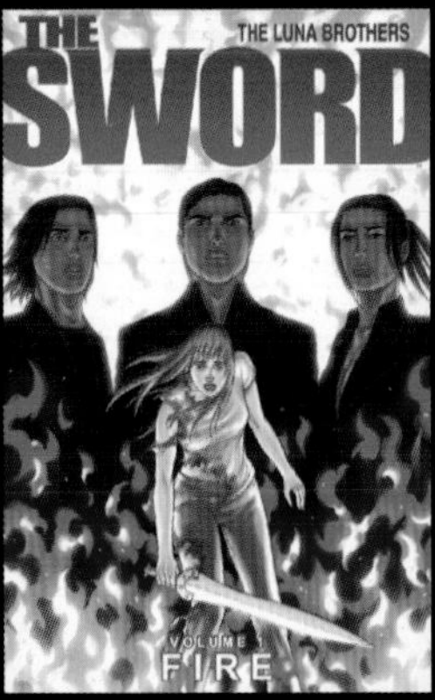
THE LUNA BROTHERS
THE SWORD
VOLUME 1
FIRE

THE SWORD
Vol. 1: FIRE
Trade Paperback
$14.99
ISBN: 978-1-58240-879-8
Collects THE SWORD #1-6
152 Pages

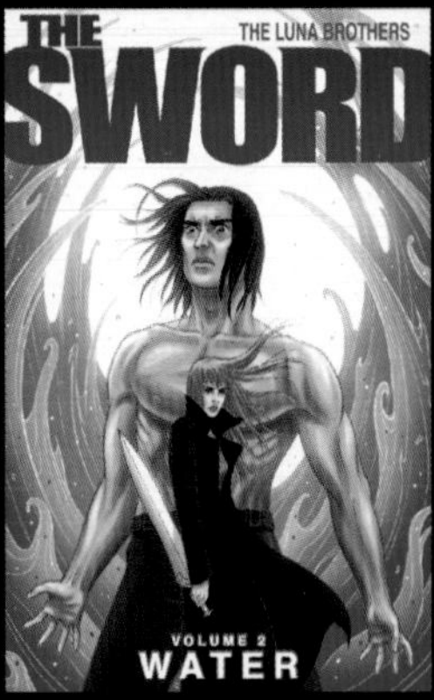
THE LUNA BROTHERS
THE SWORD
VOLUME 2
WATER

THE SWORD
Vol. 2: WATER
Trade Paperback
$14.99
ISBN: 978-1-58240-976-4
Collects THE SWORD #7-12
152 Pages

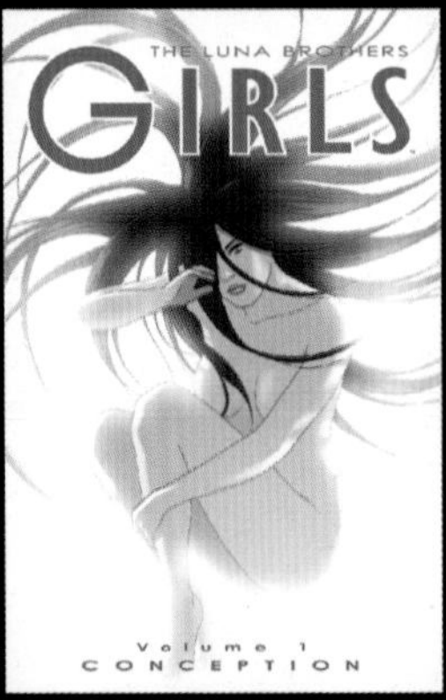
THE LUNA BROTHERS
GIRLS
Volume 1
CONCEPTION

GIRLS
Vol. 1: CONCEPTION
Trade Paperback
$14.99
ISBN: 978-1-58240-529-2
Collects GIRLS #1-6
152 Pages

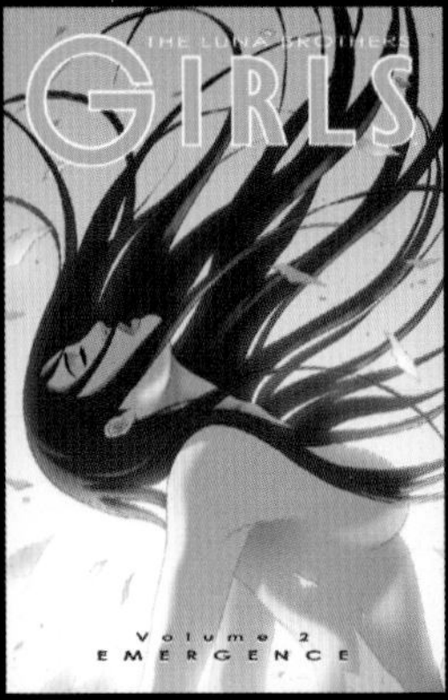
GIRLS
Volume 2
EMERGENCE

GIRLS
Vol. 2: EMERGENCE
Trade Paperback
$14.99
ISBN: 978-1-58240-608-4
Collects GIRLS #7-12
152 Pages

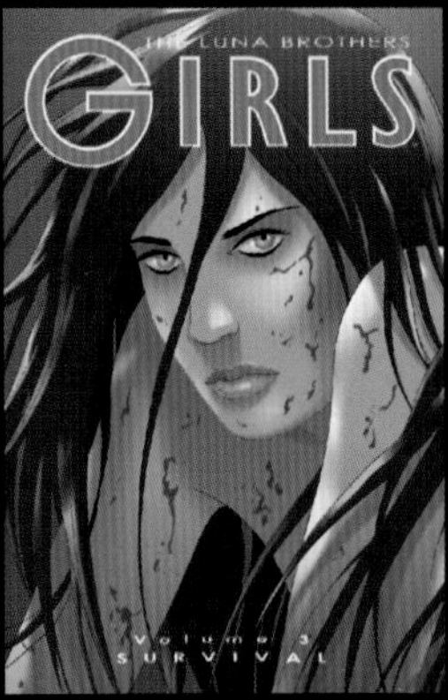
THE LUNA BROTHERS
GIRLS
SURVIVAL

GIRLS
Vol. 3: SURVIVAL
Trade Paperback
$14.99
ISBN: 978-1-58240-703-6
Collects GIRLS #13-18
152 Pages

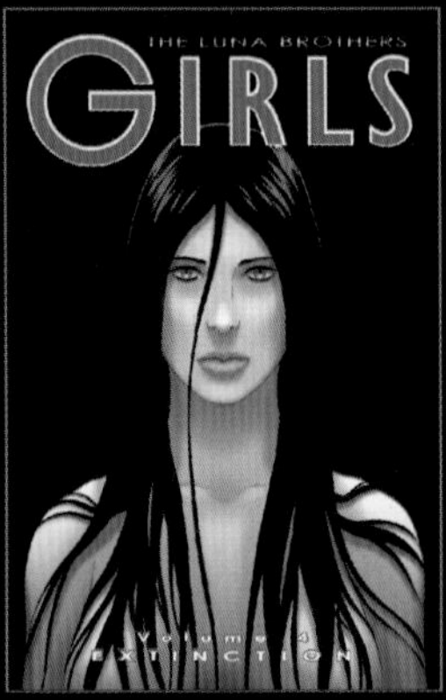
THE LUNA BROTHERS
GIRLS
EXTINCTION

GIRLS
Vol. 4: EXTINCTION
Trade Paperback
$14.99
ISBN: 978-1-58240-790-6
Collects GIRLS #19-24
168 Pages

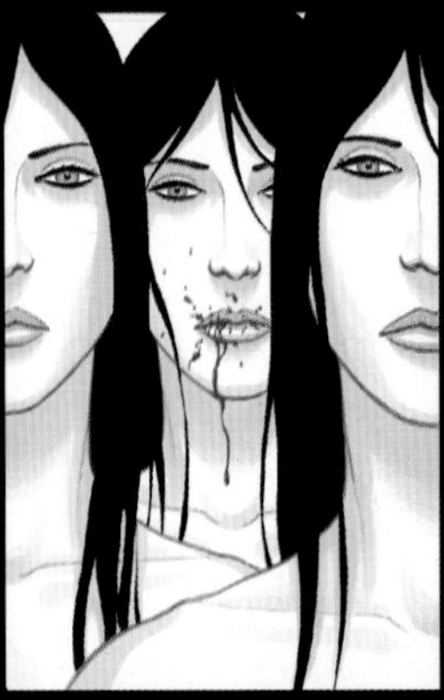

GIRLS
THE COMPLETE
COLLECTION DELUXE HC
$99.99
ISBN: 978-1-58240-826-2
Collects GIRLS #1-24
624 Pages

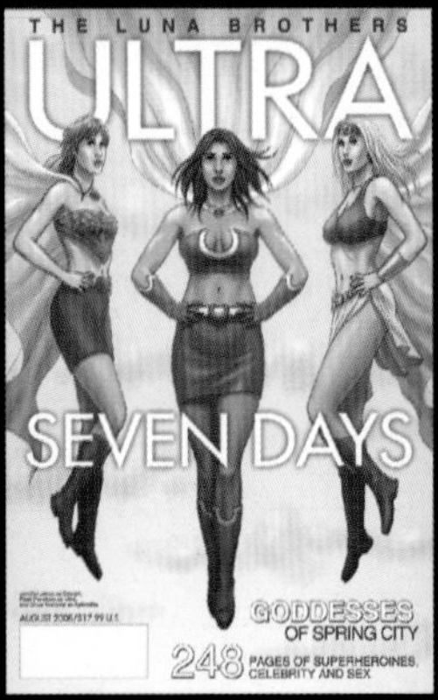
THE LUNA BROTHERS
ULTRA
SEVEN DAYS
GODDESSES OF SPRING CITY
248 PAGES OF SUPERHEROINES, CELEBRITY AND SEX

ULTRA
SEVEN DAYS
Trade Paperback
$17.99
ISBN: 978-1-58240-483-7
Collects ULTRA #1-8
248 Pages

For a comic shop near you carrying graphic novels from Image Comics, please call toll free: 1-888-COMIC-BOOK